THE SALARYMAN'S WIFE

Sujata Massey

HarperTorch
An Imprint of HarperCollinsPublishers

This is a work of fiction. Names, characters, places, and incidents are products of the author's imagination or are used fictitiously and are not to be construed as real. Any resemblance to actual events, locales, organizations, or persons, living or dead, is entirely coincidental.

HARPERTORCH
An Imprint of HarperCollins*Publishers*
10 East 53rd Street
New York, New York 10022-5299

Copyright © 1997 by Sujata Massey
Cover photo composite © 2000 by Douglas Paul Designs from photographs by Photonica
ISBN: 0-06-104443-1

First HarperTorch paperback printing: July 2003
First HarperPaperbacks printing: September 1997

HarperCollins®, HarperTorch™, and ❦™ are trademarks of HarperCollins Publishers Inc.

Printed in the United States of America

Visit HarperTorch on the World Wide Web at
www.harpercollins.com

10

Praise For *The Salaryman's Wife*

WINNER OF THE AGATHA AWARD

⬚

"Sly, sexy, and deftly done."
>—*People* (page-turner of the week)

"An impressive first novel."
>—*Baltimore Sun*

"Massey has, in this evenly paced novel of suspense ideal for a beach weekend, presented a near pitch perfect voice in modern-day Japan."
>—*Japan Times*

"Sujata Massey's hip, female Asian American twenty-something protagonist spins the story from Japan's mountain ranges to the backstreets of Tokyo in a riveting, page-turning style that will make readers late for work."
>—*A. Magazine*

"A terrific first book. . . . One can just about feel the cold draft blowing through the traditional house as Massey walks us through a foreign culture . . . enlightening and entertaining."
>—*Washington Times*

"The mystery glides along, but it's the meddling, mixed-up, manipulative Rei Shimura who supplies the real interest. Too bad she's fictional—she's the urban survivor we'd all like as a pal in Tokyo."
>—*Pacific Stars and Stripes*

BOOKS BY SUJATA MASSEY

The Salaryman's Wife
Zen Attitude
The Floating Girl
The Flower Master
The Bride's Kimono

And in Hardcover

The Samurai's Daughter

Acknowledgements

This book would not have been possible without help from wonderful people on both sides of the Pacific, and any mistakes are mine and should not be attributed to the people listed below. In Japan, I offer thanks to Carmen Nicolas and Perlita Young for a peek into hostess bars; to Margaret Uyehara of the American Embassy in Tokyo for prison protocol; to Takenori Seki for a behind-the-scenes look and history of St. Luke's International Hospital; to John Visher for sharing the trials of an expat lawyer; and Superintendent Naoto Yamagishi for insights into the National Police Agency. Thanks also to the prison visitor volunteers from Tokyo Union Church and the helpful staff members at the Tokyo American Club and Isetan department store. My long-time friends Hikari Ban, Koichi Hyogo, and Satoshi Mizushima were great fact checkers. I make an especially deep bow to Atsuko Suzuki and her family, who took such good care of me during my 1995 visit.

In the United States, I'm grateful to Malice Domestic Limited for awarding me their Grant for Unpublished Writers in 1996. More thanks go to Carolyn Marino and Robin Stamm at HarperPaperbacks for sensitive editing, and to my agent Ellen Geiger for believing in a new writer. Gordon Watson gave the best Scottish brogue on Wall Street, Masoud Javadi helped with legal language, and a number of friends offered important criticism and encouragement, especially Manami Amanai, Matthew Roshkow and Helaine Olen, Dorothy and Sarah Baker, Hikari Ban, In-Hei Hahn, Susanne Trowbridge, and my House Blend writing pals. Most of all, I thank Anthony Massey for taking me to Japan, and for all that came afterwards.

Cast Of Characters

Rei Shimura: English teacher with antique dreams

Marcelle Chapman: Roving American tourist

Mayumi Yogetsu: Innkeeper at Minshuku Yogetsu

Hugh Glendinning: Scots lawyer working for Sendai Limited in Tokyo

Setsuko Nakamura: Elegant wife of **Seiji Nakamura**, Glendinning's boss at Sendai

Kenji Yamamoto: Junior salaryman who assists Hugh Glendinning at Sendai, along with the office lady **Hikari Yasui**

Taro Ikeda: Engineer who shares an interest in ancient crime with his wife **Yuki**

Captain Jiro Okuhara: Police chief in Shiroyama

Richard Randall: Rei's Canadian roommate and fellow English teacher

Mr. Katoh: English language program director at Nichiyu

Mr. Waka: Tokyo convenience store proprietor

Tsutomu "Tom" Shimura: Rei's doctor-cousin who lives with **Aunt Norie** in Yokohama

Junichi Ota: A Tokyo lawyer

Piers Clancy: British diplomat married to **Winnie**, a socialite

Mariko Ozawa: Young hostess who toils at a bar operated by mama-san **Kiki**

Yasushi Ishida: Aged antiques dealer

Joe Roncolotta: Tokyo marketing executive

Jimmy O'Donnell: U.S. Navy veteran

Plus an assortment of students, sailors, hostesses, and gangsters who call Tokyo home

1

I suppose there are worse places to spend New Year's Eve than a crowded train with a stranger's hand inching up your thigh. A crowded train undergoing a nerve gas attack? That could mean true death instead of just an emotional one. I tried to be mature about it. After all, I'd almost convinced myself that what had been pressing against me since we'd left Nagano was somebody's suitcase handle.

He'd crept up behind me when a crush of skiers boarded and the tiny space I'd staked out had grown so tight I couldn't even move my arms. Packed *sushi-zume*—as tightly as rice balls in a box lunch—I began worrying about what might come next. I'd heard stories about the chemistry whiz who used a fluid to melt holes in clothing, and the gum-chewer who left a big wad in your hair as a memento. More than one man was known to express his pleasure deeply in your coat pocket. But those were cretins I'd assumed were native to the Tokyo subways and not long distance trains climbing the Japanese Alps.

The hand, which had been almost imperceptible at first, was becoming audacious. Exploring with my heel, I encountered a shin, slid my foot along its length and stomped the ankle underneath. A foot kicked back and a woman snapped at me to be more careful—for goodness sake didn't I know it was an overcrowded train? I ground out an apology. The hand stayed.

It was dark outside, turning the train door's glass into a mirror. I saw myself as I always appear: small, Japanese-American, and with the kind of cropped haircut that's perfect in San Francisco but a little too boyish for Japanese taste. I wished I'd had time to change into a butch pair of jeans instead of the skirt that had provided easy access for someone. I concentrated on the reflections of the three men closest to me: a young white-collar guy buried in a sports tabloid, an ancient grandpa, and a working-class tough wearing a sweatshirt with the improbable slogan "Milk Pie Club." The latter two appeared to be sleeping, but you never knew for sure. I remembered the last weapon I possessed.

"Hentai! Te o dokete yo!" I said it first in Japanese and then in English—*pervert, get your hands off me.*

I felt the hand hesitate, then depart.

"It's the guy in black! Oh, no, you aren't getting away!"

I craned my head to see a tall, stout American woman beating the thuggish-looking man's shoulders with her umbrella.

"I have done nothing! Stop it, please!" The man's apology in Japanese did no good with his foreign attacker. The formerly drowsy passengers were tittering.

"That's enough! If you keep hitting him, you could be arrested," I warned the woman as the man twisted away from us.

"I didn't have to understand what you were saying to know what was going on," the woman grumbled as she settled into a suddenly-vacated seat. "Men are bastards. All of 'em. There oughtta be a law."

As I shifted nearer, I checked her out. This was no gray-haired feminist in a patchwork jacket and peasant trousers, the kind of soul who peered enthusiastically at Japan from wire-rimmed glasses. My rescuer wore a leopard-print parka and purple Reebok sneakers. Her hair was a shade of apricot I'd never seen before.

"So, where'd you learn your good English?" she asked.

"California." That usually brought a blush to Caucasian faces, but not this one.

"You don't look it."

I let that pass. Once I would have said something, but after three years in Asia I had become too polite. Too Japanese.

"Are you going to Shiroyama?" she continued, stumbling a bit with her pronunciation.

I nodded. I was going to the 200-year-old castle town in search of antique folk art and a break from the unrelenting grayness of my life in North Tokyo. I had planned carefully, following my boss's recommendation to stay at a *minshuku*, or family-run inn. The one I'd chosen was particularly famous for its country cooking and decor. Decamping to snowy mountains while all of Japan was celebrating New Year's—the biggest party week of the year—was pretty eccentric. In fact, I couldn't believe anyone else would want to do it.

The woman was fairly clueless about rural Japan, so I explained a little about what she should expect at a Japanese inn. By the time we were talking mineral baths, I realized she was booked into the same place, and we might as well share a taxi. My solo trip had morphed into something else. I thought ruefully about the Japanese belief that there are no coincidences, that everything is part of a great cosmic plan. Considering how things turned out, I am inclined to agree.

My first view of Shiroyama was a jumble of old-fashioned shops and houses, tiled roofs loaded down with snow, and windows glowing with welcoming golden light. An old woman in a kimono bustled past, holding a parasol aloft to keep off the lightly falling flakes. I would have lingered had I not been playing bellhop for my new companion, rushing to flag down a cab before it made it to the taxi stand.

"Don't mind the Vuitton. It's fake from Hong Kong," she boasted as I lifted her pair of heavy cases into the trunk. "I didn't catch your name, young lady."

"Rei Shimura," I said slowly, as I always did growing up in the United States.

"Is that Rae with an *e*, or Ray with a *y*?"

"Neither. It's a Japanese name that rhymes with the American ones."

"Hey, Rei! It rhymes. I'm Mrs. Chapman. Marcelle," she added as an afterthought. Still, there was no question I was to call her Mrs., just as I knew she wanted me to carry her bags. She chatted all the way to Minshuku Yogetsu, which turned out to be considerably less poetic-looking than its name, which meant "night moon." Pollution had stained its stucco exterior, and windows covered by dark brown shutters made the house look like its eyes were closed to the world. Part of the garden had been converted into a parking lot holding two Toyotas: one a rusty Town Ace van, and the other a sleek black Windom. Given the high price I'd paid for my room, I could guess which one belonged to the innkeepers.

Mrs. Chapman strode past me and flung the front door open. "Yoo-hoo! Anyone around?"

A slender woman in her forties with short hair and an equally no-nonsense expression emerged from a side room and slid onto her knees, bowing her head deeply to the floor.

"Welcome. It was so rude of me not to be here to open the door for you." I recognized the voice as that of Mrs. Yogetsu, the innkeeper I had made the reservation with. Behind the courteous words, I sensed a reproach to us for having barged in. When I apologized and told her about the late train, her face tightened even more; she'd caught my slight American accent.

"You are traveling together? Surely you will prefer to have adjoining rooms?" Her offering was bland, but having experienced it many times before, I caught the sentiment underneath: *Keep the foreigners together, separate from the rest of us.*

"There's no need, absolutely no need at all." I was falling over myself. "I actually met this lady on the train."

We exchanged our shoes for house slippers, at her direction, and Mrs. Chapman painstakingly filled out the guest register while I glanced around. The place was immaculate and Zen simple, its walls hung with a few exquisite scrolls. The floor was covered by straw *tatami* mats ending at a sunken hearth where a fire burned with a low blue flame. Above it dangled an antique cast-iron kettle. Late nineteenth-century, I thought, peering at it.

I was impressed again as Mrs. Yogetsu led us past a handsome *tansu* chest decorated with a slightly unbalanced-looking New Year's arrangement of pine and flowering plum.

"How beautiful. Do you study flower arranging?" Maybe I could flatter her into a friendlier mood.

"As a matter of fact, I teach. I'm a *sensei.*"

I was startled. *Sensei* was an honorific title used to describe teachers or physicians, but was too pompous to use when introducing oneself. In describing my own work, I always used *kyoushi*, the humble word meaning tutor.

The bedroom Mrs. Yogetsu offered me was simple and extremely small, decorated with little more than a tea table and two cushions for sitting. The closet held all the bedding plus a fresh blue-and-white cotton *yukata*, the guest robe I could wear to the communal bath. The back wall of the closet had another sliding door opening into the next room. How the next-door guest and I would keep our possessions separate, I wasn't sure.

I was dying to soak my tired, stiff body. Mrs. Yogetsu pointed the way down a back staircase. As I gathered together my toiletries, I heard new arrivals downstairs: a low-pitched woman's voice speaking decorously and the more forceful growl of an older man. Another male interrupted, speaking some variation of British English, his vowels more drawn out than the BBC accents I'd grown accustomed to on the short-wave.

I hung a WOMEN ONLY sign on the blank bathroom door and entered a tidy dressing room with a glass door leading to the long, wide, sunken bath. Hefting the large plastic covers off the tub, I dipped a foot in. Like all baths in Japan, this one was oppressively over-heated.

A shower area including soap, water buckets, and wooden stools was an unspoken command to wash carefully before entering the tub, which would be shared by others. I knew all about public bath etiquette because my apartment had no bath, forcing me to travel to a public facility when I couldn't stand my trickling shower anymore. My neighborhood bathhouse was always crowded and had just a partial wall between the men's and women's sections; hearing old men talking two feet away did little for my relaxation.

This bath was mine alone and was big enough to swim in. I rested my head on its smooth wooden edge, remembering childhood summers at the pool, races from shallow to deep end that left me breathless. My body was something I didn't think about then. I wasn't a girl, I was a streamlined fish. Looking down at my small breasts breaking the water's surface, I evaluated how life in Japan had changed me. My legs had become sinewy from endless walking, and not being able to afford cheese or wine had flattened my stomach. The deprivation diet really worked.

A fuzzy feeling warned me I was close to overheating. I hauled myself out and rested until my dizziness subsided. I poured a few buckets of cool water over myself before slipping back into the cauldron. It was still blistering hot, so I cracked open the window over the bath for a rush of frosty air. I heard the bath door opening and turned around, drawing my knees together modestly and preparing to nod hello to the newcomer. I was hoping for the Japanese woman with the lovely voice.

The person who came in was a tall, athletically-built man with reddish blond hair. Also naked, but now fumbling to cover himself with a hand towel. His green eyes appeared stricken in the brief moment they met mine, just before I scrambled deeper underwater for protection.

"Wrong bathroom, please leave!" I realized after the fact that I was screaming in Japanese.

"*Sumimasen*, excuse me!" he shouted back in the strange, textured accent I had recently overheard. "It, ah, doesn't say anything on the door—"

"It says women!" I shouted in English.

"I thought these baths were communal—"

"That doesn't mean coed! What do you think this is, a soapland?"

His face reddened, giving every indication that he knew the sleazy sex baths where prostitutes used their bodies like sponges.

"I'm sorry, I meant nothing—" The man's continuing apology was cut off in midstream as the door banged shut.

My heart continued to jackhammer as I heard sounds of dressing going on in the other room, some stumbling and the zip of a fly. When I was sure he had left, I shot out of the bath and tied on my *yukata*. I exited just as Mrs. Chapman came down the hall tied up like a giant package in a yellow chenille bathrobe.

"Be careful while you bathe. The door doesn't lock." My voice shook.

"But the manager told me it would be ladies only." Mrs. Chapman scrunched up her forehead. "That sign on the door. What does it mean?"

"See this *kanji*; it looks like a woman kneeling, doesn't it? In Japanese, the word for woman is written as one who serves."

"What's a *kanji*?"

"A pictogram." At her blank expression, I tried again. "The Japanese took their system of writing from China, using pictorial symbols to represent word meanings. This is the man's symbol." I picked up the wooden sign the intruder should have known about. "What does it look like to you?"

"A blockhead on legs."

I stifled a laugh and explained, "The square is supposed to represent a rice field, and the legs underneath it represent power. So it literally means power in the rice field, which is what men did in the old agrarian culture." Next, I showed her the sign for family and explained that mixed-sex bathing was considered healthy within the family unit.

"People are perverted here," Mrs. Chapman said with a hint of excitement. "Did you ever notice you can see straight into the men's toilet at the train stations?"

"You're supposed to look away and pretend the urinals aren't there," I scolded, feeling like a hypocrite. The man had offered rather good views during his struggle to get out of the bathroom. Views I should have closed my eyes against, but didn't.

An hour later, I sat with Mrs. Chapman in the living room waiting for dinner. She had a scrapbook out with postcards of Asia. As she droned on about her favorite capital cities, my attention wandered over to the hearth where a middle-aged Japanese couple were warming their hands.

The man was pure Tokyo, wearing an expensively-cut navy suit and what looked like a permanent sneer. I dismissed him instantly as a salaryman, one of the essential office executives who filled urban Japan with an aura of cigarettes, Scotch, and exhaustion. The woman kneeling beside him was perhaps a decade younger, her long curtain of glossy black hair tied back with a silk scarf. Her eyes were rounder than mine; maybe she'd had super-expensive "Fresh Eyes" plastic surgery.

What riveted me was the fact that her ivory dress was made by Chanel—I quickly discerned from the buttons that it was the real thing. And her jewelry was Japan's best, a double-strand choker of gleaming pearls with Mikimoto's trademark gold butterfly clasp. The outfit was too expensive for a typical salaryman's wife, she'd probably bought everything overseas at a discount. Maybe they were simply rich, the sort who filled the party page of the *Tokyo Weekender*, the bi-weekly tabloid for expatriates I studied as closely as my antiques journals. As much as I scoffed at Tokyo's social lions, I was fascinated by them. This woman wasn't someone I recognized, but she seemed familiar. A memory of the bell-like voice I'd heard before my bath came back.

The sleek woman was inspecting me, taking in my ancient cashmere V-neck and the velvet leggings I'd thought would be okay for dinner. Her gaze lingered on my feet. *Yes, they are larger than yours, that's good nutrition and my American half,* I thought angrily before remembering the tiny hole in my left sock.

At dinner, Mrs. Yogetsu, the innkeeper, seated the elite couple at the head of the communal table. Mrs. Chapman and I were placed in the middle, surrounded by a sea of empty spaces.

My dinner tray looked very promising. Buckwheat noodles swam in broth that smelled deliciously of garlic and ginger. Small porcelain plates were filled with a jewel-like assortment of sashimi, as well as sweet black beans, sesame-flecked spinach, lotus root, and other artistically arranged vegetables. The only foods that made me nervous were tiny dried sardines meant to be eaten whole and paper-thin slices of raw meat I suspected was horse, a regional specialty.

Mrs. Chapman's whisper drew me away from my worries. "I can't use chopsticks. Do you think I can get a fork?"

"Don't worry. It's like working a hinge." Even though grace hadn't been said, I slipped my chopsticks from their paper wrapper and showed her how to make the subtle, pincer-like movements. As she followed my lead, two new guests slid into the cushioned places across from me. I made a slight nod of greeting to a young salaryman wearing a heavily creased navy suit that looked like a cheap cousin to the senior man's. After a panicky look, he bowed back. And then I longed to be small enough to fit into my lacquer soup bowl, because settling in right next to him was the naked giant I'd met in the bathroom.

2

He looked good in clothes, too. From beneath my lashes I took in slouchy corduroy trousers and a hand-knit Arran sweater. His hair was wet, so he must have made it into the bath after all.

"I'm sure to lose circulation in my toes before dessert, don't you think?" the foreigner said in a hearty tone to the elegant couple.

"Alcohol helps," the senior salaryman said. "Drink a lot and you will be able to sit on the floor for hours."

"Is that a charming Irish accent I hear?" Mrs. Chapman beamed at the fair-haired man.

"Scottish. We all sound alike to Yanks," the man groaned.

"Mr. Glendinning is from Glasgow, home of all that's right in the land!" said the young, rumpled-looking salaryman with whom he was sitting.

"Keep that up and I'll take you home, Yamamoto-san. Golfing in the afternoon—"

"And blazing at night!" crowed Mr. Yamamoto, whose manner changed when he turned to the big boss and switched to Japanese. "Mr. Nakamura's room is not too uncomfortable, is it? And Mrs. Nakamura, she is surely tired after the long train ride. Too many people standing around your seat, *neh*?"

"We're glad to be here, and you made acceptable arrangements," Mrs. Nakamura replied in near-perfect English, inclining her beautiful face toward the foreigner. "Hugh-san, we Japanese believe that sometimes the simplest things are the most comfortable. And I wanted very much for you to see the nostalgic way of life."

As I sucked down the savory noodles and broth, I considered Hugh Glendinning. Although his name was straight out of *Brideshead Revisited*, his accent wasn't. I thought about the working-class Glasgow accents I'd heard in the movie *Trainspotting* and concluded that also didn't fit. Hugh Glendinning's rolling *R*s and rounded vowels fell into their own uncharted territory.

"You're with these people? Did you meet them through one of the tourist agencies?" Mrs. Chapman's drawl jerked me out of my linguistic reverie.

"We work together in Tokyo. I'm going through the holidays alone, so Mr. Nakamura and his wife were kind enough to include me on their trip. I drove up separately thinking I would save time. It turned out that I could have read *Tale of the Genji* in the time it took!"

He was talking about Japan's longest and most

famous novel, a weighty tome written in the eleventh century that would probably still be sitting on my nightstand in the twenty-first. Somehow, I doubted he'd finished it either.

"Is that your Lexus in the parking lot?" Mrs. Chapman's shrewd eyes rested on Hugh Glendinning.

He grinned. "The export model's called Lexus—here it's the Windom. Ridiculous, isn't it?"

"It's just Jinglish," I said, and everyone turned to look at me. "You know, the new language created by Japanese people to express cross-cultural ideas. Here, a department store is spelled *depaato*, and a white-collar worker like you would be called *sarariman*. Or salaryman."

"So what's the meaning of Windom? It makes no bloody sense," Hugh complained.

"Mmm." His arrogance was bothering me. "Maybe a play on window and kingdom? You own all the views because you have a luxury car?"

"At least Hugh had a seat," Mrs. Chapman broke in. "The Japanese trains are terrible. No one gives up their seat to old ladies, and young gals like Rei get molested. To think I was told people in the Orient are so polite!"

Now that she had everyone's ear, Mrs. Chapman was unstoppable, plunging into a merciless replay. Thankfully, the young salaryman named Yamamoto manipulated the conversation back to the less volatile territory of Mrs. Chapman's own life in the United States. I ate my way through the fish and vegetables and took a second helping of rice while she described the retirement life in Destin, Florida, home of the most beautiful white sand beach on earth. Still, there was so much sun it got a little boring, sometimes gave a gal an itch to travel.

"Is there a Mr. Chapman?" Hugh inquired, picking up the thread. She shook her head and told him she was a widow. As he murmured in sympathy, I noticed Mrs. Nakamura giving her the evil eye. No doubt Mrs. Chapman's careless comments about meeting Asians through tourist agencies had taken their toll.

Worried an East-West table war was underway, I started a conversation about the food with a young couple who had joined the table late. Even though I was speaking Japanese, I felt Hugh Glendinning listening. When I tried to discreetly hide my serving of horse under some garnishing leaves, he picked his up and ate with gusto. I wondered if he'd be so happy knowing he was eating something that had once pranced merrily. Then again, I'd heard the Scottish national dish was something like a sheep stomach stuffed with intestines.

"You do this for a living, don't you? Talk to people. You teach, or something," he boomed when I had finally fallen silent.

"Right. It's about the best job a foreign woman can get." I would have preferred a position cataloging Japanese antiques in a small museum, but after six weeks of searching, I got realistic. My two offers were bar hostess or English teacher. I took the job with health benefits.

"I've been meaning to start language training. Tell me, do you work at Berlitz?"

"No. I'm just a contract employee at a kitchenware

company." I was starting to get embarrassed about being the poorest, most marginal person in the group.

"Kitchenware. What is it, Tiger, Nichiyu, Zojirushi?" he persisted.

"Nichiyu," I said, surprised he knew it.

"So you're from Tokyo also. I'm an international solicitor—I think Yanks would call me a lawyer? Mr. Nakamura has been good enough to let me muck about in his department at Sendai. So far, there've been no disasters."

Sendai was known to me as a historic furniture-making town, so I had been surprised to learn it was also the name of an upstart electronics company. Sendai had probably hired him to assist with overseas trade, a dubious prospect given the collapse of the bubble economy.

"Glendinning-san is a good friend." There was something oily in Mr. Nakamura's smile as he nodded toward the Scot.

"And that's why we want to share your first New Year's Eve in Japan," Mrs. Nakamura added in silvery tones.

"Setsuko knows it's a lonely night for me." Hugh rewarded his boss's wife with a crooked smile. "In Scotland, New Year's Eve is the night to end all. And January first is the best day of the year, traditionally the one people took for holiday instead of Christmas."

"That sounds un-Christian." Mrs. Chapman frowned the same way she had at the bath signs.

"But we have Pagan roots!" Hugh said cheerfully. "In one of the small towns, people still run through the streets with balls of fire, and on New Year's Eve we drink our way from house to house. Nobody locks their doors because the parties carry on into the morning."

"New Year's Eve is family time in Japan," said Setsuko Nakamura, including everyone but me in her benevolent gaze. "We spend time with the people we feel close to and dine on New Year's foods with lucky meanings. For example, these long noodles celebrate the changing of the year. Vegetables and fruits represent the harvest from field and mountain."

"Sort of like American Thanksgiving?" Mrs. Chapman looked at her dinner with new curiosity.

"Not quite. There's an interest in, how do you say, fertility . . . the small round things like the black beans and fish eggs are hope for the birth of many children," Setsuko answered.

"Fish eggs?" Mrs. Chapman faltered.

I'd crunched down on the sheet of tiny roe earlier; to me, they were a cheaper version of the Beluga my parents were probably serving at their own celebration in San Francisco.

"Not enough children are being born," Mr. Nakamura told us. "The government knows it's a problem—they pay families who have more than two children some small sum. But it's barely enough to pay for one bag of groceries."

"That's right, I can't even think of getting married or having children until I have four million yen in the bank!" Mr. Yamamoto joked.

"You'll have to work much harder at Sendai for that to happen. And on your skills with ladies as

well." Mr. Nakamura cackled, and his subordinate
flushed with embarrassment.

"We have the same problem in America," Mrs.
Chapman said. "It costs lots of money to raise kids.
But in my opinion, a family just isn't right without
young ones. I raised two of my own and to think I've
only got one grandchild! She's my everything."

"It's very sad not to have children. I have not
been fortunate." Setsuko Nakamura's smile was
tremulous.

"You're still quite young!" Hugh comforted her.

"My wife, like a fool, talks too much." Mr.
Nakamura snapped. "She's like a curse I carry, even
on holiday!"

He spoke in English, so everyone understood. I
felt Mrs. Chapman stiffen beside me. Color rose in
Hugh's face, but he said nothing.

Maybe Mr. Nakamura was just in a bad mood.
Still, I thought it was an unforgivable way to talk
to your spouse. I sneaked a glance at Setsuko
Nakamura, who was delicately cutting the raw meat
with her chopsticks. Even though her facial expression remained blank, I sensed something radiating
from her, a sharp vibration of pain. Young Mr.
Yamamoto began chatting about tourist activities
but it was too late to right the awkward stillness that
had come over us all.

After dinner, Mrs. Yogetsu brought a small television
into her pristine living room, set it up and left. I settled down amid cushions on the floor with Mrs.

Chapman, who was now complaining about the lack of back support. I tried to rig something for her, but she grumbled that she might as well go up to her room for a rest.

The young couple I'd chatted up at the table plunked down next to me.

"I travel to your country every year for Honda Motor Company," said the man whose small, rectangular glasses gave him the look of a friendly owl. "I am Taro Ikeda. My wife Yuki is too shy to speak English."

"Actually, I would like to try speaking, if you will help me?" Her hesitant English was instantly endearing. I introduced myself in my native tongue, and they both nodded with approval at my Japanese name.

"Which *kanji* do you use to write it?" Taro asked.

My second name was quite standard, but my first name had over a dozen different meanings, depending on how it was written. It could mean beauty or bowing or coldness or the number zero; the *kanji* my father had chosen was a lesser-known one that meant something akin to crystal clarity. I had to draw the *kanji* before they understood.

"My name means snow. I love snowy weather very much," Yuki chirped in her schoolgirl's English.

"Is it your first trip here?" I asked.

"No, this is our second trip. We really enjoy ski," Yuki said.

"Skiing, Yuki, skiing. And I must mention my hobby of ancient crime," Taro interjected.

"You're into crime?" I asked uneasily. It was a

strange hobby for anyone, let alone such a straight-looking young man; by the way Yuki rolled her eyes, you could tell she agreed. But the Japanese were the authors of the world's most frightening ghost stories, so I understood where his passion might be rooted.

"This is the ghost capital of Japan! Do you know its great story?" Taro asked.

I knew Shiroyama's general history. The town was once the seat of a feudal lord, Geki Uchida, who built a castle admired throughout Japan. And, Taro was telling me, Lord Uchida was the man behind Shiroyama's growth as a decorative arts center.

"Lord Uchida made much work for the people, cutting wood for furniture and designing *shunkei*. I am sorry for my poor English, but I cannot translate it exactly," Taro said.

Setsuko Nakamura, who had taken a prime spot at the hearth with Hugh, sighed impatiently. "*Shunkei* is Shiroyama's famous lacquer which is used for bowls and tableware. The lacquer is extremely thin that you can see the grain of the wood underneath. Therefore, it is considered beautiful."

"Is it possible to find antique *shunkei* around here?" I was intrigued by the idea.

"Yes, but I'm certain it would be too expensive for you." Setsuko's cold, perfectly shadowed eyes rested on me briefly, then turned back to Hugh.

"It's not the lacquer that's interesting, it's the ghost story," Taro grumbled. "Lord Uchida's eldest son ruled the house after his death, but unfortunately he was a very poor leader. Therefore, a cousin decided to take over. The eldest son was murdered. His family escaped except for one daughter, Miyo, who stayed and tried to fight with the cousin."

"Physical fighting?" I asked, a dramatic picture forming in my mind.

"Like many samurai ladies, she carried a small knife inside her kimono for possible bad situations. She used it on her cousin." Taro paused, eyes sweeping the crowd to make sure we were all with him. "It was not a deadly wound. His servant took the knife and prepared to execute her, but this cousin had a kind heart and let her live. The shame of failing was too strong for Princess Miyo. She did not want to join her family again. Perhaps they would think the new lord spared her because . . ." He pursed his lips, and I imagined he was thinking of rape.

"The soldiers released her outside the castle. She ran to the forest and was never seen again. But over time, some people who have walked in the woods tell stories about seeing a beautiful girl in a fine, old-fashioned kimono. She stands before them and then is vanished. And when it is very windy weather, people like to say Miyo is crying." Taro Ikeda bowed to applause, his story over.

"So it's really mostly superstition," I said. I didn't believe half of it, but thought that would be rude to say.

"Not for me! This is my historical project. I've done research at the museums here. With a metal detector, I have searched the forest for evidence of weapons and other things."

"He finds only beer cans," Yuki sniffed.

"Yes, I was unsuccessful." Taro didn't sound

upset. "Probably her treasures were taken many years ago."

"In my opinion, this conquering cousin sounds quite generous to his enemies. How did he perform as a leader? Was he able to build up the town's economic base?" Hugh spoke from his half-sprawled position at the fire. I had grown sick of watching Setsuko go through an elaborate ritual of warming a flask of sake over the flame before pouring a splash in a tiny lacquer saucer for him. The ritual of a woman caring for her man. Where had Mr. Nakamura gone, anyway?

Taro shrugged. "Everyone agrees that the new ruler saved the town. He forced the people to concentrate on lumber, work far more important to the future than *shunkei* lacquer."

"Is that true?" I asked Mrs. Yogetsu in Japanese when she came in to refresh Setsuko and Hugh's sake supply.

The innkeeper shrugged. "Business is good here. The runaway princess is just a story for tourists. If a daughter existed, she traveled with her family when they left the castle. As any daughter would," she added firmly.

I thought about the story as I paged through a guidebook to the Japanese Alps after the crowd drifted away from the living room. The legend was an easy way for the town to romanticize its brutal takeover. The ghostly fate of the princess was pure propaganda, a bit of sweet bean paste smeared over the ending like dessert.

A handsome man in his fifties with a thick, some-what rakish crown of silver-and-black hair came out of the kitchen. Yuki told him how much she had enjoyed the meal, and I chimed in. The man looked exhausted, but managed a polite bow of thanks before leaving.

"That man is such a talented chef. I wish my husband cooked," Yuki complained. Japanese husbands were notorious for not being able to boil water.

"He is talented. I ate so much it will take days to hike it off," I exaggerated for the sake of girlish goodwill.

"Oh! Then you must come walking with us at midnight." Yuki and Taro were going to Shiroyama's oldest temple, where the New Year would be rung in 108 times according to the Buddhist calendar. I had planned on going alone, but the thought of navigating a strange, dark town with new friends was more attractive. At Yuki's urging, I went upstairs to invite Mrs. Chapman.

I knocked several times on the door two down from mine and called her name. There was no response except the sound of a television blaring an English-language nature program. As I turned to start down the stairs, Hugh Glendinning opened his door.

"Wait just a minute. I want to say I'm sorry but hardly had a chance downstairs."

"I'm glad you didn't." It was bad enough up here, with doors as thin as paper separating us from the others.

"Now that I hear you were a victim of sexual

assault, I feel rotten. Post traumatic stress disorder
and all that." Hugh studied me like I was some
strange species, the violated woman.

"Never mind. Your walking in on me may have
been disgusting, but I doubt it will leave any psychic
scars." I made a movement to leave.

"I was an idiot. It's my fault that I'm no good
with those damned *kanji*. And when I saw you
at first—your hair—I thought you were a lad. Of
course, the minute you turned around, I realized my
error." He favored me with the same sexy, crooked
smile he'd offered Setsuko Nakamura.

"Exactly how long have you been in this country?" I demanded.

"Nine months, something like that—"

"I'd suggest you learn to read bathroom signs if
you plan to stay any longer. You are extremely lucky
you didn't walk in on a Japanese woman and offend
her beyond belief."

"But you *are* Japanese, more or less. Although I
don't understand the game you're playing with your
nationality."

Steeling myself, I replied, "It doesn't really matter where my parents come from, does it? Because
I'm not bound by tradition to let you get away with
things, take advantage."

"Take advantage?" He asked, laughter flashing
through his voice.

"Yes, the way you undoubtedly take advantage of
people in this country who are too polite to tell you
to do some things for yourself!" I ranted.

"You're a hard woman, Rei Shimura. Here I am

apologizing, when it was just as bad for me. God knows I was ashamed to be seen bare."

"Okay," I said, with a superhuman attempt at patience. "I understand it was an accident. And I know Japanese doesn't come easily. It's got to be learned."

"Well then, I'm asking for some help! Consider me your holiday tutorial project."

Again I noted his grin—had he ever really been embarrassed?—and said, "You already have access to a native speaker."

"Setsuko?"

She was the one I'd been thinking of, but he could have been decent enough to mention his male colleagues. With perfect timing, the door next to his opened. The woman in question emerged wearing just a *yukata* and her magnificent pearls.

"What is it now, Hugh?" She spoke to him as intimately as a wife.

"Ah, just practicing my English conversation skills. Bathtime, is it?"

"Yes. How about you?" Her voice was inviting.

"Done it already. Rather hot, that water. Once burned, twice shy." Hugh winked at me.

"Excuse me, but do you mean to wear your necklace in the water?" I interrupted, my eyes on Setsuko's mammoth pearls. As much as I disliked her, I couldn't stand the idea of anything precious being destroyed.

"Certainly. This particular mineral bath is excellent for pearls. It refreshes them." Setsuko caressed the pearls. "Being an American, you probably don't know that."

"Americans prefer diamonds, isn't that right?" Hugh teased.

If that was an attempt to defend me, it stank. I decided both of them deserved a short lecture of the type I used with my most unruly classes of young salesmen.

"In my museum work, I've learned an occasional salt water bath is relatively harmless for pearls." I watched with pleasure as Setsuko's posture become rigid. "However, the exact saline content of the water here is unknown. The reason I'd advise against immersing your pearls is the water will weaken the knots between them and possibly lead to a break. That's why, when you have your pearls cleaned every year, they are re-strung." I paused. "You do have your pearls professionally cleaned?"

"At Mikimoto." Setsuko narrowed her round eyes before swishing off.

Hugh gave me a mocking salute. "Well done, but do you know as much about the care of textiles? I have some ironing . . ."

"No," I spat. "And why don't you go bathe with her? Maybe this time you'll burn your problem off."

Hugh Glendinning's annoying foreign laughter followed me downstairs, and I cursed myself for not being able to leave well enough alone. It was a problem I needed to work on seriously. Maybe in the new year.

3

Sun filtered through the window's *shōji* screen and filled my bedroom on New Year's morning with pale, diffused light. I peered at my watch, which told me it was seven-thirty. I knew I'd better pry myself out of the quilts fast if I wanted the bathroom to myself.

Since I'd shut off the gas heater for safety during the night, leaving bed was painful. I flipped the heat up to high, gathered my clothing and raced downstairs.

The bathroom door already had the women's sign on but stuck when I tried to open it. I fiddled with the doorjamb, and when the door swung open, I saw the dressing room had one basket filled with clothes. The pink turtleneck, ski pants, and lacy underwear could mean one of two women. I undressed but nevertheless wrapped a towel around myself before peeking in the bath chamber.

"The shower on the left has the best spray. Come

quickly, you are surely frozen!" Yuki Ikeda, her face flushed pink, was up to her shoulders in hot water.

"What about your husband?" I couldn't believe they weren't enjoying the bath together.

"Sleeping like a big pile of garbage!" She rolled her eyes, making me laugh.

The warm shower was a joy, but slipping into the steamy bath was heaven. I took the side opposite my new friend, who politely looked at the ceiling as I laid my towel aside.

"Why are you up so early?" I asked in Japanese since there was no bossy husband around to insist on English practice.

"It's crazy! Taro and I wanted to have a romantic bath yesterday evening, but there was a WOMEN ONLY sign on all night. I tried to check the dressing room, but the door was locked."

"It was jammed with a scrap of paper. I had trouble this morning, too, but it's fixed now."

Yuki shook her head. "To be frank, I think this place is getting a little sloppy. When I came this morning, the bathroom was very messy. The bath covers—" she pointed to the three hard plastic sections neatly stacked by the side—"were all over the floor. So the water was a bit cooler than it should be."

The bath had reached the right temperature for me, but I made a properly downcast face.

"I hope there wasn't any foreigner using soap in the water. I know that Americans and English use soap in baths. Maybe they don't understand our custom of washing in the shower first."

She was giving me uncomfortable flashbacks to

the times I'd been called upon to translate for my American mother, a process that humiliated her and made me extremely defensive. I changed the subject.

"Thanks for last night."

"No, it was my pleasure! Did you enjoy it?"

"Very much." It had been worth going, although the walk I'd hoped would be private had been interrupted by Mr. Nakamura and Yamamoto, who turned up halfway along the route. Judging from their breathing, I guessed they'd started out some time after us and had run to catch up.

At the temple, I had nearly dropped my camera when I saw a group of young men wearing short cotton jackets and loincloths ringing the bell. I'd seen skimpy male attire at religious festivals in the summer, but never in ten-degree weather. I turned my head away, which had sent Yuki into a giggling fit.

"This is part of the New Year's tradition, Rei-san! To wear such light clothing shows their strength."

"It's too cold for that." My feet were going numb inside two pairs of socks and hiking boots.

"Those boys are very warm from alcohol," Taro had reassured me. "Don't worry about them."

When the youths were through, everyone cheered and lined up to try bell-ringing themselves. The act was more complicated than I'd expected; it involved tugging a cord that moved a dowel that in turn, knocked against the huge bronze bell. Mr. Nakamura went first and struggled, issuing an awkward half-note. Too much beer. He made a joke about it and passed the cord to young Mr. Yamamoto, who swung easily with powerful arms, then looked abashed and said no doubt the wind had helped him. Taro and Yuki performed respectably. When it was my turn, I found the rope slightly unwieldy but surprised myself by producing a satisfyingly mellow ring. I prayed for world peace because I couldn't think of anything personal that needed tending.

"Tremendous! You must be a baseball player." Hugh Glendinning had showed up after all. His casual step into the orderly line caused some sniping among the others waiting their turn.

"No. I've done similar things before." I walked off.

"What's that?" Hugh was refusing to go away.

I explained about my visits to the Sunday flea markets held on the grounds of Tokyo's Shinto shrines. Once there, I was always drawn toward altars rich in gold leaf and bronze. Even though Buddhism and Shintoism were different religions, they both used magnificent bells.

"Interesting," he said, but by the way he was staring over my head, I could tell he was hardly listening. "It's a shame Setsuko didn't come. She had a headache."

"I'm sorry to hear that." Even though she hadn't wanted to make the climb after her long, relaxing bath, she was with us in spirit: bad spirits.

"Are you?"

"Who cares?" I sounded juvenile but couldn't help it this time. As I stalked off to join the others, I realized Hugh had neatly crafted a love triangle in his own mind. Five days of stupid insinuation lay ahead if I didn't separate myself from the situation fast.

※   ※   ※

It was better to stick closely to women like Mrs. Chapman and Yuki. I watched surreptitiously as my new friend climbed out of the tub. She was my height, but about fifteen pounds lighter. In America, she might have been suspected of harboring an eating disorder. In reality, she just had slim Japanese bones.

"So, I think you are an unusual girl, Rei-san. What about your parents? Why aren't you with them for the New Year's holiday?" Yuki asked.

"They're the last ones I want to see." I made a face, and when Yuki shushed disapprovingly, I confessed that I didn't want to spend my few days of vacation listening to them urge me to move back. I was an only child; they could spend unlimited funds and energy on me. Idealism kept me in Tokyo, that and the fear that spending one night back in my cozy featherbed in San Francisco would make it impossible for me to re-emerge. I loved luxury. Forsaking it was one of the things I was proudest of.

"You are strange. Do you want to come skiing with us today?" Yuki asked, drying off.

"Actually, I'm more into temples and museums." I got out, sucking in my stomach a little.

"Well, then, you must come with us tomorrow when we go to the old city hall. It used to be a courthouse and prison for people in the late seventeenth century. There is an interrogation chamber where criminals were tortured. It's just horrible! Naturally, my husband must take some photographs."

After we dressed, Yuki asked me to help blow-dry

the back of her pageboy and then insisted on trying to restyle my cropped cut. She gave up quickly, saying "I like your hair! It is not typically Japanese!"

I told her about my American mother then, and she sighed. "That is romantic. I can see it in your bone structure." She pointed at my cheeks. "Strong American character. You are not a typical *konketsujin*."

The word which meant half-blooded person made me flinch. Mr. Katoh, my boss at Nichiyu, had asked about my ethnic background during my job interview and, sounding sad, advised me to keep it to myself. Blue-eyed blond teachers were always flavor of the month and landed the best-paying jobs. Looking Japanese complicated things, perhaps hinted that I was *ainoko*, a child born from a short-lived, illicit union. In reality, my mother from Baltimore and father from Yokohama had met in San Francisco at an Isamu Noguchi gallery opening. They'd married fast but had me a very respectable three years later. I had brownish-black hair, a small Japanese nose, and almond-shaped eyes. Still, I was undeniably *konketsujin*. I hated the word, even spoken by somebody meaning no offense.

The two men faced each other, blocking the hallway as I returned from my bath.

"If I could find my bloody cell phone, we could ring the police." Hugh Glendinning's voice rasped as if he'd just been awakened. He was wearing his *yukata* over pajamas and stood barefoot on the cold wood.

"There's no reason to go to extremes," said Mr. Nakamura, also in a robe but at least wearing slippers.

"You're already up and dressed, Rei." Hugh turned his sleepy gaze on me. "Have you seen Setsuko, ah, Mrs. Nakamura?"

"The last time I saw her was before her bath last night. You were there."

"That was around nine, wasn't it?" Mr. Nakamura hesitated. "I remember now. I was in my room reading. Just before midnight, I came downstairs and went out with Yamamoto."

"Hold on. Didn't you tell me your wife had a headache and didn't want to go to the temple? When did she say that to you?" Hugh moved closer to his colleague, who backed against me in his haste to achieve some distance.

"I did not want to inconvenience anyone in the group with my problem." Mr. Nakamura coughed, a hacking sound that spoke of cigarette addition.

"What about after you came home from the temple? Did you see her then?" Hugh asked.

"You were so tired that I wanted you to sleep, not to worry." He coughed again.

"You mean your wife was not in your bed and you didn't think it odd?" Hugh's voice rose to an unseemly level for New Year's morning.

"In Japan, husbands and wives . . . they have more space between them," Nakamura said weakly.

Hugh shot a questioning look at me, and I gave a tiny nod. My Aunt Norie had shared a futon with my cousin Tom until he was seven, and many of the mothers who worked at my company did the same. But Mrs. Nakamura didn't have a child.

"You were booked into the same room here,

correct?" It was as if Hugh decided to turn the hallway into his courtroom.

"Certainly, but Glendinning-san, it would not
have been polite for me to disturb you last night!"

Hugh looked at the floor for a few seconds. When
he spoke again, his voice was flat. "We'll ask that
woman about it."

"Mrs. Yogetsu," I supplied.

"Yes, Mrs. Getsu. And I suppose if Mrs. Getsu
hasn't placed your wife in a separate room, we'll start
a search."

What kind of situation would lead a woman to
sleep apart from her husband on New Year's Eve? I
thought about Setsuko and her husband after I
returned to my room and ran a comb through my
hair, trying to undo Yuki's ministrations. Setsuko—
it was funny how I knew her first name but had no
clue about her husband's. Not that I wanted to
know. The way he had spoken to his wife last night
was brutal, and I recalled him at the temple, making crude jokes to Hugh about a group of junior-
high school girls. No, he hadn't worried about her
at all.

It was difficult to enjoy breakfast, even though it was
straight out of my Zen vegetarian dreams: *zōni,* a
special New Year's vegetable broth, plus steaming rice
and saucers filled with colorful pickled vegetables. On
the side was *mochi*, a glutinous rice cake.

"I asked for toast, but I don't think she understood." Mrs. Chapman stared miserably at her meal.

"Just try it. It's really pretty good," I offered before saying half-truthfully, "I missed you last night."

"So what did you do, paint the town red?" Mrs. Chapman's sharp gaze told me she wasn't fooled.

"No, we just went to see the new year rung in at the temple. I knocked at your door, but you must have been—"

"Sound asleep," said Mrs. Chapman. "Beer always goes straight to my head. I turned on a National Geographic special and must have nodded off. When I woke up they were doing some kind of crazy exercise program."

Yamamoto and Nakamura came in wearing heavy sweaters and ski pants. A missing wife wasn't enough to cancel the day's sports. My anger surprised me, given that I didn't even like Setsuko Nakamura. Breaking his chopsticks apart, Mr. Nakamura gave me a venomous look, which I returned. I hadn't volunteered to hear the details of his problem—I'd been drafted. I continued eating my vegetables and invited Mrs. Chapman on my morning hike. She declined, saying something about souvenir shopping in town. I didn't coax her further. I liked the idea of walking fast by myself, working off the troublesome feelings I couldn't quite identify.

Ten minutes later I was outside admiring how the snow had blanketed the cars and turned the parking lot into a dazzling white field. There was a pattern in the snow, dainty tracks that could only be made by a cat. I followed the trail around to the back of the inn and found a bamboo gate, which I unlatched.

I entered a small space where snow had edged the branches of severely pruned trees like embroidery. Gusting winds shook a flurry of flakes downward, and I pulled up the hood of my down coat and trudged on, calling in a soft voice to the cat, who had to be crouching somewhere.

The paw prints ended at a heap of dead leaves and branches, a pile of rubbish out of place in the stylized garden. I fluttered my fingers in the pile, trying to encourage the animal out of hiding. As the leaves moved, I found something else.

What had looked like bark was a frozen length of human hair. And the pale, trailing branch was a slender forearm, hair shaved off in the super-feminine manner of many Japanese women. The last thing I took in before my feet gave out were glossy scarlet fingernails, one of them broken. A condition Setsuko Nakamura would not have tolerated, had she been alive.

4

Japanese police are obsessed with alien registration cards. Not having one handy is cause to be held for hours or even overnight, a misery that has befallen English teachers and bracelet-sellers alike. I wasn't surprised the Shiroyama police demanded my card when they pulled up at Minshuku Yogetsu in a salt-streaked squad car, a petite ambulance behind.

I had the card ready in my wallet and ran upstairs to get my passport. When I returned, I found Mrs. Yogetsu still hadn't moved from her courtesy kneeling position before the police.

"There's no reason why this should have happened here, I beg you to understand. I took that woman's reservation through a travel agent!" Her pleas went ignored as the officer in charge dispatched a trio of juniors outside.

Captain Jiro Okuhara appeared to have been pulled straight from home, dressed as he was in a beige

V-neck and checked golf slacks. Still, he behaved as formally as if we were at headquarters, offering me his card with a grave expression. I handled it the way I was supposed to—looking it over with great interest, something that was in fact feigned. My command of Japanese was almost exclusively spoken—although I'd been studying *kanji* characters since college, I could read only about three hundred, which left me some where in the third grade.

Captain Okuhara whisked me from the crowd of guests and concerned neighbors spilling into the entryway. In Mr. Yogetsu's kitchen, we faced off across a small table overloaded with a rice cooker, vegetable peelings, and other remnants of breakfast preparation. The kitchen wasn't as clean as I'd expected, given the New Year's scrubbing that most of the country happily took upon itself. Then again, Mr. Yogetsu hadn't been expecting a crisis.

Okuhara studied my alien card, which contained my name, photograph, and right thumbprint along with my employment and visa information. Then he switched on a cassette recorder and asked for everything that had transpired since I opened the front door.

"How distressing for you to have such trouble on New Year's Day," he said when I'd finished my account.

"It was worse for her." Setsuko had looked like she'd been packed in snow for hours.

"So, Miss Shimura, I'm wondering something." There was a perceptible change in his tone. "Why were you walking outside the inn like that? Don't you think it a little odd?"

I went rigid but answered vaguely about how I had planned to hike up to the castle ruins but decided to visit the garden first. "In Tokyo, there weren't—I mean aren't—many gardens, after all." I was stumbling over a perfectly easy sentence construction, embarrassing myself.

"How did you even know there was a garden behind the house?" He caressed a large, expensive-looking fountain pen, not writing anything down. Still, I remained hyper-conscious of the small tape recorder on the table.

"I wasn't sure there was a garden, but there were some animal feet and I followed them." It was too bad I didn't know the word for footprint.

"Was it the animal you were interested in, or the garden? You're contradicting yourself." He spoke. slowly to make sure I caught the meaning.

"It was the cat. I like cats," I added.

"Where did you touch the body?"

"I moved the leaves but didn't touch the body. In the United States, civilians never interfere with police work." I made a conscious effort to mimic his authoritarian stance.

"But how did you know who the woman was? When Mrs. Yogetsu called, she said you had made an identification."

"I heard her husband say she was missing. She was on my mind." I thought of saying something about recognizing her hairless arm and manicured fingernails but stayed quiet, not wanting to sound obsessive.

"Really! When did he report her absence?" The police chief started writing.

"Just before I went down to breakfast. I was walking to my room after bathing, and I was invited to join a conversation between him and Mr. Glendinning."

"The Englishman." Captain Okuhara nodded. "I also secured his registration card. And what was your relationship with the deceased lady?"

"I had no connection with Mrs. Nakamura." I stared at some nicks in the wooden table. "I arrived here last night at six. She and her party came about five minutes later, because I heard her voice downstairs. We sat at the same table at dinner. I saw her walk off to her bath around nine o'clock. That's it."

"How long do you plan to stay in Shiroyama?"

"Through next Sunday." I wondered if he'd try to detain me. It was his right to do so, just as it was Nichiyu's right to find a replacement for a contract worker like me should I not be around to teach English.

"And the other foreigners, what about them?"

"Mrs. Chapman is doing some kind of self-tour, but I have no idea about Mr. Glendinning. Since he's with Mr. Nakamura and Mr. Yamamoto, I imagine his plans are tied to theirs."

Captain Okuhara laid his pen down and appraised me. "For an American, you speak pretty good Japanese."

"Thank you," I said, confused at the change of manner.

"Yes, you will be fine as a translator."

"Me? I have no interpreter qualifications. I'm just an English teacher."

"Our English-speaking policeman is on holiday. Unless the other foreigners wish to wait in the prison for an interpreter to arrive, I will require your assistance. As a matter of procedure, this questioning must be done. You understand, I'm sure?"

With his eyes boring into me and his hand firmly placed over my passport, I did.

Hugh Glendinning strode in and looked at me hard. It was impossible to tell if the prospect of having me as an interpreter was worrisome or a relief. This would be almost enjoyable if the situation weren't so black.

"Your alien registration and passport are in order. I see you're a lawyer." Okuhara's voice was almost respectful.

"At Sendai. How do you like our mini-cassette recorder?" Hugh asked, and I gamely translated.

"What?" Captain Okuhara blinked a few times.

"Your recorder." Hugh tapped the small black machine. "I hope the microphone's got enough volume for you. We've had some complaints, to be frank, and are reworking the model."

"It's all right," the police captain said briskly. "When did you last see Mrs. Nakamura?"

"What kind of investigation is underway?" Hugh had carried in his own diary and pen and was beginning to make notes. "Because of my relationship with Sendai, Mr. Nakamura is effectively my client. I need to know the status of this investigation."

"I must remind the Englishman that he is under questioning, not his *client*." The police chief drew the sides of his mouth down in exaggeration, as if he found the word ridiculous.

"I'm not English. I'm a Scot." Hugh's expression remained pleasant, but I sensed anger. "I last saw Mrs. Nakamura yesterday evening, going to the bath."

"You bathed with her?" Captain Okuhara inquired.

"No, indeed. May I remind you, she is married to my colleague," Hugh reproached. "I simply saw her walking down the hallway. Nine o'clock, I think it was. She was in a bathrobe and carrying some shampoo, so I assumed she was going to the bath."

"Were there any other witnesses?" Okuhara asked.

I brought up my own presence, and Hugh shot me a surprised look. What had he thought, I'd leave him to the wolf?

"Tell me more about your relationship," the captain said, stroking his pen suggestively.

"With her? We only met at dinner." Hugh's eyes darted nervously toward me.

"No, with Mr. Nakamura's wife!"

"Oh." He exhaled, obviously relieved. "We were friends." Okuhara's eyebrows shot up at that sharp departure from Japanese male-female norms but Hugh continued, oblivious. "We've been friends for ages, ever since Mr. Nakamura asked her to help me find a decorator to furnish my flat."

"And once your residence was furnished?"

"She handled anything else I needed. Finding a maid and leasing a car . . . ordering groceries . . . the myriad things one needs to learn in a new city."

"You've been here how long, Mr. Glendinning?"

"Eight or nine months."

"And how many times did you meet with Mrs. Nakamura during this period?"

Hugh shrugged. "Often. I didn't keep count."

"Was her husband present during your meetings?" Okuhara prodded.

"Occasionally."

"Do you have any idea why she might have gone outdoors without clothing in the middle of the night?"

Hugh paused. "Actually, I thought she might have had a row with her husband."

I translated that as 'misunderstanding' for lack of a more exact word. But as euphemisms are used to describe a multitude of sins in Japanese, Captain Okuhara lit on it passionately. I haltingly translated his flood of questions about Setsuko Nakamura's relationship with her husband. Hugh drew his lips into a thin line and pleaded ignorance.

The police chief seemed unsatisfied, staring at Hugh for long periods without speaking as if to incite him into more revelations. Too much time passed. I was relieved when Mrs. Yogetsu stuck her head through the door.

"A telephone call, from the Sendai company president," she said in Japanese. I translated and Hugh bolted without apology.

"The other foreigner you mentioned, bring her to me." Captain Okuhara's voice was brusque, as if he needed to revalidate his authority.

"Heavens, this is exciting," said Mrs. Chapman after I found her eavesdropping outside the kitchen door.

Now she sat with her faux Vuitton bag on her lap, smiling at Captain Okuhara. "Can I take his picture, do you think?"

I shook my head and, anticipating his first question, asked for her documents. Because Mrs. Chapman was a tourist, she had a visitor card tucked in her passport instead of the laminated ID Hugh and I carried.

"It's in my maiden name, Marcia Smith. Marcelle is my nickname, because I never cared for Marcia." She looked at me anxiously, and I blanched. Here was something the police officer might seize upon. He looked at the picture inside, listened to the explanation, and looked back at her.

"In Japan, we have one name. After you marry, you take the man's name by law."

Even though it was out of turn, I said to him, "That might change. Japanese women are beginning to sue for the right to keep their name. Some friends of mine in a feminist organization are involved."

"It will never happen," he snorted. "Now stop pretending this is a women's liberation rally and ask the old woman about Mrs. Nakamura."

Mrs. Chapman had seen even less of Setsuko Nakamura than I had, but she had plenty of emotional impressions to offer.

"She was a quiet one: unusually quiet in my opinion. Good-looking gal, but she didn't seem very close to her husband. Not a good marriage, if you ask me."

"Please ask her to elaborate," Okuhara ordered after I translated her statement.

"Rei, you saw them." Mrs. Chapman wiggled around

in the kitchen chair that was too tight for her hips. "They didn't say a word to each other, just spoke to Glendinning and his little Japanese assistant. It was eerie, kind of like they were talking through a medium."

I knew what she meant. But in a Japanese marriage, the best communication was supposed to take place without words. A wife was supposed to anticipate her husband's needs and respond to them. What wasn't normal was the way Setsuko had stiffened, her profound aura of anger mixed with pain.

Captain Okuhara kept me for a few minutes after he was finished with Mrs. Chapman.

"You seem to have a prior relationship with the Englishman. When did you first meet?"

"Around six o'clock on New Year's Eve." I didn't want to go into the exact details of where.

"He said you met at dinner, which according to the sign in the entry hall, is always served at seven." His voice was as sharp and cold as the icicles I'd seen outside.

"I don't understand," I said, hoping to be excused.

"You're giving a very odd impression, Miss Shimura. It is apparent that either you or Mr. Glendinning is not telling the truth."

"No! I mean, I had just arrived at the inn. I was in the hallway, getting ready to walk downstairs to the bath. I didn't see him, but I heard his voice."

He nodded at last, letting me go.

The five kilometers to the castle's summit were tougher than I'd expected, a fitting penance for my half-truths to Okuhara. Plenty of ice was packed beneath the snow. Even though I followed in other people's tracks, there were some unsteady moments as I struggled to the uneven, broken-down stone wall at the summit.

This was the only remnant of the castle foundation. Yuki had warned me it was a sorry-looking ruin that didn't do the legend justice. Still, the views were good. Around me were the soft colors of old stones and evergreens and below were snow-covered roofs and the highway winding like a dark ribbon down the mountain.

The air was sharp enough to bring tears to my eyes, tears that should have come earlier. I felt disconnected, at a point somewhere above grief and shock and horror. It was a little like sitting in the balcony watching a Kabuki drama unfold beneath me. I had trouble understanding the theatrical dialogue, just as I couldn't understand the subtext behind Captain Okuhara's words. Did he suspect I'd done something wrong, perhaps in collusion with Hugh?

Going down, I took the alternate route marked DIFFUCULT through deep snow, following a path marked only by colored rope tied on trees. As I stopped to look at a twisted old plum tree that was starting to bud, I heard a crunching sound in the snow behind me. It halted abruptly and started again when I resumed walking. I spun around and saw a tall, slender figure dressed in black. Japanese eyes peered out from a woolen ski mask.

"Miss Shimura, excuse me for what I was doing. These woods are supposed to be dangerous. Bad conditions for injury." The man pulled the mask off his face and I recognized him as Yamamoto, the young assistant to Mr. Nakamura and Hugh Glendinning.

"You followed me all the way up the mountain?" I was starting to freak out.

"Yes, I walked behind a group, so you did not see." As the young man moved closer, I noticed how intense his expression was, how powerful his figure seemed looming half a foot over me. He had hit the temple bell with a lot of vigor last night, more than was necessary. A dim sense of unease prickled in me, similar to the feeling I have in certain parts of San Francisco.

"Do you want to talk to me about something?" He could probably smell my fear, the way dogs did.

"Yes. I'm very concerned about the Nakamura situation," he whispered as if there were people around to hear.

"How so?" I leaned against the plum tree and studied him warily.

"Nakamura-san's in my room. That's because the police are searching his room, I am not sure why. He's very—disturbed. As you can imagine." A short, nervous bark of laughter made me think again about dogs. "Hugh-san was on the telephone with the company president, who says we have to get this thing straightened out or we'll be fired."

"Come on, Japanese companies aren't that bad," I said. As his fear was becoming more apparent, mine began receding.

"It's terrible for Sendai, it would be a disaster if—" he stopped short.

"If what?" I was sympathetic to him, but also impatient.

"Suicide is bad enough."

"What do you mean? Do you think she lay down in the snow intentionally?" I was astounded.

"New Year's Eve is the customary time for suicide in Japan! Don't you know?" Yamamoto exclaimed. "If a man cannot pay his bills by year's end, he is extremely embarrassed. Sometimes he kills himself so his family is free of trouble for the new year."

"But I thought the Nakamuras were rich," I said.

"Wealthy? In Japan? No one is that way any longer. Mr. Nakamura is fairly thrifty, but in Japan, household money is usually managed by the woman. And Mrs. Nakamura liked to use credit cards."

"Doesn't everyone?"

"Not like this! Mrs. Nakamura was like a crazy, always shopping in the *depaato*, charging up—how do you call it?—charging up a storm. Mr. Nakamura used to complain about that. He took away her credit cards, but she found some way to get new ones."

I smiled at that. "Obviously, she knew how to preserve her power."

"Exactly. You understand." His eyes grew moist. "The reason I am coming to you is that, because you are a lady, maybe you can explain to the police chief about ladies' nature and the likely story."

My guard went up again. "You want me to feed them propaganda? Why can't you do it?"

"I work for her husband. He would fire me very quickly if I said something about this embarrassment."

I could understand that fear. Still, Yamamoto would have to do what Mrs. Chapman, Hugh, and I had already done: meet face-to-face with the unfriendly police chief and tell what he knew. Yamamoto would have a built-in advantage, being Japanese and male. I cleared my throat and said, "I can't pass on your story, Yamamoto-san. Okuhura will have all kinds of questions about times and dates that I could not answer."

Yamamoto stared past my head as if the towering evergreen trees behind me had become a major fascination. I didn't buy it.

"You know something else, don't you?" I asked.

"I know nothing else! I'm the junior assistant."

"Then why are you trying to sell me such a ridiculous, stereotyped story?" I was disturbed enough that my words flew out before I had time to think them through.

Yamamoto stepped back and sucked in his breath. "Never mind. I'm sorry I bothered you. I thought you were a *yasashii-hito*." He used an expression which translated as "easy person," but meant something closer to 'nice.'

I didn't feel nice. Yamamoto and I walked downhill in silence until we reached the Miyakawa River. He needed to return to Minshuku Yogetsu to take care of Mr. Nakamura. I pressed on, following signs for a Shinto shrine. Soon I passed under a vermilion gate and found myself in the midst of a few hundred New Year's worshipers, men wearing sensible down jackets while the women and girls froze in fancy kimonos topped only by short brocade jackets. A pair of teen-aged girls wearing the crisp cotton robes that were the uniform of shrine maidens beckoned from their souvenir stall. I shook my head, but the girls looked so disappointed I ultimately relented and bought their cheapest product, a paper fortune printed in English for international tourists. I opened the slim orange-and-white envelope to read the ironic message that I was the recipient of EXTREMELY GOOD LUCK.

The fortune read like a grocery list of guidance. *Disease: It will take a long time to get well. Believe in God. For Employment: Talk with the employer right away . . . Regarding Marriage Proposal: Remember to get married with your parents' permission.* I rambled through it without interest until I came to the statement *He who listens to one side is kept in the dark. He who listens to all sides is in the know.*

All sides. Could that mean not parroting what Yamamoto wanted me to believe, or did it mean I should listen to him? What would these Confucian fortune writers have recommended for my specific case?

I left the shrine and turned into the historic shopping and museum district. Because of the holiday, only a few antique shops were open. Although I had none of my usual enthusiasm for shopping, I decided to go into a place selling old blue-and-white china to keep from having to return to the *minshuku*. I moped around the shop examining everything until the owner finally exploded and threw me out, saying that if I was just looking, the museums would reopen tomorrow.

In a dusty little shop next door, the owner was friendlier. I dug through a large tea crate filled with miscellaneous junk and retrieved a small pine letter box decorated with a geometric pattern of brown and cream inlaid woods. Judging from its metalwork, the box appeared to be early nineteenth century. The rusty iron clasp was locked, but when I shook the box, something rattled. I wondered about what it might be, given the fancy nature of the box: old coins, or maybe a carved ivory ornament.

When it came time to talk price, I made a long face about the missing key while the shop owner argued in favor of the unknown riches inside. But he'd gone through the crate to search for it, gotten his hands dirty, and he wanted a sale to start the New Year correctly. In the end, he agreed to knock a thousand yen off his original quote. I agreed; six thousand yen, approximately fifty dollars, was a pretty decent price for something that old.

Every Japanese restaurant in town appeared to be closed for the holiday, so unless I wanted to eat sushi from a Family Mart convenience store—something I did far too often in Tokyo—I'd have to shell out for a hotel meal. I decided to go for faux Swiss at the Alpenhof, a timbered chalet sparkling with Christmas lights. The restaurant served multicourse dinners heavy on meat that started at thirty-five dollars, so I almost gave up. The maître d' confided that prices were lower in the bar across the lobby. I elbowed my way in through a mass of skiers getting drunk and singing along with The Pet Shop Boys.

When I noticed Hugh Glendinning in the corner,

I wasn't surprised. This kind of Euro-themed bar was a home away from home for *gaijin*, the slightly negative name by which foreigners were known. There were no *gaijin* here outside of us, though, and as I looked closer, I saw Hugh had buried his face in his hands. There were two glasses beside him, both empty. I waited a few beats and as no one appeared to be joining him, I did.

5

"Another Macallan neat," he said without looking up.

"Alcohol won't bring her back." I offered him the pack of tissues I always carried and he tossed it back.

"I'm just thinking. Trying to be alone, if you don't mind."

Ignoring him, I sat down and signaled the waitress to bring me a menu. "We'll both have tea," I told her firmly in Japanese and went on to order grilled cheese, a rare treat, for myself.

"You're obnoxious. Has anyone ever told you that?" Hugh muttered.

"Thanks for sending your assistant to stalk me. I almost had a heart attack!"

"Be quiet for a sec," he said as the waitress returned with a slightly different order: two grilled cheeses, two glasses of whiskey and one cup of luke-warm water with a Lipton's packet next to it. She was off to the next table before I could protest.

"You may as well try it," Hugh said, tapping his glass against mine.

I sipped. The whiskey burned and I closed my eyes tightly. Hugh poured in half the water that had come in my teacup.

"Sorry. I forget not everyone is accustomed. Try it again." After I did, he said, "Yamamoto spoke to me after the fact. I didn't ask him to bother you."

"Do you know his theory?" I asked.

"The story about suicide spurred on by financial debt? Rubbish." So he didn't believe it, either. Despite my initial impression of him on New Year's Eve, I was beginning to feel something of a bond. I decided to confide what I'd been thinking for the last few hours.

"If I hadn't made that scene last night, it might not have happened." I drank a little more whiskey.

"What scene?" Hugh's voice was slurred.

"Remember how we were talking in the hallway outside your room? Setsuko came out looking for you. She wanted you to bathe with her. My presence made you say no. Who knows what would have happened if you stayed with her?"

"You're suggesting I should have taken a bath with her?" Hugh sounded outraged. "What planet are you from? Oh, right, California. Perhaps in your society, married women bathe with their husband's colleagues all the time."

"I want the police to get their investigation right," I said, trying to stay on track. "If you hold something back, it could mean trouble for both of us."

"But you're the policeman's great pal!"

"Hardly. I found the body. People who find bodies are usually the ones who fall under suspicion. As a lawyer, don't you know that?"

"I'm a solicitor, which means I don't do criminal defense. Let me reassure you, though, that no one suspects you of any wrongdoing. And as for your supposed culpability, you've been reading far too many mysteries, I think."

"I have little time to read. Actually, all I do is work," I blazed at him. "For me, this trip—my first in two years—has gone halfway to hell. To you it may be nothing, but I paid a lot to come here and it's nonrefundable."

"Whereas in my case, I only lost one of my best friends in Japan." He looked at me with disgust.

I tried again. "So, ah, what was the basis of this friendship? All I've seen and heard is how she served you."

"I served her, too!" Hugh retorted, his face reddening as if he realized how bad that sounded. "I mean, she wanted to practice English."

"Her language skills were good enough that she hardly needed it. And for someone who likes speaking English, she had nothing friendly to say to me last night." Irrationally, the burn was still there.

"She should have. She had an absolute fascination with America. I used to help her go through the travel books in the library at Tack. . . ."

"What's Tack?" I asked as the waitress arrived with two toasted sandwiches oozing cheese. I passed one to Hugh.

"T-A-C." He spelled it out. "The Tokyo American Club."

"Cute nickname for an intense place. How on earth did you get in?" Until now, I'd believed the astronomically-priced enclave was exclusive to Americans of the *Tokyo Weekender* genus.

"Members represent over fifty countries, including Japan—and we're mostly all there because our companies pay the initiation."

I had digressed. "How terrible do you think Setsuko's life was with Mr. Nakamura? Could he have been beating her?"

"I doubt it. Nakamura would argue with her about the shopping, but that was all. Yamamoto definitely was being straight with you regarding her shopping mania." Hugh made a face. "When we went into the shops, all the clerks welcomed her by name."

"You kept shopping with her, even after your apartment was finished?"

"Yes, I, ah . . ." he faltered. "Occasionally, we shopped together."

"Even when you knew her husband didn't want her to do it?"

"It was okay. I paid," he said shortly.

"What did you buy her?" I was amazed.

"We're getting off the subject," Hugh said.

"Right." I gave him a disbelieving look. "How wealthy are they, or is that a rude question?"

"I don't think money's a rude subject at all." He raised one eyebrow, a neat trick. "Nakamura earned about fourteen million yen per annum, depending on his annual bonus. They have a large house in the suburbs I've heard was devalued to a hundred-thirty mill, given the real estate slump."

One hundred and twenty yen to the U.S. dollar. I did some rough calculations on my napkin and came up with a minimum salary of $116,000, plus a house worth almost $1.1 million. Pretty cushy for a couple with no kids. "What about his wife's net worth?"

"Setsuko didn't work, of course, and she brought no money to the marriage. She was, as you Americans say, a trophy wife. A decade younger and better looking than he deserved."

"You know a lot about them." Yesterday he had come off like the Nakamuras' new and naïve friend. Today he sounded like a spy.

"Mr. Yamamoto is a huge gossip." He grinned as if I also had an assistant at my beck and call.

"What's going on at Sendai?" I persisted. "Was anything brewing with Mr. Nakamura that might have led him to snap?"

"Do you honestly think I'd tell you if there were?" His eyebrow rose again, and I lost my temper.

"That's right, you're the company lawyer! Forget the fact that I saw you going through an emotional breakdown when I came in here, you've bounced back admirably. The Nakamuras had no problems outside of the wife who shopped until she dropped."

The Scotch must have loosened me. I had never delivered such a tirade to a stranger. The assertive American was re-emerging after three years of suppression.

"If I told you what I'd done, you'd know it was my fault." He sounded sullen.

God, what was this, a confession? Oddly, I didn't feel like running out. Taking his hand would be too forward, but I felt he needed encouragement. I closed my fingers around his wrist.

"What? What could be so bad? Come on, I've been honest with you."

He was struggling with something. I waited, feeling his pulse throb underneath my fingertips. When he finally spoke, his voice was flat.

"Divorce. She wanted one. I counseled against it. And now she's dead."

Before I could react, he had twisted his arm away from me and was gone.

The crisis must have sent Mrs. Yogetsu straight to her bed. I didn't see a trace of her all evening. Her husband, on the other hand, had come through with flying colors for New Year's Day supper. There were steaming bowls of miso soup, trays of fish and pickled vegetables, and chewy mochi cakes to round things off for dessert. I couldn't bring myself to eat much, feeling headachy from the whiskey and what Hugh had told me. Neither he nor anyone from Sendai had shown up for the meal. When Yuki asked after them, Mr. Yogetsu whispered that a company delegation had arrived on the six o'clock train. They had holed up in the living room, the sliding doors closed so tightly only the scent of their cigarettes seeped out.

I doubted Hugh would tell me what they were saying. The only communication I'd received since his flight from the Alpenhof was an envelope pushed under my bedroom door. Inside was 5000 yen and his bilingual business card with a note scrawled over the Japanese side: *Tell me if I still owe you.*

He'd gotten the accounting right—the bill had been about forty dollars for the drinks and sandwiches. I calculated my share and slid 200 yen under his door with a note saying, *Your change.* I went back to my futon and tried reading. I'd forgotten to bring the Banana Yoshimoto novel a friend had given me for Christmas, but I did have *Kodansha's Pocket Kanji Guide.* After a fruitless hour, I took my towel and toothbrush to the small women's lavatory at the end of the hall. Just as I was putting my hand on the doorknob, the men's door next to it banged open. Mr. Nakamura emerged, drying his hands with a handkerchief.

This was the first time I'd seen him since the morning and he looked like a wreck. Although I knew toilets were hardly the places for small talk, I felt to say nothing would be worse.

"About your wife . . . it was such a shock. I'm really very sorry."

"It can't be helped." Mr. Nakamura showed no reaction, just his usual displeased expression.

"Excuse me, I don't understand."

"Oh, I think you understand Japanese very well," he snapped. "You understand how to manipulate situations and get people in trouble—"

"I really don't know what you're talking about," I said, staring him down.

"The man you called a pervert and drove off the train. You picked the wrong one."

I hadn't realized the Nakamuras had been on the

same train. But it was obvious, given that his party had arrived just five minutes after me at the inn.

"What do you mean? Who was it?" I remembered the man in the "Milk Pie" sweatshirt who had dashed off the train, and guilt flooded me.

"I didn't appreciate your help as a translator this morning," he continued in the same hard voice.

"I didn't mean to intrude. Glendinning-san just asked about your wife—"

"Keep talking with the police, will you? It's important for them to know where all the foreigners were. Given that my wife was murdered."

"Really?" I forced myself to keep my voice level. "Do the police have some theory about it?"

"We'll see, won't we? I'm sure you'll stay involved." Mr. Nakamura bowed mockingly and went downstairs.

In the lavatory, I stared at myself in the mirror, trying to understand what had taken place. Nakamura had made it clear he considered me both intrusive and worthy of suspicion. And he had voiced the word *murder*, which I'd been thinking but not saying, as if it were something I could push away.

The police hadn't said anything about foul play, but Nakamura had. He knew something. My heart pounded in my ears, reminding me of what my doctor-cousin Tom had said when I worried one of my headaches might be a brain tumor: *When you hear hoof-beats, think of horses, not zebras.* Look for the obvious, not the arcane. And the obvious choice in the murder of an unhappily-married woman would be her husband.

6

"This is where they torture women. Or, I should say, torture women *and* men. Rei-san, can you understand how this terribly painful chair works?"

Taro was obviously enjoying our tour of the Shiroyama city hall's punishment room. Given the black mood I was in, it was a mistake for me to have come along. I would have checked out of the *minshuku* and said good-bye to Taro and Yuki were it not for Mrs. Yogetsu announcing there would be no refunds for anyone who wanted to leave based on irrational fears following the "freak accident." After all, the police didn't think anyone needed to leave.

I desperately wanted to tell Captain Okuhara what Hugh had said about Setsuko wanting a divorce. I planned to ask Hugh for his permission, but he had gone off somewhere with his colleagues. I was left with the Ikedas and Mrs. Chapman. And the chair.

The seat in question looked normal except for the

sharply pointed pyramid spiking up from the center of the wooden seat. As Taro began explaining in his excellent English exactly where it went, Yuki shushed him.

"No, no, Taro! I am afraid Mrs. Chapman and Rei-san will be sickness."

"Someone with a samurai name like Shimura would have been cross-examined on *tatami*," Taro continued, giving me a puckish glance. "Common people sat on the cold stone floor."

"What about foreigners?" Mrs. Chapman asked.

"Foreigners? At this point in history, Japan was closed to the world. There were no foreigners, certainly none in prison!" Taro reassured her.

Today, plenty were around. A Belgian tour group that had arrived from Kyoto were enjoying Taro's commentary about a wall decorated with whips. Soon he had hijacked half of them and the stories were only getting wilder.

"Rei? I'm feeling poorly." For once, Mrs. Chapman's florid face was pale.

Yuki and I exchanged glances and took her across the freezing courtyard to more neutral civil buildings. I became interested in a group of storehouses where rice was once kept as tax revenue for the shogun; the buildings were decorated with exquisite stamped metal nail covers that looked like long-eared rabbits. I asked Yuki if they were fertility symbols and she giggled as if I'd said something naughty.

"No! The brochure says it symbolizes the power of the shogunate, that its ears are long and can hear everything that happens here, no matter the distance."

Like Sendai Electronics, sensing trouble and coming directly to stifle it. I thought of the corporate officers who had come down last night and were now sleeping next door to me, smoking nonstop. They made rotten neighbors; I hoped they wouldn't stay all week.

After the museum, we decided to have lunch in a modest snack shop that the Ikedas enjoyed during their last trip. I had a vegetarian sautéed noodle dish and was glad to see Mrs. Chapman liked her crispy pork cutlet, the first food I'd seen her finish. We ate in enthusiastic silence, and as I sipped my second cup of tea, I decided to bring up what we had suppressed from our conversation all morning. "So, what do you think is going to happen with Mrs. Nakamura's death?"

"It depends whether they rule it murder or suicide," Taro promptly replied.

"What makes you think it might be murder? Couldn't she have died naturally?" I asked.

"Watch out, Taro, you'll damage yourself! Rei-san is very close to the police." Yuki pressed her raspberry-glossed lips together in disapproval. I remembered Japanese citizens were sometimes wary about the police. After World War II, many former military officers were absorbed into the police. There was a hard and secretive edge to the organization, and some recent corruption charges hadn't improved things much.

"I was drafted to do the translations. I had no choice in it," I smiled at Yuki to put her at ease.

"You were wonderful, sugar. Like those translators on TV." Mrs. Chapman patted my knee.

"It must be murder because of Mrs. Nakamura's

state. I saw when I followed the husband outside. No clothes! Obscene." Taro looked more excited than upset, I noted.

"What do the ladies think? They are experts because of the many murders in America!" Yuki said.

"I heard every family has a gun inside the house. True?" Taro's eyes glittered.

"Well, we certainly do have a right to bear arms. Out in the country—" Mrs. Chapman began.

"Not *all* of us have guns," I interrupted. Lately, almost everyone I met wanted to know whether I packed a .45. Sometimes it was really embarrassing to be an American.

"Just because someone's powerful doesn't mean he's innocent. Look at all the political scandals in Japan. Bribery, corruption, blackmail . . ."

"This is serious business. The police returned to the *minshuku* this morning. I think there's every chance the death could be foul play." Taro held up his empty teacup to the waitress, who languidly came to refill it.

"Why didn't they move us out to search for evidence? It just doesn't make sense," I said.

"Mrs. Nakamura surely killed herself. She seemed plenty unhappy at dinner." Mrs. Chapman gave me a significant glance.

"You have been spending time with Glendinning-san, haven't you? Surely he knows more than the rest of us," Yuki coaxed.

"Do tell." Mrs. Chapman appeared to be salivating, even though her plate was clean.

"He's pretty close-mouthed. He wants to be loyal

to the company, I guess." I decided to keep quiet about Hugh's anguish the day before.

"Aha. Very Japanese. He must be getting along well within the ranks!" Taro slurped down the remains of his tea.

"Rei-san, I've been thinking maybe he has some interest in you," Yuki chimed in. "He kept speaking to you at New Year's Eve dinner."

I shook my head violently, not liking the conversation's turn.

"Perhaps you prefer a Japanese or another *konketsujin*?" Yuki's expression turned calculating. "How old are you, anyway? If you wait too long, you'll be Christmas Cake."

"I'm past that," I said, making a face. Single women were called all kinds of things—"unsold goods," "old miss" or, like Yuki was saying, "Christmas cake." The whipped-cream-and-strawberry confection was full-price right up to December twenty-fifth but couldn't be sold the day after, just like no man in his right mind was supposed to want a girl older than twenty-five.

"Career women marry later," Taro consoled me. "Yuki was twenty-eight."

"Baka!" Yuki cursed. But from the way her husband grinned, I could tell how lucky he thought he was.

Taro and Yuki made love that afternoon. Their door was shut for the four hours between the time we all arrived home and dinner was served. They came down sleepy-looking and all smiles to join me at the hearth where I was showing Mrs. Chapman the antique box I'd bought on New Year's Day. When Mrs. Yogetsu called us to dinner, she looked at it, too.

"This is not from Shiroyama." Her voice was almost triumphant.

"Where, then?" I challenged. She could have been right, but it infuriated me, with my master's degree in Asian art history, to be shown up like this.

"I think a place like Hakone. Yes, that type of wood inlay is popular there. Someone must have found it as a souvenir, and brought it here. Now it's for sale in Shiroyama because tourists buy anything."

"What's she saying? Is it valuable or fake?" Mrs. Chapman had become impatient listening to the Japanese.

"Neither. She just thinks it was not made locally. If I could open it up there might be a clue, since something's rattling around inside."

"Let me try. I'll need something sharp." Taro began prying at the box.

Mrs. Chapman pulled a bobby pin out of her fluffy orange halo and Taro set to work. I looked away, unable to stand seeing my treasure broken.

"Here you go." He handed the box back to me. "You look first, in case it's something deadly!"

I lifted the lid and found an inch-long polished piece of blue-and-white porcelain. I passed it around and everyone agreed it had to be a *hashi-oki*, a small ornamental piece used to place chopsticks on while dining.

"I don't think it's very old because it's decorated with acrylic paint," I told them. "But the box might be. Look at its paper lining."

"Old newspaper. May I borrow this to study?" Taro looked really excited.

"Sure," I said, handing it over but tucking the chopstick rest in a scrap of paper to put away upstairs. Worthless as it might be, I could use it as tableware at home.

"Where is Glendinning-san?" Yuki was starting to sound like a broken record.

I didn't speak up, so Mrs. Yogetsu did. "The press conference for the autopsy took place at police head-quarters this afternoon. All the men from Sendai were there."

"The autopsy! What do you think the coroner's finding was?" Taro looked like an electric bulb had been switched on underneath his skin.

"Mr. Yamamoto says it's suicide," Mrs. Chapman interrupted. "Something about money. In my opin-ion, the woman probably couldn't handle life with that wretched man anymore. It's just like my cousin, Maureen, whose husband couldn't keep his pants on. Poor gal spent twenty years depressed and drinking. One day she just decided to leave the life and washed down some sleeping pills with half a bottle of white Zinfandel wine . . ."

"A sad story, but not Setsuko's." Hugh Glendinning spoke from where he stood in the doorway with Yamamoto. Both were dressed formally in dark suits: Yamamoto's the one from New Year's Eve and Hugh's a wide-shouldered charcoal wool worn with a crisp white shirt and a Sulka tie.

"Eavesdropper!" Mrs. Chapman was furious to have been shut up.

"Sorry. I was wrong—I am a poor conversation-alist," Taro apologized.

"Gossip is only to be expected, living in the fishbowl that this place is." Hugh glanced at me and sat down, Yamamoto shadowing his movements. "For your information, the coroner ruled it an accident. It's believed that Mrs. Nakamura lost consciousness and froze to death."

"It couldn't be," I said under my breath.

"It's official," Hugh said crisply.

None of us had the nerve to ask more questions. The easy traveler's rapport that had developed between us on the first night was gone. There were two camps now—Sendai and the rest of us.

After dinner the Ikedas and I drifted into the sitting room to watch a televised performance of Beethoven's Ninth, the quintessential Japanese holiday concert. Taro and Yuki smiled and hummed along. I shut my eyes until the news came on at ten, with a feature on the Shiroyama press conference regarding Setsuko Nakamura's murder. Listening carefully, I realized Hugh had told us exactly what was available for public consumption. No more, and no less.

When I went up to bed an hour later, Hugh surprised me in the hallway.

"I need a word with you," he said.

"Okay." I leaned against the wall outside my room, glad Taro and Yuki were out of earshot.

"What the hell have you been telling people about Setsuko?"

"What is this, the Scottish inquisition?" The nervousness I'd tried to subdue all day flared.

"Oh, come on," he chided me. "You were giving them all an earful about possibilities of suicide and murder. I thought that was between us."

"People thought up those things on their own. Besides, why do you care? As you said, the uncertainties surrounding her death have been solved."

"Nothing's been solved. Just a lot of bows made and *sayonaras* said before Nakamura hopped the four-thirty limited express to make funeral arrangements. As I'd expected."

This was the first time since the divorce comment he had said anything remotely suspicious of Nakamura.

"What can you do about it?" I whispered. "You're in an impossible position."

"But you aren't." He looked steadily at me. "You're a naturally nosy person and you pass for Japanese. With your language and looks you can ask questions that I can't."

"Hah. You don't know the trouble that looking like this causes," I said, thinking of the many rude discussions about my ethnicity I'd endured.

"I do know. That's why I tried to buy you lunch yesterday." As I started telling him I was immune to his blather, he touched a finger to my lips. A spark flew, and we both jumped back.

"You can help me. You're already doing it, just with no sense of discretion."

"I don't want to." I felt belligerent. Setsuko Nakamura had eaten out of his hand, and I saw where it had gotten her. Death in the snow, a quick write-off by the coroner.

"Why don't we talk about it again tomorrow? Just

sleep on it." He leaned down, bringing his face so close I could practically inhale him. Sensing he was slightly off balance, I ducked under his arm.

"You're violating my space," I hissed. "Good night."

Safely inside my room, I collapsed. Doing anything with Hugh Glendinning was a very bad idea. It would be one thing to assist out of the goodness of my heart, but the fact was I had disliked Setsuko Nakamura. My initial passion to learn about her background was for my own self-preservation. Now that I was out of harm's way, any passion I felt had a different origin.

This was a dangerous trajectory, the worst since Shin Hatsuda, the ponytailed painter who had swept me off my feet at a party in Harajuku. Shin's crime had been departing ten months ago with half my art books and more of my self esteem; Hugh Glendinning could reap even more damage. *I don't do gaijin*, I once said to Karen when she wanted to fix me up with a blue-eyed investment banker. It was not why I'd traveled halfway around the world.

I pulled off my sweater, belatedly remembering the window exposing me to the street. I grabbed my *yukata* around my shoulders and turned, finding the screen in place after all. I was losing my mind. I snapped off the light and burrowed into the chilly futon.

I had been dreaming about being on my high school debate team, lined up to go on stage with my teammates: Mr. Nakamura, Mr. Yamamoto, Mrs. Chapman, and Hugh. Standing at the podium in her ivory Chanel dress, Setsuko Nakamura was ready to lead us. She opened her mouth to say something. Then she pulled out a perfume atomizer and started spraying the audience with a noxious chemical scent.

I awakened in blackness. A burnt odor filled my nose: gas, strong enough that I was choking. I pulled myself out of the blankets and began crawling to the heater. There was no flame, but I could feel with my hand that the control switch was rigged between on and off. I tried turning it, but it wouldn't budge.

Oh, God. The personal prayer I hadn't been able to think of on New Year's Eve came to me now. I needed to get out. I pulled myself along on my stomach toward the thin wedge of light shining under the door.

I had locked the door before bed. Now the knob wouldn't turn at all; some force held it tight. I pounded and tried to call out, but couldn't manage more than a cough. Feeling along the wall for the switch to the fluorescent overhead light, I flipped it with no effect. My energy spent, I curled up on the floor for a minute, trying to calm myself. As my hand stretched up once again to try the door, it suddenly opened. I fell gasping into the lighted hallway and onto a pair of large, Argyle-covered feet.

7

"What are you doing in there? The smell!" Hugh coughed.

I sucked in the hall's fresh, frigid air for a minute before croaking, "Gas leak."

He swept past me into the bedroom, and I heard first a tearing sound of the *shōji* paper screen and then the window slamming open. The next sound was of the heater's tubing being yanked from the wall. He came back and half-dragged me across the hall and into his room.

From my place on his futon, the shadowy room seemed to spin in a cool white light flowing from a laptop computer on the tea table.

"Don't be sick, I beg you." I heard him pouring liquid, and he put a glass to my lips.

"That smell," I said before sucking down the most delicious glass of water I'd ever had.

"A harmless hydrocarbon mixed in with the natural

gas. It's there to warn you, thank God for it." Hugh coughed again and drank straight from the thermos.

"Someone rigged the heater," I said after I'd regained my normal breathing. "And my light wouldn't turn on, and the door was locked!"

"My overhead light's not working either, so it's probably a tripped fuse." Hugh sounded thoughtful.

"Why were you outside my room in the middle of the night? What time is it?"

"It's just after midnight. I've been awake, working. A few minutes ago I heard a pounding sound which made me think either the Ikedas were having an awfully good time or someone was meeting his maker."

We both jumped at a new sound, three sharp knocks on the door. Before Hugh could move, the door was thrown open by Mr. Yamamoto, whose eyes widened at the sight of me sprawled on the futon.

"Excuse me for intruding, but I heard something—I was worried—"

"Rei had a wee accident, left her heater halfway on, and woke up to a bad smell," Hugh said. "We're airing the room. In the meantime, she'll rest here."

I started to shake my head, but Hugh camouflaged that by laying his hand heavily on my hair. "She's feeling a bit grim, but it's nothing serious."

"I smelled gas when I came down the hall," said Yamamoto. "It is very dangerous and also difficult for foreigners to understand."

"Yes, you always tell me that," Hugh was trying to close the door, but Yamamoto stayed squarely in the way. "My heater's on now, but I promise to extinguish it when I go to sleep."

"That's a good idea, I am very glad Miss Shimura is safe. Do you wish me to wake the innkeepers and see if another room can be found for her? Or if it is more convenient, she can have my room and I will sleep with you, Hugh-san."

"Are you kidding?" Hugh's low chuckle was full of innuendo. "Do me a favor and keep things quiet. I'll see you in the morning."

"You had no right to say that," I protested when Yamamoto was gone and Hugh began shaking a second futon out of the closet. "This is Japan. I'm supposed to be an innocent flower, especially when I'm traveling alone."

"Stay where you are. You'll have your own bed, but you shouldn't be alone tonight." Hugh tucked the blankets around me tightly, as if to prevent escape. "We'll talk more about what happened tomorrow."

I closed my eyes. I didn't trust him one hundred percent, but I didn't want to go back to my room. Like him or not, he was the closest thing I had to an ally.

"Do you mind if I stay on the computer a while longer? I have some work . . ."

I was relieved he would remain awake, but I couldn't muster the energy to say it. Instead, I sighed, pulled the blanket over my head, and drifted into a thick, restless sleep.

When I awoke, I felt unusually warm. Hugh sat cross-legged before the small tea table, still tapping at his computer. The *shōji* screen was pulled away from the window to reveal the sun dappling snowy mountains. It was a perfect morning.

"Didn't you sleep?" I squinted at him, a vision in a fresh white shirt and charcoal trousers.

"I slept from two to seven. And don't worry, the heater wasn't on all night. Just since I've been awake."

I sat up, hugging the quilt to me. "Would you bring me a *yukata*?"

"There's an extra in the closet." Hugh didn't seem willing to get it, so I slunk out of bed and got it.

"That's what American girls wear to bed? Hardly feminine, but on you it's okay."

"This is Japanese thermal underwear, and it's perfectly normal and practical in this weather. Why are you so dressed up?" I challenged.

"Strategy meeting at the Alpenhof. Yamamoto booked a conference room so we can troubleshoot with the guys who came up from Sendai."

"If you've got so much work, you should just go back to Tokyo. What are you doing?" When I knelt behind him, he instantly switched screens to a boring menu, which made me wonder what he wanted to hide.

"Nice, hmm? One of Sendai's products in development."

"It looks about the same as the Toshiba I have at work."

"There's something quite visibly different about it, though. Can you tell?"

I looked over the computer and shrugged.

"It's not plugged in," Hugh said triumphantly. "That's how I kept working last night when the power was gone."

"Well, they all can run on batteries, right?"

"Not for more than a few hours. You can safely

work on this for up to sixty hours, and the battery holds a charge for two years."

"Wow!" I wouldn't mind something like that for myself.

"It's an advanced lithium ion battery called the Eterna, and it is still in development." He stopped, then laughed. "Look how I'm opening up, sharing trade secrets even. And you say I'm not frank with you!"

"Who designed it?"

"A brilliant young engineer from Bombay. He was glad for the cash, and now we've got exclusive rights. None of the market leaders can touch it."

"That's too bad," I mused. "Your engineer would have done better if he were able to sell it to more companies. And in turn, society would have benefited. Everyone could share the technology."

"What are you, a Communist? Come on, a fair price is one that makes both parties happy." Hugh turned off the computer and snapped it closed. "I'm off."

"I'm going back. I'm sure my room is well-aired by now." I shifted from foot to foot, knowing I owed him something. "Thank you for taking me in last night."

"I do have a minute to get your thoughts on what might have happened." He paused, the joviality gone. "Last night, you were speaking hysterically of someone rigging the gas."

"It really happened. Whoever did it jammed the door so I couldn't get out." I spoke in what I hoped was a reasonable manner, adding, "The whole episode makes me curious whether Mr. Nakamura really left town yesterday evening."

"Of course he did. Yamamoto and I saw him off."
Hugh dug through his suitcase for a tie.

"He could have traveled to the next station
and returned to set the gas. Or had somebody else do
it," I suggested, watching him loop the tie and
straighten it.

"What's the motivation for Nakamura to gas
you?" Hugh looped and straightened his tie without
so much as a glance in a mirror.

"He hates me." Haltingly, I told the details of
how Nakamura had confronted me outside the *minshuku* bathroom and practically accused me of mur-
dering his wife.

"You're overreacting. But what about your chums
Mr. and Mrs. Crime? The husband's an engineer,
which he means he's rather adept at mechanical things.
If he could open your souvenir box, he could surely
tamper with your heater and trip the right fuse."

"Taro Ikeda is my friend," I protested, thinking
uneasily of his and Yuki's unexplained absence during
the afternoon.

"He's mad for murder and mayhem! Mrs.
Chapman told me how he got his thrills in the torture
chamber. Sometimes, there's a thin line between fantasy and action."

"What's your excuse? You vanished after dinner."

"Like I told you, I was upstairs working. Ask
Yamamoto, he'll vouch for me." Hugh paused.
"Surely you don't think I fixed the gas to drive you
into my bedroom?"

"Don't be an idiot." Upset at his accurate guess,
there was nothing for me to do but leave.

※   ※   ※

Even after a long, hot shower I had a headache, and the smell of gas hung heavy in my memory. I shut the window in my cold room and began searching for aspirin. A tiny enameled pillbox had spilled open in my backpack, and the business cards and receipts in another pocket were crumpled and out of order. My natural tendency toward disorder appeared to be spiraling.

I wasn't *that* messy, I thought, going over to my duffel bag. Unzipping it, my fears were confirmed. Someone had tossed everything about and even rifled through the pages of the *kanji* dictionary. My passport and money were still intact, which made me relieved until I began wondering what the intruder had wanted. When had he or she been in the room? *After the accident.*

Not bothering to pour myself water, I swallowed the aspirin and went downstairs.

"Sleep well? You're down late today," Mrs. Chapman commented when I dragged myself to the table.

"Not really. There was a problem with my gas heater, and I was overcome by some fumes. I suppose it was a malfunction, so I'm going to see if I can get it replaced," I said, watching people's faces.

"Gas heaters are extremely safe—in fact, there's an automatic shut-off bar in the case of earthquake. You must have made a mistake, Rei-san," Taro said sternly.

"You sure you want to stay on here, honey? For what we're paying, you'd expect central heating!" Mrs. Chapman was outraged.

"Actually I don't expect it," I said, sensing more disapproval from Yuki and Taro. "I don't expect this to be a little America."

"Well, I've done all I can with no heat and the rabbit diet." Mrs. Chapman peered into her bowl of miso soup and put the lid back on. "I'll get on to Singapore and some real food, if I can get a flight out today."

"Today? You need to talk to a travel agent because it's the middle of the holiday season! What are you going to do in Osaka if there's no connecting flight?" I had a terrible vision of her with a pile of luggage and no one to help.

She refused all logical arguments, though, and wound up having Taro call an agent. No space, as I'd expected. Since she was so sulky, Taro helped book her on a day tour of the Alps with an English-speaking guide. I agreed to take her to Alpenhof myself to meet the bus.

Half an hour later, as I slipped into my boots at the *minshuku* entrance, Mrs. Yogetsu marched up to me.

"You made a lot of noise last night and tore the *shoji* paper over your window." Her voice was as frigid as the wind that had blown through it.

"That's because the heater in my room broke. I could have died from gas poisoning!"

"If you don't know how to use a heater, please ask for help."

She had a lot of nerve to treat me like a foreigner, given all her lectures to me were in Japanese. I figured the only way to fight back would be to give her a taste of my American mother's haughtiness. In a cold voice, I told her, "I do know how to use a heater, and I know the one in my room is broken. I'll need a new appliance or a new room tonight—your choice. Just have it done by the time I come back."

At the Alpenhof Hotel, I carried Mrs. Chapman's overweight carry-on bag into the bus and saw her settled among a nice group of senior citizens from Canada. I waved until the bus disappeared into a red blur against the winter landscape. Then I was alone, feeling worse than I'd expected.

I had to do something. Anything. I wandered like a zombie through the town until I found the Shiroyama Folk Art Center, a gallery nestled in the downstairs rooms of an old merchant's house. The curators had assembled an excellent exhibit on three centuries of regional lacquerware, so I forced myself to study the spare elegance of the *shunkei* handicrafts Setsuko Nakamura had lectured us about in the living room on New Year's Eve.

Thinking of her made me sad again. If I had gotten off on the right foot, we could have become confidantes. I could have told her about the Tokyo group I knew who helped women break away from abusive marriages. I might have given her a reason not to walk out in the snow to her death.

Back at the *minshuku* in mid-afternoon, I struggled to open my bedroom door, this time from the outside. I fiddled with it and at last the obstruction, a small, stiff wedge of paper, dropped to the ground. I lay on my futon and unfurled it. A Lotte chewing-gum wrapper. What did it remind me of?

When it hit me I was off the futon and groping wildly in the pockets of the jeans I had worn the two previous days. I slid my hands to the very corners. Nothing.

I must have thrown away the similarly tiny scrap of paper that had been stuck in the bathroom door New Year's morning. But there wasn't a waste basket in the dressing room; I'd taken it with me. Then I'd reused it. I closed my eyes, recalling the feel of the paper in my hands, how I'd unfolded it to wrap the chopstick rest before taking it upstairs for safe-keeping.

I began rummaging through the tea caddy where I'd stashed the chopstick rest. My hands quickly sorted the spare coins and receipts I'd been collecting and pulled up the small piece of blue and white ceramic. Its wrapper was gone.

8

Hugh had not returned from the Sendai meeting at the Alpenhof, although Mr. Yamamoto had. He answered my questions about Hugh's whereabouts in a sullen tone that made me think he had been closed out of something. It was tough to be the youngest person in a Japanese company, I knew from experience. I offered a sympathetic look which was not returned.

I went back to my room, combed my hair, and changed into the plaid miniskirt I'd worn on the train. It had a slimy residual feeling about it, but it would look better than my snow- and salt-drenched jeans. It was already five P.M. and dark; I thought Hugh might be knocking off in the bar with his colleagues.

I'd guessed wrong. The concierge told me the Sendai group was still in session. All the tables in the bar were taken, so I wound up leaning against the circular wooden bar with a half-pint of Asahi Super Dry beer. I eventually found a seat next to a middle-aged skier who couldn't get over my funny accent—did I come from Hokkaido or somewhere like that? I didn't agree or disagree, just wondered how long I could last.

On my way through the lobby a half-hour later, the concierge caught my eye and inclined her head toward a bank of elevators where Hugh was huddled with two of his Japanese colleagues. As the elevator doors opened, all the men boarded and faced outward. Hugh looked straight through me as the doors closed.

I reentered the bar feeling miffed and let the skier buy me another beer. A rotten idea. Forty minutes later, I was running through a variety of excuses for not wanting to go to dinner with him. I was feeling pretty desperate when Hugh finally came in, briefcase in hand and a luxurious shearling jacket slung over his shoulder. He ordered two bottles of McEwans Lager in English; the bartender rolled his eyes. The skier settled his bill, muttering something in Japanese about whores.

"That's a Campbell tartan you're wearing." Hugh was scrutinizing my short skirt. "I don't suppose you're related to any Campbells?"

"Of course not! And what was that business in the elevator?"

"I pretended not to see you. My colleagues haven't stopped giving me hell about the girl who stayed with me last night."

"Yamamoto must have told. I could kill him!"

"He's just a boy looking for attention, the last

person to worry about. Now tell me what's so bloody urgent you tore yourself away from your museum schedule?"

I took a deep breath. "I need you. You have to come back to the *minshuku* bath."

"What are you, mad? At least wait until my colleagues depart on the evening train."

I waved the torn paper in his face. "What I'm trying to tell you is that this gum wrapper was stuck in my door; just like another paper jammed the bathroom door on New Year's Eve."

"Where's the first piece of paper?" Hugh tapped impatiently on the bar.

"Stolen from the tea caddy in my room."

"You call not being able to locate a piece of rubbish an act of theft?" He gave me the same exasperated look as when I'd argued with him about Sendai's monopoly on the Eterna battery.

"Between last night and this morning someone went through my room. Everything was out of order. Now I know what they wanted, it's so obvious—"

"What's obvious?"

"On New Year's Eve, someone intentionally jammed the bathroom door so he wouldn't be interrupted while killing Setsuko."

"But Setsuko's body was outside," he said as if I hadn't been the one to find her in the first place.

"She was *naked*. I always thought it was strange she was lying unclothed in the snow. Maybe she was killed in the bath or the shower. This afternoon I tried to go down there and look around, but the men's sign was on."

"So you wanted me to go into the bath to serve your purposes," he said slowly.

"That's right. But I've been waiting here so long"—I made a pitiful face—"I'm sure the man inside is gone. If it's ladies only, I'll go in. Or if no one's inside, we can put the family sign on and search together."

"What's this change of heart? You couldn't get far enough away from me when I asked for your help last night." He swiveled around on his barstool to face me, his knees bumping up against mine.

"That was before someone tried to kill me," I said, moving my legs away.

"Why would anyone want to kill you? Setsuko's the one we should worry about. Now that I have a copy of the autopsy, we can see—"

"The police gave you the autopsy?" I interrupted. "Don't they know you're illiterate?"

"Actually, I nicked it from Nakamura and photocopied it at the hotel desk."

"You mean you stole it?"

"Oh, just temporarily. Do you think you can translate it?"

"Of course I can." A vast exaggeration, but he didn't need to know. "Let's go back to the inn and get started."

"No, we need to talk things through." He drained his bottle. "We'd best not linger here, though. If my colleagues see me, I'm done for."

Five minutes later, we were in a taxi I'd hailed outside the Alpenhof. I pulled out my copy of *Gateway to Japan* and suggested Furukawa, the next town over.

"My guide mentions a charming little shop that sells *zōsui* for just four-hundred yen!" I told Hugh. "That's a type of rice stew. We could get a bite there— I'm going to need something after all those drinks."

"Why not a charming little steak house?" Hugh countered.

"We'll talk about it when we get there," I said diplomatically. "Food is hardly the issue. I just need to know the truth about Mr. Nakamura."

"The truth?"

"Everything you know about Mr. Nakamura, and at this point, don't you dare plead company privacy. Not when my life's in danger."

"Okay, okay." He held up his hands in mock surrender. "What I know from company records is his full name—Seiji Nakamura—although you can probably imagine we've never been casual enough to be on a first-name basis. Anyway, he graduated from university in the mid-sixties and went straight to Sansonic Stereo. Seven years ago, he had risen to a midmanagement position in strategic planning, which he resigned to join Sendai."

"I wouldn't have left a famous company like Sansonic. Sendai is newer, so the benefits probably aren't as good. And Japanese men in his age group usually work at the same company for life."

"That's right. Setsuko told me that as the younger generation was coming up through the ranks, her husband began struggling. He ignored some good ideas because he couldn't stand the thought of his employees showing him up."

"Madogiwa-zoku," I murmured. At Hugh's blank

expression, I explained, "It's a slang expression that literally means window-side tribe. At my company, it's what they call the older men who are assigned desks by the windows because they're not in the heat of things anymore."

"Really? I have windows in my office." Hugh sounded pensive. "Getting back to my story, Sendai recruited key employees from its competitors. They threw a lot of money at people, and Nakamura did the smart thing and went over."

"Why would they want an old window-tribe member?"

"He's an aged, well-connected negotiator who knows a million people in the government, including the fellows who regulate exports and patents."

"So he *was* appreciated."

"Until recently. In strict confidence, I'll tell you that the Sendai auditors have discovered he's abusing his company credit cards. Charges for entertainment expenses: half a million yen spent during one evening at a hostess bar none of us have even heard of. He's living like its the bloody eighties. No one can afford expenses like that anymore."

More than $4,000 dollars spent at a hostess bar? It almost made me think I'd picked the wrong career. I asked why Nakamura hadn't been fired yet.

"They were planning to ask him to account for it all, but now that he's lost his wife, that plan's on hold." He stared down my outrage. "Yes, we talked about it today. I advised them to wait because the charges could have been related to demands Setsuko was making and might very well end with her death."

I shook my head, remembering how passively

she'd accepted her husband's verbal jabs. It was impossible to think of her holding the reins.

As we entered Furukawa, I asked the driver for some recommendations. We settled on a small, cheerful-looking restaurant that served *yosenabe*, simmered one-pot dishes that were a specialty of the mountain region.

"Does this include eel or octopus or anything really dreadful?" Hugh asked when we entered a spacious *tatami* room decorated with large neon sea creatures.

"Don't worry. You'll love it," I said and ordered seafood *nabe* for two, a platter of crab legs and artfully sliced raw vegetables we cooked by dipping them into a pot of broth bubbling on a small fire built into the table. It was a pleasure to eat simply after the elaborate, tense dinners at Minshuku Yogetsu.

"I don't miss eating with everyone, but I want to go back soon." Using a sharp metal skewer, I pulled a long strip of crab meat from a claw and placed it on Hugh's rice bowl, tired of watching his futile antics with chopsticks. "We should be there already. I just know she died in the bathroom. If only Yuki and Taro had gotten inside that night!"

"Maybe they did."

"You're joking," I said, nevertheless recalling how Yuki had spoken of the mess in the bath New Year's morning. What had she seen, and why had she moved things instead of waiting for Mrs. Yogetsu to do it?

"If you think I'm joking, why don't you laugh? You're far too sober for twenty-seven."

"How do you know my age?" I was taken aback.

"Mrs. Chapman's a talker, and we both think it's a shame you've limited yourself to the teaching ghetto. Had you done law instead of art history, you'd be at the top of corporate Japan."

I wrinkled my nose. "Lawyers don't make money anymore. In America, things are so bad that half the young graduates are moonlighting as shoe salesmen."

"Really? Tell me more."

"About lawyers in America?"

"No. About how you grew up and came here to blaze a trail through the blackboard jungle."

Since he was making fun of me, I wouldn't. Never at a loss for words, he launched into his own stories about how he had grown up in a small village in the Lowlands, studied at Glasgow University, and prac- ticed law for two years in London before signing with an international firm. By thirty-two, he'd consulted for companies in Barcelona, New York, Düsseldorf, and Buenos Aires; Tokyo was his first posting in Asia.

"Where does your wife live?" I asked, having heard on the Tokyo grapevine that Brits never wore their wedding rings.

"I'm alone. I thought it was obvious." He looked slightly amused, as if he sensed the real motivation behind my question.

"Given your age I would expect one." I still didn't know how much to believe about him.

"I'm not that old. I'm practically a member of Generation X." He cleared his throat. "Actually, I'm not very successful with women. The ones I know want country houses and babies instead of city flats and ski holidays. Besides, who could tolerate moving every eighteen months?"

"Poor guy," I said, refusing to rise to his barb about women. What was I expected to do, tell him I was his kind of girl? My nervousness accelerated when he picked up the check the waitress had left dead-center between us.

"I'd really like to pay," he said when I also reached for it.

"It's not as if I'm impoverished," I said, struggling to read upside down and calculate my share.

"Since you refuse to tell me anything about your background in America, what can I do but assume that?" Hugh peeled money out of his clip.

"Assume away, then," I said as we slid into the taxi. The driver had preceded us outside and already had it warmed up. I closed my eyes and settled in for the long ride home.

"Why the secrets? I know less about you than anyone at the inn," Hugh complained.

"Could you go a little more slowly, please?" I begged the driver, who was zipping through downhill turns as if there were no snow or ice anywhere. A familiar, unpleasant feeling was beginning in my stomach and I now regretted the distance and topography between Shiroyama and Furukawa.

"At least tell me why you came to the Alps by yourself for a holiday. If you ask me, you're the suspicious one."

"Look, I can't talk about this." Perspiration broke out on my forehead as the taxi went into a start-stop routine waiting to enter the freeway. Once we got on, it would be only twenty kilometers home. I should be able to survive that.

"You're sick?"

Hugh's intuition surprised me. In a low voice, I said, "I'm sorry. Maybe I should get him to drop me off where there's a train station. I do better in steady vehicles—"

"The best thing is to rest. Here, I volunteer my shoulder."

I could not let myself vomit on his beautiful suit, I thought, backing as far as possible into the corner, resting my head against the hard glass window. The vibrations were jarring, so I allowed my head to slump against the seat back covered by a polyester doily. Then I felt Hugh's hand in my hair.

"Much better," he murmured, pulling me firmly against his shoulder. It was surprisingly comfortable, cozier still when he arranged his shearling jacket over me. His neck smelled very good, a mixture of soap and leather and something indefinable. "Do you want the window open?"

"Yes. Thank you." I was able to get the few words out before curling my legs up on the seat and sinking into a half-coma with the chill wind in my face. After a while, I felt the car accelerate and knew we had made it to the highway. Now as the road curved, I felt a pleasant, rhythmic sensation, throwing me a little deeper against Hugh's shoulder from time to time.

When I opened my eyes again, it was dark. I was definitely on the mend. Hugh's hands were now caressing my scalp; I moved closer, willing it to go on. He had an annoying personality but physically, he was heaven.

"Feeling better?" he asked.

"Mmm. What time is it?" I felt something brush against my lips.

"Late." Hugh kissed me again. Despite the gentleness of his mouth, the chastity of it, I felt something start simmering inside me. "Is it all right?" He pulled away and traced my cheek with his finger.

"You ask too many questions," I mumbled, thinking that despite his gaffes and inability with chopsticks, I found him too sexy for words.

He knew. His arms came around, crushing me close, and his tongue flashed into my mouth. It had been too long since I'd been touched like this; when his lips traveled down my neck, I arched against him, completely lost.

The car stopped abruptly, smashing me against the door. I had forgotten about the driver, forgotten we were anything but a man and woman alone in the dark. A street light shone in the car window, revealing us to be in the *minshuku* parking lot.

"I'd laugh if I weren't in such a state of physical distress," Hugh said. "I can't even get out of the car."

"Oh, you mean—"

"I like you too much," Hugh said raggedly.

"It's just a physical reaction. It was bound to happen, given the way we met." I straightened my Campbell tartan skirt, which had ridden up to a perilous level, and jumped out.

"Wait." I looked back to see he had paid the driver

and followed me out of the car, wrapping his coat around himself. "What exactly is so offensive about me?"

"I don't want you—intellectually." It was painful to spell out that although he was so attractive, he was all wrong. There was the baggage with Setsuko, and a sense of inexplicable danger.

"You little snob! Who are you holding out for, someone who went to Cambridge?" His voice was mocking.

"It's not that. You're just—too old, too Scottish, too . . ." I fumbled for the words.

"Too *gaijin*." He found the last word.

I didn't reply, just stood beside the *minshuku* door, shivering. He walked past without looking and closed the door in my face.

9

"Skiing tomorrow, so early to bed for us tonight, neh? Now that the terrible business is over, we can get a taste of what we came here for." Yamamoto was talking to Hugh when I came in after waiting a miserable five minutes outside to fake a separate entrance.

"You'll have a great day tomorrow. The snow is pure powder," Taro told him.

"Rei-san! Where have you been? You missed dinner." Yuki was there, with Mrs. Chapman at her side. It was a veritable conference.

"I've been, ah, exploring." As soon as the word was out, I started blushing, although only Hugh would catch the double meaning. "I'm cold. Very cold! I think I'll take a bath."

Upstairs, I changed into my nightclothes before going downstairs to the bath, which, in fact, had become free. I didn't need Hugh after all. I simply hung the FAMILY ONLY sign on the door and went in.

I looked over the dressing room's neat trio of sinks and the stack of empty bamboo baskets where bathers would leave their clothes. I slipped out of my slippers here and trod barefoot into the bath chamber. A monotonous drip ran from a shower along the wall. I walked across the wet wooden floor to pull it closed, and then turned my attention on the long rectangular bath. As I'd remembered, there was a low, wide window running along one side. I leaned over the side of the bath and slid open the window. There was no screen, just a four-foot drop to the roped off, trampled area where Setsuko had lain.

The bath was covered with heavy lids, just as I'd seen it the first time. I lifted the lids off the tub to peer into its copper-lined depths. The underwater bench ran around all four sides; it looked to be only two and a half feet below the surface. I rolled up the sleeve of my *yukata* as best as I could and reached in, feeling for anything that might have been left behind. I stopped moving when the outer dressing room door opened.

"Excuse me?" Hugh's voice was tentative. He didn't enter the bath chamber until I'd opened the door.

"I didn't think you'd come." I squinted at his weird ensemble: the shirt and trousers he'd worn earlier, plus black leather gloves.

"You should be wearing gloves, Rei. Did you touch the window?" he scolded.

The criticism relieved me. Clearly, we were going to pretend the taxi incident never happened. I said, "If you come over here and look outside, you can see how easily she was dropped. Which explains why there were no footprints leading away from the body."

"I remember you fiddling with the window on New Year's Eve." Hugh came up behind me to look. "I closed it when I came back later with Yamamoto."

"So?" I asked, not seeing what he was getting at.

"So we have your and my prints on the window, while, for all we know, Setsuko's killer wore gloves."

"We shouldn't wipe it clean, I suppose."

"Certainly not. Can you imagine if we have to explain it to a judge one day?"

I resumed my search of the bathtub, thinking that if I'd been alone, I could have taken off my clothes and gone underwater. I could still do it tomorrow.

"Look at these bath covers." Hugh held up one of the large plastic pieces I had put to the side. "Lightweight, but stiff as hell. I could crack one over your head, and you'd be out. Then I could have my way with you—say, hold you under water until you drowned." He chuckled. "Hypothetical, my dear."

Feeling disquieted, I said, "They look pretty clean to me, although anyone could have washed them off under a shower."

"Very true," Hugh said, going over to fiddle with the shower drain. It was disgusting work; I was glad I wasn't doing it.

"You're not finding anything, are you?" I asked after I'd spent ten more minutes trolling for evidence in the bath.

"Nothing you'd want to touch. Clumps of hair, mostly Japanese, though there are some light ones, probably mine or Chapman's. It's impossible to tell in this muck."

We gave up after a while and went into the dressing room to dry off. Hugh was washing his hands when I heard a squeaking of vinyl against wood: the sound of someone walking quietly in slippers before halting at the door.

"Busted," I mouthed at Hugh.

"Don't worry. We'll pretend we really went in," he whispered, turning on the sink. He plunged his head under the faucet and I did the same.

Outside the door, Mrs. Yogetsu was waiting for us, her face wrinkled in a prune-like expression of disgust.

"Oh!" I said, for want of anything better.

"Is there a problem, darling?" Hugh murmured, kissing the top of my head.

"This is not a love hotel! It's a decent place, and I will not stand for your screwing in public rooms." Mrs. Yogetsu was using plain verb forms meant for inferiors, a slur I'd understand.

Hugh nuzzled my neck, continuing to play the role of lover. I kicked him and started apologizing.

"I am very, very sorry. It was a mistake we made, as foreigners. I'm so sorry, I won't do it again."

"*Sumimasen.*" Hugh apologized with one of his sporadic Japanese expressions. Despite the humility of his words, I felt his body rumbling with silent laughter.

"People who walk in the night come into danger. It happened to the Nakamura woman. Watch that it doesn't happen to you," Mrs. Yogetsu spat before storming off to one of the nearby doors, presumably her private quarters. The belt to her robe caught in the door as she slammed it. The door creaked open again, and the belt was whipped inside.

I wanted to laugh, despite the gravity of the situation. But there was no place to do it.

"Come. I want you to have the autopsy," Hugh whispered when we got upstairs

"Can't we do this later?" I was still nerved out by Mrs. Yogetsu.

"It's got to be now. I'm leaving at seven o'clock to ski." He pushed me inside and locked the door.

"I don't know why you insisted on concocting that false love scene if your reputation is so precious. What about your colleagues and Yamamoto?" As I shook out the wet robe and spread it to dry near the space heater, I answered the question for myself. The Japanese people around us would consider him virile; I'd be the tramp.

"She's the important one. And the crucial thing is that she not know what we were up to. Here you are, Miss Prim." He pulled a packet of papers out of his suitcase.

"Can I take this, work on it a little while?" I scanned four pages of tiny typed characters and realized how impossible it would be to translate.

"By all means. It does no good in my hands."

"In the museum, I overheard some docents saying they didn't like Mrs. Yogetsu. She overcharges them for flower-arranging lessons." I sunk down on the edge of his futon. "I think she's horribly arrogant but that's not enough—"

"Not enough to make a murderer. Come here. If you go to sleep with a wet head, you'll catch cold." Hugh knelt behind me and started rubbing my wet hair with a towel like I was a dog that got caught in the rain.

"That's not very Scottish of you. I hear your countrymen tramp around wintry moors wearing kilts with nothing underneath." I spoke lightly to cover up the fact that his touch was making goose bumps break out all over me.

"A kilt is good cover, unlike that obscene sleeping costume you affect."

"I explained to you earlier that this is Japanese thermal underwear. It's indigenous clothing."

"But you run around in it like you're some kind of American boy! Let me advise you that you aren't."

I pulled away as the towel chafed my neck. "Oh, I forgot. *Gaijin* prefer an Oriental fantasy girl who always agrees."

"I think you know me better than that," he said shortly.

"I don't think I know you at all," I said, although in a way, I did. He anticipated my thoughts, finished up my sentences. And I knew the way his hands felt on me, which was another reality unto itself.

"If you are going to leave, do it now." He'd taken away the towel and was stroking his fingers through my hair. "And I don't want any changed minds or midnight visits where I have to tuck you in and lie awake the rest of the night slowly going mad—"

"That's how you felt last night?" I twisted around and saw something desperate in his eyes.

"Yes. You were so sick and fragile, and all I wanted

to do was this." As his mouth drifted over mine, he pushed me backward on the soft mattress.

It's what I want. That thought flashed through me as I kissed him back, my hands gripping his shoulders.

"I'm not so awful, am I?" he breathed when we came up for air.

Not replying, I offered him my neck. Yes, he remembered the spot that had sent me reeling across the taxi seat. He knew that, and more. Soon I was tugging at his starched cotton shirt and then, his belt. I couldn't let go.

"Be careful," he chided, disappearing beneath the quilt. "I'm too old, too Scottish . . ."

"But I want you anyway," I sighed. It was chemistry, pure and simple. I stretched my hands down his body and found him the way I'd expected: rocklike.

"Say that to me tomorrow." His mouth was on my navel.

"Do you want to, ah . . ." It was as if some second, renegade voice within me had spoken, the one that told me if I halted this erotic journey I'd wonder forever about roads not taken.

"I'm not prepared. Are you?" He pulled the covers back and regarded me with astonishment.

"No. I came for the museums." A crazy laugh started somewhere inside me.

"Maybe I have something else for you then," he murmured, and his mouth and fingers trailed downward. He was a Pagan all right. In the space of a few minutes I exploded, gasping, into his hand which had flashed up to cover my mouth.

"You're delicious. I could have you for breakfast,

lunch, and dinner." He resurfaced and drew me into a kiss. I was incapable of speech. When he stroked me again, I flicked away his hand. It was my turn. I broke away and slid down the length of his lightly furred chest and stomach, lingering long enough on his thighs that his rough breathing told me he couldn't stand it anymore. Then I closed my mouth over him and began learning the track of his desires.

"What happened to Miss Prim?" Hugh whispered afterward. "I'm not going to ask how you knew, just feel grateful."

"I was listening to you breathe." I could talk again and felt wonderful.

"Darling, you've got to admit what happened was beyond physical."

"Metaphysical?" I traced the ridge between his pectorals, now slick with sweat, enjoying the sound of our shared laughter, low and intimate.

"Sssh," Hugh cautioned. "We'll rouse Yamamoto."

"Do you think anyone heard?" I would die a thousand deaths for having forgotten about the thin walls. "Not likely, as it's the only time we ever shut up." I felt him holding my hand, a curiously innocent gesture after all we had done. "Will you be around tomorrow when I come back from skiing? Things have changed for us, and there's something I want to tell you."

"It's tomorrow already. This is about Setsuko, isn't it?"

His silence told me yes.

"You're a bastard," I said and rolled away from him. He pulled me back.

"I brought the matter up now so I can reserve

you for the evening. We'll get out of here to talk.
Wait for me?"

"I'm not exactly the waiting type." The comfortable feeling I had allowed myself to be lulled into was
almost completely gone. "And going to be busy."

"More museums to see? I'll take my chances,
then." He ran his tongue over the nape of my neck.

"I should go back to my room. So you can rest up
for your skiing," I whispered.

"Please don't." Hugh threw a leg over me, and his
voice softened. "This is the going to be the best part."

Neither of us spoke again, as if willing it to be so.

When I awoke, the room was bright and he was gone.
From my cozy spot under the blankets, I saw a neatly
folded pile of my thermal underwear and his *yukata*. I
smiled at that; clearly, he wanted me to be covered for
my trip back across the hall.

I'd make an effort to be tidy for him, too. I rolled
up the bedding and slid it into the closet, stopping
when I heard something knock against the back wall.
I pulled the futon back out and crawled in to investigate. My hand closed around a gray velvet jewelry
box.

I sat back on my heels and considered things. I
knew it could be nothing for me. What had happened
between us physically—and, I grudgingly admitted,
emotionally—had surprised both of us. Even if he
had bought me a present in advance, all that could be
had in Shiroyama was lacquered wood.

I popped open the box and looked down at something

sickeningly familiar—a choker of eight-millimeter, perfectly matched pearls in the pinkish shade Japanese women preferred. Pearls with a twenty-four karat butterfly clasp that was broken along the edge, as if someone had yanked it hard.

I had to get out. I didn't even finish putting the blankets away, just threw the box back in the general area it had been. What excuse would there be this time? I'd been doing a fine job building support for his innocence. I guess he'd thanked me in his own manner.

I gave myself a quick sponge bath in the lavatory, scrubbing everywhere his mouth had been. Then I dressed and began making plans for my trip back to Tokyo.

10

"But the holiday week isn't over yet. You have not visited the ghost museum." Taro Ikeda pushed his glasses higher on the bridge of his nose as if examining me for my true intent. We were eating our last breakfast together, and he and Yuki had vehemently protested my early departure. Mrs. Yogetsu remained silent as she moved between us, scooping hot rice into the breakfast bowls.

"*Boyfriendo* trouble." Yuki's Jinglish didn't make me smile. How had they picked up on things?

"Yes, Rei, don't you want to wait to say bye to Hugh and Mr. Yamamoto?" Mrs. Chapman asked. "I think they'll be back from skiing by mid-afternoon."

"I'm sorry, but I can't. The death—I've never been exposed to anything like that. And I booked myself on the morning train. I'll beat the U-turn rush of travelers going back to the city."

You're going back to Tokyo, then?" Mrs. Chapman's voice was all business.

"That's right." Back to my crummy flat and my best friend Richard Randall and a job that, on the best days, could only be called tolerable. Back to life and not death.

"Don't worry, honey. I'll tag along with you. I've seen all these mountains. What I need is to experience a world-class Japanese city. I'll stay with you until I find a hotel."

How to best discourage her? "Mrs. Chapman, I live in a fourth floor walk-up. One and a half rooms with no heat. Also, the neighborhood is a magnet for the homeless."

"That sounds interesting!"

Taro grunted and Yuki put her hand over her mouth, hiding her giggle.

Remembering Mrs. Chapman's conservative nature, I brought out the artillery. "My roommate is gay or bisexual, he's not sure which. We'd have to all sleep together. . . ."

"Well, I could just as easily find a hotel. With heat." She blinked rapidly. "Mr. Ikeda, would you be kind enough to set something up with your reservations person? So it's ready when we arrive?"

We had seats on the train and slept half the way to Tokyo. Once there, we went straight to the touristy southwestern part. Taro's agent had found a single room with private bath and central heat in Roppongi for $150; the only explanation for the deal was that everyone was out of town for the holidays. Mrs. Chapman was pleased with the price and the sight of all the Western restaurants in the area.

"We'll talk first thing tomorrow morning," she said, writing down my telephone number and address in the hotel lobby. "You'll take me to Tokyo Tower and the Meiji Shrine and maybe Disneyland."

"Why don't you try another bus tour? There are organized excursions to all those places . . ." I had escaped my holiday in hell only to find it wouldn't let me go.

She got my message, because her voice came more slowly. "Gosh, I'm chattering on, when you probably left Shiroyama to get away from me! My husband always said I was pushy. I'm sorry."

"No, I'm sorry," I said. "It is hard to be a stranger in a foreign city. I'm sure we'll be able to meet some time . . . maybe for lunch early next week?"

"You've got a deal, Rei Shimura." She sighed happily, looking around the cozy lobby decorated in pink and teal. "Hey, do you think there's a bellhop in this place?"

I could have used assistance by the time I finally got home, humping my heavy bag up the stairwell into a dark and freezing apartment. Richard should have been home, but then again, I hadn't called ahead to tell him about my premature arrival.

Saturday morning, the kitchen was so cold I had to turn the broiler on for warmth while I made toast and coffee. Going through the stack of newspapers that had piled up, I began looking for mention of Setsuko Nakamura's death.

I was midway through the first article when Richard opened his bedroom door. He was wearing a set of long underwear like mine topped with a droopy Norwegian sweater that hung past his narrow hips. He must have tiptoed in after I was asleep.

"Telephone, baby. Long-distance." He handed me the cordless and settled down across from me.

It was Yuki Ikeda. "Rei-san! I was worried you were not safe."

I had promised to call, but was so exhausted and depressed when I'd finally gotten in that I couldn't bring myself to do it. "*Sumimasen*. Sorry. I came in so late, I didn't want to wake you with a phone call."

"We're leaving today, so I had to call you. Things here are . . . strange. Mr. Yamamoto got lost."

"What do you mean?" I stared out the window into the grayness of my neighborhood. I couldn't imagine a tourist getting lost in tiny Shiroyama, where every corner had a sign directing you to this or that temple.

"There was a skiing accident, they think. Yamamoto-san vanished yesterday morning. Hugh-san searched many hours at the ski park. Then it started snowing heavily, which made vision impossible."

It was terrible to think of Mr. Yamamoto's body buried by mounds of snow. I'd been mad at him for gossiping about me, but now I remembered the humor and compassion he'd shown at New Year's Eve dinner. He was a young man full of energy and dreams that were probably over.

"I have another thing to mention. We still have your antique box. Taro hasn't finished reading the newspaper lining, but he's sure he can date it," Yuki said earnestly.

"That really doesn't matter anymore . . . How can you think about it now?" I was amazed at her digression, given the seriousness of Yamamoto's disappearance.

"We will return it, I promise. It was so irresponsible, you must think we are thieves!"

"Please take as long as you like. I have no real use for it." I liked Yuki, but I hadn't really thought we'd see each other again. Making friends while traveling was one thing, keeping them was another. Now she was chattering on, making me open my calendar and set up a coffee date for the following Sunday.

"Very good, we will take care of your box. And Rei-san, maybe it is better that you left. Because of how Hugh-san behaves now."

"Oh?" I tried to sound uninterested.

"When he came in yesterday he was very angry, especially when Taro mentioned you were gone. Such a frightening personality! No, you would not like him anymore."

"What's going on, sugarplum?" Richard pounced when I got off.

"Don't you read the papers?" I would have thought he'd kept abreast of the fact that I'd landed smack-dab in the middle of a scandal.

"Only for Ann Landers and the Canadian hockey scores. You know that."

I handed him the *Japan Times* January 3rd edition with a front page photograph of Hugh Glendinning and the Nakamuras snapped at a cherry blossom viewing festival last spring. Setsuko, wearing a stunning gold-embroidered kimono, stared straight into the camera's eye with the slightest hint of a smile; her husband looked appropriately sober. Hugh was laughing at something off-camera.

Richard read the story, then went back to the picture on the front. "This *gaijin* was involved? He looks yummy."

"He was," I said without thinking.

Richard yelped. "Asian girl goes on sex holiday! Tell me or else." He brandished my dull vegetable knife.

I gave in quickly, as we both knew I would. Partly because Richard was a good amateur therapist, given his years reading Landers; also because he was my best friend, probably the only person willing to share the rent on a tin-roofed hovel miles from the plush neighborhoods where most foreigners congregated.

"That's a lot more interesting than what was in the paper," he said when I was through. And then, irrelevantly, "So, how does this affect your feelings for Shin?"

"Shin Hatsuda?" I had almost forgotten about the last heartbreaker in my life. "There's nothing I feel for him. Not an ounce of emotion."

"Then why has there been nobody since? You should trust again, realize not all boys are going to paint third-rate nudes with your face on them."

"Now Shin seems so young, so fledgling." I paused. "No offense."

"Hey, I'm glad I'm under twenty-five, and I

wouldn't recommend anyone over thirty. They've
got expense accounts but none of the crucial drives."
Richard waved his coffee cup at me, sloshing a bit of
the dark brown liquid over the art deco ice cream
parlor table we'd carried home from the Togo shrine
sale a year ago.

"Our drives were equal. It was a shame." I said
glumly, wiping up the spill.

I'd picked the wrong words; they set Richard off
on his favorite Lemonheads song, the one that mis-
appropriated my name.

"*It's a shame about Ray!*" Richard belted.

"*If I make it through today, I know tomorrow not to
leave my feelings out on display. I'll put the cobwebs
back in place . . .*"

"That song is about a man named R-A-Y." I cov-
ered my ears with my hands. But he'd turned on the
CD player and was singing at full throttle along with
Evan Dando.

"*It's a shame about Ray! In the stone under the dust
his name is still engraved. Some things need to go away.
It's a shame about Ray!*"

Hugh Glendinning's name would be engraved on
my lower body for the rest of the year, if not the rest
of my life. As Richard quieted down, I tried to
explain how depressing that was. "The problem is he
paid attention to me for the wrong reason, to get
something—"

"Absolutely! If he had you in rapture, he knew
you wouldn't give a flying leap what he'd done. Do
you really think he killed her?"

"I don't know." I shut my eyes, wishing none of

it had happened. "There was something he wanted to tell me, but I wasn't going to wait around for it."

"Smart, Rei, very smart. And to think you have a Phi Beta Kappa certificate rolled up somewhere behind your bookcase!"

The morning paper ran a short follow-up on the tragic, accidental death of Setsuko Nakamura. Speaking for Sendai, Hugh Glendinning relayed the fact Mr. Nakamura was grieving the loss of his wife and, after a short absence, would return to his position overseeing strategic planning at Sendai.

Richard drifted into the bathroom to shower, and I pulled out the Nakamura autopsy. If I understood it, I might be able to believe that I had overreacted to Setsuka's death. After studying it for twenty minutes, I found I could only make out a few *kanji*. I could fax it to my father and have him explain the medical parts. Then again, I didn't know how I'd present it without getting him riled up about the dangers of my life in Japan.

While I was looking through a stack of New Year's postcards half an hour later, a name leaped out at me. Here was someone who knew even more than my father. Not pausing to read the card's greeting, I went to the phone.

The switchboard operator at St. Luke's International Hospital was unexcited that Dr. Tsutomu Shimura had a female cousin. I got the feeling that young women called on a regular basis for the thirty-three-year-old, still-unmarried *oisha-san*, as physicians were fawningly called. The operator informed me that Tom had gone to an emergency medicine conference and would get my message upon return.

"Tell him it's Rei, his cousin in Tokyo who's home for the holidays," I begged. The fact was I'd met him just a couple of times, first when he'd stayed with my family in California, and years later at my aunt's house in Yokohama. He'd been pretty friendly, saying he admired me for living where I did. I had a strong feeling he'd come through for me.

I went out with a load of clothing for the dry-cleaner, and on the way back, stopped at the Family Mart convenience store. I needed to pick up a few groceries and see Mr. Waka.

I made my way through the aisles of toiletries and snacks to where the fifty-something man of my dreams was ringing up some candy for a junior high student. He'd lost most of his hair and had a small soccer ball for a stomach, but we had lots in common: chiefly, a passion for society gossip. Mr. Waka was a big fan of Japan's imperial family. When business was slow, he translated for me all the best tabloid stories about its younger members.

"*Irasshaimase,* Shimura-san," he sang out in welcome when I placed milk and a small box of sushi on the counter in front of him. "What an honor to see you again! I thought you had given up eating."

"Waka-san, I can't believe you forgot about my vacation. Don't I mean anything to you?" I made a long face.

"Such money you throw around traveling. It must be very nice." Mr. Waka began to bag the food.

"Where did you go? I can't remember. So many nice young misses come in and talk to me that I cannot keep their lives apart."

"I went to Shiroyama—"

"Oh, yes! I believe you saw many TV crews up there!" An excited look crept across his face. Within seconds, I was seated behind the counter with him, a complimentary box of Almond Pocky pretzels between us. As I munched one of the salty-sweet sticks, I described the scene and people involved.

Mr. Waka, as I could have expected, promptly decided Setsuko's accidental death was murder. "*Wah!* It must be one of the foreigners. The *Scotlandjin*, or the old lady, or you!"

"Don't be like everyone else in this country, assuming the worst of foreigners! What about Mr. Nakamura, Mrs. Yogetsu, or the Ikedas?"

"But you didn't like the Nakamura woman," Mr. Waka pointed out. "You were jealous because of the *Scotlandjin*. If anyone has motive, it's you."

"It's not like that." The police had no problem with me. I mean, the chief gave me back my passport."

"Just wait for them to come. They come often enough in this neighborhood. But don't worry." He gave me an angelic smile. "I will offer you a personal reference."

It was pitch black when I turned the corner to my apartment. I stumbled over something on the pavement by my house, and when I heard a groan I knew

I'd bumped one of my homeless neighbors. They usually stretched out on newspapers and blankets under the awning of a permanently-closed factory farther down on the block.

"*Gomennasai*," I apologized. "I didn't mean to step on you."

The man flicked his cigarette lighter. In its flame, his craggy face appeared baffled. I had done something weird again. One wasn't supposed to talk to vagrants.

"Please take this." A sudden impulse made me thrust the dinner I'd bought at Family Mart into his hands. The homeless never begged; what I was doing was radical and might be unwelcome. Nervous about his reaction, I sidestepped him and quickly ran into my building.

I had forgotten it was *kanji* study night. Richard, Simone, and Karen were clustered around my low *kotatsu* table, their toes pressed against the electric heater underneath. A neat stack of flash cards waited on the low table's center, ready for the contest.

"It's about time you got home," Richard complained as if I were some kind of reckless gadabout.

"I forgot about the time. I had a lot on my mind." Since I'd given up my dinner, I needed to make something. On the stove, I surveyed the leftovers of a pasta dinner made from the last of my shiitake mushrooms and some linguine my mother had mailed last month.

"We saved you the work of cooking for us," Karen said sweetly.

"Rei, I cannot believe about this Shiroyama. We

must make a group trip there next time," Simone said between puffs on a Galoise.

The phone rang, and Richard rolled across the *tatami* to pick it up. *"Moshi-moshi*. Yes, I speak English. But not with an accent like *yours*." He listened for a minute. "My name is Richard. And I have a feeling I know yours, babe."

It could only be one person. I grabbed the phone away and said a breathless hello.

"You didn't tell me you live with a guy!" As I'd suspected, Hugh Glendinning was on the other end.

"It wasn't any of your business," I said, watching Richard stick out his tongue, which now had a gold ball in it. "Ooh, that's awful!"

"See what you missed at the New Year's Eve party?" Simone lifted her sweater to show off a gold-ringed navel. "You also could have gotten pierced."

"What's going on, some kind of party?" Hugh sounded furious.

"No, it's just my study group. Maybe you could call back later. . . how did you even get this number?" I demanded. It was only listed under Richard Randall.

"I squeezed it out of your chum Yuki, and I'm not ringing off until you tell me why you left."

"You ask too many questions." It was out before I recalled having said the same thing between our first kisses in the car. There was a long silence, and I supposed Hugh was remembering as well.

"Did you leave because of the necklace?" he asked.

"Yes. It was interesting how something so precious wound up in your closet."

"I don't suppose you'd believe me if I told you it was planted."

"No, I wouldn't." When he didn't respond I said, "Tell me about Yamamoto."

"Still missing. I've been searching the slopes since yesterday. Today I wiped out on one of the tougher courses and sprained my ankle. I was in hospital all afternoon."

"How miserable for you. Could you communicate with the doctors?"

"Not really. It would have been helpful to have you translate." He paused. "At least I didn't fall the way Yamamoto did. They spotted his skis sticking out of a ravine but are unable to go down."

"So they believe he is—" I couldn't say dead, that was too terrible. "Do you think this accident might be connected to anything that happened earlier? Maybe someone chucked him over the mountain because he knows too much?"

"Of course it could, which brings me back to the autopsy! You'll need to translate it pronto, all right?"

"I'll mail it to your office so you can get it done professionally. There's no connection between us, Hugh." His casual orders irritated me enough that I didn't mention how I'd thought of asking my cousin Tom for help.

"Split personality time, hmm? I remember you becoming rather connected to me in the early hours yesterday. In fact, you made me promise to do something again and again—"

"Watch it. I presume you're talking in the hallway?" Not that I was any better off, as my friends had completely stopped their conversation to listen.

"Actually, I'm on my cell phone standing on crutches in a foot of snow because I don't trust a damn person inside the inn!" Hugh had lost all control and was shouting in the receiver. "Because I've lost two friends and the only person who can help me won't. Think about that, Miss Prim!"

He clicked off, and somehow, I was left holding more than the phone.

I was a terror at the *kanji* game that night, surprising everyone. Granted, I'd had nothing to read except the dictionary in Shiroyama. I found myself drawing characters on Richard's portable whiteboard with unusual speed. We played for a hundred yen coins, and by the end of the night I had collected twenty of them.

"Enough to buy a small piece of Roquefort cheese! You may serve it to me on a baguette next week," Simone suggested.

"Or a ten-minute telephone call home. My parents would like that," I countered.

"You could always spring for a five-pack of rubbers from Condomania!" Richard smirked.

"You are so vile," Karen said, speaking for all the women. "It's a wonder we let you stay in this group."

It was odd we had all come together, I mused while washing out the pasta saucepan after Karen and Simone left for their train home. Richard and I were a natural team, struggling to teach English at Nichiyu.

We'd met Simone selling Moroccan bracelets in Ueno Park. Simone had it tough, perpetually fleeing the Tokyo police with her briefcase of questionable baubles and sharing an apartment smaller than ours with three other French girls.

Karen, on the other hand, lived a life of relative luxury. As a magazine and TV model, she made enough to share a large one-bedroom with a Japanese boyfriend. It was true that blondes had an easier time than anyone in Tokyo, but I still liked Karen. She reminded me of the good-natured athletic girls who had taught me to swim, and she cut my hair for free. Above all, her earnest desire to learn to read and write Japanese impressed me, given that her career certainly didn't demand it.

These were my friends, the people I belonged with. I reminded myself of that as I prepared for bed, but was unable to keep myself from dreaming that night about a mountain four hundred miles away with two men on it—one lame, the other probably dead.

11

When my parents telephoned the next morning, they received an account of my New Year's trip that excluded murder, disappearances, and sex. I did mention that I had called Tom, which I thought would make my father happy—after all, he'd cinched my cousin's medical fellowship in San Francisco. But I'd overlooked what mentioning my father's family would do to my mother.

"I owe them a Christmas present," she fretted. "Do you suppose it's too late to send something?"

Even after thirty years with my father, my American mother remained deeply intimidated by Japanese etiquette. The handful of visits we'd made during my childhood always meant crash courses at Berlitz and tea ceremony school; when we reached Japan, she was understandably upset that my father's family still treated her like a foreigner.

"People don't usually give Christmas presents in

Japan, Catherine," my father said from the other extension, where he had been fairly silent up to now. "And I already sent a New Year's greeting."

"I could mail them some sun-dried tomatoes, the great big ones in extra virgin olive oil from Sonoma. When I brought them with me last time they seemed to like them. Rei, do you think that would be repetitive?"

"It's a great idea. And send me some, while you're at it. The dry kind. If olive oil leaks through the package, the post office will think it's a bomb."

"If you came home for Christmas you could have eaten all your favorite foods," my mother sniffed, starting on a familiar theme.

"I know. I meant to come home. I just couldn't afford it."

"What are you talking about? We sent you a ticket last year that you still haven't used," my father grumbled.

"One way," I reminded him. "You want me to come back and stay."

"Every year that you delay work on a doctorate is a waste," my father said. "You did so well with your master's degree that you could resume your studies very easily."

"Rei's done enough graduate school," my mother cut in. "She is going to work as an art consultant in my firm. It's exactly what she wants to do."

"If you want to see me, come here. You're always welcome," I said, striving for control.

"I don't know, Rei. That terrible room you live in with that effeminate boy . . ." my mother's voice trailed off.

"I'll book you into the Prince Hotel! Come on, I could use some company at the shrine sales."

"I'll think about it. But I've got two new houses to do, and Daddy's teaching at the medical school this semester so he can't possibly get away. You know I can't handle the Shimuras without him."

"I've got to run," I said, sensing a new list of their alleged slights was forthcoming. The problem was separation: the way the Shimura men whisked my father off to the golf course, leaving my mother with Aunt Norie, who always forgot she didn't like fish or other foods of the sea. My aunt had also laughed at my mother when she wanted to ship home an antique ceramic urinal. I was with my mother on that one. The blue-and-white urinal looked great planted with California poppies.

"What are you doing today?" My mother was unwilling to let me go.

"Oh, I thought I'd go shopping, maybe look for some wood-block illustrations," I improvised.

"Really! Keep an eye out for me. Remember, I don't care about age, I'm looking for color and line and as little water damage as possible . . ."

My mother and I both loved Japanese antiques. Since she was an interior decorator, looks were more important than history. I was more into age, but my budget limited me to small, often damaged pieces. Still, everything I bought filled me with joy. I also realized that if you hung enough kimono and wood-block prints on the walls, it diverted the eye from peeling paint and made things cozy enough that you almost forgot the lack of central heat.

I hung up the phone and started doing dishes

under a trickle of cold water that I knew wouldn't heat up until I was through. I thought about my mother's request; it would be easy to go to Oriental Bazaar, a gleaming emporium aimed at foreigners, to find the kind of prints she wanted. That held no challenge, though.

The telephone rang again and I let the answering machine kick on. When I heard the voice of a Japanese man speaking fluent English, I shut off the sniveling tap and ran to pick up.

"You're back sooner than I expected, cuz," I greeted Tom Shimura, son of my mother's mortal enemy.

"I'm still en route—at the train station, actually—but called in and got the message. What is up?" Tom's enthusiasm for colloquialisms always made me smile.

"I have a Japanese medical document that I can't understand."

Tom's voice lowered to a confidential level. "Is it your medical record? Don't tell me you finally went in for your annual?"

The fact my cousin knew I was overdue for any kind of doctor visit annoyed me. Had he been through my St. Luke's records himself? I steeled myself into politeness and said, "Actually, I haven't. But I was wondering whether you know anything about autopsies?"

"Sure. I dictated plenty of them when I was training. Why?"

"I'll tell you when we get together."

"You want to see me today? I'll be in Yokohama by lunchtime."

"Tell me where," I said, astounded at my luck. Tom was the busiest man I knew.

"Could you stand a trip to the suburbs? My father's gone back to work in Hiroshima, so we've been quite lonely. *Okāsan*—Mom—will be thrilled to have somebody new to cook for."

"Please tell her not to go to any trouble."

"Trouble? We're still eating our way through the New Year's leftovers. Consider yourself performing a public service."

On the well-groomed street leading to my cousin's house, every driveway held a car sparkling from the culturally-mandated New Year's washing, some with holiday ornaments decorating the grilles. Tom's Honda Accord was no exception. The decoration of pine twigs tied with *washi* paper looked like it had been crafted by the same person who had done the exuberant arrangement of pine, bamboo, and plum by the front door: Aunt Norie, Yokohama's own Martha Stewart.

"Rei-chan, you shouldn't have!" my aunt said when I presented her with a small jar of Indonesian vanilla beans. I would probably be "little Rei" to her the rest of my life, but didn't really mind.

Tom came downstairs and gave me an awkward, light embrace that he'd probably learned in America, as no one else in his family had gotten to the point of touching me yet. Some things were just too foreign.

"Can you recognize me? This overwork at the hospital . . . I need to join a health club or something." Tom poked at his barely rounded stomach.

"You look great, Tom," I said. Aunt Norie had confided she'd received almost a dozen calls from brokers active in the arranged marriage scene. Tom, however, would have none of it.

For lunch, Aunt Norie served scallops au gratin, a cucumber salad, sake-simmered lotus root, spinach-sesame rolls, and pickled eggplant left over from New Year's. She said, "Please tell your mother how much we enjoy that vinegar she sent for my birthday! It's on the salad. But I don't understand what it is, exactly."

"Balsamic," I guessed. And too much of it. I had to keep from puckering my mouth as I ate.

"I mean to go on a *natto* diet, but *Okāsan* keeps stuffing me with high-cholesterol meals," Tom said, not looking like he minded a bit.

"You eat *natto*? I'm glad I don't have to work with you." I made a face at him. The smell of fermented soybeans was just as bad as its stringy texture, although millions swore it was a font of good health.

"Tomatsu, if you want to lose weight, get married. None of the girls today cook! Oh, I'm sorry, Rei-chan. You surely are an exception?"

"I hope so!" Had she forgotten the time I brought her imperfectly rolled, but nonetheless delicious, vegetarian sushi?

"How is the romantic life? Any nice new boyfriends?" My aunt probed.

Before I could say no, Tom came to my defense. "Leave Rei alone. After all, she came over for a professional consultation."

Aunt Norie blushed and made excuses to do some

vacuuming upstairs, perhaps fearing Tom would order me atop the dining table for some kind of exam. Instead, he led me into the living room and settled into a plush recliner. The chair uttered an electric groan and began vibrating along his shoulders. Tom sighed happily, reinforcing my suspicion he wouldn't leave home anytime soon. He'd live in the massage chair until Aunt Norie finally found a bride with acceptable culinary skills.

As Tom read the autopsy, I wandered through the minimalist beige living room, sliding the floor-to-ceiling *shōji* screens aside to look at the garden, where plum trees were already budding. Maybe my aunt would let me cut a branch to take back to my room.

"This reads like it was written twenty years ago. Country doctors!" Tom snorted.

"Tell me about it." I sat down on the couch and opened the notebook I'd brought with me.

"It starts out quite normally, describing the subject as a forty-one-year-old female weighing forty-nine kilograms," Tom told me. "The stomach contents were partially digested rice, fish, and vegetables, giving the impression she died four to six hours after eating."

That would have been between eleven and one, when I'd gone out to hear the temple bells ring.

"Moving on, general X rays showed no fractures. The X ray of the skull revealed no fractures, although the coroner noted bruising behind both ears. A dental exam showed teeth to be intact with no lacerations of the tongue."

So she hadn't bit her tongue or had it pierced, I wrote, thinking of Richard.

"A pelvic exam revealed that she had given birth previously, and there was evidence of a well-healed tubal ligation."

I was stunned. "It can't be. She said she didn't have children!"

"People lie. The body can't." Tom looked at me significantly. "The coroner went on to perform toxicology tests. In thirty cubic centimeters of blood taken from the left ventricle, there was a blood alcohol content of one hundred and five milligrams per deciliter."

"The police said she was extremely drunk and passed out in the snow."

Tom shook his head. "If she had been driving a car and been stopped by the police, she probably would have tested positive for alcohol. But given this very slight blood alcohol content, she wouldn't have been falling-down drunk."

"She seemed perfectly sharp when I talked to her after dinner that night. She drank a little sake." I remembered with a pang the ceremonious way she had poured for Hugh.

"Eighteen c.c.s of water were present in her lungs. It looks like the coroner assumed it to be melted snow."

That made me think of the bath. "Wait a minute. If someone were forcibly held underwater, how much water would show up in their lungs?"

"Not much, since the throat contracts against foreign substances. Drowning victims typically have twenty c.c.s or less in their lungs." Tom handed the papers back. "They should have tested for liver and kidney disease but didn't. That's what I'm upset about. They shortcut things, *neh*?"

I didn't want to discuss such boring things as livers and kidneys. "What about the possibility of assault? You mentioned some bruises behind the ears."

"It could be that because she was lying down, her blood flowed to the back of her head and caused the marking."

"The bath contained some special kind of mineral water," I mused. "Why didn't they test it? Then they could tell it wasn't snow—"

"It looked clear to them, I assume." Tom looked at me. "Now are you going to tell me why you even have a copy of this document?"

I hesitated before saying, I can't tell you. It's confidential."

"But this is Setsuko Nakamura, the woman who's been in all the newspapers for the last three days. How did you get hold of her autopsy?"

"I'm helping a friend of hers. We have a theory that she was drowned by her husband. What you told me about the autopsy shows that he certainly had the time to do it."

"*Maybe* had the time. Nothing about the autopsy's firm, Rei."

"What do you mean?"

Tom chucked me under the chin. "Forensics cannot offer firm answers."

"Then what's the point?" I let my exasperation show.

"Listen, cousin. This woman died between four and six hours after eating dinner—no one can say for certain. The water might have been snow, or it could have been from the bath. And she may or may not have had a head injury."

"Okay," I said, standing up to go. Maybe was not as good as certainly, but it was a step in the right direction. And now I knew she'd had a child.

"I'm really grateful, Tom," I began. "I owe you."

"That's all right." He gestured at the papers I was tucking away. "What are you going to do with it?"

"I'll return the autopsy to my friend. Case closed," I said, wishing I could believe it.

I carried three curved plum branches home and arranged them in a chipped Satsuma vase I'd rescued from the neighborhood's oversized trash pickup a month ago. Even with the addition of flowers, I found myself thinking my small apartment was a dump compared to Aunt Norie's house. Kimono and wood-block prints couldn't hide the electrical cords draping the walls like an ugly spider web, and nothing could be done to camouflage the ancient linoleum floor. What finished the disaster off were my cardboard boxes overflowing with books and shrine sale miscellany, and my sorry wardrobe hanging on a rod that spanned the length of one short wall. No wonder my mother refused to stay with me.

I slid the *kotatsu* table on its side against the wall so I'd have room for to unroll my futon. I laid across it with the autopsy notes in front of me. I wished I'd studied Setsuko more closely when I found her. All I really had was a memory of her snow-shrouded figure and her long, black hair frozen stiff like a piece of bark. Her hair. I thought about it and suddenly had another question.

Aunt Norie said Tom had gone to the hospital. The St. Luke's operator told me he was unavailable. I tapped a pen restlessly against the table, thinking. Tomorrow I had to go back to work. I needed to put this problem away.

Thirty minutes later I was outside St. Luke's, the sleek, sand-colored building which was perhaps the most luxurious hospital in Japan. St. Luke's had been founded in 1900 by an American doctor, a fact that protected it from U.S. bombs during World War II. The hospital was haven again following the 1995 subway gas attack by members of the Aum Shinrikyo cult. Five cult members punctured bags containing nerve gas on several commuter trains; when the fumes began to escape, people began pouring off the trains, half-blinded and ill.

Eleven died and approximately 3,800 people were injured, many of them going to St. Luke's. Tom had overseen the emergency room that morning. He told me the most amazing thing had been the stoic calm of the victims. Nobody cried, just waited patiently for their turn.

Unlike me. I walked straight into the emergency room, presented my card to the head nurse and demanded to see Dr. Shimura immediately. Shortly thereafter my cousin emerged from a curtained-off area wearing a white coat and look of irritation.

"Just five minutes," I said. "I want to ask you more about bruises."

"If I don't come with you, I suppose you'll never leave." Tom sighed and showed me into the hospital café, a cheerful blue and yellow room decorated with faux Grecian columns. A table full of nurses stared at my cousin with undisguised longing. He didn't seem to notice.

"So you want to know about bruises." Tom swirled cream into a small cup of coffee. "On a most basic level, they form when some kind of trauma breaks the blood vessels and allows blood to seep through tissue."

"And blood always flows downward, according to gravity?"

"Sure." Tom twisted his watch around so he could look at it without being obvious.

"She couldn't have died naturally, then." My voice rose and the nurses swiveled around to look at us again. "When I found her, she was lying face down. I'm sure of it because her hair had fallen over her face."

Tom's beeper went off. He unclipped it from his waist and studied the number blinking on it.

"Bruises wouldn't have formed on the back of her head if she fell face down. Don't you get it?" I beseeched him.

"I have to answer this page." Tom walked over to a telephone on the wall and lifted the receiver. He spoke animatedly and gave a slight bow at conversation's end, but I was too wound up to find it amusing.

"I've bought myself ten more minutes," Tom said when he came back. "Did you bring the autopsy?"

"Of course." I chewed on my thumbnail as Tom read it again.

"Yes, you're right," he said at last. "Given the circumstances, this is very likely the Battle sign."

"You mean she fought somebody?"

"No, cousin. Battle is the name of the physician who identified a special type of bruise. He studied head injuries and found that when someone is hit hard on the back of the head, it fractures the cranium and also bursts the capillaries so blood seeps through tissue and pools behind the ears. This creates dark bruises now known as the Battle sign."

"But didn't you tell me the X ray showed no fractures?"

"Often fractures don't show up. Even having been in medicine for ten years, I can tell you it's extremely difficult to look at a film and discern a hairline fracture from a vein or even a normal joining of the skull bones."

"So, you're telling me you believe she was hit on the back of the head?"

"Yes," Tom said, after a second's pause. "Looking at the time the coroner did the exam—10 A.M. on January 2—there was a very reasonable amount of time for the sign to appear, even allowing that she was packed in snow for a night."

"We've got to do something."

"Well, the ideal situation would be to have the coroner revise his findings. But it's not likely that he will admit to any mistake."

"So no one will ever find out." I didn't hide my disgust. "She'll have died and been written off all because of some mighty *oisha-san*'s incompetence.

Or maybe, because the company involved is Sendai, they had everything smoothed over."

"If you want to put your mind at ease, call the police," Tom said. "Tell them you talked to me and I suggested they take the autopsy to a different coroner for a second opinion."

"The captain won't listen to me. He hates foreigners."

"Try. Your Japanese is good enough."

"But it's not medical! If I call him, could I give him your number, too? So you could explain everything?" I hated myself for being so dependent, but I knew how much weight Tom's words would carry.

"If you insist." Tom didn't look happy. "Cousin, I'm going to just say this once. After you speak to the police, this mission of yours should end. This friend who asked you to do things should realize you're an English teacher, not a crime fighter."

"Crime fighter?" I raised my eyebrows. "You've been reading too many comic books."

Tom didn't smile. Instead, he changed languages. "In Japan, young people listen to their elders. So I'm telling you as an older cousin to younger, that whoever struck this woman thinks he got away with it. You're not the one to tell him otherwise."

Nobody could possibly know why I'd gone to St. Luke's, but I was on hyper alert as I edged my way into the train station. I watched the people who boarded the train, but seats were plentiful at this hour and no one came near me.

I was the only one to get off at Minami-Senju, my subway stop. I walked fast over the steel pedestrian overpass and down its steps to the sidewalk, passing Family Mart and the liquor store. A large group of *bōsōzoku*, young motorcycle hoodlums, roared past me. They had lately taken to congregating outside the liquor store, revving their engines for the fun of it. Nobody dared complain because *bōsōzoku* were rumored to be junior workers for the *yakuza*, organized crime gangs similar to the American Mafia.

Compared to them, my homeless neighbors were absolute gentlemen. Tonight they had a bottle of beer between them and were pouring it out into small glasses. One of them called out an invitation that I pretended not to hear.

The first thing I did when I got into my apartment was lock and chain the door. Then I telephoned Minshuku Yogetsu. My relief that Mr. Yogetsu answered instead of his wife was short-lived.

"Miss Shimura! Such luck you called. My wife wants to talk to you. May I put her on?"

She had probably decided to charge me for the broken *shōji* screen. I did not want to talk to her about it. "Actually, I can't stay on the phone. I just wanted to leave a message for Hugh Glendinning."

"Oh, he's out drinking at the Alpenhof. He does that every night, now. I'm surprised he doesn't move there." Mr. Yogetsu sounded hurt.

How interesting. Was he drowning his sorrows or entertaining someone new? I pictured a slim Japanese girl in tight ski pants. I hastily rang off, hoping Mr. Yogetsu would not encourage his wife to call me

back. I phoned the Alpenhof, where the bartender
answering the phone sounded like he was in the middle of a brawl. When I asked him to check for a white
man, he shouted "No *gaijin*!" and hung up.

I would have to contact Captain Okuhara first and
then relay the message to Hugh. I dialed the number
on the business card the police chief had given me. A
desk sergeant answered, and I identified myself as the
Japanese-American woman who had found Setsuko
Nakamura's body at Minshuku Yogetsu. There was a
series of clicking noises, and I thought I'd been disconnected until I heard a new voice.

"Okuhara here."

"This is Rei Shimura. Do you remember me?" I
asked hesitantly.

"The amateur translator. I recognize your accent."

"I have some more information about your case."

"The Nakamura accident?" He sounded bored.

"I'm telephoning about the autopsy, which is . . .
perhaps not correct after all." Taking a deep breath, I
launched a translation of the high points Tom had
told me.

"Yes, I know what the Battle sign is. The coroner
did not mention it." Captain Okuhara spoke firmly.

"The thing is, we know the last thing she did that
night was take a bath," I reminded him. "If she had
been struck in the head and then held underwater,
she could have drowned. Do you remember how she
had water in her lungs as well as the bruises behind
the ears?"

"How did you reach this rather astonishing con-
clusion, Miss Shimura?"

"A Saint Luke's physician provided this analysis, so if you don't believe me, just call him! But please look around before all the evidence is gone—look in the bath at least—"

"She was found outside. You of all people, should remember that."

"Yes, I found her under the bathroom window, with no footprints leading to, or away, from her body. She lay face down, which means there was no reason for her to have bruises behind her ears. No reason except for the fact that somebody hit her in the head. Think about it!" I dropped the formal language I'd started with, had no more patience for honorifics. There was a long silence.

"How did you get the autopsy?" When he spoke again he sounded friendlier, but I still felt ruled by caution.

"It was given to me."

"The only person who had a copy was Mr. Nakamura."

"Mr. Glendinning obtained a photocopy because he was concerned. He knew Mrs. Nakamura had wanted a divorce. There's every reason to believe her husband was the person who struck her." There, I'd said it at last.

Captain Okuhara wanted to know more. Now that I had his complete, uncritical attention, my words slowed and my grammar fell back into place. I told him about the papers in my door, the gas accident, and the scenario Hugh and I had constructed in the bathroom.

"You were correct to call, Miss Shimura," he said

at the end of my outpouring. Correct. That was an improvement over the way he'd been treating me. Cheered, I asked him what the next step would be.

"First, I will call this doctor at St. Luke's you told me about. Then, if I see fit, I will order the autopsy redone."

Feeling giddy I hung up and went to bed, but found I could not sleep. I fixed myself a cup of cocoa, trying to will myself into relaxation. Captain Okuhara had listened. He had thanked me. Vindication would never again feel so sweet.

12

The crackers and candy piled up next to the coffee-maker had been thoroughly pawed over, but they still tempted me on my first evening back at work. Everyone had brought a souvenir from their vacation travels. I added a small sampler of Shiroyama's sweet bean cakes to the display and wondered if there would be time for a cup of tea and a quick bite before I started teaching.

"You look like the cat who got the cream. Did the flying Scotsman call back yet?" Richard's sibilant whisper in my ear made me jump. I shook my head. I'd waited all weekend and was heartily sick of it. Richard opened his mouth, probably on the verge of offering condolences, but I interrupted him.

"You took that earring out of your mouth!"

"It's a tongue stud," Richard corrected. "This dress code sucks. I don't know how much longer I can take it."

It was a minor miracle that Richard managed to

squeeze himself four nights a week into the button-down shirt, blazer, and trousers Nichiyu required of him. If he had his way, he'd dress in the black T-shirt, leather jeans, and multiple earrings he wore constantly on his jaunts into Roppongi and Shinjuku. No one at work was aware of his sexual orientation. This made him complain that our living together ruined his image. Still, he needed me as much for close companionship as my share in the rent payment.

Richard was everything to me. Having grown up an only child, I felt cheated that I'd never had anyone with whom to sing in the car or play secret games. Karen and Simone, who had experience in such things, assured me brothers really weren't that fun, but I still chose to define my three years with Richard in sibling terms.

"I hope you remember to remove your stud when you drink hot liquids," I faux-lectured Richard as the electronic melody chimed over the intercom to tell us the regular workday had officially ended. It hadn't. Most salarymen spent at least four more unproductive hours at their desks or in Richard's and my English classes.

Not only did we have to teach at night, we had to teach groups Nichiyu management assisted on arranging according to work section and not language level. This meant bossy men who couldn't put together two sentences dominated each class, while better speakers of lower rank were afraid to open their mouths. Today when I asked "What was the best thing about your vacation?" three times at slow speed, it met with dead silence.

"The best thing was sleep!" Mr. Fukuda bellowed

at last, and there was nervous laughter from the group of adults clustered around the U-shaped table.

"Sleeping! Surely, Mr. Fukuda, you didn't sleep the whole five days?"

Yes, he had. So had Mr. Nigawa. The only person who admitted to doing anything was Ms. Mori, who had made a cake for her family.

"No one went away?" I asked skeptically, remembering all the souvenir sweets.

"You, *Sensei*!" someone asked me. "Where did you go? Mr. Randall said you left him alonely in Tokyo."

"Alone in Tokyo and no, let's not talk about me today." I knew why my students begged me for monologues—it enabled them to glaze over into sleep. "Come on, let's all ask our neighbor what the best thing about vacation time was, and also what we missed about work. I'll model this with Ms. Shinchi." I motioned my best student to her feet. "Hello, Ms. Shinchi!"

I held out my hand for her to shake. The shy woman pumped it up and down while bowing slightly.

"Hello, Ms. Shimura."

"Did you return from New Year's vacation?"

"Yes, I returned from New Year's vacation," she parroted back.

"What was the best thing about your vacation?"

"The best thing about my vacation was seeing my mother in her house." She stared at her feet.

"Can you tell me more about that?"

"I had not seen her for one year's time."

"Mmm. Is there any reason you're glad to be back at work?" I prompted.

"I like returning to work to earn some money."

"There! Let's see how many different answers we can find in ten minutes, and I don't want to hear any Japanese."

We got home late, but Richard persuaded me to stay up to watch a Junzo Itami comedy called *Funeral*. It was surprisingly hilarious. I was laughing at a greedy priest trying to make off with a mourner's precious tiled table when Richard hit the VCR's PAUSE button.

"Someone's in the hallway."

"Mr. Noguchi's drunk and searching for his key again," I guessed. We had another neighbor one landing below, a widower who lived on shrimp chips and Yebisu beer. When he was really badly off, he sometimes stumbled up an extra floor.

"Nope. He's knocking on our door," Richard insisted, so I got up and looked through the peephole. The man standing outside was not Mr. Noguchi, but he wore a business suit and carried a briefcase. A lost salaryman? I opened up.

"Miss Shimura?" The stranger looked like he wanted to flee. Maybe it was my long underwear, but what did he expect at a quarter past ten? I tugged my *yukata* more tightly around myself and took the card he handed me. The side printed in English identified him as Junichi Ota, Attorney at Law.

"I'm not looking for any representation, thank you." I started to close the door.

"I have been sent by my client, Hugh Glendinning." As Mr. Ota spoke, my sense of gravity shifted, and I grabbed at the door frame for stability.

"I did not know you had a husband." Mr. Ota was looking past my shoulder at Richard sprawled across my futon in his long underwear.

"He's nothing. I mean, he's a colleague, not a husband, and he was getting ready to go to his room."

"Goodnight Miss Shimura, my honorable colleague." Richard slouched off without protest, since he would be able to hear everything through the paper thin door.

"What happened?" I asked Mr. Ota when we were alone, gesturing for him to sit down with me at the tea table.

"Mr. Glendinning was arrested yesterday morning in connection with Setsuko Nakamura's death and Kenji Yamamoto's disappearance." There was a rushing in my ears, but faintly in the distance, Mr. Ota continued. "According to Japanese law, a civilian can be arrested and detained without bail for forty-eight hours on the suspicion of having committed a crime. After that a public prosecutor must rule whether there is enough evidence to keep him in custody. Unfortunately, I believe this may happen to my client."

Captain Okuhara must have gone crazy with what I told him two days ago. I would call him back, straighten things out.

"The police chief is obviously refusing to consider Mr. Nakamura because it's easier to blame a foreigner. I'll talk to him." I headed for the telephone.

"Please do not do that!" Mr. Ota issued as much of a command as was possible in polite Japanese.

"Anything you say can be used against Mr. Glendinning.
It happened before."

"All I told him was that the autopsy should be re-
evaluated because it showed signs of a head injury!
Nothing about Hugh."

"You told the captain that Mr. Glendinning stole
the autopsy. That made him look very bad," Mr. Ota
said sternly. I wondered if he'd come just to make me
feel guilty. Well, it was my fault. My new year's resolu-
tion had been to think before speaking, and I'd failed.

Mr. Ota's accusing litany continued. "Miss Shimura,
you also put forth a theory about a bathroom killing.
Based on that, the police found evidence at the bottom
of the bath, part of Mrs. Nakamura's fingernail. And
they say Mr. Glendinning's fingerprints were on the window from where the body was dropped. The deceased
lady's jewelry was in his room, and now Mrs. Yogetsu,
the innkeeper, swears that she heard the two of them
together in the bathroom that night, arguing."

"My fingerprints were there, too. On the window
and on the pearls. And I—I was arguing with him in
the bath. Why didn't they hold me for questioning?"

"Maybe because you called it in. Good scout, *neh*?
Count your blessings." He looked pained as he spoke.
"If things were more ambiguous, we'd have a better
chance for my client's release. But the testimony from
the innkeeper's wife was very bad luck."

"Are you a criminal lawyer? Do you have experience?" I looked at Mr. Ota's suit, a polyester-wool
blend that hung limply from his small shoulders. He
didn't give the impression he had won enough cases to
afford a decent tailor.

"If Mr. Glendinning goes to trial, he won't need a lawyer. Just God." At my blank expression, he said, "Ninety-nine percent of cases that are brought to trial result in conviction."

I couldn't let myself think of that possibility. I had to stay calm. I said in my coolest voice, "I guess your role is to stop the indictment?"

"Precisely." Mr. Ota sounded relieved I was no longer arguing with him. "Even if the decision is made tomorrow to keep him, I'll have twenty-five days to gather enough evidence to stop the indictment. And Mr. Glendinning has many friends in the legal and business communities who may be able to help. High on our list is Mr. Piers Clancy, an attaché at the British Embassy."

"You still need me," I said. "I'll go back to Shiroyama. Hugh's Japanese is terrible. If he's being abused in some way, I could talk to the police—Captain Okuhara knows me."

"That's a very bad idea! Mr. Glendinning believes there is some danger of you being charged as an accessory to the crime. You must not appear close in the least."

I thought about it. Even more damning than my fingerprints was the contact we'd had: drinks at a hotel, dinner in another town, two nights in his room. And we both came from Tokyo where we might have had prior acquaintance. Given the way I'd behaved, anyone would think I would have benefited from Setsuko's death.

"Why did you come to me, then?"

"My client has made a request." Mr. Ota unzipped

his simulated leather briefcase and withdrew some papers. "The *tsuya* for Setsuko Nakamura is tomorrow night. Mr. Glendinning asks that you speak to Miss Hikari Yasui, his office lady, about attending it together. He wants you to look for anyone you might recognize from Shiroyama, and to make contact with Setsuko Nakamura's relatives. Watch closely and tell us later. Because you are so good at finding the hidden truth."

He'd sent a jab from behind bars that only I'd understand. I didn't know what a *tsuya* was, but I had a feeling it had something to do with funerals, and wouldn't be funny like the movie I'd been watching.

"I can't go anywhere that Mr. Nakamura might be. He might recognize me and become furious—he already thinks I'm too nosy," I explained.

"Your nose is fine. But you must change the hair, and perhaps wear some spectacles?" Mr. Ota handed me a single page from the midst of his stack of dog-eared documents. It contained two telephone numbers for Hikari Yasui and Piers Clancy.

"How much does Hikari Yasui know?" I asked.

"Yasui-san knows that her boss is in trouble. She is a girl with a loyal heart."

I wonder if Hugh had also told him that part. I cleared my throat and asked, "Will you stay in touch with me? Can you tell me what happens with the prosecutor?"

"Certainly. Tomorrow I will be staying overnight in Shiroyama, but I'll call when I return."

I watched Mr. Ota from the window as he left

fifteen minutes later, slipping on the wet pavement as he walked with arm outstretched, trying to hail a cab. They don't come this far down, I wanted to say to him. In this neighborhood, you were lucky if they came at all.

I called Piers Clancy promptly at nine the next morning.

"Your English is very good, Miss Shimura," he said snidely after I'd introduced myself.

"So is yours. Despite the accent." The few words he'd uttered sounded like a bad imitation of *Masterpiece Theatre*.

"Well, then." A moment of chilly silence. I pictured him sitting at a large desk wearing a starched shirt with cuff links made of some precious metal. "Let me advise you that this is a rather unusual case for the consulate. I've seen subjects jailed for drunk and disorderly conduct, drugs, that sort of thing. Nothing like murder."

"I thought you were his friend. You can't believe he did it?"

"I didn't go to the Japanese police, Miss Shimura. You did."

"About my calling the police—it was a well-meaning move that was unfortunately misinterpreted. What I want to know is where we go from here, and how Hugh's holding up in prison."

Piers Clancy coughed as if something irritating had caught in his throat.

"I haven't been to Shiroyama. However, our consul has toured various detainment facilities in this region and found them generally Spartan but safe. No chance of inmate rape or violence, given that prisoners are forbidden to mix."

"But the police are known to be brutal. I heard about an Iranian jewelry vendor who was beaten so badly that he went deaf!"

"They'd be mad to beat a British solicitor." Piers laughed a bit cruelly. "It's all a matter of knowing the rules. I've spoken to Hugh about etiquette: not looking or speaking to the guards until told, and so on. If he is harmed, he is to notify us and we will make a formal protest."

"Wonderful," I said, sarcasm heavy. "What else can you do for him?"

"Foreign consulates are neither expected nor allowed to interfere in the Japanese legal system. As a private citizen, though, I will submit a character reference, which can at least be brought to the judge's attention when he has his preliminary hearing."

"I don't suppose it would help if Sendai sent anyone to vouch for him? The company chairman or executive officer?" A mid-level foreign diplomat wasn't worth half a Japanese business leader.

"We have dead silence from that quarter, except for a comment that they'd understand if he felt the need to resign."

"Don't they know he was the one who wanted the autopsy looked into and the bathroom searched? If Hugh killed somebody and was lucky enough to have the thing ruled an accident, wouldn't he just have kept quiet?" The words tumbled out of me.

"Hugh will employ refined versions of some of

those arguments, certainly. And he's working with Ota on establishing an alibi for the time he was allegedly bathing with that woman—"

"He didn't go with her. I know it because his hair was wet before dinner. His and Mr. Yamamoto's."

"I appreciate your memories, but as Yamamoto is missing and presumed dead, we're not too well off."

Piers Clancy clearly didn't want to work with me. I was going to have to fall on his mercy for the slightest morsel. I asked, "Will you talk to Hugh again today? Can you tell him that I'm sorry?"

"Miss Shimura, please. I'll let you know when, or if, he is allowed out." The diplomat's voice was fading as if he were already onto some new order of business. "Until then, be a good girl and stay away from the journalists, will you?"

The next person on my list, Hikari Yasui, was considerably kinder.

"The problem will be straightened out soon, Miss Shimura. Everyone is helping," she said in good English with the high-pitched, eager-to-please intonation that told me she was close to my age and probably very pretty. The office lady voice; I sounded like a bear in comparison.

"What exactly is a *tsuya*? Is it the funeral?" I asked.

"No. The cremation ceremony is for relatives only. The *tsuya* comes first, so friends and neighbors can say good-bye to the deceased. There will be an altar in the home where people will offer prayers and discuss with each other their remembrance of the loved one."

"I don't know the etiquette." With my face, I couldn't get away with social blunders.

"You must wear black, and the only acceptable jewelry is pearls, which of course represent tears. Also, if you can bring a *kōden*, it would look right."

She was talking about a gift of money—Japan's favorite, all-purpose present—tied up in a ceremonial envelope with black and silver cords. I could find it at any stationer. I started worrying about the proper amount to enclose and whether I'd need to present a name card or some evidence of my identity.

"I've thought about this. You will be a new O.L.—an office lady—from Sendai. Mr. Ota said you are young, so—" she gave a wistful laugh—"what else could you be but an O.L.?"

"I don't look right. My hair . . ."

"Yes, I heard. I am reserving a wig at the beauty salon so you will be more normal."

My day had become very complicated. I needed to borrow a black suit from Karen, get fitted for the wig, and keep the lunch date I'd set up with Mrs. Chapman. After that I had to show up at Nichiyu, where I'd concoct an excuse to leave two hours early. Then I would take a long ride in a packed commuter train to Setsuko's *tsuya* in the suburbs. I became tired just thinking about it.

I decided to combine Mrs. Chapman and the beauty parlor. When I called, she said she was due for a styling anyway. We met at Hibiya Station and followed the directions to one of Tokyo's few surviving art deco buildings in a cluster of pricey real estate near Hibiya Park.

"It's like my beauty operator's back home!" Mrs. Chapman said as I held open the Oi Beauty Salon's frosted-glass door. Inside my eye was caught by a deserted row of old-fashioned bubble hairdryers, and a wall full of foam heads topped by horrible fluffy wigs. The place was a postwar treasure. I could imagine General MacArthur's wife sauntering in for a comb-out prior to lunching at the Imperial Hotel a few blocks away.

Mrs. Oi, a tiny wrinkled woman who looked like she'd been working since the Occupation, bowed deeply to Mrs. Chapman and shouted for the shampoo girl to bring coffee. When Mrs. Oi turned to me, I tried not to flinch as she stroked through my hair, commenting on its barbaric shortness. Yes, a wig would be just the thing to make me over until I grew my hair out to a proper womanly length.

"Are you going to a wedding or something? Would madam like a traditional hairstyle?" She scrutinized me closely.

"Actually, a party," I said. Mrs. Oi looked surprised; maybe people didn't rent wigs for parties. I improvised, "My in-laws will be there, and they cannot know I cut my hair last month."

"We always have to please the husband's family, *neh*? It's the woman's way," Mrs. Oi trilled, leading me to a selection of dark Japanese wigs. There were two basic styles: either long, straight and modern, or ornately upswept in the manner of a nineteenth-century geisha.

She placed a half-dozen wigs over my head until we were both satisfied with a silky, synthetic mane that hung straight to the middle of my back. For the first time in my life, I looked totally Japanese.

"This is your look," Mrs. Oi said firmly. "You should not have cut your hair. If you are serious about having long hair, maybe you should buy the wig and wear it until your short hair grows out."

"No, a rental is perfect. To tell the truth, I'd like to go back and forth between short and long. I'm sort of impulsive that way."

"Not so many ladies rent wigs these days. It is a shame. It's a good way to change your look, put a little spice back in the marriage." She began laboriously writing a receipt with gnarled fingers decorated with heavy jade and pearl rings.

After finishing my business, I poured my own cup of coffee and sat down to wait for Mrs. Chapman. She'd been shampooed and was now sitting under one of the large bubble dryers with a *Tokyo Weekender* on her lap. She shouted something at me which I couldn't hear over the whine of the dryer.

"What's that?" I came closer.

"I was wondering what you were doing with that wig! I thought you were coming here for a shampoo and set just like me."

I had been vague and just asked her meet me at the salon so we could go to lunch at a little Italian restaurant nearby. Now I lied, "I've been invited to a party and need a new look."

"If you wear that, you don't look at all American. You might as well put on a kimono." Her voice was teasing, but I had the feeling the sentiment behind it wasn't.

"The only kimonos I have are antique. They're not exactly wearable." I didn't like the conversation's turn, so I put the wig in my backpack and made an excuse about going off to find the ladies room.

She was finished and raring to go when I came back. It was such a pleasantly balmy day that I suggested we forget Italian and simply get takeout food to take into Hibiya Park. At the Sogo department store's massive food market, I found delicious Chinese noodles and she chose fried chicken. Both of us were content.

"So how much longer are you staying?" I asked as we settled down on a bench facing the duck pond.

"It's indefinite." Mrs. Chapman sighed heavily. "The travel agent promised I'd be able to fly out tomorrow, but when I showed up at her agency, she told me the New Year's travelers had booked up everything. I called the airline and they said the same thing."

"I'm sorry."

"That's what she said. Very, very sorry. So much for my open-return ticket." She pressed tangerine-frosted lips together.

"So what have you seen of Tokyo?" I dug into my spicy noodles, wondering whether I would have to entertain Mrs. Chapman forever.

"I went to that shrine you told me about and Disneyland by bus, like you suggested. I've also done quite a bit of shopping for my granddaughter on the Ginza, the big shopping street."

"Just like Setsuko. Shopping, I mean."

"I can't stop thinking about her, either." Mrs. Chapman sighed again. "It's on the English language news every night. I heard Hugh Glendinning was arrested."

"The police are just questioning him." I couldn't bear to say he was the main suspect.

"Really? It sounds like you're still involved. Do tell!" She leaned in so close one of her chicken legs dropped on my noodles.

"Not exactly." I gave her back the chicken leg and picked up my can of hot green tea. "I think all of us might have some information that could help the police. I just don't know what it is."

"Maybe we should brainstorm. If you could just give me a timeline of the events again—the news had it all muddled."

I supposed it wouldn't hurt to go over the scene again. "The autopsy suggested Setsuko died between eleven P.M. and one A.M. We were all there until about ten minutes to midnight. Then the Ikedas and I took a walk to the temple. Mr. Nakamura and Yamamoto caught up with us halfway. Hugh arrived a half-hour later."

"What about the innkeepers and the family?" Mrs. Chapman asked. "Where were they?"

"With us. It seems like you were the only person at the inn the whole time. You and Setsuko, I mean. Can you remember hearing her moving around the inn? Going up or down the back staircase, maybe?"

Mrs. Chapman chewed thoroughly before answering, "Like I said before, it was hard to hear over the TV. Then I fell asleep."

"Yes, that's what you told me before." I was disappointed all over again.

"Can I give you a piece of advice, honey? Keep your emotions in check, just in case the police have the right man. Hugh Glendinning was straight out of the movies, so good-looking and all, but you never know." She paused, studying my face. "You think the situation's different. I've hurt your tender young feelings."

"You haven't. It's nice to have a friend with the insights of age." Unlike Richard, who thought the whole situation was a joke. At least Mrs. Chapman, in her own bossy way, was trying to help.

At work, I decided to offer Mr. Katoh the truth—that someone I knew had unexpectedly died, and my presence was requested at her farewell ceremony. I'd done right; he took death ceremonies very seriously. Of course I could attend. My boss assured me Richard would gladly take my evening students.

Hikari and I met at six o'clock in front of a fast food stall in Shinagawa. Because we were the only women under thirty dressed head to toe in black and carrying *kōden*, identification was a cinch. She enthused about the long, phony hair and the ladylike Junko Shimada suit I'd borrowed from Karen. You could hardly tell I'd hitched the waist around with safety pins. I felt like a Japanese Barbie doll; the only thing subverting the look was a pair of black-rimmed glasses I'd borrowed from Richard.

My vision was slightly blurred, but I nevertheless checked out Hikari. She was tall, like all the best-looking girls in the Roppongi clubs. Her naturally-black hair swung all the way to her waist, and she had a tiny frizzed set of bangs. The conservative black suit she wore could be kindly described as Chanel-inspired, the double-C imperfectly stamped on gold buttons. She had a powdery smell I recognized as my deodorant; there, our similarities ended.

We stood the first half hour on the train but squeezed into seats after a big exodus at Yokohama Station. I pulled from my backpack three English language dailies with articles about Hugh's detainment. The one in the *Japan Times* was headlined RAKE'S PROGRESS and narrated how Hugh had ripped apart the Nakamura's idyllic marriage. The writer noted that Hugh had worked for short stretches at six different companies, lived in a Roppongi apartment with a monthly rent of 600,000 yen and had been charged with several parking violations since his arrival in Japan. An investment banker in London was the last girlfriend before Setsuko Nakamura, according to anonymous sources within the expatriate community. The article had a quote from Piers Clancy urging the public to remember Mr. Glendinning had not been indicted, much less convicted, and had a stellar reputation in the international legal community. Not surprisingly, Sendai's public relations office had no comment.

Hikari was looking over my shoulder, so I handed

her each paper as I finished. After looking at the *Japan Times*, she asked if the word "rake" meant something other than a garden tool.

"In this case, it means a playboy," I said. "Do you know about playboys?"

"I know." She shot me a pained look and read on silently until we got to the final stop, Zushi. Taxis were lined up at the curb, and she ushered me in ahead of her. We were transported along a rocky seashore to Hayama, the nearby town where Mr. Nakamura lived.

"So what do you think about my hair? Does it look as fake as it feels?" I was beginning to worry I wouldn't be able to pull something over a man who already knew me.

"I think you look very Japanese. Like my sister, maybe." Hikari flipped open a glow-in-the-dark compact and repowdered her perfect face.

I took off Richard's glasses to stare out the window at sprawling suburban houses, each with a garden lot large enough to erect another dwelling, which would have happened had it been Tokyo.

"I heard that in the mid-seventies, a rice farmer sold his land. If you bought then, maybe you could afford it. Today it would be impossible," Hikari said, as if she knew what I was thinking.

Each house appeared to have been designed with a restrained splendor true to Japanese roots; low structures in spotless cream or white stucco, topped by sloping tiled roofs in gray or blue. The gardens were walled so you couldn't see the treasures within, but I did catch a glimpse of a soaring fountain through one bamboo gate. I found myself wishing I could bail out of the cab and the ominous *tsuya* to seriously investigate these palaces of the bourgeoisie.

"I don't really want to go in. I have no idea what I'm going to do," I confessed.

"Rei-san, do not doubt your strength." Her voice was reassuring. "I received a faxed message from Hugh through his lawyer which said to trust you, because you are good at finding hidden truth."

So he was sending the same ironic commentary to everyone. She also had warranted a fax and I hadn't. "Did Hugh mention any names of Setsuko's relatives? Mother, father, what did she have?" The word *child* popped into my mind, but I didn't think it would be wise to tell Hikari everything.

"No parents living, as far as I know. This is the house. Please stop." It was too dark to see Hikari's expression, but in her voice I heard fear.

13

The *kanji* character for death glowed darkly on the surface of white paper lanterns flanking the Nakamura house. People wearing sober black suits and kimonos streamed past a small army of reporters clogging the street with bright lights and microphones. Some guests responded to their shouted pleas, but I kept my head down and followed Hikari inside, placing my *kōden* on a tray monitored by a pair of mean-looking men in black suits. On the back of the envelope I'd written the amount being given, 5,000 yen, and my aunt's maiden name, which I had decided to use as my cover.

Setsuko's good taste was as apparent in her home as it had been on her person. Calligraphy scrolls hung on the walls, and small antique ceramic and lacquer pieces were arranged on glossy *tansu* chests. The living room bustled with well-dressed guests and tuxedoed waiters offering whiskey and beer. The overall effect was of a very fashionable cocktail party.

A second room with *tatami* flooring had been designated for mourning and was filled with flashy golden funeral trappings and the spicy scent of a few hundred potted chrysanthemums. More flowers bordered the frame of a large photograph of Setsuko, who surveyed us with her cool half-smile from atop the three-tiered golden altar decorated with bowls of apples and oranges, offerings meant for Buddha.

Contemplating these decorations allowed me to delay approaching the brocade-covered box resting in front of the altar. It was closed, no doubt a necessity due to the gruesome slicing that would have been done in the course of two autopsies.

Hikari and I followed the lead of a woman who went up to the altar and bowed before it, clapping her hands together soundlessly in prayer. It was all over within a minute. I guessed it would be up to her relatives to kneel and pray for hours at the funeral tomorrow. Not many seemed to be in attendance: as Hikari and I traveled back to the living room, she identified almost everyone as Sendai salarymen and their spouses.

"Do you know all of them?" I was awed.

"Almost everyone. Over there is the company president."

"Masuhiro Sendai?"

"Yes. But it's best if you don't introduce yourself. He takes an interest in all his employees."

All except the ones in disgrace, I thought, looking at the doll-sized man with a thick shock of gray hair. He was conferring in a corner with a large foreigner, which made my hackles rise.

"Who's the *gaijin*?"

"He doesn't work at Sendai."

The man wore a Brooks Brothers suit and the smug, prosperous air of an expatriate executive in his early sixties. Maybe he was a lawyer, a contender for Hugh's job.

"Can I get a list of the people who gave *kōden*?" I asked, thinking a foreigner's name would pop right out.

"Oh, no! That goes straight to Mr. Nakamura."

"How about a guest list?"

"I doubt it. It is difficult to talk to Mr. Nakamura's secretary." Hikari looked unhappy, and I wondered what position she would move to now that Hugh was in prison. "Are you all right being alone for a while? I have some responsibilities." Hikari gestured to a group of her fellow office ladies clustered in a doorway.

I slipped back into the mourning room, figuring that anyone who really cared about Setsuko would be praying for her.

The attractive woman I had seen earlier at the coffin was back and seemed unable to tear herself away. I lowered my glasses slightly to inspect her. She had the same sleek hair as Setsuko, and she wore a slim-fitting black suit that looked like a Hanae Mori design. A handkerchief was pressed to her eyes. I was mustering the courage to approach her when I heard my name spoken softly in my ear.

"Miss Shimura." It was Captain Okuhara, this time in a highly official-looking uniform. "I thought you didn't know Mrs. Nakamura. It's surprising to find you at her *tsuya*."

"I wish I could say the same for you." Of course he would have spotted me; the question was whether he'd turn me in to Mr. Nakamura. If I could convince him I was on the guest list, maybe he would be thrown off. I ventured, "Mr. Nakamura has been so—reflective—about his wife's final days, that I got word he wanted us all to come to say good-bye. Have you seen the others?"

"No." A smile tugged at the corners of the policeman's mouth. "Actually, he is most interested in having his wife's killer apprehended."

"I thought you already had your killer in custody." I couldn't keep the bitterness out of my voice.

"Did Glendinning tell you where he is?" Captain Okuhara demanded.

"I heard it from his lawyer. You know you don't allow him phone calls."

"If Glendinning would do some talking instead of leaving it all to his lawyer, things would go better for him. As things stand, I have a feeling he will be with us for a long time."

I felt hot and cold in the space of a few seconds and had to put my drink down. One of Hikari's office lady colleagues thrust a napkin in my hand. I passed it over the wet spot I'd made on an antique *Tansu* chest.

"It's tough for you, isn't it?" His voice lowered to a sadistic purr. "Tough to realize that Mrs. Nakamura and your boyfriend did more than shop together. We have sworn testimony from the Yogetsu wife that Glendinning bathed with Mrs. Nakamura on New Year's Eve. She heard voices raised, voices speaking English."

"My voice and his." I met his gaze squarely. "Hugh and I were together. Bathing became our hobby. Ask Mrs. Yogetsu! She caught us the last evening I stayed there."

"A cute story, but I don't think it happened at eleven o'clock," he said. "You were watching television with the Ikedas."

I couldn't deny that, so I said, "I'd like to know how Mrs. Yogetsu could be snooping around the bath when she was busy serving me and the others. If you ask me, she just has a bad attitude toward about foreigners."

"Walls are quite thin in Japanese houses, and foreigners behave quite strangely. For instance, others heard you and our suspect—the man you claim not to have known—enjoying each other like, shall we say, old friends. First you played in the bath and then you rolled across the futon . . ."

I swore under my breath in English, and Okuhara laughed.

"You know a lot about our suspect, Shimura-san. I'd like to talk to you in more official circumstances."

I shook my head. "You twist everything I say to your own benefit."

"You'll have to talk sometime, you know."

"I'm getting a lawyer." I glanced out the side of my glasses to confirm who was entering the room. Yes, it was Seiji Nakamura looking in our direction. *"Sayonara,"* I said to the police chief and shot back into the hallway.

I caught up with the good-looking mourner outside the powder room. In my breathiest Japanese, I gave my cover name and said I worked at Sendai. She introduced herself as Mrs. Matsuda, a friend who had been studying the tea ceremony with Setsuko at one of the posh tea societies in Tokyo.

"I've always wanted to learn tea, but I hear it's very difficult," I said, disappointed she wasn't Setsuko's sister.

"It's a necessity if you plan to marry. Also, have you thought of trying contact lenses?" She added the last in a conspiratorial whisper.

"Mmm," I said, sizing her up. "But where do good looks take a woman, really? Mrs. Nakamura was lovely, but so unhappy."

"She could not have children. She tried everything. Finally, her age . . . it was too late."

"A woman's greatest joy is a baby." I employed one of Aunt Norie's stock phrases.

"Yes, thanks to God, I was blessed with three. Setsuko was like an aunt to them, always bringing gifts and so on." A tiny smile creased Mrs. Matsuda's perfect maquillage.

"She sounds like a very kind person. I feel badly for her husband, all alone now."

"Plenty of the office ladies will be feeling that way, I'm sure." Her voice had an edge.

"Of course, she was planning to leave him . . . the divorce . . ."

"I have no idea what you're talking about!"

I realized then that they must have been friends who stayed strictly on the surface. I asked, "Are any of her family members here? I would like to express my sympathies."

"Just her aunt is left. A very sad lady. I don't think she had seen Setsuko in years."

"She lives far away?"

"Not at all. But who knows when a loved one's life will be taken? It's all so arbitrary, really." She was drifting into the tearful state I'd first seen her in.

"Could you please show this lady to me? I would like to offer my respects . . ."

"She's getting a glass of sake over there—do you see the old lady with the bad back? I have been trying to tell her to sit down, but she is very determined. You know how ridiculously proud the elderly are."

I practically mowed down a trio of waiters carrying a large iced salmon in my efforts to catch up with the small woman whose figure was curved like a question mark.

"Excuse me, but were you Nakamura-san's aunt?" I asked.

"Oh, yes! Are you Mariko-chan?" Her weak voice filled with joy. It was too bad I had to introduce myself as Norie Fujita, a new office lady at Sendai.

"Forgive me, but I think you are probably the age of my great-niece. My name is Ozawa, and I am so pleased to meet you."

Mrs. Ozawa bowed dangerously low, and I reached out my hand to steady her elbow and asked, "Would you sit down with me for a minute, Mrs. Ozawa? I'd like to find a place where it isn't so crowded."

"Yes, it's a very well-attended event, isn't it?" she sounded proud. "All these high-class people and television cameras. Setsuko would have liked it . . ."

My thoughts exactly. We walked together down the hallway, and I located a room without guests, a tiny study where cheap plywood bookcases were filled with old electronics magazines, and a Sendai laptop computer like Hugh's rested on a desk scattered with papers. It had to be Mr. Nakamura's study. There was a small tweed couch which looked like a good place to put Mrs. Ozawa, so I coaxed her in and closed the door.

"I am ashamed to say I have never seen my great-niece, but I imagine she must be very similar to you. You are also a *konketsujin*?"

"Mmm. I grew up in the United States," I said, thinking she'd probably caught my slight accent.

"You grew up like a princess, then." Mrs. Ozawa gave a brief, tinny-sounding laugh. "No trouble with the neighbors. For Harumi, who was Setsuko's mother, it was very hard. After the war, when Japanese women delivered half-American babies, they were treated like refuse. The smart ones managed to get their sailors to take them to America."

"What do you mean?"

"Harumi was married to my brother Ryu, and they had Setsuko while living with our family. Ryu passed away in the early 1950s—old war injuries, you know. After he was gone, it was very hard for our family. And there was so little food . . . Harumi and Setsuko were considered a burden."

"I suppose Harumi worked to help your family?" I asked, feeling sorry for the widowed, beleaguered daughter-in-law.

"Yes, the poor woman went to work near the American navy base in Yokosuka. She shined sailors' shoes, but my parents thought there was more to it." She lowered her voice and said, "Harumi became pregnant. It was unmistakable after a while, so she left the household."

"You mean she was cast out?" I was horrified.

"Yes, because they knew it was an American sailor after the birth of their daughter, Keiko. Unbelievably, the American stayed with her. He could not marry her, but he set her up in a small house which had, of all things, a washing machine!"

"Did Setsuko's mother live forever after with this man? Why isn't he here?"

"He was shipped back to the United States after two years. Harumi sold me her washing machine because she could not keep the house, and she returned to shine shoes near the base again. The last time I saw her, she had both Setsuko and Keiko sleeping in a cardboard box at her side."

So the woman I'd thought was born privileged had once slept under cardboard just like the vagrants in my neighborhood. It was unfathomable.

"I continued visiting from time to time to bring old clothes and so on. But they were growing up in a terrible environment, it killed Harumi and Keiko both!"

"How?" I nearly jumped on her.

"Harumi was killed by a drunk American driving on the wrong side of the road. I was very worried about the daughters, but by then I had married and was living with my husband's family, so I could not take care of the girls. Harumi had a friend who raised them in Yokosuka."

"How did Setsuko's sister, Keiko, die?" I wanted to stay on track.

"Setsuko told me that in her teens, Keiko became

very wild. She gave birth to Mariko outside of marriage and spent her time in the bars taking drugs with the American sailors. One time she had a bad reaction. She jumped off a building, and that was it."

"And Keiko's little daughter Mariko?" This was one of the saddest stories I'd ever heard.

"Setsuko made sure she was taken care of, and she is now working at a bank . . . quite a suitable place for a young lady. Of course I haven't seen her. I would like to, now that she is the only one left."

"Which bank?"

"I don't know exactly, but it is a good one in Tokyo." Mrs. Ozawa paused. "The last time we met, Setsuko asked me to consider leaving some inheritance for Mariko. She said the Ozawa family's pattern of casting off women must be broken. At the time, I said to her, dear niece, I am sympathetic, but the young woman in question is not any kind of blood relation." She blinked back tears. "I was wrong. Setsuko walked out on me when I told her I wouldn't help Mariko. I never heard from her again."

In the space of this conversation, my picture of Setsuko Nakamura had altered. If Mariko really existed—I reminded myself that Mrs. Ozawa had never seen her, and Mariko's mother, Keiko, was conveniently dead—Setsuko had tried to do a great thing for her.

"I am not feeling so well. I would like some more sake . . ." Mrs. Ozawa was struggling to stand. I helped her up and commandeered her out the room, thinking more sake was probably not a good idea for a depressed woman who weighed less than ninety pounds. I would have to watch over her. Hearing brisk steps coming toward us, I looked up and saw Mr. Nakamura.

"What is it?" Mrs. Ozawa asked, not understanding why I'd stopped moving.

"Please go ahead, Mrs. Ozawa. I'll meet you," I said, going into a deep bow and mumbling the customary funeral greeting Hikari had told me would be correct should I come face to face with the impossible.

"Fujita-san? Thank you for coming. Have you spoken to Arae-san?" he said softly, not at all his usual manner.

"*Eh to . . .*" I hedged.

"Well, please see her about what to do. The toilet room needs to be cleaned up, fresh soaps and towels set out . . ."

If I were a Sendai employee, I'd obey him without question. Maybe this was some sort of test. I murmured my agreement and kept bowing until he turned on his heel. When Hikari had run off to the kitchen to take care of responsibilities, I had thought it strange. Now I understood the reality of O.L. Hell.

I found the powder room in the hallway near the front door. Rummaging below the sink, I came up with a powdered cleanser. Just behind the toilet was a little brush in a stand decorated with a snowman. I knelt to dislodge the brush and was drenched by a jet of water that shot up from the center of the toilet.

Water continued to spray upward as I sprang back, realizing I'd set off the toilet's bidet function. I found the STOP button on the side of the seat a few seconds too late. The floor, cabinet, and walls were sprayed with water. Karen's suit, too.

I mopped it all up with the three tiny towels Mr. Nakamura had asked me to replace and cast about in vain for fresh towels. Someone knocked on the door and I knocked back, signaling my occupation.

"Rei?" Hikari's voice at the door led me to crack it open at last.

"I've created a flood here," I said needlessly as she looked in and gasped.

"People have been noticing you!" Hikari moaned. "Miss Arae asked me who you were. I told her you were from the daughter of somebody in Mrs. Nakamura's tea society, but she heard from somebody else that you were a Sendai O.L.!"

"Who's Miss Arae?" I was lost.

"Miss Arae is head of the secretarial group. She is talking to Mr. Nakamura right now. I'll get the coats. We've got to get out."

Hikari and I jogged down the cul-de-sac slowly because of our high heels and caught a taxi on the main road. Once inside, Hikari pulled a small red leather book out of her handbag. "Setsuko's telephone book. I found it in the kitchen."

I flipped on the taxi's dome light and began leafing through tiny pages filled with handwritten *kanji*. "Thanks. I can follow up on anyone who looks interesting."

"Don't you want me to look at it first?" Hikari sounded crushed.

"Well, I'm sure I have more time to work on it than you. Maybe I should go through it myself." I didn't trust her to know the things I wanted to find.

"Really? I heard you had to have the autopsy translated."

"Well, medical language isn't my thing, but personal names are easy. I've studied *kanji* for years." Not very successfully, but she didn't need to know that.

"May I see the book once more?"

"Sure." I handed it back, thinking that I couldn't believe we were fighting over it. Maybe we were fighting about something else.

She returned the book after a minute and I slipped it into my purse.

"It's kind of you to lend it to me," I said, trying to make up for my rudeness. "You must be very fond of Hugh to go to this trouble."

Her face flushed. "Not so fond. Not fond enough to be stupid."

"That makes two of us." Yet, as we lurched over the pitted road leading to the train station, I doubted myself.

14

Mariko was going to be one in twelve million, if she had stayed put within Tokyo city limits. I spent Wednesday searching through Setsuko's book without luck. Neither was she among the many Ozawas listed with Tokyo directory assistance. Thinking it over, I concluded that she might have married and changed her name, or might have no telephone at all.

Mr. Ota called to get a report on how the *tsuya* had gone, and I asked immediately for the latest on Hugh.

"Things are proceeding. While I was visiting, the British consul made a visit to ensure his conditions were adequate. We all had a chance to talk."

"Do you think he'll get out? The two day period is up today."

"The police chief in Shiroyama is keeping him longer. There's a legal loophole he's using while he tries to gather evidence."

"Can't the consul help?"

"The British consul cannot supersede the Japanese police. By the way, what's this about your withholding the address book? Miss Yasui could have had it translated in a matter of hours."

"I'm using it for my research," I said, although I'd only made out half the names so far. "If you want me to give it up, have Hugh confirm it. I'm not giving it up until then."

"I thought I told you he's not allowed telephone calls. The most he could provide was a floppy disc. He had messages on it to half of Tokyo, a big headache for me."

"Is there a message for me?"

"Yes, there is," he said grumpily. "I will fax it to you."

"When?" I couldn't believe he hadn't volunteered the information earlier.

"This afternoon, maybe."

"Listen, the only fax I have access to is at Nichiyu. If you could send the document at a set time, I'd be able to intercept it without anyone noticing. What about five minutes after three?"

"Three-oh-five then, Miss Shimura, and don't forget to bring me the address book soon, please."

Mrs. Bun watched me run to the fax machine when it suddenly stuttered at four minutes after three. It was only a report for Mr. Katoh.

"Rei's doctor is faxing her medical record, and she's afraid we'll all snoop in it," Richard smoothly lied. He made me blush, adding to the effectiveness of the ploy. At 3:08, the machine started again, spitting out a cover sheet with Mr. Ota's letterhead. A second page followed with blurry typed writing. I grabbed them tightly against my chest and sprinted from the room, Richard at my heels.

"Come on, Rei. I'm involved!"

"Sorry, babe." I slammed the women's lavatory door in his face, curled up on the cracked vinyl chair by the sinks and began reading. The message had been neatly typeset into a memo form addressed *To Rei Shimura, from HG, regarding incarceration.* I half-smiled at that, but stopped quickly as I read on.

> Alive and well in an unheated prison with no telephone privileges, to put it mildly. For reasons of security I cannot discuss elements of my defense, but Mr. Ota and I are both working hard. I am unsure whether the answer to Setsuko's death lies here or in Tokyo, which is why I asked you to help.
>
> I understand from everyone who's spoken with you that you are remorseful about your telephone call to the police. I was quite angry at first; I'd be lying if I didn't tell you that. But I've thought things through and have come to the conclusion that you intended no malice. I hope Mr. Ota has communicated my feelings, as well as the fact that I remain grateful for whatever you can do. You are

a woman of considerable talents. Still, I
request that whatever you learn should be
solely communicated to my lawyer, who
will in turn share the news with me.

It wasn't the way he talked, this patronizing, unemo-
tional set of commands. Yet I had no doubt he'd
written it. I read it over a few more times and wandered slowly out to the hall, where Richard was waiting. Without saying anything, I gave him the letter.

"He sounds stodgy. Like an old man," Richard
concluded.

"It's probably the way lawyers are trained to
write." Irrationally, I was upset at my friend's criticism. Maybe Richard was right; it certainly wasn't the
kind of letter a person would write to someone he
was romantically interested in.

"Mmm, I don't know. He seems to be taking
things too seriously. He's got no sense of humor."

"Richard, prison is a serious place!" The letter was
so depressing that only one thing was clear in my
mind: he needed to get out. Then I could look into
his eyes and figure out where we stood. And I would
find Mariko, even if I had to visit every bank in town.

I started the next morning with the English-language
telephone directory. I tried bank personnel departments in alphabetic order, identifying myself as a
long-lost friend of Mariko Ozawa's. I quickly found
out Aoyama Bank didn't release personal information
about employees. The same policy was in effect at the

next two banks. I needed a more compelling story. Then I came up with a truly devious idea.

"I wish to register a complaint about a bank employee who made an error with my account last week, Mariko Ozawa . . ."

The receptionists all instantly went into a defensive, hyper-courteous mode. "Could you please wait for a minute? We will check that . . ." They would come back, triumphant. "We have no employee by that name. Perhaps the honorable customer was mistaken?"

I had luck midway down the list when I called JaBank. "Mariko Ozawa? In foreign exchange at the Shinjuku branch? The personnel manager you need to speak to is named . . ." I took down the name carefully and assured the clerk I'd follow up.

That afternoon, Richard and I were sent to a kitchen store in Shinjuku to look at the English language signs that had been created for a Nichiyu espresso maker that could also steam milk to make caffe latte. "Latte" had been misspelled "ratte", and Richard argued it wasn't worth changing because there was no letter *L* in Japanese. We pronounced the word "ratte" ourselves to be understood by anyone at Nichiyu.

"The problem is the word looks like *rat*," I said. "Who'd want to drink something called caffe rat?"

"Rats are considered very clever animals in Japanese folktales. They're loved by everyone! Let's keep it." Richard had the kitchen section manager and two clerks nodding in support.

"If we allow one misspelled sign, the misspelling might make its way into the brochures and packaging. How can Nichiyu ever hope to compete against Braun and Krups if our brochures are written in Jinglish?"

"Find me one expert who says people even read the brochures," Richard scoffed.

"Okay, I'll find a second opinion," I insisted, wondering who I could ask. Mrs. Chapman, maybe? She was as typical an American as I could think of, and I doubted she'd approve of any Jinglish brochure.

The argument over the espresso maker was postponed for now. We said our good-byes to the department store team and walked toward the train station, Richard pointing out how close we were to Mariko's bank.

"Lets go there. It's just one subway stop away."

"Richard, we're working! I don't know about you, but this job means something to me. I'd like to keep it."

"We're not expected back for a while. If we're a half hour late, what's the problem? We can say we got caught in bus traffic. Vouch for me, and I'll vouch for you."

He became distracted on the way when he spotted a branch of his favorite source for leather and denim, New Boys Look. I had no patience to wait while he shopped, so we agreed to meet after I found Mariko. It was almost three o'clock, bank closing time.

JaBank was on Shinjuku Dori, underneath the super-sized TV screen where Chisato Moritaka was singing "Jin Jin Jinglebell." The bank was considerably more sedate, with a cordial employee who showed me upstairs to the foreign exchange section. A moon-faced woman in her mid-twenties was counting out yen to a foreigner with a backpack.

"Is Miss Ozawa here?" I asked as she finished the transaction and prepared to call the next person in line. I was surprised that someone sharing Setsuko's bloodline could be so plain.

"Please take a number if you want assistance," the clerk sing-songed.

"Don't be so uptight, Hatsue!" A young woman with dark curls rose from a sea of desks behind the customer service counter. "I'm Ozawa."

There was something undeniably cocky about the way Mariko Ozawa stood with her hands on her hips. Her navy uniform fitted her a little too tightly and her makeup was exaggerated, as if she were trying to put ten years on top of her twenty-something. She tapped a scuffed high heeled shoe impatiently and stared me down.

"I'm here on a family matter." I handed her my card and bowed.

"I have no family." She chewed on her full lower lip, smearing purple lipstick.

"I'm from America," I said, deliberately vague in the face of her eavesdropping coworkers. "My Japanese isn't so good."

She gave me a long look. "I'll be off in ten minutes. Wait right there." She pointed with a dragon-lady fingernail to a small couch in the customer waiting area. I opened the latest edition of *Tokyo*

Weekender but kept sneaking looks upward to make sure she wouldn't vanish on me.

Promptly at three she came back, carrying a fake fur coat and a black bag with MOSCHINO written across it in big brass letters. I watched it swing against her hip as she led me out a back exit, past a guard who looked at both of us carefully and recorded something in a notebook.

"Your bank has a lot of security," I commented.

"A teller was attacked a couple of weeks ago, so they're being careful."

"Robbery?"

"More likely someone's lunatic boyfriend."

"I met your great aunt, Mrs. Ozawa. She had no idea what had become of you,"

"It's supposed to be that way," she snapped. "I'll have nothing to do with the Ozawas."

"You look so different from the Ozawas, with your height and that great curly hair—where do you get it done?"

"It's not a perm, okay? It's natural, and I hate it. In junior high, the girls pulled it all the time to make it more straight, more Japanese. It got so bad I dropped out."

"What happened to you after that?" I'd heard how terrible bullying was in the schools.

"I started working." She glared at me and I kept quiet during the rest of our walk through the east side, watching the businesses around us change from clothing stores to slightly seedier pachinko parlors to strip bars and the soaplands where prostitutes worked. This was Kabuki-cho, the infamous red light district I'd blundered into while naively searching for "public relations" work during my early days in Tokyo. I pulled my parka around my body and tried to ignore the doorway droolers.

"Don't speak. You'll embarrass yourself and me," Mariko said, pausing at the entrance to an establishment with the proverbial green door— this one decorated with a neon silhouette of a woman's hourglass figure. We entered a small, extremely dark room. I quickly deduced it was a hostess bar from the couples at tables: businessmen with large tumblers of whiskey, brightly-dressed younger women nursing doll-sized glasses of oolong tea. All were enjoying a late liquid lunch or early happy hour. I gave a Western man with a teen-age Asian girl in his lap a particularly dirty look as Mariko hustled me by.

A middle-aged woman with eyeliner drawn up garishly around the corners of her eyes strode out from a bar loaded with glistening bottles of liquor. Judging from her glittering gold and diamond jewelry, she was probably the Mama-san who ran the place.

"We aren't hiring," she called out to me. I smiled and bobbed my head while Mariko yelled back I was just a friend. She led me into a back room cramped with racks of clothing and lingerie, shut the door and started undressing.

"This must be your part-time job?" I was at a loss for better words.

"You have a problem with it?" Mariko challenged.

"No. It's just that I only knew about JaBank."

"How was that, anyway? You're such a snoop."

"Mrs. Ozawa knew that you were at a bank somewhere, so I made some phone calls." I paused. "I actually called bank headquarters and said I had a complaint against you in order to find out where you worked. I hope it doesn't get back to you."

"I got some stupid phone call, but because I don't work with customers, it made no sense. I told them it was a mistake." She walked directly in front of me and turned around, indicating I should zip up her short, spangled blue dress. Her back was as smooth and golden as her face; she must have lain nude in a tanning bed to achieve that look in the Tokyo winter. "You still haven't told me how you met the Ozawas."

"We met at your aunt's *tsuya*." Mariko said nothing, so I clarified, "The one for Setsuko Nakamura in Hayama."

Mariko was fussing with her hair, attempting to pin it up, seated in front of a mirror. "*Obasan* hosted somebody's *tsuya*? I can only hope it was her husband."

"Your aunt . . ." I was going to have to break the news of the death. I swallowed hard and said, "Setsuko is the one who passed away. I'm so sorry."

Mariko sat still for a long moment. Then she swiveled around on the dressing table stool, half of her hair up and the other half hanging down. "Tell me again."

She sounded genuinely stunned, but it could have been an act; hostesses were trained to read people, give them whatever made them feel comfortable. Mindful of this, I spoke carefully. "She froze to death outside a *minshuku* in Shiroyama. It was ruled an accident but now the police think she might have been slain."

"I don't believe it. Aunt Setsuko was the last family member I had." Her purple mouth quivered.

"Your mother died when you were little, right?"

She nodded. "I was just a baby. My father didn't think he could take care of me and work, so he went off to Okinawa, Aunt Setsuko told me. I don't remember him at all."

"Who raised you?" She was alone in a way that was so complete that my suspicions toward her started to fade, replaced by pity.

"Kiki, you saw her out there."

"Why do you even work at the bank?" I was curious about that, because I knew hostessing paid at least twice as much as clerical work.

"It was a deal I had with Setsuko. She said she wanted me to have other choices. But I like the bar, and Kiki needs me." Mariko looked at my clothes, then my face. "Have you thought of becoming a hostess? That's kind of an Audrey Hepburn thing you have going on with your hair. And your English . . ."

"Setsuko was right, you're too smart to be wasting your time like this. Why don't you go into marketing?" I stopped, realizing she was diverting her grief or trying to distract me. "How often did you see Setsuko?"

"Once a month—for lunch—and then she'd give me the money."

"What money?" I thought her bluntness was pretty un-Japanese.

"My due from my grandfather."

"He was American?" I recalled the sailor Mrs. Ozawa had mentioned.

"Yes, ma'am," she said in a mocking American voice, before switching back to her slangy Japanese. "He was in the Korean war. I think he was home-ported to a ship based here, and he met my grand-mother. The other thing I know is he had money and did not forget his daughters. He knew about me because Aunt Setsuko wrote to him."

"Tell me more about your aunt," I said, watching Mariko transform her eyelashes into long, navy blue spikes.

"She was very kind to me, usually took me shop-ping at Mitsutan or Mitsukoshi for a new outfit every couple of months—"

"When was the last time you met?" I interrupted.

"Two months ago. She called in the meantime but said she couldn't get away to see me." She wiped off the purple lipstick, applying a dark red Chanel color and checking her teeth for smudges.

"Mariko, can we meet this weekend and talk some more?"

"Why do you care?" Mariko was asking as the dressing room door banged open. Kiki, the Mama-san, walked in and tapped sharply on her watch.

Mariko sighed. "I've got to start work."

"Let me be your first customer. I'll buy you a drink." I started to follow her out, but Kiki blocked the door.

"Who are you?" Kiki surveyed my checked suit, turtleneck, and low-heeled shoes with disdain. There was something threatening about her, so I gave my name in a cold voice and left it at that.

"You're not one of the Ozawas?" She looked me over a second time, and when I shook my head, said, "It's a good thing. Setsuko was bad enough."

Her use of the past tense hinted that she knew about the death. Knew, but hadn't told Mariko. I asked her, "May I ask how you came to know Setsuko?"

"You think she was too high to know me?" Kiki shot back.

"Not at all. She grew up poor and had no employment. And you look like you've done very well."

"What are you, some kind of girl-detective-in-training trying to get dirt on my business? We pay all the right people to avoid these problems."

"I'm a teacher, actually." Striving to present myself with authority, I added, "I don't feel right leaving Mariko now. She's been through a shock, not knowing anything about her aunt's death until five minutes ago."

"It's a little strange, a lady teacher visiting us." A furrow developed between Kiki's sharp eyes.

"When will Mariko be free?"

"Never," she answered, taking me by the arm and escorting me into the hall.

"But I need to ask her something—"

She cut off my protest with directions. "I'll send you out the back way. Just around the corner to the right and you'll be on the main street."

I obeyed, but once outside, walked the opposite way to get to the front of the club and note its name, Club Marimba. I'd be back.

New Boys Look opened to the street. Richard was right up front, preening not in the jacket he had talked about, but a shiny leather vest and jeans.

"I'm thinking of taking these instead of the jacket. What do you think?" Richard's eyes remained locked on himself in the mirror. I knew from experience this could last an hour.

"Special price," one of the clerks said in English.

"Gee, I don't know, honey," I teased. "You look fabulous, but will it play in Nova Scotia?"

That did it—Richard hated any mention of the place where he'd spent his tormented teen years. He handed the clerk his Mastercard.

"Gift wrap, please." To me, he said, "They told me about a dance club with an amazing eighties theme night. Depeche Mode, Eurythmics, all our favorites. But ladies aren't allowed."

"That's right." The salesclerk winked at him, and Richard gave him a sly smile. I'd had enough.

"Come back later to do your flirting," I said. When he started whining, I tapped my watch the way Kiki had done it.

As we crowded on the subway to work, Richard remained sulky. "I don't know why you're complaining about my behavior. You're the rude one. You were fifteen minutes late!"

"What would you say if I told you I was hanging out at a hostess bar?"

"I'd say you were full of it."

"Sssh, you're teaching the wrong kind of

English," I cautioned, aware of the curious teenagers across the aisle.

"I thought female customers weren't allowed into hostess bars."

"I think it's okay if you're escorted. I met Mariko at JaBank and then she took me to where she works."

"Your little bank teller is a lady of the evening?" Richard's jaw dropped.

"Richard, all hostesses do is talk to men, light their cigarettes, et cetera. In sexy clothes. While we talked she was changing into a dress you wouldn't believe."

"Something delish? Tell me."

"It's not your scene, Richard," I said, opening up the *Weekender* to cut him off for a while. The party page was as tranquil as ever. The Japanese College Women's Association had sponsored a sale of contemporary Japanese prints at the Tokyo American Club. Everyone who was anyone had gone. From amongst the *gaijin* and Asian elite smiling in black and white, a face tugged at me. I pulled the paper closer.

"Hey, share with me!"

"I know this man," I said, examining the florid face I'd seen less than twenty-four hours ago.

"Joseph Roncolotta, marketing guru and director of Far East Ventures? Rei, the bonnie prince was far cuter."

"This is the man I saw talking to Masuhiro Sendai at Setsuko's farewell party. Oh, wow. He's rich and American and old! Do you know what I'm thinking?"

"Well, we both could use a sugar daddy, I

suppose." Richard lounged against the phone booth as I called information to get the number for Far East Ventures. Luckily, it was a small enough company that I was transferred right to the boss's voice mail. I spoke in English, leaving my number and describing myself as an American wanting to consult with him. Posthaste.

15

It was raining so brutally when I came home from work that my homeless neighbors had moved their gathering into the abandoned sandal factory across the street. I could see a light flickering on the ground floor and hoped they had a heater. At times like these, my cramped apartment felt like a palace. I switched on my own heater and ran to the ringing telephone.

Mrs. Chapman was on the line, wanting company for dinner. The last thing I wanted was to go out again, but there was such pathos in her voice I found myself agreeing.

After hanging up, I noticed the message light blinking. Joe Roncolotta had telephoned and said he'd be working late. I called him back, and was pleased that he answered his phone himself, speaking accented but serviceable Japanese.

"Hi, it's Rei Shimura."

"Hell of a day, isn't it?" he said.

"Yeah, I look like a drowned rat."

"Hard to believe from the sound of you," Joe said smoothly. "Tell me you're one of the Shimura steel heiresses and I'll believe I died and went to heaven."

I gulped. "Sorry. I work for Nichiyu."

"Nichiyu! Excellent rice cookers, and you have a new coffee-maker in development, don't you?" He didn't sound displeased, and I envisioned a new set of wheels turning.

"Mr. Roncolotta, I need to talk to you about something sensitive. It would be better face-to-face."

"Please call me Joe, and I stand ready to serve. How about dinner tonight? I'll make myself free."

I stalled, remembering my date with Mrs. Chapman. The chance to talk to him this soon, before he had any time to investigate exactly how powerless I was at Nichiyu, was too good to pass up.

"I'd love it," I said firmly. "The only problem is, I already made plans with a friend. Could she join us?"

"Sure, do you ladies know Trader Vic's in the New Otani?"

"Near Akasaka-Mitsuke Station, right?" I cringed at his expensive choice.

"Yep, but you'd be better off to take a taxi on a night like this."

"Okay," I agreed, intending nothing of the sort. I'd taken a Tokyo taxi just once in the last two years, and what I paid had made me nearly hysterical.

❖   ❖   ❖

Mrs. Chapman hadn't taken the subway yet, and found it entertaining. As we rode into central Tokyo, I filled her in about how we would ask him about Setsuko Nakamura. But Mrs. Chapman seemed more interested in his *Weekender* photograph and a short item about his business acumen.

We made it to Trader Vic's at five after nine, perfect timing. Most of the businessmen sitting in the cozy faux Polynesian bar looked up when we came in, reinforcing my feeling I may not have looked like a Nichiyu executive, but had done right to wear high heels and Karen's suit. Either that or Mrs. Chapman's rejuvenated hairstyle was the attraction.

Joe wasn't there yet; perhaps keeping me waiting was a power technique. Mrs. Chapman had an old-fashioned and I ordered whiskey on the rocks. While my friend chatted on about Tokyo Disneyland, I paged idly through a copy of *The Arts of Asia* I'd brought with me. I was nervous about the whole thing.

"Very industrious," boomed a foreign voice in my ear when I was midway through an article on little-known landscape prints by the wood-block artist Keisai Yeisen. "Make me a Suffering Bastard, will you, Mori-san? Put it on the dinner check, along with these ladies' drinks."

Despite his forty or so spare pounds, Joe Roncolotta had an aura of energy that I found intriguing. His thick silver hair was brushed into a shiny gloss, and his clear blue eyes seemed, implausibly, to be flirting with both Mrs. Chapman and me.

"How nice to meet a gentleman. Marcelle Chapman

of Destin, Florida." Mrs. Chapman sparkled, holding out her hand.

"How did you recognize us? I didn't tell you my friend would be American," I asked when we had been seated in the center of the small, darkly romantic dining room that adjoined the bar.

"You wore the same suit at Seiji Nakamura's house."

I winced. My subtle plan for interrogation was dissolving faster than the ice cubes in my drink.

"What's that?" Mrs. Chapman sounded peeved, and I remembered I hadn't told her about the *tsuya*. No time now.

"So tell me how Nichiyu connects to Sendai? And why a girl with a Japanese name is reading about wood-block prints in English?" Joe's laugh rolled across the dining room, causing a few people to look up.

"I really came to talk about you. How you got your start and became so successful, and, of course, to introduce Mrs. Chapman. She's looking for unusual things to do in the city."

"Sightseeing I can tell you," he said, smiling at Mrs. Chapman. "But I'm sure neither of you gals want to hear about the old days, it'll put you to sleep."

"But you're a self-made man, I'm fascinated by that!" Mrs. Chapman flirted, helping me out.

"The Navy brought me to Japan." Joe leaned back in his chair. "I was a young seaman based in Yokosuka, where the Americans had taken over the old Imperial Navy shipyard. People were struggling even ten years after the war. The only business booming was the black market."

Yokosuka. Something flared in my memory but before I could speak, the waiter had arrived to take our order. Joe recommended the filet mignon. Mrs. Chapman went along with his suggestion, but I chose a Southeast-Asian style prawn dish.

"You were telling us about the black market. How did it work?" I asked when the waiter departed.

"The merchandise came mostly from the military commissaries: cigarettes, nylon stockings, Milky Way bars, Scotch like you're drinking tonight. I got into the game like any sailor, carrying the stuff through the gate and handing it off to a guy I didn't know. Then I started thinking I would earn more if I could organize sailors to work for me."

"You saw a business opportunity!" It was pretty distasteful to me, but I tried to hide my feelings.

"That's right. By the time my tour was over, I was making far more through the black market than I could hope to earn back in the States."

"You could have gone to school on the GI bill, like my husband," Mrs. Chapman suggested.

"I'm probably not as smart as your husband," Joe said with a chuckle.

"He's deceased." Mrs. Chapman batted her eyes.

"Far East Ventures isn't still in the black market?" I strove to return to business.

Joe shook his head. "By the early sixties, the American efforts to help rebuild the economy were finally getting somewhere. People had solid employment and enough money saved to afford things like washing machines and television sets. The American manufacturers wanted to reach them, but hadn't the foggiest notion of how marketing and distribution worked here. I got involved."

"What do you do now that nobody buys American televisions anymore?" I asked.

"I go the other way, advising Japanese companies on marketing strategies for the States. And I still market the foreign goods that can't be duplicated here— designer jeans, status handbags, that kind of thing." His smile oozed prosperity.

"Weren't the, ah, Japanese Mafia"—it was rash to utter the word *yakuza* in a room full of wealthy Japanese people—"involved in the black market?"

"Sure. My partner paid the protection money so we could stay in business. When we became involved with big corporate clients, organized crime was less of a worry. Now we find ourselves dealing in board-rooms rather than run-down hostess bars."

"Hostess bars! Were you married at this time? What did your wife think?" Mrs. Chapman har-rumphed a bit.

"She was a Japanese girl, so she knew the game."

"Was? What is she now?" Mrs. Chapman asked.

"Dead," he said, without changing expression.

"I'm sorry," I said. It was sounding more and more like he could have been involved with Setsuko's mother, but I didn't know how I'd get there, if Mrs. Chapman continued her romantic attack.

"So, tell me how I can help you." Joe leaned back in his chair and looked at us both.

"My business relates to a woman I thought you might know. Her name was Harumi Ozawa."

"That doesn't ring a bell, but honey, there are a

few hundred names in my Rolodex, it's hard to keep them all straight."

"She was Setsuko Nakamura's mother," I said, watching his face.

"I must have missed her last night." He shook his head. "It's hard to meet everyone you need to."

"Harumi is no longer living. But when she was a young woman, she worked in the slummy area near the Navy base in Yokosuka. She became involved with a sailor who was here in the early fifties," I said.

"Why are we talking about this?"

"I thought you might be Setsuko's father."

Something flashed in Joe's sharp blue eyes and when he spoke the good-old-boy accent was almost all gone. "My wife's name was Seiho Yamazaki. If you go back to the papers from 1959, you can read plenty about her."

"In the society column? Rei says you're the toast of the town," Mrs. Chapman gushed.

"No, the regular news. I killed her."

Mrs. Chapman squealed, and I tried to keep from gasping.

"It happened during one of those blinding storms in typhoon season. We were driving home. I didn't see the streetcar coming and it hit Seiho's side. She was pregnant. I killed the baby, too."

The waiter descended with the entrees. I was glad for the interruption, a chance to think up an appropriate response. All I came up with in the end was, "I think you're being extremely hard on yourself."

"This was never about marketing rice cookers, was it? What can I really do for you, Rei?"

I paused. "Like I said before, I'm looking for

information about Setsuko's parents. Maybe you know Harumi's sailor."

"Listen, if you're trying to identify a sailor who fathered a bar girl's baby, there must have been tens of thousands, and they weren't all bad. Many guys could afford to set their girl up in a small house and feed not only her but her parents and brothers and sisters. If a girl was smart, when her sailor shipped out, she found another." Joe sliced into his steak, and I watched a river of blood run across his plate.

"Mr. Roncolotta, I'm sorry Rei's putting you through this." Mrs. Chapman glared at me.

"Harumi was a shoe-shine girl, not a prostitute," I insisted. "The only reason she was in tough circumstances was because her Japanese husband died and her in-laws cast her out."

"Yeah, yeah." Joe rolled his eyes. "You don't have to tell me how snobbish those ex-samurai families are. That's why I married a working-class girl."

"Why you were at the *tsuya*?" I asked.

"Business." Joe popped a chunk of steak into his mouth and chewed.

"What kind of business?"

"With Masuhiro Sendai. I've been trying to get an introduction for the last two years, without success. I knew he'd be there. Do you think that's tacky?"

I shook my head, thinking of my own reasons for being there. "Do you even know Mr. Nakamura?"

"Yes, but I don't like him. He's a double-crosser." Joe paused. "Chilies got to you, huh? You look like you could use a glass of water. Waiter!"

"I'm fine," I said, but took the refilled glass gratefully.

"That Nakamura is an extremely unfriendly man," Mrs. Chapman added. "I wouldn't be surprised if he killed his wife."

"Do you know his history, that he left Sansonic for Sendai?" Joe asked. I remained quiet, because I wanted to see if his version of the story differed from Hugh's. "The gossip is that he took some key files with him. When Sansonic found out, half the people in his section lost their jobs, and the posts Nakamura had promised them at Sendai never materialized. What's really strange is that Nakamura never presented the Sansonic files to Sendai, but they kept him. Japanese manners."

"What would you have done if you were at Sendai?" I challenged.

"I would have told him to take the proverbial long walk off the short pier! Why's a gal like you mixed up with him, anyway? I thought he only played inside the company."

"I'm not mixed up with him. My interest, like I told you before, relates to Setsuko."

"She's interested in a young man, really," Mrs. Chapman cut in with a patronizing smile.

"Both of you—all these questions—I just don't understand it!" Joe Roncolotta threw up his hands.

"We were in the wrong place at the wrong time. That is, we were at the inn when Setsuko died," Mrs. Chapman volunteered.

"I was close to the situation." I paused, not wanting to go into the horror of my discovery of Setsuro's body. "I said something which led to a person getting slammed with her murder."

"The Scottish lawyer?" Joe perked up. "As far as his innocence goes, I don't know him well enough to have an opinion. Hell of a squash player, though his ankles are a little creaky. A lot of power in those arms."

"Where were you on New Year's Eve?" I asked. There were still too many coincidences for me to be comfortable.

"Getting sloshed with a few friends at TAC—the Tokyo American Club. You can ask the doorman about it." Joe ordered coffee for all of us. I shook my head at dessert. Looking regretful, Joe also declined. Mrs. Chapman picked at a piece of chocolate cake.

"Tell you what," he said after he'd flooded his beverage with cream and sugar. "If you're serious about this search, take the train down to Yokosuka. A master chief, Jimmy O'Donnell, hangs out at the veterans' club. This fella had his nose in everyone's business from the late forties through the sixties. If anyone would remember your sailor, it would be Jimmy."

"That's a good idea. Thanks." I was slightly cheered.

"You're welcome. I can't remember when I've had a more surprising dinner meeting. It makes me wonder who you are, really."

"Not party page material," I said, my defenses going up.

"Tell me and I'll judge for myself."

"Rei's an antiques expert who's pitifully under-employed. What do they call those kids who can't find good jobs, slickers?" Mrs. Chapman mused.

"Slackers," I told her, by now really annoyed I'd invited her along. In a monotone, I gave Joe my five-minute résumé: the Berkeley master's degree that didn't pay off, the disastrous job interviews, my choice of bar hostessing or teaching at Nichiyu.

"It's hard to be here, unconnected," Joe said when I was finished. "I tell you, my business would never have gotten off the ground without my Japanese partners. I know a fellow on the board at the Tokyo National Museum, if you want me to put in a word for you."

"I don't believe in favors." It sounded obnoxiously pious, but people who chose to employ only their friends' friends had kept me from finding a decent job in Tokyo. The last thing I wanted was to become someone like them.

"You're not very Japanese then." He chuckled.

"I'm half, and I don't appreciate comments like that."

"If Seiho and I had been lucky enough to have a child, I wonder what she would have looked like. Maybe you."

Joe's eyes rested on me for longer than I was comfortable, and Mrs. Chapman yawned loudly. I guess it wasn't much fun to go to dinner with a handsome man your age and find him neglecting you for a slacker.

"We should go," I said, getting out my wallet.

"It's my treat." Joe signaled for the waiter to bring him the check. "And even if you don't believe in favors, Rei, I do. You owe me something for the money and time I've invested in you."

"Oh!" I was horrified by the connotations, especially after he'd spoken of me like a daughter.

"Sweetheart, I want your best Japanese antique shopping tip. Painted screens are more or less gone forever, *tansu* are selling sky-high, and you can't find truly fine pieces anymore." He looked so comically distraught that I laughed.

"Haven't you tried going to Heiwajima?"

"That God-awful fair in the Ryūtsu Center?" Joe looked pained. "It's pitiful to see my friends' wives begging for discounts with their terrible Japanese. They wind up lugging home things that probably cost more here than it would in L.A. I've been here forty years and I'm beginning to think there's no point in even shopping anymore!"

"You need to shop smart," I told him.

"How's that?"

"Three steps," I said. "The first is to realize you can't be an expert in everything. You need to concentrate on what you really love, whether it's furniture or blue-and-white china. Step two is going to museums, and combining that study with window-shopping every antique store in town. Finally, when you're shopping at a big sale like Heiwajima, pick up a business card at every stall and look at the address. The dealers from far away would sooner discount their antiques than carry them back."

"When is this sale?" Mrs. Chapman asked.

"Not until the spring, but I can send you something, if you like. Old fabrics and china are really all I can afford, but my serious love is nineteenth-century wooden furniture. I've only bought one big piece. For my parents."

"How's that? Don't they live in California?" Joe asked.

I told him the story of how my mother had begged me to find her a *tansu* straight out of an art book. The chest had to be made of zelkova wood with iron fittings and a special lacquer finish, and be reasonably old although not decrepit. It took three weekends of combing shops and flea-markets until I found a superb example for a fair price. I paid a teacher returning to the States $300 to include it in her shipment, saving thousands off the cost of private shipping.

"And you want to know the kicker? My mother had it appraised in San Francisco for seven thousand dollars more than I'd paid."

"Maybe I could do this for the ladies in my retirement community," Mrs. Chapman looked excited. "That's the focus for the rest of my stay here— antiques!"

Joe toasted me with his coffee cup. "Why are you even wasting your time teaching English?"

"Nichiyu is a good employer. Sooner or later they'll let me run the language program."

"If you really want to work with antiques, you should just do it," he insisted.

"I've heard that before." I didn't try to hide my bitterness. "The people who've interviewed me here all say go back to the States, maybe I can find a job in San Diego or Seattle where it won't matter when I can't read and write *kanji*. The problem is I don't want to leave Japan."

"I see." Joe paused. "Have you heard of personal shoppers?"

"I used one a few years ago to get all my Christmas shopping done. The problem is they stuck to one store and certainly didn't look for bargains!" Mrs. Chapman wiped daintily at her mouth with a napkin.

"Exactly. Rei could become a freelance antiques shopper specializing in overseas clients and the expatriate community in Tokyo. It would be easier and cheaper than opening a store."

"I never thought about retail. Just museums." I contemplated the dark, sugary sludge at the bottom of my coffee cup, thinking if I drank it, I'd be up all night.

"If you want to be highbrow, give them lectures and trips to museums. I'll think about it some more." It was as if an electric light had switched on inside Joe; I knew why Far East Ventures had succeeded.

"The foreigners I know would never go for that," I protested. "They have enough trouble paying their rent, the telephone, that kind of thing."

"What about my friends? Corporate couples, military hot shots? I could get you a few introductions." He pulled an appointment book from his breast pocket. "Let's do an open house in, say, six weeks?"

"Unlike your hot shots, I don't have the funds to start a business." I felt regretful for a moment, thinking of my small savings account, the CDs that couldn't be touched for ages. I shook myself. It was odd Joe had come up with such generous career advice. Perhaps he was trying to distract me from the search for Setsuko's relatives.

"With a business like that, you don't need any capital. Just contacts, PR, a will to succeed!" Joe wouldn't stop talking.

"I don't think so." It was a phenomenal idea for

another person. "I'm sorry I took your time. It wasn't honest of me. Here, please let me share the cost." I gestured toward his gold American Express card lying atop the dinner check.

"Eight of my friends are watching us. Are you really going to shame me in front of them?" he asked.

I supposed it would look odd if we went Dutch in such a fancy place with such a well-known man. I gave him a half-smile and acquiesced, thinking it best not to end the evening with a scene.

"I do have a marketing question for you," I said as the three of us zoomed down to the lobby in the New Otani elevator. "We have a situation where we're trying to promote caffe latte drinks. The question is whether to say latte or ratte. Does it matter?"

"Ratte for all your signs and brochures here and latte overseas." Joe's answer came quickly.

"But don't you think rat looks awful? Won't people laugh?"

"Why are you working at Nichiyu, to look smart or help sell their products?" Joe challenged. "If you want to move products in this country, you've got to adapt."

On New Year's Eve, I'd used virtually the same words to criticize Hugh Glendinning. How self-righteous I'd been, priding myself on my encyclopedic knowledge of Japan. Talking to Joe Roncolotta made me realize how much of the book I had left to read.

16

When the telephone shrilled somewhere in the tunnel between night and morning, it took me away from a horrible dream that Mr. Nakamura had become my boss at Nichiyu and Hugh my student. The three of us stood in a classroom filled with giant Almond Pocky sticks that I knew would tumble if anyone moved.

I groped for the telephone in a haze. *"Moshi-moshi?"*

"My apologies, Shimura-san. It's Okuhara."

I snapped on an old, tin lantern I'd electrified into usefulness and squinted at my Seiko alarm clock. It said two-fifteen.

"I'm calling about Mayumi Yogetsu," The police captain spoke crisply.

"The innkeeper?" If it's about the torn *shōji* paper, I'm willing to pay."

"It's not. Mrs. Yogetsu died in the ambulance this evening, following a fall at eleven o'clock at your neighborhood train station, Minami-Senju."

I sucked in my breath as Okuhara continued. The engineer had been pulling into the station's southbound platform and observed a middle-aged woman waiting alone on the platform. Then, from out of the shadows, another person ran up and shoved her onto the track. The engineer, aiming to stop at a prefixed point at the far end of the track, couldn't help running over Mrs. Yogetsu. By the time the train stopped and doors opened, the person who pushed her was gone.

"You can't blame this on Hugh."

"Certainly not. He's spent this evening pacing his cell, complaining that we should return his laptop computer! Shimura-san, the reason I'm calling is in regard to your role in this incident."

"My role? I don't understand."

"The handbag belonging to the deceased was crushed flat. However, we found a paper inside with your address and telephone number."

"Oh, no." I remembered my last call to the inn. Mr. Yogetsu had said his wife wanted to talk with me, and I'd hung up fast.

"When did you return home from work this evening? Is there someone who can verify your presence?"

"I went out again." I stammered out something about dinner at Trader Vic's, glad that Joe had paraded me and Mrs. Chapman before so many people. He'd insisted on sending us home in a taxi; the driver would remember us. Still, for Joe to be hassled by a police captain would be a pretty dismal follow-up to the event. "Please wait to call my companion until the morning, I'm sure he's sleeping now—"

"Wait to call until you've prepared him, you mean? I need the name now, so I can put the English-speaking officer in Tokyo on it."

After Captain Okuhara hung up on me, I sat for a few seconds, trying to absorb things. Ironically, I needn't have hurried from Shiroyama; it seemed death had followed me. Now I could only rack my brain over what Mrs. Yogetsu had wanted to say to me.

Mr. Yogetsu might know. I dialed Minshuku Yogetsu, rehearsing what I'd ask. A policeman answered, so I hung up.

The telephone rang again and Richard groaned in protest from the other side of the wall. I picked up, expecting Okuhara again. What I heard was my name spoken through sniffles. It took a few tries before I could figure out that it was Mariko Ozawa. She apparently had decided to make use of the business card I'd given her.

"Rei-san? I need you," she whimpered.

"What is it?" I asked with foreboding.

"It's somebody—somebody's trying to kill me."

"What?" I repeated, drawing the covers around me. The temperature in the room seemed to have plummeted.

"Someone grabbed me outside the bar. He put a small sack or something over my head and started choking me. If it wasn't for the bar's bouncer coming out, I would have been dead."

My mind whirled with possibilities, but I forced myself to calm down and ask where she was. She told me Narita, a city northeast of Tokyo known chiefly for its airport.

"Are you planning to fly somewhere?" I asked.

"Yes. That's why I called, to see if you could lend me your passport and some money."

"Mariko, we look nothing like each other, and people holding American passports usually speak English. And as for money, I doubt I even make half of what you do!"

"I know, but you seem like the kind of person who saves."

"Pitifully little. Tell me where you're staying tonight." I had a terrible vision of her leaning up against a telephone outside a lonely, closed-up train station.

"Violet Venus."

"Where?"

"It's a love hotel. I'm here because it's cheap and you don't have to give your name."

"Tell me exactly what happened." I drew the receiver under the covers with me to preserve what warmth remained.

"At eight o'clock, I stepped out of the club to get a liter of cream for the white Russians." It took me a second to realize she was talking about drinks, not people. "Someone was waiting behind the backdoor. I stepped out, and he grabbed me and wrapped something white around my head. I swung back to hit him in the balls, and he started choking me." A long, shuddering sob. "Then our bouncer opened the back door. The guy threw me on the ground and was gone."

"Did you get a good look at him?"

"He was behind me, I told you!"

"What about the bouncer?"

"He couldn't see around the corner to where we were."

Anticipating a bad answer, I asked, "What did the police say about it?"

"I didn't call them. Kiki says the less we do with the police, the better. There was a problem some time back about the liquor license."

"But someone's after you. You can't lose your life because your Mama-san has legal difficulties!"

"I'm not going back." She was sobbing again. "Even though Kiki is probably going to send out some of her friends to find me."

Given Kiki's trade, her friends were likely to be gangsters. I could understand why Mariko didn't want to be found.

"Leaving the bar tonight was very brave and intelligent of you," I said, trying to convince myself. "I'll pick you up as soon as the trains start running. And don't worry, okay? We're together from now on."

Mariko reluctantly agreed to return to Tokyo and meet me the following morning outside Shibuya Station at the statue of Hachikō, Tokyo's most famous dog. Urban legend said that the male Akita breed had been the faithful companion to a professor, meeting his train every evening so they could walk home together. The owner died sometime during the twenties and the dog became a stray. Still, he returned to Shibuya every night for more than ten years in the hopes his master's train would come in. The aged canine became a national symbol of loyalty; when he finally went to doggy heaven in 1935, a bronze replica went up. Hachikō's statue was so popular you had to designate his head or tail as a meeting point.

Pushing my way through hundreds of junior high school students assembling for a field trip, I wondered if, like Hachikō, I'd be stood up. But after a minute there was a tug on my sleeve.

"Mariko?" I asked tentatively. The person standing before me wore blond dreadlocks and a black leather jacket, with bootleg jeans worn over platform-heeled boots. Faint bruises showed under a long chiffon scarf that had slipped sideways on her neck.

"Urusai wa yo." You're too loud, she whispered.

"Let's go quickly, then." I scanned the crowd and spotted Richard's blond hair flip-flopping as he strode toward us. I'd told him to wait by the Williams-Sonoma window until I'd given him a signal, but as usual, he jumped the gun.

"Your dreads are to die for. Are you in a band or something?" Richard gushed in slangy Japanese.

Mariko shook her head and blushed. Richard's blue-eyed blond magic seemed to be doing its usual trick.

"This is Richard," I said. "He's sort of like my brother. We share the apartment, I didn't get the chance to tell you last night."

"I'll be your bodyguard, okay?" He moved his hands in a phony karate chop that made a cluster of junior high school girls giggle. "I've planned a return trip that's rather indirect. We'll switch back and forth between the Ginza and Hanzomon lines to throw off anyone who might be following us."

"Don't worry, you look nothing like yourself with that hair," I told her. Frankly, it made me cringe.

"It's a wig," she said with pride. "I thought about bleaching, but there wasn't time."

"I know a girl who does it half-price. By the way, I love that jacket. I have a vest that would be amazing with it."

"You like it? I bought it in Shinjuku at New Boys Look."

"Tell me about it!" Richard crowed. To me, he mouthed, "Thank you, baby."

As we traveled north on the subway, the two of them chatted about clothes, which I took as a sign she was beginning to feel safe. When we got out at Minami-Senju Station and started crossing the steel pedestrian bridge that led to the busy main road, Mariko wrinkled her nose at the ever-present stench of diesel fuel.

"This isn't where I'd expect *gaijin* to live," she said.

"It's what we can afford," I said, showing her into our building. She complained all the way up the three flights of stairs. When I opened the door to the apartment she brushed past me, treading straight over the linoleum I tried in vain to keep clean.

"Your boots!" I called out.

"I thought foreigners wore shoes inside their homes. What's all this history stuff?" Mariko was gawking at my walls decorated with kimono and wood-block prints.

"It's part of your heritage. Do you like it?" I hung her leather jacket on a lacquered Kimono rack.

"Aunt Setsuko liked antiques. I prefer the seventies, Pink Lady and all that stuff."

It was clear to me that Mariko was a master at

diversion; she probably was a great hostess. I cut off a stream of comments about the long-gone Pink Lady pop group and insisted she tell Richard and me about her assault.

"What more can I say? I told you everything. I don't really want to think about it, I just want to be safe again." She slumped slightly, and Richard was quickly at her side.

"Rei, you have no sensitivity." He shot me an indignant glance.

"I don't want what happened to Setsuko to recur," I told them both. "Mariko, think about who's been in the bar lately—"

"I talk to a lot of men, and sometimes they get angry when I don't want to see them privately. There are so many, at least twelve on a slow night and up to twenty when it's busy . . . I can't keep track. It's also hard to think when I'm hungry," she said in a little-girl voice.

"Okay, we'll have breakfast." I went into the kitchenette and started chopping *shītake* mushrooms and one limp scallion. I would make a six-egg omelet and cut it three ways.

"Rei, you need to get a better knife. Look how unevenly it slices things," Richard nagged, as if he ever did more in the kitchen than pop the top off a beer.

"My knife is fine." I gave him a dirty look. "When the sharpening man comes around again, I'll go to him. By the way, Mariko, there are a stack of newspapers by the futon, articles I've saved about your aunt's death. You might want to read them."

She glanced at the *Japan Times* and put it down. "I can't read much English. I'm pretty stupid, I guess."

"That's not true! You're smart enough to speak your mind and finally leave that hostess bar." I would have gone on, but Richard shut me up by offering to translate the *Japan Times* article into Japanese. Mariko quickly agreed, moving over so Richard could lounge next to her on my futon. They made a cozy pair, Richard stumbling over the occasional phrase in his translation and Mariko snickering. He was making her feel good about herself. I liked that, although it could mean trouble later on.

She could be trouble herself. As I flicked on the gas burner, I thought about how Mrs. Yogetsu had been killed at Minami-Senju station at eleven o'clock, after Mariko had left Club Marimba. If she'd gone straight from the bar to Narita, she could have called me around eleven. Instead she had waited till two-thirty.

"This guy in the picture, he's been in the bar!" Mariko interrupted my uneasy digression by waving a newspaper at me.

"How can you be sure? Foreigners all look alike." I didn't want to hear her rip into Hugh Glendinning. I threw mushrooms in the pan and concentrated on sautéing.

"She's talking about Mr. Nakamura," Richard said sharply.

"This was old Seiji? Disgusting!" Mariko's long white fingernail jabbed through the paper.

"Easy, it's my only copy," I begged. "When did you see Mr. Nakamura?"

"Let me think." Mariko paused. "The first time was about two weeks before New Year's. He came back last Friday. Both times he spent about an hour talking with Kiki. I was ticked off because if he didn't go to anyone's table, none of us could earn a commission. I went up to him and flirted a little, to see if I could encourage him to join me. Kiki yelled at me to mind my own business"

"Kiki's the Mama-san, right? What was he saying to her?" Richard asked.

"I couldn't tell. She made me sit in the back."

"She probably wanted to keep you from getting in a situation where he might grope you—or do you think he knew you were his niece?"

"He paid no attention to me. He seemed nervous." Mariko sounded thoughtful.

"Did you ever hear anything about Setsuko having a child?" I went back to the stove.

"Are you crazy? She doesn't like children at all! When I was little, I never saw her. She only became interested in me when I was around fifteen. All of a sudden she wanted to dress me, fix my hair, teach me the right way to talk. I was annoyed at first, but then she started bringing me stuff and I figured she was pretty cool."

Pretty cool. By no stretch was that a declaration of love. How far would she go to avenge Setsuko's death? I lowered the flame and put a lid on the pan.

"Mariko, I need to ask you to do something with me."

"I'll wash the dishes, *okay*?"

"Please don't worry about housework." I would treat Mariko like a queen if she'd do what I wanted.

"Would you take a look at Setsuko's address book? I'm hoping you can tell me if there are names you recognize."

"Okay. That's easy." Mariko pondered the book while I made toast. At the table, munching away, she told me what I'd already figured out—that most of the names and addresses were stores. It was more a shopaholic's record than anything.

"At Mitsutan, let's see, she was super-friendly with one of the clerks, Yumiko Yokoyama. They talked all the time."

"Is there a number or address for your grand-father I could have missed?" I didn't want to let go of the idea of Setsuko's phantom parent.

"I told you that she never gave me as much as his name. I looked in the *F*'s for father and *O*'s for *Otōsan*. Under *O* there is something strange: an address in Kawasaki City and a long number. It's too long to be a phone number and the area code would be wrong, anyway."

She passed the open book to me. This entry, the first on the page, was different from the others, which generally were a name, phone number, and address. Here the address was simply followed by the number 63992 and the code 62–22–3. Didn't soldiers and sailors have serial numbers? Here was more evidence I could bring to Yokosuka.

"You're right, it really is weird," I said. "We can stop in at the address and see who's there. It will fit in nicely on the way back from Yokosuka."

"What are you talking about?" She sounded unenthusiastic.

"I need to run down to Yokosuka for a couple of hours today and thought you might want to come. You want to find out who your grandfather is, don't you?"

"As the bodyguard, I ought to have a word in this," Richard interjected. "*Yakuza* are everywhere. Personally, I think Mariko should stay home to redo her nails and watch videos with me."

"Mariko's got her dreads on, and it will just be for a little while. I need to talk to a retired sailor in Yokosuka who may remember your grandfather. If she introduces herself, I'm sure he'd be compelled to help."

"Talk to me straight, not to him!" Mariko complained.

"Okay, Mariko, it's only an hour away," I entreated.

"I know," she said impatiently. "It's my birthplace. I lived there with Kiki when I was small."

"You can guide me, then!" I was thrilled.

"I'll come. Given one condition," Mariko said.

"Anything," I said rashly.

"Richard comes with us, too."

17

At first glance, Yokosuka seemed a fusion of small-city Japan and big-city America. Young men in over-sized jeans tripped to a break-dance beat that blared from a boom box held on someone's shoulders. Billboards advertised corn dogs and American-sized Levi's jeans. Beyond a traffic circle filled with taxis and Japanese buses lay the sparkling blue bay and ruins of an old military watchtower and broken-down cement wall.

"That part was Imperial Navy ground before Americans came," Mariko told me. "See the old railway treads in the grass? They brought weapons and supplies in that way. Now it's all a community park. I learned to swim in the pool over there."

"You must have been adorable!" Richard had flirted with her steadily, making me wonder if it was possible for a leopard to develop stripes.

"So adorable half the mothers wanted me out

of the pool." Mariko chewed her lower lip. "After we got out of the water, they used to warn the girls to dry off in the shade so they wouldn't get tan like me."

"You know a lot about Japanese history," I said to change the subject and make her feel better.

"All I know is my stupid, lousy life!"

We walked about ten minutes, passing a gleaming hotel tower and a giant shopping mall Mariko said were new. At the base entrance, an actual yellow line was drawn on the road, a border between U.S. and Japanese territories. I hadn't expected to see that, nor the dark gray police bus parked on the sidewalk.

Something was up, I judged from the line of tense-looking officers wearing riot gear. I followed their line of unblinking observation across the street to a cluster of twenty or so middle-aged Japanese people dressed in business suits. They stood silently, holding signs in Japanese and English reading REMEMBER HIROSHIMA AND NAGASAKI and STOP NUCLEAR WAR FOREVER.

I watched Americans and Japanese enter the base through separate passages, opening wallets to show identification and holding open shopping bags for inspection. Taking a deep breath, I started off for the entrance marked AMERICAN.

A polite Marine who looked barely eighteen sent me into a small office where a different guard sat underneath a sign reading A MARINE ON DUTY HAS NO FRIENDS.

Accordingly, I used my warmest voice to ask him the whereabouts of the veterans' club.

"You're not a military service member, ma'am?" His voice was startlingly deep for such a young man.

"I'm an American citizen." I took out my California driver's license, which he looked at briefly and dismissed.

"I can't do anything with this. Not without a military sponsor."

"I'm not trying to get on base," I insisted. "I'm just trying to get some information."

When a second guard moved in, I realized I appeared as potentially dangerous as the protesters outside. Paranoia had infused everyone. I gave up, feeling them watch me as I walked out to rejoin Richard and Mariko.

Somebody in town had to know about the club. I started with the protesters, who unfortunately had little more than pamphlets to offer. Then I surveyed the string of businesses along the road, dusty little places that looked as if they'd been around for many decades before the new mall.

A shop advertising military embroidery and patches seemed perfect. Inside, an elderly Japanese grandmother type was bent over a sewing machine. I was shaken when she looked up, scowled, and crossed her hands into an X of refusal.

"No more Jesus stuff, OK? I already buy *Watchtower*."

"Excuse me?" I asked in Japanese.

"Baptist or Jehovah? You born-again, from that church, *neh*?" Annoyingly, she persisted in English.

"Because of the base there are all kinds of weir-does running around with pamphlets, Americans and converted Japanese," Mariko muttered. "It was like this when I was a kid."

I looked down at the sensible navy suit with the skirt that ended a proper yen note's width above my knee and resolved to tell my mother to cancel my subscription to the Talbots catalog.

"I don't practice any religion," I said firmly. "What I'm really looking for is the club for retired chief petty officers. Do you know it?"

"A bar so early on Saturday morning? What kind girl are you?" the woman exclaimed.

"A complete naughty-bones!" Richard was delighted.

"It's for research purposes only," I said, trying to preserve my dignity.

"I don't know nobody no more." The seamstress opened a drawer, took out a small pipe and lit it.

"Surely lots of military come in here, given that you take dollars," I prodded.

"The old men have retired back to States. They say Japan too expensive now. Even the young sailors don't buy so many patches." She gestured toward a counter displaying hundreds of patches with appliquéd motorcycle, ship, and heavy metal music motifs. "I had to put away the skeleton patch because of missionaries."

"You mean you bow to censorship? Look at your countrymen outside, standing up to the invader!" Richard cried.

The woman smiled at him and pulled a Grateful Dead patch out of a drawer. "You like? For you, a special price. Because not missionary."

This was exactly his and Mariko's cup of tea. The two began debating the virtues of skulls versus the Harley Davidson eagle and I kept my eyes on the window, watching the flow of Americans amongst the Japanese. A gray-haired man in uniform had stopped to frown at the protesters. He appeared to be the right age. I told Richard and Mariko to stay put.

As I approached the man, he made a dismissive motion with his hand. "I go to mass every Sunday, all right?"

"I'm not a fundamentalist, I'm just looking for directions to an off-base club for retired chief petty officers." I gave him my most engaging smile.

"Young lady, you're talking to a captain, not a chief," he barked, placing his hand on the gold monstrosity that decorated his hat.

"Congratulations, then," I said. "But have you heard of this club?"

"I don't fraternize with the enlisted." He moved off, superbly dignified.

I made a face at his back and slumped back to Richard and Mariko, who had been joined at the store counter by two American sailors wearing jackets so covered by patches it was difficult for me to see why they were in the market for anymore.

"It's not the kind of place that rocks much, you know?" The tall one with a bandanna stylishly wrapped around his head was slouched against the counter talking to Richard.

"You say it's the next right, go two blocks, and then left again?" Richard asked, shooting me a victorious look.

"Does the club even have a name?" I asked the bandanna-wearing man.

"The unofficial name is Old Salts. I call it Old Farts. But it's got cheap beer, and you can pay in dollars." The sailor appeared to be evaluating me. "So what rate's your friend that he's got two babes in arms?"

When Richard looked blank, I nudged him and said, "I think he's asking about your military rank."

"Do I look like an American squid?" Richard grinned and ran his fingers through his short gelled hair with a flourish.

Richard had spoken the wrong body language.

"You a fag or something?" The tall sailor gaped, and his friend made a rumbling sound in the back of his throat.

"Let's go," I said in Japanese, fearing Richard might make a guns-of-pride response. We were down the block within seconds. I turned back to see the old woman looking after us anxiously while the two sailors hooted disparagingly.

"What if they come after us?" I panicked as we headed deep into a district of tiny bars and snack shops.

"Then we fight," Richard said. "You two will defend wimpy little me."

Old Salts was exactly where the sailors had told us. Richard opened the door to a smoky cavern decorated with the famous mid-seventies poster of Farrah Fawcett in an athletic swimsuit.

"Son, take your gals back to the A Club. This club is chiefs-only." Our greeter was a balding man with a belly that strained at the confines of his Pepsi T-shirt. Still, his voice wasn't as harsh as the captain who'd brushed me off.

"I know this is unorthodox, but Joe Roncolotta sent me." I spoke up before Richard had a chance to inflict any damage.

"Joe's doing all right for a guy who never made it past second class." There was a scraping sound, and a second man spoke up from the darkness. "You're from Tokyo?"

"Yes. I came all the way down to see Jimmy O'Donnell." My eyes searched through the gloom and found a snowy-haired man with dark blue eyes fixed on me.

"Have a seat," the man said with authority in his voice.

"I brought two friends," I said, indicating Richard and Mariko.

"Okay. But you'll have to pay for your drinks at nonmember prices."

"Two Buds and a canned coffee for Rei," Richard said, affecting a super-masculine octave. "My treat."

"A gal named Ray? Your Mom and Dad must have really wanted a son," the man who had let me enter said.

"It's a Japanese name," I said, handing him my business card. "Is Mr. O'Donnell around?"

Pepsi started to say something but the leader cut him off.

"The master chief is fairly hard to get hold of these days. Living the quiet life in the mountains."

"Which mountain?" I didn't believe him.

"A very distant one. We could give Jimmy a message. What's the problem, exactly?" the leader asked.

As I hesitated, wondering how much was safe to offer, Mariko spoke up in accented but surprisingly good English. "The problem is me."

"Not another one of them." Pepsi, upset at having been left out too long, sat down next to her. "Looking for your husband, right? Shipped out on you?"

"Are you crazy? I'm too young to be married!"

"We're looking for her grandfather. While he was stationed here in the early fifties, he fell in love with a woman named Harumi Ozawa. He had a daughter with her, then went back to America," I said.

"Poor little cherry blossom," Pepsi smirked.

"Give her some respect," the leader snapped. "The girl could be yours, for all you know."

"No way. My grandfather had money, and wouldn't have ended his life in a run-down bar," Mariko said nastily.

"What we know is he went back to the States and married there, although he continued to support Harumi and, even after she passed away, he kept sending money to Japan."

"So where's the problem?" The white-haired man sounded reasonable.

"The problem is Mariko's aunt was the only living member of the family who was corresponding with him. She died recently, of unnatural causes. Her name after marriage was Setsuko Nakamura."

"I saw that," Pepsi said. "I'm surprised they didn't say a sailor did it, we get blamed for every damn thing."

"Okinawa, yeah, that was the damnedest thing," Richard said with irony, referring to the horrific gang rape of a young schoolgirl committed in 1995 by three U.S. servicemen.

"Hey, watch it!" said Pepsi. "They were Marines anyway, at least two of 'em."

"If you haven't talked to your grandfather before, why start now?" The white-haired leader addressed Mariko directly. "Even if you are his granddaughter, there's no guarantee he'd leave you anything."

"I don't care," Mariko shot back.

"Tell me something more about your grandfather." He was staying remarkably patient.

"Why? As rude as you are to us?" Mariko closed her hand over Richard's arm.

It was time for me to step in. "I think we may have something that relates to the father, perhaps a military serial number."

The two men crowded around the address book, shutting us out. When they broke apart, the whitehaired man spoke.

"This isn't a serial number. There are too many digits."

"Are you positive?" I felt deflated.

"Serial numbers are social security numbers, right? Nine digits. You've got ten if you count the long number and the code."

"You've been very helpful, but couldn't we just telephone Mr. O'Donnell?"

"He'd know nothing more than us."

"But don't master chiefs take care of their sailors?" I tried catering to their egos. "If a sailor loved his Japanese girlfriend but had to go back, wouldn't he have asked the master chief for advice?"

"It's not that big a deal, really. You're talking about a situation that literally thousands of sailors were involved in. We ain't proud of them. After all, I stayed here and married my girl." Pepsi told me.

"Did you, now? How caring," Richard's voice had a dangerous level of sarcasm and from his smile, appeared ready to start some kind of confrontation.

"Births and deaths are registered with city hall," the white-haired man offered.

"Thanks." It would mean a trip back on a workday, but I could swing it.

"Do you know where Missouri is?" Mariko asked unexpectedly when we stood up to leave.

"Between Kentucky and Kansas," said Pepsi, a real wise guy.

"No, the bar," Mariko said. "There used to be a bar around here called Missouri."

"Oh, sure!" Pepsi said. "Bar Missouri. A real whippersnapper of a gal ran it, smart-mouthed like you wouldn't believe."

Mariko nodded. "Where was it?"

"Where the JaBank is now, on the street that we call the Ginza because it has all the department stores. Not that it compares with the real thing in Tokyo. Why?"

"I want to see the place where I grew up," Mariko said, startling me.

"How about that!" Pepsi looked speculative. "So tell me what happened to the gals who worked there?"

"The rent went up, so we moved." Mariko's eyes flickered to me, as if she worried I might say something. I didn't. I wanted to hear more about her childhood, but I knew it would come bit by bit, on her own time.

To appease Mariko, we went straight to the Yokosuka JaBank. My annoyance at the way she'd sabotaged things in Old Salts had given way to self-criticism. Bringing her to Yokosuka had been a bad idea, given her trauma only a few hours earlier.

Standing outside the glassed-in vestibule where the cash machine was located, I watched Mariko walk around restlessly. Then while Richard was punching in his access code to withdraw cash, she hovered behind. She appeared to be reading over his shoulder.

I tried to catch Richard's eye when he came out, but he was full of talk about a curry restaurant Mariko remembered from her girlhood. We walked twenty minutes until we found a grimy little shop with no Indians in evidence. Instead, a moon-faced Japanese woman in late middle age doled a soupy mixture over a scoop of sticky Japanese rice, slapping a fried egg on top.

"This place sucks." Mariko was speaking Japanese again, now that it was just us three. "I want to get out of here."

"I thought you wanted to come here," I reminded her. "This isn't my taste, either. For real Indian food, you have to go to Moti in Ropppongi."

"Don't be a control freak, Rei," Richard chided.

I blew up. "What kind of crap is this, the second you have a new friend I metamorphose into some kind of villain? Watch your back, Richard. That's all I'll say."

Mariko cleared her throat. "Richard-san? What did it mean when those sailor boys called you that thing—*fag*?"

"It's slang for guys who like guys. You know, homosexuals." Richard raised his eyebrows teasingly.

"Well, why did they call you that?" Mariko sounded cross. "What did you say to annoy them?"

"Nothing, really. Sometimes people can just tell."

"Poor, poor Richard-san!" She put her arms around him. "You can change if you want to. I know a girl who specializes in boys who like boys."

"But I don't want to," Richard said. "Ask Rei. Life's too good the way it is."

If she were to ask me, I could tell her his video collection had *Debbie Does Dallas* and *Harry Does Hong Kong*. But I was sick of them both.

"I can't eat this, and I want to stop in Kawasaki to follow up on that address Mariko showed me," I said.

"I'm not going there, I've done enough for you today. Talking to those disgusting old men was like being at work!" Mariko grumbled.

"How many nights a week were you working at Marimba?" I asked.

"Six! It was exhausting."

"What about New Year's Eve?"

"That too. Why?" She stared at me, the reality slowly dawning. "You're pathetic. You want to blame me for my aunt's murder!"

"Was Kiki, the Mama-san, also working?"

She tossed her dreadlocks. "Of course! If you don't believe me, ask one of the losers I had to entertain. I have their cards at the Marimba."

"Rei's not going to bother you anymore," Richard promised her. "At least you know I'm here to protect you."

Richard patted her dreadlocks, and Mariko snuggled into his chest. They seemed happy in their embrace. Too happy. When I got up and said goodbye, only the curry cook acknowledged me.

I was in Kawasaki forty minutes later. Armed with the address I'd found in Setsuko's book, I went to a police box. The officer on duty located the address for me on an oversized map that decorated the wall.

"It's best to take the bus, because a taxi will cost a lot," he advised, deciding to treat me like a backpacker. "But you should go next week. It closed today at noon."

I didn't understand what he meant.

"The post office." He tapped significantly on the map. "You're asking for directions to the Northern District post office."

Damn them for building up the country so quickly, I thought as I rode the bus anyway, to make sure he was right. Whoever had lived on the property where the shiny white post office now stood was long gone. I went to the fruit vendor on the left and the stationer on the right but no one knew anything about a house that had once stood there and where its owners might have moved.

It took twelve minutes to get back to Tokyo, long enough for depression to roll over me like a heavy blanket. That's what I needed, to curl up in bed and put everything away for the night. I'd ignore my worries that Mariko was about to rip off Richard's bank account or had any knowledge of Setsuko's death. I'd push aside my brutal mental picture of Mrs. Yogetsu falling to her death because of a secret I'd refused to hear. And I wouldn't dare let myself think of Hugh.

I had intended to lie down for an hour, but when I awoke it was pitch black and freezing. I stuck an arm out from the futon and grabbed the last pair of jeans I'd worn. I pulled on one of Richard's oxford shirts and my parka before looking around for something to eat. Nothing. The only solution was a snack from Family Mart. I hurried through the neighborhood thinking of my favorite *onigiri*, a seaweed-wrapped rice ball with a tangy pickled plum buried in the middle. I was deep enough into fantasy that I didn't see a black sedan speeding around the corner, but jumped back just in time.

"What's new?" Mr. Waka laid aside his tabloid when I entered his store.

"Not much. I'm alone tonight. Richard's out having the time of his life with a girl who's moved in and replaced me."

"Here, have some of my *oden*. It's good for the troubled heart." Mr. Waka went to the counter and stirred a cauldron of golden-brown fluid, bringing a few odd pieces of sausage and fish cake bobbing to the surface.

"Mmm, I had something less rich in mind," I demurred. "Just some rice. Any *onigiri* around?"

Mr. Waka shook his head, sorrowful. "None. Except for salmon, which you do not like."

I poked around the refrigerator and freezer cases, eventually settling on a Sweet Sixteen ice cream cone. Bland and soothing, it would stay cold on the trip home.

As I walked back holding the ice cream in my gloved hand, my footsteps sounded loud, perhaps because the neighborhood was so quiet. Saturday night in one of the world's most densely populated cities and not a soul around. I craved a sign of life, something to convince me I wasn't Tokyo's loneliest person.

I took back my wish the instant that I rounded the corner to my street. There, parked squarely in front of the door, was the black sedan that had clipped me, hazard lights flashing.

18

Looking up at my lit window, I could make out the shadows of two people. Were they Richard and Mariko, or Kiki's mobsters? I tried to melt into the sandal factory doorway.

The car started, its headlights blazing on and temporarily blinding me. An electronic window whizzed down on the driver's side.

"All alone on a Saturday night, Rei Shimura. You surprise me."

I was shaken in a different way as Hugh Glendinning's rounded vowels washed over me. He flipped on the interior light, and I got a good look at him. He was clean shaven and pale, wearing his shearling jacket and corduroy jeans. As he adjusted his position, I caught a glimpse of his bandaged ankle.

"They hurt you!" I said, getting in the car.

"No, I sprained it skiing. Remember?" He put the car in reverse and executed an incredible turn on my dead-end street. I looked over my shoulder at my apartment window, and the figures in the window were waving: Richard and Mariko, after all.

"I've had this car for six months. Not bad, eh?" Hugh said, turning the radio on to J-WAVE, a pop station with English programming.

"You almost ran me over back by the Family Mart."

"Don't tell me you were the idiot running around in black in the middle of the night?" He looked at my parka. "So you were."

"How did you find me?" I unwrapped the ice cream I'd almost forgotten.

"Mr. Ota gave me directions. I can't believe you live here. This district is seedier than hell."

"It's poor but safe." As we passed the liquor store, the door opened and, as if programmed, a drunk emerged, vomiting a plume of liquid onto the sidewalk.

"Not from a public health standpoint. Did you see that?" Hugh exclaimed.

"It's no worse than the trains. Come on, tell me how you got out!"

"I'm ashamed to admit it now that the Getsu woman is dead—"

"Yogetsu," I corrected.

"Right." Hugh picked up speed and headed for the Shuto Expressway. "Because Mrs. Yogetsu was the witness with the most damning story against me, I suggested Ota dig around in her background. He found something interesting: her flower arranging licenses weren't in order. She'd been passing herself off as a master teacher when she was only third degree. Whatever that means."

"It means she was practically a rookie! I never liked her flower arrangements. I should have known something was off."

"Mr. Ota told her that if I went to trial, her misrepresentation would be made public. With that in mind, she amended her previous claim that she'd overheard me with Setsuko in the bath."

"She saved you." The woman I'd disliked so much had come through. So what if it was chiefly to save her reputation?

"Mr. Ota sensed there was something else she wasn't telling him or the police. After signing the new statement, Mrs. Yogetsu shot off for Tokyo, presumably to see you."

"I was out that night, so she missed me. And then she was killed at my train station. If I'd spoken to her on the telephone, it might never have happened," I confessed.

"It was tragic. I didn't learn about it until my hearing this morning, when the prosecutor decided to let me go."

"So you're free and clear?" I was astounded.

"Not really. Captain Okuhara is still poking around for a way to bring me back in. If Yamamoto's body is found with signs of foul play, I may be charged."

"I'm so sorry," I said. "For everything."

"I wrote that you were forgiven." His voice didn't sound particularly warm.

"Yes, Mr. Ota sent me your fax. And did he tell you I went to Setsuko's farewell ceremony?"

"I know all that. Hikari said you took an address book she'd planned to give Mr. Ota. I'd like you to hand it over. Your work is done, Rei. I don't want you to feel driven by guilt or something as daft as the fact that we spent one night together."

"Don't talk to me like that!" So what I'd read in the fax, the distanced, cold prose, was true. A tense silence descended, broken only when Hugh took a handkerchief out of the glove compartment and handed it to me.

"You're not worth tears." I balled it up and threw it back at him.

"Thanks, but you're still dripping ice cream on the car seat."

I hadn't seen the small chunk of strawberry ice cream that had fallen. I hastily wiped it up.

"So what's in the address book?" He tried again.

"Names. I'm looking up the important people."

"And why would you be better at it than my lawyer?"

"Because I'm finding people all the time. In fact, I already have her niece Mariko under my care."

"What! How old is this child?" Hugh braked sharply to avoid hitting a minivan.

"Twenty-four. She's staying in my apartment right now, if you want me to prove that she really exists—"

"I believe you," he said grudgingly. "Tell me more."

I recounted what I'd learned about Setsuko's humble background and her few remaining relatives. When I got to the story of Mariko's attack, he clucked disapprovingly.

"So is the niece really safe with you? You live in a building without a concierge, let alone any kind of security system."

"Did you go upstairs?" I shouldn't be surprised that Mariko and Richard had opened the door to him. Too bad I'd left the apartment so messy.

"No. I shouted upward, and they called back that you were out. They invited me up, but I can't climb stairs. So I decided to wait in the comfort of my car."

Hugh decelerated off the expressway for Roppongi Crossing, the center of young foreign and Japanese night life. It took three changes of the stoplight to make it through the intersection jammed with luxury motorcycles and taxis, but at least I could watch the mob scene: the drama of leather-clad lovers reuniting, young girls stomping off to discotheques, and hawkers in tuxedos and miniskirts, not always according to sex. Hugh turned left at the Roi Building, travelling down a short, steep hill. He stopped in a no-parking zone bordering a cemetery.

"Could you give me a hand getting out?" He asked, extracting crutches from the back seat. "My favorite little place is just over there." He pointed to a basement-level pub flying the Union Jack.

As we hobbled toward it, a Japanese doorman dressed like a rugby player sprang into action.

"Hugh-san, Hugh-san! You are returned at last, but you have some injury—"

"Nothing permanent, Kozo," Hugh said as the strong young man took over for me.

"*Abunai*, Hugh-san. Please be safety . . ." Kozo scrambled to find chairs for a tiny table in the corner of the dark, smoky room filled with red-faced, primarily middle-aged foreigners.

"Hugh-san will be comfortable, I think," the waiter said, propping Hugh's leg up on another chair.

"Thanks, Kozo," Hugh said, and by the time I had shrugged out of my coat we were surrounded by voices from all corners of the old British empire.

"It's Shug, back at last!"

"Did they break your leg to exert a confession?"

"It figures you'd land a female police escort!"

"About the only decent thing I accomplished in the Japanese Alps was finding another English speaker to join our ranks," Hugh grumbled when they were through. "Though I'm stunned to find you here so early on a Saturday night. Don't you have anything better to do?"

"We had a feeling something interesting might turn up. Got a tip from a good source," an Australian answered with a smirk.

"Piers." Hugh's attention had flashed to a very pale man in business clothes who had come up. "An excellent piece of negotiation. I'm indebted."

"Stay in town and out of trouble, Hugh. That's all I ask." Piers Clancy's eyes landed on me for a half-second before averting them as if he'd seen something distasteful. "Do you plan to retain Ota?"

When Hugh nodded, Piers said, "You should consider Ichikawa, the one who got Raymond off for sexual battery. He's formidable."

"I'm not as badly off as Raymond. After all, I didn't do it," Hugh snapped.

There was a chorus of things like "Get off, we

know you're clean!" and "Your mates are with you, Shug!" that trailed off when Piers gathered up his Burberry and stalked out into the night.

"He must have work to do," I said, trying to put a good face on things.

"It's been fun, Hugh, but I must be off." A lanky Englishman clapped Hugh on the shoulder. Another friend suddenly remembered he had to be at the flat to take a call from the London office and the Australians were off to meet some models at Motown.

"Don't reckon you're much for dancing with that leg," one of them said as he swung out the door.

"Ta." Hugh looked at his watch. "So, it took just five minutes to be reclassified as a virtual pariah."

"What's this Shug stuff?" I asked.

"Just a nickname for Hugh. It's a Scottish thing you wouldn't understand."

"That's right, I'm so terrible with languages. Why did you bring me here? It's like meeting in Tokyo Station."

"I didn't want to be alone with you," Hugh said, looking past me and out the window at traffic. "The last time, we had those complications. I apologize for losing control."

Kozo reappeared, taking Hugh's order for Tennent's Lager. I stuck with Perrier, given my empty stomach.

"What was I saying?" Hugh asked after Kozo had gone.

"Just that you aren't interested in me anymore." I stared him down, willing him to deny it.

"You wouldn't want me if you knew the truth. I guarantee it."

"The truth? You mean what you were going to tell me in Shiroyama?" When he nodded, I said, "Try me."

"Right, here goes. Do you remember the *Japan Times* piece a while ago about American expatriate businessmen paying Japanese businessmen for privileged information?"

"The economic spies," I remembered. "It turned out the CIA was behind it. Stories like that make me ashamed to carry an American passport."

"Right. Some European nations began thinking it would make sense to do the same for the betterment of its trade interests. So I—well, you can imagine."

The thought of a man who spoke no Japanese and could barely handle chopsticks sneaking around to gather company secrets was ludicrous. I started laughing, a reaction that didn't please him.

"Damn it, Rei, can't you see what could happen? If Okuhara digs enough, I'll be out of the country faster than a subway ride from Roppongi to Hiroo."

"But how does this relate to Setsuko?" I asked, struggling to be serious.

"She was one of my sources." As he spoke, I felt like he'd punched me in the stomach. I couldn't look at him anymore, just stared down at my mineral water, watching the bubbles pop. "Do you remember how you attacked me for buying her gifts? It wasn't me, really. It was a multinational government group."

"Oh, that makes it better! You come to this country and stretch out your right hand to be paid. All the while you're stealing with your left!"

"I don't believe what I'm doing is so wrong." He

raised his eyebrow, a gesture I would never again consider cute. "Do you have any idea of what the annual
trade imbalance is with your own country? Over fifty
billion a year. My work is simply greasing the wheels
for free trade."

"The trade imbalance is rising not because the
Japanese are nefarious, but because the U.S. dollar is
strengthening! Face it, what you're doing isn't *honest*."

"You and your honesty. The way you rushed to
ring up Okuhara without talking to me first!" Hugh's
rage was finally out in the open.

"I have a problem with the partial truth. I telephoned Okuhara because I was trying to put together
the pieces. When things are held back, you can't."

"If only Setsuko had held back." Hugh stared
into the golden depths of his beer. "She had no problem listening in to her husband's telephone conversa-
tions, thought it a lark because she hated him."

"And because she wanted you," I said, having
become painfully aware of how desire could make
one do very stupid things.

"She did fancy me a bit. I suppose that I played it
to my advantage."

"Like you do with all of us, I suppose."

"You want me to have my heart carved up and
served along with the drinks? I'm through with flir-
tations with you." Hugh made a move to leave his
seat, but I wanted out before him.

"Thanks for reminding me. I'll be going, then." I
motioned for Kozo to bring the check. I would put
both drinks on my credit card as my parting shot.

"You going to end it like this?" Hugh winced when his left foot touched the floor.

"End what?"

"You're driving me home," he said. "It's the least you can do. I'm lame and under the influence and Roppongi Hills is only five minutes away."

"Haven't you heard of taxis? I'm sure your friend Kozo can hail one for you, and if you're broke, I'll lend you the money."

"I'm illegally parked. If I leave the car overnight, it will be gone tomorrow."

"I can't drive in Japan!" Although I had an international driver's license, it had expired and I'd never driven on the left, let alone in Tokyo. I explained this all to Hugh and he waved it away.

"You're sober, the right color, and they won't stop you in a hundred years! Come on, Rei, if it's the last thing you do for me, I want you to take me home."

All I had to do was stay on the left, I repeated to myself like a mantra. I drove like a terrified zombie down Roppongi Dori, but once we got onto a quieter side street I started to unclench. The car wasn't that hard to drive. In fact, it had a whimsical sensor that chimed when you approached objects too closely. I couldn't hit anything with a system like this.

By the time I'd started fantasizing about what it would be like to drive the Windom on the freeway, the twin towers of Hugh's building had risen up like a sterile monster colony. At Hugh's direction, I passed the main entrance to Roppongi Hills and swung around a corner to enter an underground garage. I pulled into a spot marked with his name. A classy touch, along with the Acuras and Mercedes that filled the neighboring parking places.

"Aren't we locking the doors?" I asked after I'd lifted his garment bag and laptop out of the back seat.

"This is one of the cheaper cars in the garage. No one with half a brain would think of touching it." Hugh limped off toward the elevator, and feeling like his mule, I picked up the luggage and followed.

The elevator doors opened with an electronic chirp on the twenty-second floor to a hall carpeted in cream wool. I glanced in the mirrored wall and frowned at my windblown, exhausted appearance.

"I know it's ridiculously seventies," Hugh said, as if my unhappy face was a reaction to the decor. "Inside the flat it's the same. Almost everything's rented, so don't slag me off."

That relaxed me enough to anticipate something truly wretched. The door opened to a tiled entryway hung with a large, expensively framed print of rugby players locked in a mud-covered embrace.

"You're such a guy!" I was blown away.

"I thought I turned the lights off when I went off for the holiday. My electric bill's going to be a nightmare," Hugh moaned as I slipped off my shoes and followed beige wall-to-wall carpeting into a giant living room where a solid glass wall revealed Tokyo Tower and Hotel Okura lit up gorgeously against the dark sky.

The view was the best thing in the huge room furnished with sterile leather furniture in a shade that matched the carpet. The dining room was hardly

better, dominated by a glossy rosewood table and six
rigid-looking chairs. One wall was mirrored and the
other held a pair of reproduction screens depicting a
flowing river banked by plum trees. I'd studied it as
an undergraduate, so the identification came easily:
Red and White Plum Blossoms by Ogata Kōrin, an
early eighteenth-century artist.

"Setsuko chose that." Hugh sensed my unasked
question about the only Japanese thing in sight.

"No wonder. From you, I would have expected
Sumo wrestlers or something more akin to your
rugby players."

"The wrestlers are in the bedroom," he said with
a ghost of his old smile.

"You have more room than you need, don't
you?" I was trying hard to keep my cool. In the two
rooms I'd seen so far, I could fit my apartment five
times over. I had a fleeting thought of how my art
and textile collections could warm the environment
but pushed it away.

"Excuse me," I said, noticing a half-opened door
to what looked like a powder room. Walking in, I
caught a quick movement in the mirror. I yelped and
started to step back, but my hand had already hit the
light switch. In a millisecond, track lights shone down
on the man slammed up against the linen closet: Kenji
Yamamoto, looking frightened but very much alive.

19

"The exterminators were here scarcely a month ago, so please don't tell me—" Hugh stopped short.

"*Sumimasen*, I'm so sorry!" Yamamoto, wearing what looked like one of Hugh's expensive Scottish sweaters over his ski pants, dropped to the ground and began the kind of bowing appropriate for temples.

"Sorry? I damn near broke my ankle because of you!" Hugh waved a crutch at him.

"Please forgive me. Please understand!" Yamamoto cried.

"Do you mind?" I looked at the two of them significantly. Yamamoto got to his feet and Hugh limped out after him.

When I emerged a few minutes later, the two were sitting at the dining table with a bottle of Scotch between them.

"This is Cadenhead's, one of my favorite single

malt whiskeys. You haven't tried it yet." Hugh held out a glass to me.

"You're drinking with someone who might have killed Setsuko and was willing to let you take the fall. Why not lie down and hand him a knife to finish you off!" I stormed away from them and into the kitchen, where I was hit with multiple shocks at the sight of the full-sized stove and oven, the dishwasher, the small center island with a butcher-block top. It was unbelievable. I hadn't seen a kitchen this luxurious since I'd left America.

"While you're in there, could you pull some shepherd's pies from the freezer? I think everyone could use a bite," Hugh called after me.

What did he think this was, a dinner party? I rummaged around the freezer, setting aside packages of ice cream, fish fingers, and lamb curry until I came up with a two-pack of shepherd's pie. I slid it into a spotless microwave mounted on the wall and began looking for something for myself. I wound up with French crackers—it seemed none of his food was Japanese—spread with Patak's Original Lime Pickle and some thin slices of a wan tomato.

"Do you have place mats?" I asked when I came out.

"Second drawer in the sideboard. Thanks. But you're not eating a pie?"

"You know I don't touch meat." I watched him cut through mashed potatoes to dead-looking green peas and oily ground meat before turning my attention to Yamamoto. "So, how did you break in?"

"A long time ago Hugh-san gave me a key. He said when I needed some privacy, I could come."

"That was to be negotiated beforehand—remember?" Hugh said.

"There was no time. I had to leave Shiroyama. I couldn't continue with Sendai, so the practical thing was to disappear."

"What about resigning?" I asked.

"You cannot resign from the *yakuza*."

I felt like my stomach was falling out of me, straight down to the soft Chinese rug under the table. I stared at Hugh. "You're part of the Japanese mob? I didn't know they took . . . foreigners."

"I wish I had a camera to freeze the greatest look of indignation yet." Hugh was laughing outright.

"So you could send our snapshots around the country and put a contract out on us?" I stretched out a hand to his colleague. "Yamamoto-san, if you're telling the truth, you shouldn't have come to *him*."

"But this *yakuza* business does not concern Hugh-san! It is about Nakamura-san and the Eterna." Yamamoto shrunk from me.

"The Eterna?" I was confused.

"The long-life battery we're developing for our laptops. I told you about it," Hugh said.

"It was my special project. The week before we went to Shiroyama, I worked late every night—later than you and Nakamura-san," Yamamoto said pointedly. "I went into his office to drop off the plans for expansion into Singapore. On his desk, I saw a floppy disc labeled Taipei."

"Taipei? We're not doing anything there." Hugh stopped eating.

"Exactly! I was curious, so I read the disc. I am not

an engineer, but I noticed that it mentioned lithium ion, an important element in the battery design."

"The formula's still classified because the patents aren't in order yet. Why would Nakamura have it?" Hugh asked.

"He intends to sell the plans outside the company through the *yakuza*, like I have been saying."

"I'd have to see a copy of the disc to believe it," Hugh said.

"I made one and brought it to give you at the *minshuku*." It disappeared from my suitcase. I noticed on New Year's Day."

"I suppose you left a hard copy on your computer at work?" Hugh asked.

"If I did that, I could be accused! I could not risk leaving it anywhere."

"I want to hear more about the *yakuza*." I interrupted.

"There is a man Mr. Nakamura sometimes has drinks with on Thursday afternoons at the café across the street." Yamamoto paused. "Ichiro Fukujima, who is said to be a member of the Saito family."

"Nakamura may have a gangster pal, but Sendai is not a *yakuza* company. Masuhiro Sendai would never tolerate anything that might bring a whiff of scandal. Look at how quickly I was suspended from work!" Hugh said.

"Gangsters make many secret movements," Yamamoto insisted. "At the *minshuku* on January third, someone entered my room again, leaving some very expensive jewelry. Pearls I recognized from Mrs. Nakamura's neck."

I gasped as Hugh asked calmly, "So, what did you do with the jewelry?"

"I threw it in the back of my closet. I meant to talk to you that night, but you went to dinner with Rei. When you came back you stayed together." He gave me a resentful look. "All night long, I think, because it was not quiet."

"Tea, anyone?" I scooted into the kitchen. As I searched for a kettle, I thought about how the jewelry had been hidden. Yamamoto and Hugh had side-by-side rooms. The closet in the middle could be accessed by either man. I'd misjudged the situation, and so had the police.

I emerged with a tray bearing a teapot, sugar, and a small pitcher of soured milk I found in the fridge. As I poured for the two of them, I asked Yamamoto the question that still burned for me—why he believed the necklace had been placed in his suitcase.

"I thought if Mr. Nakamura was a *yakuza* member, maybe he was not afraid to kill. When I found the necklace, I thought he was giving me a warning," Yamamoto said.

"So that's why you ran," Hugh said, grimacing when he tasted his milky tea.

"I didn't know what trouble it would cause," Yamamoto sounded tearful. "When I finished the first ski run ahead of you, I dropped my skis in a ravine and caught a taxi back into Shiroyama. I traveled by train to Yokohama and stayed for a few days with an old friend. But his parents were coming back from their New Year's holiday, so I had to leave."

"Why didn't you stay with your parents?" Hugh

pushed his tea cup aside and poured himself more whiskey. "They could have helped you come up with a more realistic exit."

"They know nothing. How could I say I was running from Sendai? Such a famous, excellent employer? They would never understand!"

"Do you realize they're probably in the process of planning your funeral? You must ring them," Hugh insisted.

"But Sendai can't find out—I could die!"

"Could you call the National Police Agency?" I asked. "They oversee all of Japan's police departments and are trying hard to make inroads against organized crime."

Hugh creaked to his feet. "In exchange for another night here, will you please telephone home?"

"I'd like to, but Yokohama is long distance."

"Call them now! Please!" Hugh barked.

"You should call the National Police Agency yourself," I muttered when Yamamoto had gone into Hugh's study to use the telephone. "I don't trust him. Besides, the police need to know the truth about the pearls."

"I'm not calling anybody," Hugh said. "The pearls are no worry—I'm out of prison, aren't I? And I'd like to figure out this mess regarding the Eterna battery."

"Why, so you can get your job back? Forget Sendai. You could work anywhere else in the world. I thought you were a man on the move, a new job every eighteen months—"

"I want to stay *here*." His voice was obstinate.

I looked at the brass captain's clock on the sideboard.

It was after midnight, which meant the subway had stopped running. I would have to find a taxi.

"I'm out of here." I carried the plates and glasses into the kitchen, noticing Yamamoto hadn't touched his Scotch. I deliberated whether to load the dishwasher but decided against it, in the interest of giving them something to do.

Hugh swung up behind me on his crutches as I was gathering together my parka and shoes.

"I'll give you a run back in the car. Your lousy tea sobered me up."

"No chance. You need to keep an eye on Yamamoto, and it's easier for me to take a taxi."

"It's just a few hours until the morning trains start up. Don't go." Hugh was studying me in a way that reminded me of the last night we'd spent together, the night before everything went to hell.

"I've had enough. Good-bye, Shug." I peeked over my shoulder to catch his reaction and was annoyed to see he wasn't even watching. He was talking into his hallway intercom, already with something new.

Outside the building, a taxi had just pulled up. Lucky for me. I smiled gratefully at the Roppongi Hills doorman who handed me in, but did a double-take when he gave the driver my address and a crisp 5,000 yen note.

"Glendinning-san requested," the doorman said to me in explanation.

Hugh must have organized this subversive act of charity using the intercom.

I should have been humiliated, but the hard fact
was that a crosstown taxi ride would have been cata-
strophic for my personal finances. So as dirty as Hugh
Glendinning's money might be, I'd take it.

20

I dressed in the bathroom the next morning to avoid waking Mariko snoring gently on the spare futon. I would have also liked to sleep in, but Sunday was the busiest shopping day of the week. It would be an advantage to show up at Mitsutan before Setsuko's favorite salesclerk, the one Mariko had told me about, got too busy.

As I rode the subway to Shinjuku, I pictured the mysterious Miss Yokoyama folding Chanel scarves or arranging Prada handbags in glass display cases. I was pretty disappointed when the information desk clerk sent me to the children's department. What interest did Setsuko have in children's clothes, besides the occasional present for her friends' offspring? Maybe it had something to do with her secret baby. Wondering, I rode the escalator up to the land of infant Moschino and headed to a pair of female salesclerks folding the smallest sweaters I had ever seen.

"Does a Miss Yokoyama work here?" I looked at them without hope.

"I am Yokoyama. How can I help you?" The smaller one wearing her hair in a neat braid smiled at me with slightly buck teeth, wholly too unglamorous to be a friend of Setsuko's.

"I'm looking for something... a nice sweat-shirt," I said, hoping to draw her away from her colleague to the other side of the department. "Something for an older girl."

"Do you know her size?" Miss Yokoyama began leading me deep into racks of pink and red outfits.

"Actually, I came to ask you about Setsuko Nakamura. I'm not sure if you know she passed away?"

"Oh, yes. It was tragic." Miss Yokoyama looked over her shoulder at the other salesclerk, then back at me. "Did you go to the *tsuya*? What was she wear-ing?"

"The casket was closed because of the autopsy." I was surprised at her question before remembering she was in the business of selling clothes. "I'm here because I had a few questions about her shopping. I'm putting the family finances in order."

"Oh?" Miss Yokoyama sucked air between her teeth. "I'm afraid I don't understand."

"You waited on her when she came in, didn't you? I know she used to spend a lot."

"I don't know about that." Miss Yokoyama's answer came before I'd stopped talking.

"This is confidential, so please don't worry about anything." I fingered a sweater, marveling at the price of one hundred percent acrylic. Antique silk kimonos went for less at the shrine sales.

"I'm sorry, but I really don't think I have anything to say."

"Can I meet you in the ladies' room or somewhere like that?"

"No breaks allowed until one o'clock."

"I'll wait for you!"

"Will you buy something from me?" she asked suddenly. "If anyone asks what we're doing so long together, I can explain you had a problem deciding."

"Okay." I'd have a horrendous Visa bill this month, but so be it.

"Get a T-shirt," she advised. "It's cheaper, and I think I can find something that will fit you. You're small enough."

"What do you mean?" I wasn't *that* flat.

"It's a style! Tiny, tiny T-shirts show off the bosom. You're a foreigner, aren't you?" Miss Yokoyama beckoned me to follow her into the pre-teen department. "No wonder Setsuko-san was friends with you. She liked foreigners."

"You met Mr. Glendinning?"

She nodded, blushing a little.

"What did they buy?" I asked.

"Oh, anything. A dress if she had a party to attend. Spanish porcelain figures. She liked English china, too."

"But I don't understand. If you sell only children's clothes—"

"I worked in customer service before."

"Ah. Mariko didn't say that."

"You know Mariko-san?" Miss Yokoyama smiled briefly. "That crazy girl. So different from Setsuko-san."

"Did Mrs. Nakamura try to get her into Chanel?"

"Oh, yes. But Mariko-san always preferred *bodi-kon*. You know, the clothes that fit like a glove."

"So who won?" I shook my head at the preppy-looking Elle T-shirt she held out.

"Mariko-san," Miss Yokoyama smiled, showing her teeth. "Those clothes were never returned."

"Not returned?" I was confused.

"Setsuko-san often changed her mind." A veil seemed to drop over Miss Yokoyama's face.

Setsuko often changed her mind. Even if you paid for something with a credit card at a Japanese department store, you could usually get a cash refund without question. If Setsuko returned most of what Hugh bought her, she could have profited.

"I've got to get back to work. Just take this one, it's on sale." Miss Yokoyama held out a white top decorated with two kissing cats and the slogan LOVE CATS FRIENDSHIP, QUALITY CLOTHING SINCE 1981 WE MAKE FOR YOU.

"You made sure she was able to return everything she bought, didn't you?" I smiled as I spoke, hoping not to frighten her.

"I knew it was a bad idea, but now it's all over. Please don't say anything." Miss Yokoyama looked ready to jump out of her skin.

"What do you mean?"

"I've told you all that I know." The salesclerk hurried off to the register near her colleague with the T-shirt and my credit card in her hands. Walking downstairs a few minutes later, I realized the price of information had worked out to a whopping 3,200 yen plus tax. But, I could return it. Just like Setsuko.

The next people on my list were Taro and Yuki Ikeda. I arrived at our meeting point in Omotesandō a little early and decided to look around. Just like Roppongi, the stores were packed with luxury imported goods, and this was reflected in a residential mix of wealthy Japanese and company-funded foreigners.

Outside Tokyo Union Church, I watched foreigners arrive for the multidenominational English language service. My attention was caught by a silver-haired man in a long overcoat, with a flashy-looking older woman at his side. Joe Roncolotta and Mrs. Chapman. Joe had seemed mildly courteous to Mrs. Chapman during the Trader Vic's dinner. I was stunned they were dating. I hurried toward them.

Joe did a mock double-take and Mrs. Chapman turned and giggled, hoisting a plastic bag aloft. "Rei, you should have been with us this morning! There was an antiques flea market just up the street."

"The Togo Shrine! It's great, isn't it?" I said.

"I got a call from the police about you the other night." Joe scrutinized me. "We should talk about it. Where are you headed?"

"Actually, I'm on my way to meet some friends. Taro and Yuki, you'll remember them, Mrs. Chapman." I would have loved for Yuki Ikeda, with her interest in matchmaking, to see Mrs. Chapman's escort.

"The last thing I need is cake," Mrs. Chapman

cooed. So she was dieting now. It was incredible what love had done to the woman who had once opined to me that all men were bastards.

"How about joining us tomorrow?" Joe persisted. "I was going to show Marcelle the Tokyo Stock Exchange in the afternoon, and then we were going to TAC for an early happy hour."

I glanced at Mrs. Chapman, and I saw her face was rather oddly screwed up. Probably she was signaling for me to decline.

"Monday's my busiest teaching day, I'm sorry," I said. "I do want to see you again—both of you—how much longer are you staying?"

"Oh, I'm wait-listed for a flight later this week. Can you believe how badly organized the airport is?"

"Call me if you have any more trouble with the airline," I said, imagining that as long as things were humming along with Joe, her plans might be delayed. "If you phone during the afternoon when I'm out, you might get Mariko. She understands English, but you have to speak slowly."

"Another roommate? Dear, I thought you just lived with the fruit loop in your apartment. Remember, there was no room for me?" There was an injured undertone to her voice, and I cursed myself for being so careless.

"It's temporary. She's just a girlfriend in trouble who had to leave her home . . . I'm helping her find something."

"That's kind of you. Let me know if I can help— is she bilingual?" Joe asked.

"Sort of." Unfortunately, what came out of

Mariko's mouth these days was mostly the obscene English Richard had been teaching her. I wasn't going to mention that.

I got to the Hanae Mori Building about nine minutes late. Yuki was watching through the window and gave me a big wave when I jogged up.

"I'm sorry you had to wait," I panted. "You'll never guess who I met."

"You should have brought them along! I think it is beautiful, this second chance at life and love," Yuki said when I had told them about Mrs. Chapman.

"Next time. Where's the menu?" I was weak from having skipped lunch, so I ordered the biggest cake in the glass showcase: apple strudel. Taro cheered my choice; he was going for the Black Forest cherry cake himself. Yuki, true to her New Year's diet, stuck to black coffee.

After the waitress set up our dainty meal, Taro placed my antique box on the table. I opened it and found the newsprint that had lined the interior had been removed. Small strips of paper and glue remained.

"What happened here?" I didn't hide my dismay.

"Oh, I already read the paper and could tell it was from the early sixties because there was some article with mention of the crown prince Naruhito. See, I made you a translation." Taro handed me a typed piece of paper. "You seem sad. Look inside the box again."

I peered at the box's interior, running my finger over the scarred wood. The original lacquer finish was rubbed off and I saw, suddenly, what he wanted me to: letters carved in *hiragana*, Japan's phonetic alphabet. The easiest alphabet, the one I'd known since I was nine.

"Shiroyama," I spelled out. "So maybe the box comes from there, after all."

"There's more writing," Yuki said.

I looked closely again and read "Uchida Miyo," the name of the lost princess of the Shiroyama legend Taro had retold on New Year's Eve.

"We don't know that it's real," I said, trying to control my excitement. Anyone could have done it as a joke. Still, the grooves of the letters were worn smoothly, as if they'd been cut long ago.

"We could have it appraised at one of the antique stores around here," Taro suggested.

"All those people know is how to mark things up for tourists. I'd rather take it to Mr. Ishida." Yasushi Ishida was the man who had sold me the marvelous *tansu* chest a year ago. I could visit his shop on my way home.

"In any case, it's a nice thing to take your mind off the trouble," Yuki offered.

"Trouble?" I repeated.

"Hugh-san is in prison, to be tried for the murder. You didn't know?" Yuki's eyes were big.

"He's been released," I said shortly.

"Oh, really?" Taro asked.

"Rei-san, you surely haven't seen him?" Yuki wailed.

The coffee went down the wrong way, and I began coughing into my napkin.

"This is not a good idea. Hugh-san may be free at the moment, but most people believe he is a criminal!" Taro's voice was sharp enough that the two grandmothers dining quietly at the next table turned their heads.

"I thought you liked him," I said.

"He was very kind and funny, but the police do not hold prisoners unless they have a very strong case." Taro said. "His true character must be different than our first impression!"

If he is indicted, just remember the judge convicts in ninety-nine percent of all cases. It's the Japanese system," Yuki said soberly.

"This Japanese system, I guess I don't understand it, Yuki. I wonder why, for instance, you and your husband found it so crucial to share my sex life with Captain Okuhara." The fury that had simmered in me for a week spilled over.

"I told you not to tell!" Yuki shrieked at her husband.

"When a policeman asks, you must tell the truth," Taro argued back. "Rei-san needs to be protected! She's a girl who knows nothing about men's nature."

"Excuse me," I said, waving a hand in his face. "If you're going to insult me, do it directly, please."

"Rei-san, I am not your relative, so I cannot tell you what to do. But please, you must not see him again. You must be careful," Taro said.

"I always am." I whisked the check out of the tiny silver holder where the waitress had placed it, trying to quash the anger rising in me. I owed a lot to the Ikedas. They had shown me around Shiroyama, uncovered the box's carving and even handcarried it into the city to return to me. But they had also brought me something that I didn't want: the old nagging doubts.

Ishida Antiques had closed by the time I arrived at the dingy 1930s house where Mr. Ishida worked and slept among his Japanese treasures. I figured he was probably home and knocked until he craned his head out of an upstairs window.

"Shimura-san! Wait shortly, please!" A smile creased the face of the man who looked as devout as a monk whenever I spied on him at the shrine sales.

I waited for him to unbolt the door that creaked like something out of a horror movie but led to a paradise crowded with dusty furniture: table standing atop table, ceramic urns stacked in precarious towers that leaned but never fell. Today the shop smelled like oranges. I finally spotted an offering of tangerines at the base of a beautifully carved miniature shrine hanging over the entrance.

"I've brought something mysterious for you." I pulled my box out of the Mitsutan shopping bag. As Mr. Ishida examined it, I started to narrate the legend of Princess Miyo.

"I know the story, of course. I presume you're interested in learning if your purchase connects to the legend." He set down the box.

"Could it be genuine?" I asked.

"It is interesting. Especially since the name is inscribed in *hiragana* and not *kanji*."

"Mostly women wrote in *hiragana*, right?"

"Yes, they wrote in phonetics for the centuries before they were allowed to study *kanji*. But Princess Miyo was a young lady in the 1860s, when national reforms were beginning to include an education curriculum for all. A princess, especially, would have had a private teacher." Mr. Ishida scratched his cheek.

"What about the carving? Do you think a woman might have been trained to do that?"

"Certainly. Noblewomen often carried knives so they could be prepared to commit suicide, should enemies take over."

"So maybe it isn't a fake." My spirits rose.

"Even if she didn't carve this herself, it was surely done in the nineteenth century. I'll show you something for comparison." Mr. Ishida rummaged in a corner, coming back with a small wooden hibachi— a brazier in which coals were once burned for warmth in the household. The hibachi had calligraphy running down one side that had been smoothly worn down by age; this, we compared to the carving on my small box.

"The wood used for your box is lighter and cheaper, but both are from the same era. I feel it." Mr. Ishida held my box almost reverently. "Most likely someone between 1830 to 1870 has carved this name. Probably a child."

"It could have been her." I pictured a beautiful little girl in a handmade silk kimono, her head bent industriously over the box as she whittled away.

"May I keep this for a few days?" Mr. Ishida interrupted my daydreaming. "I have a colleague at the

Tokyo National Museum with an interest in the aristocracy."

"Of course," I murmured before wondering what Miyo would want. I closed my eyes, feeling the uncanny connection again. Only it wasn't just a little girl in an exquisite kimono enjoying a way of life soon coming to an end, it was myself in the first grade, panicked over what crayon to use when drawing my skin color. It was young Setsuko huddled in a cardboard box, and Mariko shunned at the swimming pool. We four, a number considered bad luck because it was pronounced *shi*, the homonym for death.

21

I'd almost forgotten Monday was nonburnable garbage day, so after I'd gotten my backpack and lunch together and walked out the door I had to double back to get the bag of bottles and cans. The phone was ringing inside the apartment. I ran past Mariko, who was cuddled deep in her futon.

"Hey, Rei. What's new?" It was Hugh Glendinning.

"What happened with Yamamoto?" It bothered me that he hadn't reported in the day before.

"I drove him home yesterday, where he met his mother and father. Tearful reunion and all that."

"Has he talked to the police yet?" When Hugh didn't answer, I exploded. "You're killing yourself, do you know that? You could very well be charged as the accomplice in his trumped-up death!"

"Accessory," he corrected. "But I'm fairly certain he's innocent. Remember the disc, the one he said contained the battery formula? Hikari can't find it in the office. Just like Yamamoto thought, Nakamura must have gotten nervous and taken it home."

"Unless Yamamoto is lying about everything." I glanced at Mariko, whose ponytail was peeping a bit higher out of the blankets. She was listening.

"Wait to sling your arrows until I find the disc," Hugh told me.

"Until you find it? What are you going to do, break into his house?"

"Technically, it won't be a forced entry. You'll see."

"What do you mean by that?"

"I need you, Rei." Hugh's voice was silky. "You know how to get to the house. And as far as physical searching goes—crawling under tables and such—I'm still incapacitated."

"Why not hire a professional detective to help you?" I cast about for a logical alternative.

"Impossible. If Ota got wind of the business, he'd drop me."

"Because you'd be breaking and entering," I pointed out.

"No, what we're doing is more akin to gaining access to the house through a ruse. We'll be cleaning the house in lieu of the regular maid."

"Gee, you really know how to get me excited." First the Nakamura bathroom, now the whole house. I was upwardly mobile.

"I've already asked the girl who cleans my flat to bring a spare maid's uniform for you. We'll go over there tomorrow, and if it makes things more attractive, I'll pay you out of my government account."

"Having you pay for dinner and taxis is humiliating enough, and the only reason I've let you do that is I simply can't afford it. Talking to me about your spy fund is insulting beyond belief. Even if I wanted to go, I have a midday tutoring session!"

"Couldn't you come down with cramps or one of those mysterious girls' things bosses are loathe to explore?"

"Don't be sexist." I said, all the while thinking that if I got into Setsuko's house to look around, I might find some real evidence of the American father. I could perhaps prove to Hugh that Setsuko's death had less to do with high-tech thievery than dysfunctional family relations.

"Richard could fill in for me, I suppose. But if I do go—"

"I know." He was laughing. "You'll do the driving."

I would feel safer in a car than a train, I thought as I walked to Minami-Senju station to catch my ride to work. These days, I couldn't stop brooding about how Mrs. Yogetsu had died at my station. It gave me the chills to pace the platform from where she'd been pushed, but none of the commuters who regularly waited there had talked about the incident.

For me, the train station had become a sinister place. When I was alone, I imagined a stalker in the shadows, and when hordes surrounded me, I imagined an anonymous knife in my back or shove onto the tracks. Some people believed there was safety in numbers, but for me, there was only paranoia.

※   ※   ※

I made it to work in one piece to find Richard await-
ing me with a telephone message slip in hand.

"Guess who called?" He held out an imaginary
kilt and did an imitation of Scottish dancing.

"He called here, too? I don't know what's wrong
with the man." I rolled the message into a spiral
before tucking it in my pocket.

"Miss Bun gave the phone to me because he
couldn't speak any Japanese. He said something
about an urgent message for you. Baby, if you play
this right, you could move to Roppongi Hills."

"Or prison! Did he say he was all right?"

"He's at home among all his dreamy luxury appliances and the view of Tokyo Tower." Richard sighed.
"I'm so annoyed you didn't see the bedroom. I asked
about it but he said no, you absolutely did not roll
between the sheets."

"You didn't!" I was horrified.

"Of course I did. He said something terribly
dry and British and laughed afterward. Very sexy
laugh."

"Richard, you've got to help me." I drew him
into a corner and told him about my need to leave. I
couldn't tell Mr. Katoh I had another farewell ceremony to attend. After a few minutes of bitching,
Richard agreed to help. We were cementing the
details when Mr. Katoh walked in.

I hadn't expected to see him at an hour when he
usually was closeted with the other section heads. I
slid off the desk where I'd been sitting and threw

myself into a bow. Mr. Katoh greeted both of us pleasantly, then fixed his attention on me.

"Bad weather today, isn't it, Miss Shimura? Not like your California."

"Well, rain at this time of the year, I've grown to expect it," I said, sensing from his tone that something else was brewing. Richard caught it, too, and fled with some excuse about papers left in a classroom.

"Shall we go in the conference room? I have a problem I hope you can assist with. As you perhaps already know, our company plans to expand English instruction."

"Are you hiring new teachers?" I sat down across from him on one of the nice leather chairs the senior executives used at their board meetings.

"Eventually. But it is a big expansion from just the Tokyo headquarters to our factory and offices in Osaka."

Osaka was a booming business city, arguably the heart of capitalist Japan. Still, it had a crushing reputation for dullness. Nobody I knew would want to trade multicultural, cutting-edge Tokyo for Osaka. Still, my boss was counting on me.

"I could probably locate some potential teachers through the English Teachers' Association," I offered.

"That is considerate." Something about my boss' language told me that wasn't precisely what he was after. "Miss Shimura, we are very happy with your work."

"Thank you," I said, ducking my head a bit to show appreciation.

"In fact, the company would like to offer you a

promotion." The miserable look on his face contradicted his words. "After your years of loyal service, we plan to upgrade your status from a contract worker to company employee with full benefits. We would like to start you in Osaka."

"Permanently?" I croaked.

"Yes. You could live in the female employee dormitory."

Great. From what I'd heard, shared corporate dorm rooms were minuscule, with barely enough room to hang clothes, let alone house my antiques. Living in the dorm would be like college revisited, with the addition of a curfew and a surly matron at the door.

"Why aren't you sending Richard?" I felt overcome by bad fortune.

"Mr. Randall is not so comfortable with the Japanese culture. We especially thought of you."

"It's a lot to think about." I didn't ask about the money, because I found myself suddenly feeling that no amount would be enough to compensate for the loss of friends and relatives and the life I had painstakingly built.

"Miss Shimura, what do you think?" Mr. Katoh's tired brown eyes pleaded with me.

"May I give you my answer later?"

"Of course." Mr. Katoh sounded startled, which reinforced my feeling that his offer was actually an order that had come down from above.

I felt so stunned by Mr. Katoh's proposal that my feigned physical collapse just before lunchtime was fairly realistic. Mr. Katoh became extremely upset and wanted to call an ambulance, but Richard came up

with the perfect solution of putting me in a taxi
ostensibly headed to St. Luke's. The taxi stopped at
the train station, per my request, where I hopped the
Hibiya line over to Roppongi.

When Hugh opened the door to his apartment, I
could tell the maid had been there. Tidy before, his
living space was now fanatically organized. The CDs
and magazines appeared alphabetized, the windows
gleamed without a single streak, and the scent of pine
cleaner was everywhere. If this was the kind of performance I had to imitate, I was in trouble.

"Why did you call me at the office? You could
have blown everything," I said, shaking my head at
the cup of tea he was offering.

"I was trying to check your clothing size. You
didn't call me back, so I had to simply accept what
Fumie brought me."

"Your maid really wears this?" I held up the black
polyester uniform with a ruffled white apron that
looked straight out of an adult video.

"Don't worry, it's freshly washed." He showed
me into his room and left. I looked around and saw
there actually was a triptych of sumo wrestlers on the
wall, although I couldn't discern the artist's seal.
Trying to get closer, I stubbed my heel on the corner
of a rowing machine and swore.

The only other piece of furniture in the room was
a massive sleigh bed. I sat down on the edge and
began taking off my conservative work suit.
Something was bothering me. I realized when I was
fully undressed that it was my lack of goose bumps. I
scanned the room and saw no space heaters. Hugh

had central heating, the first I'd encountered in a Japanese residence.

I hung up my clothes in his closet and couldn't help running my hand through his long row of suits, noting the fine textures and colors too expensive to be defined: taupish browns and bluish grays and charcoals. What did it say about him, that he chose such expensive things? I closed the closet and went out to the living room, hoping my face wouldn't give away my snooping.

"That's a good length for you," Hugh said, looking at the too-short uniform. He had been making notes on the fold-out map, his bad ankle propped on the coffee table. A few inches of the bandage showed from underneath his gray flannel trousers. Although he'd come to the door without crutches, he still had a slight limp.

"Do you have a Bible?" I asked, suddenly inspired.

"Sorry, I'm rather lapsed in terms of religion!"

"One of those will do." I went to the bookshelves and gave him a large, faux-leather-bound law book. "Now you look like a Jehovah's Witness."

As we loaded the car with a plastic bucket and cleaning supplies, I explained the concept. There was no good reason for a business-suited *gaijin* to roam a suburban neighborhood. Unless, of course, he had a religious mission.

"If I open my mouth, I'll be lost," Hugh groaned.

"Nobody will expect you to speak much Japanese. But if you're supposed to be ex-American military, you'll need to keep the Scottish accent to a minimum."

"No way, man." He practiced a California Valley boy accent which made me snicker until we entered the Shuto Expressway, where sudden lane changes sent me into a state of confusion. There was no time to read the *kanji* on the signs; here, Hugh guided me and I simply obeyed.

"How much longer? That wasn't fun at all." I rubbed at the tension in my neck and shoulders when we finally made it past the traffic jams of Yokohama and onto an uncrowded toll road.

"Judging from the signs, it's about an hour. You can speed up, but you'll see no one goes over one-hundred kilometers per hour." Hugh hit his seat's RECLINE button and stretched back.

"You're one to talk, given all your tickets," I said, accelerating.

"It's only parking tickets. Why would I want to speed? If you pass one hundred, this obnoxious little bell rings. Listen, it's happening now! Rei Shimura, I have a cell phone in hand. I could call the police right now!"

"You wouldn't." I stayed at 110 for a few minutes, slowing down when the bell started driving me crazy. The Toyota-installed Big Brother stuff really worked.

"You're good for someone who's never been on the left before. Not too much wavering into the shoulder, and your turns in the city were impressive," Hugh told me.

"Thanks." I felt pleased in spite of myself.

"You should get your own car," he continued. "Everyone sells after a few years to avoid the taxes, so you can get a bargain on something used. Although I reckon its hard to find a parking garage in your ghetto."

"Find me something on the radio, will you?" Thinking about leaving Tokyo for Osaka was upsetting me.

Hugh clicked the radio to the station I woke up with every morning.

"Good afternoon, it's two o'clock from the J-WAVE singing clock!" I sang along with the corny station identification, which was followed by a Spice Girls hit. The British pop group segued into an old favorite from Echo and the Bunnymen, and Hugh joined in with a rich tenor. Somehow, it didn't surprise me that he could carry a tune. What did jolt me was the fact he knew the lyrics to "Lips Like Sugar" as well as I did.

"How old did you say you were?" I asked.

"Thirty-two. I'm ancient, remember? This is eighties music, I danced to it all over Germany and New York."

"We're five years apart." Half a decade.

"Good at math, why don't you teach that? Or music. I like your voice."

We sang companionably for a while longer, Hugh doing an imitation of Robert Smith, The Cure's mournful lead singer, that made me laugh so hard I almost missed the Hayama exit. I wondered why I could be so cheerful in the face of committing a crime and, as if on cue, got lost. It turned out the toll road entrance into Hayama was different than the taxi ride Hikari and I had taken. After driving aimlessly for a while, I admitted to Hugh I had no clue how to proceed.

"Hikari said to go north." Hugh pulled out his map again.

"Hikari says a lot I don't believe. I'd rather just stop at a police box to get directions," I told him.

"Are you insane? Do you plan to register our names and faces with the police again?"

"Nobody knows me. I could go in and you could hide. Just get down low in the passenger seat. No, not with your head in my lap." I pushed him off and kept driving. Where was the ocean? I was surrounded by hills. Finally I saw the convenience store I remembered as the turning point for Nakamura's neighborhood.

"I'll stay down in the car, so as not to blow your maid's image." Hugh looked like a giant, gray flannel-covered snail curled up between the car seat and floor. It would be funny if it weren't so dangerous.

We went over the plan one last time. I would drive the car around to the back of the house and get out with the cleaning supplies. Hugh would wait a few minutes to ensure no one was looking, then drive on to a discreet parking place and return on foot.

A couple of neighborhood housewives were chatting and sweeping leaves from the street in front of the Nakamura house. I passed them, turning into the narrow alley running behind the block. I parked outside the Nakamura's garden gate.

"If we get out of this unscathed, you owe me," I said in parting.

"I offered you money before." He peered up at me from his uncomfortable position.

"That's not what I want." I slid out and slammed the door.

22

My first feeling upon entering the Nakamura house was gratitude. Gratitude that the key had worked and no one was inside and the caterers had cleaned up the *tsuya* so well that my stab at cleaning would be minimal. Taking my shoes off and walking through the first floor, I decided the only place I'd have to expend serious energy was the kitchen.

Japanese kitchens were awful. It always amazed me that the zealous hygiene applied to the human body did not enter areas of food preparation. In the Nakamura kitchen, the small sink and counter were coated with grime. Oil-filmed cabinets were crammed every which way with boxes and jars. Atop the cabinets, blenders, and other small appliances had their cords hanging down, inviting accident. The drying rack was overloaded with a precarious array of dishes and cutlery; one false move and it could all crash down.

I switched on the hot water heater to fill my bucket.

As I surveyed the dull linoleum floor, a steel-edged square in the middle caught my eye. The *yukashita*, the under-the-floor storage pocket, was a prime hiding place. I used the one in my kitchen to store favorite foods I didn't want Richard to consume.

Prying the lid up, I looked into a neatly organized space containing a crock of miso and a bag of onions. There was also a very large, dead spider, which led me to breathe a little faster and slam down the lid.

I went through the cupboards, finding no secrets but enough space to store the dishes and cutlery from the counter. I was wiping everything down with a lot of detergent when the doorbell sounded.

I cracked open the back door and didn't see Hugh. For some reason, he must have gone to the front. I padded out to the entryway and whispered a greeting into the intercom.

"Konnichiwa," Hugh greeted me heartily, holding the large book aloft. "Jehovah's Witness calling."

I put my shoes on and walked outside, keeping my head down. There I bowed, opened the gate, and led him inward.

"Some housewives were staring at me when I parked the car, so I felt I had to stick to the main road. Remember how my head was down in the car? I never saw the house! It took me a while to identify the gate, but I recognized the name over the post box because the *kanji* is like the one in your surname."

"Mura, which means village. What have you been doing, studying?"

"I can see my breath in here. It's like Shiroyama."

Hugh strode into the dining room and switched on an electric heater mounted high on a wall. Warm, dry air rushed out. "Shall I start here?"

"As long as you remember to vacuum and dust." I was determined that he clean along with me. When I came back half an hour later, my work in the kitchen done, I found him making faint dusting gestures around a *tansu*.

"Come see what's in this chest." He slid open the ornamental front panel to show a steel safe.

"Can't you open it?" I asked.

"I'm not *that* kind of spy."

"Wait a minute." In my handbag, I had a scrap of paper with the code Mariko had found in Setsuko's address book. I elbowed Hugh aside and tried it three times without success.

"What was that all about?" Hugh's voice was impatient. "There's nothing more we can do in here. I have to hurry if I'm going to find the discs."

"Try Mr. Nakamura's study. End of the hall, to the right."

"Thanks." He hobbled away and I went into the room where the coffin had been. All funeral trappings were gone, and a low table was in the center, stacked with a few magazines and photo albums. I set aside the one with the oldest-looking pictures to look at later.

Upstairs, I started in a small bedroom that was probably designed for a child—or husband, judging from the single bed that was unmade. I changed the sheets and straightened up before attacking the book-case. I paged through some Japanese classics and thrillers I decided were Mr. Nakamura's books, and the ones I guessed were Setsuko's: international and Japanese travel guides, Shizuko Natsuki mysteries, and a few books on Japanese art and antiques. I began methodically going through her collection, shaking each book open to look for hidden papers. When I found a book of wood-blocks by Utamaro, the foremost painter of courtesans in the Edo period, I paged more slowly. I paused at a picture of a lovely young woman with a glass of sake in one hand and a steamed crab in the other. The translated title was something like "Young Hussy Viewed Through the Moralizing Spectacles of Her Parents." I smiled.

"This isn't a library." Hugh spoke in my ear, making me jump.

"You're finished downstairs?" I slammed the book shut.

"Yes madam. I found a cache of discs, none labeled the way Yamamoto had described, but I've copied it all to go through at home."

"I've found a lot of travel books on California, Florida, the East Coast . . . also England and Scotland. Were you planning to take Setsuko back to the UK?"

"No! How many times must I tell you we weren't together?" Hugh sounded irate.

"There are also a couple of American phone books from Dallas and San Diego. Maybe she was looking for someone in America," I quickly said.

"But you told me she knew her father." Hugh took the Dallas book from me and looked at the spine. "Damn it, these were taken from the TAC library. They'll have my head."

"Maybe her father's name is inside . . . or some other family members?"

"Well, there's no time for reading now." He loaded the books into an opaque trash bag.

This master bedroom was utterly Setsuko, furnished only by a bed set on a black lacquered platform and covered in mauve silk. A long, gilded screen painted with butterflies and summer grasses hung over the bed, which was flanked by a couple of low *tansu* chests. Very Zen, very elegant. A thin layer of dust over the furniture and the tucked-in covers told me Mr. Nakamura probably hadn't slept there in a while.

I went through the chests, finding toiletries and Setsuko's undergarments, soft swirls of silk and nylon that were a lot nicer than anything I owned. We surveyed the closet. Nakamura's side was obvious: suits, shirts, and golf clothes. A black lace teddy was tucked in with them which Hugh pulled out with a flourish.

"You think he's a cross-dresser?" Hugh asked.

"Too small. This is practically my size," I said.

"But the fabric's too cheap to have been something of Setsuko's, and her unmentionables are in the chest." Hugh eyed me as I sniffed at the underarms, which bore traces of a powdery deodorant. When the telephone rang, we both jumped.

"Maybe it's someone from the neighborhood, checking." Despite the cold, I felt myself start to sweat in the black polyester uniform.

"The answering machine should kick in," Hugh said.

It didn't. I counted six peals before the caller hung up.

"We should get out of here," I said, but Hugh continued as deliberately as before, moving on to Setsuko's side of the closet. I watched his hands move gently through the pale silk blouses and the delicate knit suits. As if they were still a part of her, I thought with a sick lurch in my stomach.

"I wonder when he'll get rid of her things," I said, but Hugh didn't seem to hear me. He was moving faster through the clothes, checking the labels.

"It's not here," he said. "A red Gianni Versace suit I bought for her at Mitsutan. Was she buried in it?"

"The coffin was closed so I don't know for certain, but I really doubt the funeral people would dress her in red. Too loud."

"Where could the Versace be, then?" He paced the room.

"She probably returned it," I told him.

"She wouldn't! It was fabulous on her. Besides, I had the credit card and receipt."

"At Japanese department stores you can return things you charged for a cash refund, no questions asked. Setsuko did that a lot. I found out last Sunday."

"So you're saying she cheated me?" Hugh sat down on the bed, denting the immaculate coverlet.

"Come on, you were paying for information! Does it matter whether it was in the form of goods or cash?" I explained what Miss Yokoyama had intimated.

"It's being tricked that bothers me," Hugh muttered as we made a final clean sweep upstairs. "If I had known she wanted money I would have gladly paid it. But she seemed thrilled about the clothes."

"Women in Japan aren't supposed to desire money. That's reflected in the salaries paid to those of us who do work. You earn five times what I do," I said, bumping the heavy bag filled with the telephone books downstairs.

"I didn't know that. Still, aren't you're doing what you love?" He began a slower descent behind me.

Ha. A picture of myself riding the bullet train to my horrible new job in Osaka ran through my mind as I walked around turning off lights and heaters. We had a short spat over whether the living room door had been open or not; I threw up my hands at last and allowed him to close it.

"Is the front door locked?"

"Check!" I called back. In the kitchen, I remembered to turn off the water heater and collected my cleaning supplies in the pail. Then Hugh slipped out the back door with his law book and I began the process of waiting. Somehow, those last minutes alone were the worst; what my watch told me was really twelve minutes felt like half an hour. At last I heard the Windom purring down the back alley, and I slipped out of the door with the books and my trash bags.

I had miscalculated. The car that stopped at the gate was a white Mercedes. I darted behind a camellia bush and listened. The car door opened and footsteps clipped the garden path. I caught a glimpse of shiny black wing-tip shoes and dark blue trousers.

I looked further up to Seiji Nakamura's face.

He paused, looking around. He obviously knew a maid was scheduled, because he'd left an envelope with cash payment in the entry hall. We'd taken it to avoid causing suspicion.

Another thought hit me—what if he had been hoping to rendezvous with the maid? Why else would he be out, driving around, during work hours? I remembered the lace teddy hanging in Setsuko's closet.

The footsteps came closer. I couldn't let myself be found. Equally nightmarish was the prospect of Hugh arriving. Nakamura had passed me without seeming to notice and was now creeping along the kitchen wall, looking in the windows. He was suspicious.

Escape would be now or never. I straightened up from my hiding position and started tiptoeing toward the garden gate.

Wind rushed against the garbage bags full of supplies that I was carrying, creating a crinkling sound. I picked up my pace, intent on getting off the property as fast as I could. I heard the scraping of Nakamura's steps on the cement path, coming back.

The humming sound of an engine approached. *Don't stop here*, I thought as I fumbled with the latch and at last pushed through to the alley.

"Who's that?" Seiji Nakamura's voice bellowed behind me as Hugh drove into the alley. I sprinted past Nakamura's Mercedes, counting on Hugh to keep driving at a slow pace, following and picking me up on the main road.

That didn't happen. Hugh put the Windom in reverse and backed up, smoothly sailing around the corner and vanishing to points unknown.

I kept running, moving like someone had poured

super-strength gas in my tank. I heard Mr. Nakamura yelling as I ran past a couple of gawking housewives. Initially, I was only afraid of being nabbed by Nakamura, but now I thought of the police.

I jerked a glance over my shoulder and did not see Nakamura; I slowed to a walk, gasping as much from terror as the exertion. My situation was bad. I was lost without money in a Japanese suburb several miles from a train station. I also had no idea how I'd find Hugh. The creamy houses that had looked so enticing the first time I'd entered the neighborhood now looked alternately mocking and menacing. I was out of my league, they seemed to tell me. I'd failed.

I'd walked all the way down the hill to the convenience store when the Windom pulled up.

"He saw me!" I fell into the car with the torn garbage bags I'd carried the whole way.

"Who? What? And why did you take off like a ninny just when I was arriving?"

"Nakamura! He came in that white Mercedes. I thought you saw it."

"That car was blocking the alley. I couldn't get through, so I reversed. I never thought—"

"He saw the back of me. Maybe he'll think the maid was shy. He'll certainly find his house clean," I added glumly.

"Right. We must not panic," Hugh said as if to convince himself while making a dangerous right in front of oncoming traffic. I screamed. He ran two red lights on the way out of town. I shut my eyes and didn't open them until he'd gotten on the toll road and set the cruise control to ninety-eight kilometers per hour.

"It was a set-up," I decided. "The maid must have told him we were coming. Or your secretary, Hikari."

Hugh shook his head, remaining silent. After a while I couldn't stand it and stretched my hand toward the radio dial.

"Do you mind?" Hugh barked, snapping J-WAVE off. He was obviously quite shaken. Well, he had more to lose than I did.

After fifteen minutes, he took his left hand off the steering wheel and closed it over my right. He was probably trying to apologize or needed some comfort. I squeezed his hand back and then made a move to release it. But he hung on, his fingers tracing my ring finger.

"What's this?" He took his eyes off the road for a moment.

"I got it for Christmas." It was a piece of modern sterling silver set with onyx and mother-of-pearl that my mother had sent me.

"Why didn't you wear it in Shiroyama?"

"I don't travel with valuables."

Hugh put his hand back on the wheel. I stared out the window, watching the evergreens and mountains slowly give way to gray forests of skyscrapers and factories. When the Shuto Expressway loomed, I started reading him the directions we had assembled before starting the trip.

"I'm fine from here, thanks," he snapped.

It was dark when we arrived back at Roppongi Hills, where the portico was filled by a mini-traffic jam of media vehicles. Hugh sped past and turned to enter the garage. But a young man waiting by the entrance swung a camera toward us while darting under the rising door. Hugh backed up with a horrible screech and shot down an alley.

"Drop me off near the train, will you? I'll get home on my own." The style in which he was driving was bound to lead to arrest, and I didn't want to be involved.

"What about me? I won't be able to go home for hours and I'm not in the mood to drink in Roppongi. There's nowhere I can go that people don't know my sorry foreign face." His desolation reminded me of the way he'd appeared on New Year's Day drinking by himself.

"You could try a really crummy neighborhood like mine," I suggested, expecting him to complain about its shabbiness.

"There's an idea. We could kill time by going through the telephone books." Hugh sounded thoughtful.

"That sounds like fun." I yawned, thinking of the huge task ahead.

"Darling, are you saying you'd rather do something else?"

"I'm not, and you're only conditionally invited," I warned.

"And what are these conditions?" There was laughter in his voice.

"First, you've got to start driving like a law-abiding man. And second, the only one who gets called darling is Richard, okay?"

23

As if anticipating good times to come, Richard's head poked out the apartment door as I helped Hugh upstairs. He held out his arm for my parka and, upon seeing the maid's uniform I was still wearing, yelped.

"Nothing like acting out one's fantasies, eh?"

"Where's Mariko?" I slipped off my shoes and motioned for Hugh to do the same.

"She left a note saying she had to hurry to work."

"Back to work! Do you believe it?" I asked.

"Well, she had plenty of time to go through the bathroom to take my Super Hard gel and your favorite MAC lipstick."

"Just great." Mariko hadn't done much to prove her innocence, but I still was going to worry about her. I slumped against a wall, knocking a kimono askew.

Hugh had moved in from the doorway and was evaluating the apartment. I followed his eyes over the brick-and-plank bookcases holding my art books and Richard's Japanese comics, my laundry drying near the heaters and finally, the rumpled futon I'd neglected to roll up in the morning.

"This reminds me of my younger brother's room," Hugh said, smiling. "Not the antiques, mind you, but the mess."

"It's all Rei," Richard said. "My section of the apartment begins beyond those doors. I don't suppose you'd want to see my adult video collection?"

I hadn't been so embarrassed in ages. I ran around, stuffing stray clothing into the closet while Richard showed Hugh around—a five-second tour, given the size of the place.

"Do you own a telephone?" Hugh asked cautiously.

"Of course. But no long distance!" Richard ordered.

"Just calling my answering machine, I promise." Hugh's shoulders were shaking with laughter as he started punching his number in. I frowned at Richard—I didn't like how swiftly he had appropriated Hugh—and pulled the photo album from one of the garbage bags. I settled down near the heater to look at it while Richard hung over my shoulder.

"Which one is Setsuko?"

"The pretty one on the left." A nine- or ten-year-old Setsuko stared out of the page at us in a navy blue sailor suit. A slightly older, stout girl stood with her in front of a small, crumbling house with a tiled roof, the kind that didn't get built much anymore.

"Is the plain Jane with her the sister?" Richard asked.

"Maybe." I squinted at the faded picture. "No.

It's got to be Kiki, Mariko's guardian." There was something hard about Kiki's mouth, even then, and I recognized her flat nose. Kiki was wearing her uniform as provocatively as she could given the circumstances, her skirt hitched up a bit, which only did the unfortunate thing of accenting her thick legs.

"Come on, it has to be Setsuko's sister," Richard insisted, flipping back through the album. "Even though they don't look exactly like each other, they're together in all these pictures." There they were, dressed in flowery kimonos for the children's coming-of-age holiday. I slowly paged through more pictures showing them in later childhood and adolescence. The last picture was most telling: teen-aged Setsuko and Kiki wearing tight mini-dresses, posing in a smoky nightclub with Japanese businessmen more than twice their age. So they had been hostesses together.

"What do we know about Mariko's mother?" Hugh hung up the telephone and joined us, stretching out on the floor so he could rest his ankle.

"Setsuko's sister Keiko died after giving birth to Mariko," I said. "That's what the aunt told me. I meant to research it at Yokosuka City Hall but haven't had the time yet."

"Mr. Ota did." Hugh sounded smug. "I just received a message saying there's no death record for Keiko Ozawa. He did locate a 1954 birth record for Keiko, and one showing Setsuko born in 1956. Keiko had the Japanese father and was listed as a legitimate, first-born daughter. Because Setsuko was illegitimate, her listing was something different—"

"*Onna*," I said. It was a blunt term for woman

that was rarely spoken. "This is completely different from what Mrs. Ozawa, the great aunt, said. She told me Setsuko was the older, legitimate one!"

"Not by any Japanese government records. Either Auntie was lying or we can be generous and say she might have Alzheimer's."

The heater had caused steam to condense on my window, and I rubbed a finger on the glass to see out into the street. And suddenly the truth was as clear as the neon sign flashing SAPPORO in stylized letters over the liquor store.

"If Setsuko was the younger sister, the American was *her* father. What Mariko told us was true," I said.

"And Kiki is Mariko's mother?" Richard quizzed me.

"Maybe not. Setsuko's autopsy showed she had a baby," I remembered. "Let's see, Mariko is twenty-four. If she was born in 1973, Setsuko would have been only seventeen. I can understand why she gave up her own daughter."

"To a sister just three years older?" Richard objected.

"But not as pretty. With fewer chances," I said.

"I think it's time for drinks at the Marimba, don't you? Drinks and conversation with Mariko and Kiki." Hugh looked at his watch.

"You'll need me there, because I'm the one Mariko's closest to," Richard offered.

Hugh stiffened, but I glared at him until he said, "Men do usually attend these places in groups."

"Naturally!" Richard was acting like he went to hostess bars on a regular basis.

"And they're dressed well because they've come from the office," Hugh challenged him.

"You want to be my fashion advisor?" Rambling about the merits of Hugo Boss versus Junko Shimada for Men, Richard led Hugh into his room.

I went into the bathroom where I had a fast shower, shaving my legs so fast I nicked both knees. Mindful of what Kiki had said about my looks last time, I wore Karen's black cocktail suit the way I had for dinner with Joe, a black bra underneath but no blouse and sheer black stockings. I fiddled around with my arsenal of Shiseido makeup samples and the one lipstick Mariko had left me.

"You look like an extremely bad deed," Hugh said when I emerged from the bathroom.

"I wore this to dinner at Trader Vic's and it was acceptable." I began searching around in my shoe boxes for the solitary pair of spike heels I owned.

"It's quite appropriate, but don't be surprised if someone asks you to sit on his lap."

"Mariko says that kind of thing usually goes on with foreigners. You are going to control yourself, aren't you?" I carefully slid the photo album into my backpack. It was not an evening bag, but at least it was black.

"I'll be better than Richard. It was hell trying to talk him out of his tongue and ear jewelry."

"Now you see what I have to live with."

"I like him, although when you showed him the photo album I wanted to strangle you." Hugh held his arm out for me to balance as I stepped into my highest heels. The three extra inches made me feel tough.

"He knows everything about Mariko. Like he said, they're close. That's why he should come with us."

"You must understand the more people we involve, the riskier things get. I can picture young Richard called to my burglary trial."

"He'd lie for you. He lies for me all the time," I assured him.

"But you're not supposed to lie in court!" Hugh protested.

"You and your honesty." I parroted back what he'd said derisively to me in the English Pub. This time, we both laughed.

Hugh handled the admissions at the door—a whopping 7,500 yen per person, which included a bottle of rail whiskey. As we handed our coats to a bouncer with a bruised-looking face, I muttered to Hugh that I hoped the European Union was paying. He nodded and put a finger to his lips.

The club was busier now than it had been the afternoon I'd visited before, almost every table filled. I was the only woman present who wasn't in the business. I had no illusions about why I'd been allowed in; the men with me were simply so dishy they couldn't be turned away.

"We want to see Mariko-san," Hugh said to Esmerelda, the Filipina in a burgundy lace slip dress who led us to a table with much swishing of the hips.

"There's no Mariko here," she said uneasily. "Do you mean Mimi-chan?"

"Yeah, yeah. The girls all have bar names," Richard said.

"What's wrong with me?" Esmerelda pouted.

"Absolutely nothing, darling," Hugh assured her. "It's just that the wee man fancies Mimi." He gestured toward Richard, who gave a brilliant smile.

"Ah, you want doubles. Double pay?" Esmerelda appraised Hugh's suit before looking deep into his eyes.

"No problem," Richard said as if he were the one holding the credit card.

"I think I see her," I said, gazing a few tables away at the back of a slender girl with a head of springy curls.

"She'll be glad we asked for her by name," Richard said. "It means a two thousand yen bonus."

A couple of salarymen who had followed us in took the next table. Country bumpkins, I guessed from their cheap suits and the way one of them whipped out a camera and trained it on his hostess's low neckline. Richard craned his head to see better, and I kicked him back into place.

Within minutes, Esmerelda brought Mariko. The two hostesses approached us arm-in-arm with big smiles. When Mariko was close enough to distinguish our faces, she swore and hustled back to where she'd come from.

"Mimi-chan . . ." Esmerelda's voice trailed off, and she slid into the banquette next to Hugh. "I think she's not feeling well. Cramps, or something."

Hugh winked at me and there was a blinding flash of light from somewhere. I shut my eyes fast.

"Let me pour for everyone." Esmerelda leaned so her dress fell away from her bosom. She brushed her fingers against Hugh's when handing him his drink, but filled my glass only halfway and set it down squarely on the table.

"How about some games?" Esmerelda whipped a deck of cards out of a tiny black handbag containing a wad of money and a Chanel compact.

"I'm good at games, how about you?" Hugh smiled at her.

"Is the Mama-san here tonight?" I interrupted.

"Yes, but if you're asking for a job, I'm sorry. Mama likes younger girls." Esmerelda began distributing the cards with a practiced hand. "What shall we play? Strip poker? For that we need a privacy booth."

"A private booth?" Richard sniffed. "I'm not shy, baby."

"I'm feeling nauseated. I'd better go to the bathroom." I swung my backpack over my shoulder and got up, unable to watch the two men I was closest to dissolve into a molten pool of testosterone. Hugh I could understand, but Richard?

"In the back." Esmerelda didn't look away from her conquests.

As I sauntered past the table where Mariko had rejoined her customers, one of them said something and gestured to me. I smiled, angling to join them. Mariko shook her head.

"Hey, I like your lipstick. Meet you in the ladies' room?" I said to her in English.

I never made it there. In the unlit hallway that sprung off from the main room, I was grabbed. I struggled briefly against the arm that cut in below the rib cage and knocked the wind out of me. *They'll never know what happened,* I thought as a large, sweaty hand clamped over my mouth and a knee shot into the back of my thigh.

24

My moan was absorbed by the attacker's hand, and I was propelled into a dark, overheated room that stank of fuel. I flashed back to my nightmare with the gas heater in Shiroyama and realized this time I might really die. Hugh and Richard would be consumed for at least an hour with the tantalizing Esmerelda.

A fluorescent light came on overhead, revealing I was with Mariko's Mama-san in the dressing room. A kerosene heater burned, smelly but not lethal.

"We have a lot to talk about, Keiko." I swayed a little as I took the stool in front of the mirror, the room's only seat, a power play she couldn't miss. I looked at her leaning against the door as if to revalidate her authority. Now I saw past the grape-colored velvet dress stretched too tightly around the abdomen and the unflattering feathered haircut to hard, cool eyes that were very much like Setsuko's.

"My name is Kiki." Her voice remained calm.

"Being a foreigner, Japanese is a little hard for you, maybe."

"Kiki is a nickname for a hostess who wants to disguise who she really is. And the blood that runs through me is Japanese and American, like your sister's."

"Setsuko wasn't my sister," Her eyes darted to the door. Who did she think might enter?

"I didn't say she was Setsuko, but I thank you for confirming it." I unzipped my backpack and pulled out the photo album, flipping to the picture of the two teen-aged girls in the arms of the businessmen.

"This was back in Yokosuka, wasn't it? In the nightclub that's now a bank."

As Keiko glanced at the picture, her expression changed. I let her take the album in her hands, go through the pages herself.

"I want to know why the daughter with pure blood wound up working in a bar while the *konketsu-jin* got the salaryman and house in the suburbs," I said, my fear starting to subside.

"There's nothing wrong with what I do. I pay my rent and taxes and employ twelve people—how many women in this country can say they do that?" Keiko pushed the album back at me.

"But you can't tell me the bar has been a good environment for Mariko. Where will she be in ten years? She has no security, must rely completely on men."

"Men rule the world, don't they?" Keiko stared at her sagging face in the mirror.

"Tell me about Mariko's father," I said, pushing my luck.

"He was an American soldier here on R&R." She spoke in a monotone. "When he went back to Vietnam, he stepped on a mine. Setsuko heard about it just before Mariko was born."

"Really?" If this was true, it would mean Mariko was more American than me—three-quarter's worth.

"Look here." Keiko took the album back and showed me a group shot I'd glanced at without much interest before. A young Setsuko sat cozily on the lap of a good-looking, light-skinned black man who looked around twenty, clearly military from the cropped hair and the dog tags he wore around his neck. I judged the time period to be the early 1970s based on her short, flared dress. I had the same reaction as I did to the picture of her with the Japanese businessmen—she was too young for this. Her open, excited expression reminded me of uniformed schoolgirls I saw giggling on the subway.

"Setsuko was stupid to get pregnant just as she was starting in the business. Stupider still to go ahead and have the baby, someone you could never pass off."

"Because she's half-black?"

"Yes. It's girls like her who fill the strip bars and soaplands—exotics, they're considered. She could never be hired at a high-class company. It was a miracle Setsuko even found her that bank job," Keiko said.

"Mariko might be okay in the United States. After all, her American grandfather has some money—"

"Forget about the American," she said tightly.

"You knew him when you were little. What was he like?"

"I remember a man who gave me chocolate. He was around for a few years and left. He married someone suitable, my mother told me." Keiko moved to the clothing rack and began fiddling with a cocktail dress.

"Surely you remember his name," I wheedled.

"Listen, I brought you back here to warn you that I've had enough. Tonight two customers asked to have you sent to them! I had to say you weren't my girl."

"If you give me the name of Setsuko's father, I won't ever come back."

She knew the name. It was clear from the way she paused before exhaling, her boozy breath hitting my face. "I've had enough! You and your friends finish the whiskey and get out."

"If I go, I want to be assured of Mariko's security. Did your *yakuza* friends—"

"Don't say that word. The walls have ears!"

"Okay, did *they* find who attacked her?" She did not answer me, so I asked, "What makes you think she'll be safe here?"

"I don't believe anyone was after Mariko in particular. Esmerelda was also mugged, but she kept her head and didn't run away to foreigners for shelter," Keiko blazed. "And I have a question for you—why do you even care? You have your own life."

"I'm fond of Mariko," I said. It was true, despite my nagging worries about her intentions. I liked her straightforward style and thought she deserved a better life. Maybe she could be steered into taking her bank job more seriously, or even a better career.

"That's American bullshit. People from your

country say they are in love after one night, I've heard it before."

"I do like her! We aren't soul mates, but we get along. I also know she's truly attached to my roommate Richard."

"Infatuated," Keiko spat. "It's older than the war but still goes on, the Japanese girl falling for the foreign man. He thinks she's a geisha to serve his every need, and she thinks he's stronger than her own people. You too. It's like that opera, what do they call it?"

"*Madame Butterfly*. What do you mean?"

"Why are you with Big Red instead of a Japanese man?"

Hugh and I weren't together, and the hard truth was most Japanese men were not interested in someone as mixed-up as I was.

"You want the foreign man, they want him all over Asia. My girls from Thailand and Philippines and Singapore are all the same. It's like one hundred years ago, still."

And with that, Keiko threw me out.

Hugh and Esmerelda were playing patty-cake when I limped back to the opposing banquette.

"How was the card game?" I took a small sip of whiskey and put it down. I preferred the Scotch version.

"I taught Esmerelda rummy and she won quite handily." Hugh raised an eyebrow at me.

"I'll bet. Where's Richard?"

"He went to chat up Mariko. Didn't you see him in back?"

Catching Esmerelda's eye, I said, "I was in the dressing room. I had a long talk with your Mama-san. She mentioned that you were recently attacked."

"What happened, Esmerelda? Tell me," Hugh entreated.

Esmerelda's face blossomed into radiance. "Oh, that is not a happy story! You should not hear—"

"On the contrary." Hugh slid an arm around her. "I want to know everything about you."

"I'd gone out to buy cigarettes." She paused. "I know you do not smoke, but I do. The life of a hostess is high stress."

"Talk about stress!" Richard rejoined us, and I made space for him beside me.

"Go on, sweetheart. What day was it?" Hugh toyed idly with Esmerelda's spaghetti strap.

"The Wednesday before New Year's Eve. At night it was very cold weather. I am not used to it, coming from Manila." Esmerelda shivered, which made me wonder why she hadn't worn a sweater over her skimpy silk dress. "I had just stepped outside when I felt someone grab me from behind. A pillowcase went over my head, two hands around my throat. And a voice. English."

"A British accent?" I asked, remembering that Hugh had been in Tokyo prior to the New Year.

"I do not know. She said it funny. Mary-ko. I said to her in English, no, no! I am Esmerelda! I threw out my purse with the alien worker's card on the ground. Then she kicked me so I fell. While I lay there I heard her pick it up. She kicked me again and told me to count to one hundred or she'd kill me. Then she left."

"Do you think it was a woman?" I asked carefully. Japanese people speaking English sometimes mixed up "she" and "he"; I didn't know whether the same was true for people from the Philippines.

"I cannot say for sure. The hands were rough, rough like a man, but the voice was maybe a woman. I am not sure. I just say it because . . ." she batted her eyes.

"Yes?" Richard breathed.

"When I was pulled against this person's body, I felt—" Esmerelda gave a coy smile and gestured to her breasts. "How do you call them politely in English?"

Hugh choked. I refused to look at him, but noted that Richard's eyes were sparkling.

"Breasts," I said in a no-nonsense voice. "What happened to the pillowcase?"

"I left it there." Esmerelda shrugged. "I think the garbage man removed it later."

I threw up my hands. "You lost important evidence."

"I could not return it! It would only cause questions."

"Where would you return it?" Hugh asked.

"A hotel," Esmerelda replied shyly.

"What makes you think of hotels?" His voice was casual.

"It was foreign size, big enough to go over my head and shoulders. And good white cotton, like they have at the New Otani. I once spent an afternoon there. So I know."

I thought of Joe Roncolotta and his familiarity with the hotel. He could have padded his chest to resemble a woman's, and his Southern accent could have confused someone not fluent in English. "What happened to your purse?" I asked.

"The person did not take it. I still have it here." She patted the expensive little bag.

As Hugh asked Esmerelda to describe the scene once more for him, I turned my attention on Richard.

"I tried to talk to Mariko in the back alley," Richard whispered. "I apologized for . . . some awkwardness that happened. Then the bouncer came out and told me to get going. Mariko had to beg him to let me back in the club."

"What do you mean, awkwardness that happened? Did you make Mariko leave the apartment?"

"That's not it." Richard looked nervously toward Hugh and Esmerelda, who were paying us no attention.

"I tell you everything!" I hissed in my roommate's ear.

"Okay." Richard sounded miserable. "When you were gone this afternoon, she tried to convert me."

"Oh, no!"

"She couldn't comprehend I wasn't interested, so she split."

Keiko passed our table, slapping the check in front of Hugh. "If you go now, you won't miss the last train."

"No worries. I drove." He looked up and smiled.

"Really? Is your car the black Windom I called the towing company about?" Keiko said in a mock-concerned voice.

"Will you give me your card?" Esmerelda looked forlorn as Hugh started counting out cash for the bill.

"With pleasure." Hugh handed her his card and a five thousand yen note. "Please keep Mariko safe. And yourself, of course."

"You shouldn't be so kind. It's really not necessary," she beamed, tucking the tip into her little bag.

"Oh, it's just a token of a Scot's gratitude. Remember, I'm not English." He laughed as if that were an old joke they shared.

"Not English," she repeated, as if trying to memorize that. "Come back soon!"

25

I pulled a parking ticket off the windshield and handed it to Hugh before getting behind the wheel.

"I promise I'll pay it. Sooner or later." He stuffed it in his jacket and slid into the passenger seat. Richard was curled up in the back with his feet against the window.

"Where do you want to go?" I was filled with a crazy energy.

"Let's drop off your roommate first, then decide." Hugh looked over the seat at Richard. "He's sleeping like a baby. Now can you tell me why I had to entertain that junior Joan Collins by myself?"

I told him about how Keiko had grabbed me and how I'd turned the tables on her enough to learn something about Mariko's parentage.

"So she's the violent type." Hugh clicked the door locks shut, as if there were some danger in the streets of brightly-lit Kabuki-cho. "She could have easily gone after Mariko and Esmerelda."

I thought that was unlikely since the young women worked for her and shared a quasi-mother-daughter relationship. I explained my doubts.

"If Keiko attacked Esmerelda while *calling* her by another woman's name, it would make her seem like an outsider who didn't know the bar," Hugh suggested.

"That's too convoluted." Hugh's comment had triggered a memory of my visit to JaBank, when Mariko had told me a young woman teller had been attacked by an unknown person. Three attacks at the two locales where Mariko worked; it seemed likely someone was looking for her. But why? "Maybe Keiko eliminated Setsuko and is trying to kill Mariko so she can make a claim on the American's estate," I said.

"Why would she want to kill them now as opposed to decades earlier? Where does my laptop battery come in?"

"Your battery's not important. But Keiko—I could tell from the way she was looking at old photographs of Setsuko, she was moved. No matter how many names she calls Setsuko, she still cares about her."

"Emotion runs high in family situations. Perhaps the sister who had to scrabble for a living envied the one who landed the salaryman and life in the suburbs. One day, it got to be too much."

"Why did Mr. Nakamura come to her bar twice? I didn't ask Keiko. I should have." I was in north Tokyo now, sailing through dark and lonely streets. In no time, I was in front of my apartment building.

Hugh reached back to shake Richard's shoulder. "Time to get up, laddie."

"What about Rei?" Richard mumbled.

"She's driving me home," Hugh said as if I'd already agreed.

"Do you have your key?" I worried. My roommate waved it at me and ambled sleepily toward the building.

"I'll only be a minute," I promised Hugh and jumped out, feeling strangely maternal toward my roommate.

The entry hall was dark. The cheapskate landlord had installed a light rigged on a timer, meaning that when we came in, we had only three minutes of illumination while traveling upstairs.

"Out like a light," Richard cackled, fumbling at the switch. I reached over him and clicked up and down a few times without success. The bulb must have burned out. There were only two other tenants in the building, and unfortunately neither of them had taken the initiative to replace the bulb. As always, I would do it the next morning.

I knew by heart the steps leading to the apartment and would have bounded upward were it not for the listless roommate I was helping along. It took forever to reach the last flight leading to our landing. Richard was giggling about the fact I was holding his hand.

Only five more steps to go. I resolutely put my foot forward and stepped into air.

I grabbed Richard tightly with one arm, and with the other sought the railing. I had no idea of what had happened to the staircase. I searched again and found that the step I'd been heading for had been knocked out. There was nothing above it either. I stretched out my hand and touched the rough, splintering edges around where the wooden stairs had been.

"Whassit, Rei? Hurry up, I've got to take a leak."

"Richard, the stairs are gone!"

The light bulb could not have died a natural death, just as the missing steps hadn't broken with age. The person who had done the damage had selected the stairs leading to where Richard and I lived. It would have been easy to do the job between the time we had left for the club and the other building residents hadn't yet returned from work.

The trap had been laid for me. I had been meant to fall. Even if I made it past the monstrous gap, I didn't know what was waiting on the landing. Another hole, or maybe the person who had chopped out the stairs.

"We're going downstairs," I whispered to Richard. "Let me lead."

We made it out faster than we'd gone up. As Richard stumbled to the curb and relieved himself in the moonlight, I told Hugh about the stairs.

"I'm going back in with a torch," he said immediately, pulling a flashlight out of the glove compartment.

"You're too weak! I practically had to carry you upstairs earlier this evening. And it's very dangerous."

"What's the alternative, then? The police?"

"I don't want them." The police would ask about our day's activities, and if they entered the apartment to look around, they'd notice Setsuko Nakamura's photo album lying prominently on the *kotatsu* table.

"What can we do with him?" Hugh gestured toward Richard, who had zipped himself up and was weaving toward us singing "It's a Shame About Ray."

"He can sleep at Simone's," I said, thinking fast. Two of her roommates were still on vacation in France, so there would be space for him on a futon. I called Simone on the car phone and she agreed, urging me to join them. I declined; I had other plans for myself.

As we drove south, Hugh tuned the radio to a night jazz program. Akiko Yano sang in her high, sweet voice about memories the color of the wind. Keiko's memories were much darker. Black enough, perhaps, to send me a swift, dangerous message.

I had laid the groundwork for my accident. On my first visit to Club Marimba, I'd given Mariko my card, which had my business and home addresses in both English and Japanese. She'd slipped it in her purse, which lay open on the dressing table when Keiko had walked in on us. Either the Mama-san had taken the card, or Mariko had given it to her.

We dropped off Richard at Simone's cramped but safe apartment in Ebisu and continued on to Roppongi, where I stared out the window at cross-cultural couples. Peroxide-blond hostesses were slipping into the flash cars of old, wealthy Japanese men; more natural-looking Japanese O.L.s walked hand-in-hand with ruddy-faced foreigners they'd probably met at work. I thought about what Keiko had said about warped relationships between foreigners and Japanese.

"I have a question for you." I kept my voice light. "Do you think of me as Japanese or American?"

"I don't know why you're worrying about things like this after the night we've had—you could have lost your life on those stairs—"

"You pointed out once that I had a problem defining myself. I wanted to hear what you thought. I'm curious," I added, feeling his eyes on me.

"Both," he said at last. "Turn here. I want to avoid Roppongi Crossing."

"It's impossible to be both!" I was irritated at his cop-out.

"What do you want me to say? That you have the face and figure of the woman in the Japanese art book, but a meaner streak than Tonya Harding? That despite your tea ceremony manners, you're absolutely undaunted by power? I heard about how you treated Piers Clancy." Hugh sighed, making me think they'd had an argument.

"He deserved it." I recognized where we were and proceeded slowly into the Roppongi Hills driveway, looking out for photographers. No one was visible except for a good-looking blond woman pulling shopping bags from the trunk of a Volvo. She hastened her step so we all reached the elevator at the same time. I was glad there was no staircase; I couldn't have handled one tonight, even with the lights on.

"Hallo, Hugh! I suppose you know those television people were waiting outside all afternoon and evening? I was thinking of making them all a cup of tea." To me, she said in an overly slow and loud voice, *"Konnichiwa."*

"Konbanwa," I replied, the teacher in me unable to resist correcting her *good day* to *evening.*

"Yes, yes. Four years here and I still can't keep it straight." Her throaty laugh matched her lean, tall figure and the black mink that stretched to her slim ankles. Faint lines around her hard blue eyes told me she was either a fanatic sun-worshipper or a few years older than Hugh.

"Rei, this is Winnie Clancy." Hugh was yawning twice as much as he had in the car. "You know her husband Piers."

"Ah so desu ka?" Is that so? I asked. But Winnie didn't seem interested in anyone but Hugh.

"Now that you're out of that tiresome prison, you can come to the black-and-white party benefiting the International School's swimming pool next weekend." Winnie placed her massive shopping bags on the elevator floor, cordoning me off into a corner. "If you buy a table of ten, that would cover the cost of the diving board. I've got a dinner partner for you already, a lovely girl from Wiltshire who's working with the cultural attaché . . ."

I smiled. It was interesting what people would say if they thought you didn't understand their language.

"Winnie, please." Hugh looked mortified.

"Oh, how impolite of me. You have a *guest* this evening." The door opened at her floor but Winnie leaned in the doorway, unwilling to depart. "After your little friend leaves, come by for a sherry."

"I'm exhausted. Better not." Hugh waved and pressed the CLOSE button.

"I don't know, Hugh. You seem to have a bizarre connection with older, married women." I lifted the back of my skirt to rub my thigh still sore from Keiko's blow.

"If it weren't for Winnie, I'm sure Piers would have left me to rot in Shiroyama." Hugh's eyes were focused straight ahead. I followed his gaze and realized he was watching my actions in the mirror. I took a while dropping the hem of my skirt and stepped off the elevator in front of him.

"Don't go before I take a look at your leg," he offered while turning the key in his door.

"Did I miss seeing the M.D. on your card?" I kicked off my shoes and descended on the sofa.

"I'm the king of sports injuries! My medicine chest has everything. Sticking plasters, hot packs, cold packs, anti-inflammatory tablets . . ."

"Good." I reached under my skirt and began tugging down my pantyhose.

"What do you think you're doing?" Hugh demanded.

"Wouldn't someone descended from the Pagans know? Help me here, I can't quite reach." I laid my legs across his, leaving him to pull the stockings down the rest of the way. He shook them out and folded them into a small square.

"You're so tidy you could get a job folding underwear at Mitsutan," I teased, savoring the feeling of his hands gliding up the back of my thighs. The horror of the staircase seem very far away.

"I forgot which leg it was." He appeared more flustered than I'd ever seen him, I realized with a rush of happiness.

"Should I turn over for you to look?"

"This game of yours, Rei, I can't be held responsible."

"It's not a game. You owe me." I leaned over and, very slowly, touched my lips against his. He held back for a second and then groaned, crushing me against him. By the time we broke, both our jackets were on the floor and he was regarding the safety pins cinching the waist of my skirt with a tender expression.

"I thought you would never let me near you again," he said.

"That's not what you said to me in the English Pub." It still hurt, remembering.

"I was trying to make it easier for you, more graceful." He kissed his way down my neck.

"And you say I'm the one with tea ceremony manners! Tell me, are we staying on this slippery leather sofa all night?"

"I don't expect you to come to my bedroom. There's no rush." Hugh sat back and looked at me.

"Why not? I was in there earlier today and it looks fine. You could move the rowing machine to a better place, but I liked the sumo wrestlers and your closet full of cashmere." I was already unbuttoning his shirt.

"Even if that's a back-handed compliment, I'll take it." His eyes locked with mine. "I'll take you."

True to his word, Hugh took a long time with me. It was after one o'clock when the last layers of clothing came off and we rolled across the sleigh bed. The next set of explorations seemed to last a century.

When Hugh finally entered me, he stopped midway and ran his finger across the wetness on my cheek. "Am I hurting you?" he whispered.

It wasn't pain I felt, just a startling rush of emotion. I pulled him closer, whispering that if he didn't start moving, I'd die. Had I known it would be like this? *Yes*, I thought as we began. There was no space between us anymore. With each stroke, I felt myself changing into something else, someone different.

"You're my obsession." The words choked out of Hugh as my body seemed to splinter off in a hundred different directions. I rode out the rest of his passion, soaring as his breath caught and he made a final great push.

Hugh curled his arms around me after he'd taken care of the condom. Both of us were breathing like we'd run for an hour.

"Was that the way you like it?" he murmured.

"I'd probably like it every way with you." Just thinking about what had happened made me press my legs together.

"Why is it you can be so honest about sex and dishonest about your other feelings, so brutal to me?" The voice was warm and teasing, but I stiffened.

"You're the brutal one, starting an argument when I'm lost in the most delicious afterglow."

"Afterglow?" His tongue lapped at the back of my neck. "Who says it's time for afters?"

"I thought men couldn't, so soon . . ." I reached down to find evidence to the contrary.

"Let's see what happens," he suggested, and we did.

We must have slept briefly toward morning. In the next minute, it seemed, J-WAVE's morning man was bellowing "London, eleven P.M. . . . Moscow, one A.M. . . . Tokyo, seven A.M. It's Tokyo today!"

Hugh kissed my shoulder and floated the sheet off my body.

"Wakey, wakey, darling. Time to get up."

"Why?" I moaned, covered my head with a down pillow.

"You're going to sub for Richard's class in two hours, and we can't miss breakfast."

"What are you, a morning person?" I lifted the pillow to squint at him.

He laughed. "It's a very good morning because we're going to change history, aren't we?"

"I can't tolerate lectures this early in the morning."

"In our past, whenever you've left my arms, we've had a terrible row. You're coming back to me tonight in a good mood, aren't you?"

"Who can predict the future?" I asked.

Easing out of bed wearing nothing but the bandage around his ankle, Hugh looked pretty divine. Rolling on my side to watch him, I smiled like the Cheshire cat.

"How about a shower? There's room for two."

He went into the bathroom, turned on the water, and began singing what vaguely sounded like the Eurythmics' "Obsession."

"I never knew a man without a job or future could be so cheerful," I chided, following him under the spray.

"I have a tremendous future: burglar, spy, or assassin . . . I can't imagine you've had the pleasure of shagging someone like me before?"

I hesitated just long enough to make him wonder. After all, I was from the USA, crime capital of the world. "I haven't." I wrapped my arms around him.

"Prosecution rests, then."

Our combined laughter splashed across the tiled room as if there were nothing to worry about at all.

As we ate breakfast, we kept looking at each other. Hugh was wearing a white terry cloth robe and I was in one of his Thomas Pink shirts, cuffs turned over twice. He had fiddled with the buttons down the front. "It shouldn't be too low because you're teaching salesmen, and I know what they're like. But open enough that it shows your lovely collarbone."

"I've never spent this much time worrying about what I wear to work. Do you do this every morning when you go off to Sendai?" I grumbled.

"Never. When I'm employed again, maybe you'll worry for me?" He smiled, handing me a cup of Darjeeling with the milk and sugar already mixed in.

I shrugged, thinking he needed no help in the clothes department. He could probably tell the skirt

I was wearing for work was a polyester-wool blend, and my evening shoes were from Washington Shoes' bargain section. It was a pretty odd combination, but there was no way I dared repeat the outfit I'd worn to work the previous day.

Breakfast was simple. Hugh fix himself a soggy English cereal called Weetabix, which I declined. He made me toast and went back to the *Asian Wall Street Journal*. As I sipped the pleasantly sweet tea, my eyes strayed to the robe falling slightly open around his thighs and I wished I were staying in. As it was, I spent a good half hour on the telephone talking to my landlord about the urgent repairs needed, and after that, explaining to poor hungover Richard why he couldn't go home yet.

"What's on your schedule today?" I asked when finally readying myself to leave.

"I'll start out with a massage at TAC and then have lunch with Mr. Ota. This afternoon, I'm going to see Setsuko's travel agent. Ota got the name and number, but I told him I wanted to go myself. I thought I'd try to work a little harder at integrating in the culture." He tied my belt and kissed me deeply, smelling of toothpaste and shaving cream. "Are you satisfied?"

"Temporarily," I said, tearing myself away before I was lost. I rode down in the elevator with two businessmen and shot through the lobby, my evening shoes clicking against the marble floor. I walked outside into blinding sun and half-tripped when I heard my name.

"Shimura-san, Shimura-san!"

I turned around like a fool into the face of two cameras.

"Aren't you a friend of the accused murderer Glendinning-san?"

"Are you hoping to become a hostess at Club Marimba?"

"Chigai-masu," I said. The expression translating as "it's different" was the polite way to deny something. But the questions kept coming and if I'd understood correctly, the last one was about whether I'd enjoyed a night in Glendinning's bed. I cast about desperately for escape and spotted a taxi, its passenger door already swung open in welcome.

I jumped in and locked both doors, ignoring the elderly salaryman with a cane who had been making painstaking progress toward the vehicle.

"Bakayaro!" The salaryman swore and waved his fist as the taxi drove off. But the driver was twinkling at me in the rearview mirror, and I realized that for the first time in Tokyo, I was behaving like I was somebody.

26

At Nichiyu, Mr. Katoh was waiting by my desk, anxious for an update on my health. I assured him that aspirin and sleep had brought me to a near-perfect recovery.

"Maybe you came back too early." My boss studied me with concern. "Your face is flushed and your mouth is swollen, perhaps you should take your temperature . . ."

In other words, my night showed. I hoped I would be strong enough to handle the salesmen, a particularly noxious all-male assortment of junior executives. We had a history of bad blood since last summer's company retreat, when the men had asked me to stand atop a table for a casual photograph. Before I realized what was going on, somebody had darted the camera under my skirt and snapped a picture. I'd reported it to Mr. Katoh as an incident of *seku hara*—sexual harassment—but all that happened was I received a mysterious extra two weeks' pay and Richard took over the salesmen's instruction.

At nine o'clock I strode into their classroom carrying the new espresso maker like armor before my body. According to Richard's plan, today's task was teaching all parts of the machine in English plus some fancy coffee talk in French and Italian. There was giggling at first, but I ignored it and got down to business, asking two students to role-play an encounter between customer and salesclerk.

"What is caffe rat-te?" Mr. Takeuchi asked his partner, Mr. So.

"Caffe rat-te is a delicious beverage made from milks and exsu-presso—"

"Espresso!" Mr. Nara, the know-it-all, shouted from the back row.

"Espresso," continued Mr. Takeuchi. "For added delicious taste, please try a sprinkle of cinnamon or nutmeg or cocoa."

"Beautifully said. Now, can Mr. So explain the perfect formula for caffe latte?"

"One half milks, one half *kohi*," said Mr. So.

"No, two parts milk, one part *kohi*," corrected Mr. Takeuchi.

"Mr. Takeuchi is right, but please remember we must not call it coffee or *kohi*. We need to use the Italian word espresso to show how special the product is." It wasn't my favorite machine. I'd burned my hand trying to steam milk with it two weeks ago. This wasn't the time or place for my opinions, though. The men ran through the lesson in a remarkably ordered format, leaving the last fifteen minutes free.

"Miss Shimura, please may we have conversation time?" Mr. So begged. I was surprised; usually, the students didn't like exercises where they couldn't crib from the book. I readily agreed.

"What shall we talk about today, then? Any suggestions from the floor?" I asked.

"Current event!" shouted Mr. Nara.

"Sure. What's in the news?" I'd seen only the *Asian Wall Street Journal* that morning and had no idea about anything beyond a brief surge in the U.S. dollar.

"Mr. Nara, did you watch television this morning?" Mr. So asked so stiffly I wondered if he had rehearsed.

"Why, yes! I watched *News to You*. There was some very interesting news on that program." Mr. Nara grinned and rubbed his hands together.

"So, what's up?" I asked, trying to teach a colloquialism but making half the class squirm with laughter.

"The program say Miss Shimura is friends with a *satsujin-han*."

"The word in English is murderer," I said, feeling cold.

"This murderer is a *gaijin* from Scotland. Scotland is a part of Great Britain, you know." Mr. Nara smirked, playing to his crowd.

"Selfridges," said someone from the back, mentioning our biggest British vendor.

"Does your murderer know about Selfridges?" Mr. So turned an innocent face toward me.

"It's interesting that you choose to call this person

a murderer," I replied. "In Japan, as in the United States, a person cannot be called a murderer unless he or she is convicted. And as you may have heard, Mr. Glendinning was questioned and released."

"Convicted?" Someone in the class asked for a translation.

"Miss Shimura, is he your boyfriend?" Mr. Nara advanced on my desk, crossing both physical and emotional boundaries.

Talking about personal life was so off-limits that when Mr. Katoh's wife was expecting a baby, nobody knew until the day after it happened. If pregnancy within the bonds of marriage was taboo, what was an affair between single people? I hesitated a moment too long before saying, "I'm not sure."

"No *commento*!" some wit said.

"This class is for conversation about you, not me." I turned my back and started to write on the blackboard. "Here's a conversation topic: quickly, I want everyone to tell me how they plan to attain their sales goals in a new and interesting way."

"But Miss Shimura, you are more new and interesting!" Mr. So whined.

How could a good thing turn bad so fast? I pushed Hugh to the back of my mind and willed myself to get through the rest of the class. When the electronic melody finally chimed, the answer came to me. Things had been bad all along. I'd just forgotten.

Strangely, Richard didn't come in to teach his evening class. He had left a message with the office that an emergency had arisen; I prayed he hadn't returned to the apartment and encountered some new menace. I wound up having to take his night students with mine, suffering double the questions and snickering.

After work, I stayed at my desk. Now that I'd been on television, I needed a disguise. I called Oi Beauty Salon. Mrs. Oi had seen the noon news and offered to send a wig by courier—her grandson, who she assured me was entirely trustworthy.

It was dark by the time the courier showed up. I transformed myself into Japanese Barbie and threw Richard's old raincoat over me and left Nichiyu through the service entrance.

At the apartment building, the light was working and the stairs had been repaired with brand new, tough-looking boards. I trod up carefully. Opening the apartment door was a little scary, but once I stepped inside I felt the rush of comfort that I always did upon arriving home.

Richard had evidently come and gone. A trail of water told me he must have run from bathroom to telephone fairly recently. I looked at the answering machine and saw eleven calls had come in.

The first message had been recorded at twelve-thirty and was from Hugh.

"Darling, Winnie told me you were on the morning and lunchtime news. If anyone calls, stay mellow and just refer them to Mr. Ota. And don't worry."

"Hello, Miss Shimura? This is Manami Tsureta." A confident woman's voice. "I am a reporter from the *Japan Times* working on a story about the Sendai murder. I would like a comment on your relationship with Hugh Glendinning. Please call me back."

I had previously been a fan of Ms. Tsureta's investigative journalism, but there was no way I wanted to be her fodder. I fast-forwarded through her number to the next call, which was from a man with a rasping, uncultured voice.

"This is Nao from *News to You*. We're doing a story called the murderer's mistresses and need you to respond to various charges. It's in your interest, I'm sure you'll agree."

"It's Karen. I see you're still wearing my Junko Shimada suit about town, huh? I liked the shot they got of you in the evening without a blouse underneath. I'd try it but with my size, I'd probably get arrested. What were you doing wearing stilettos to work this morning, though? Totally tacky!"

"It's Okuhara, from the Shiroyama Police. I need to speak to you again."

"This is Ishida, calling about your antique box. I have some news from the museum. Please call me very soon, if you have time."

"Hi, Rei, it's Joe Roncolotta. It's about noon on Wednesday. Listen, you had fabulous exposure on the news this morning. I want you to know that now would be the optimum time to open your antique shopping service. Call me, ya hear?"

"Rei, it's your mother. Where were you last weekend and why haven't you called me back? We'd like to know if you're alive."

"This is Wakajima from the *Yomiuri Shibum*. We're going to press with a story about Hugh

Glendinning and need your comment. I'll try you at your office."

"It's your lover again. I've finished up with Setsuko's travel agent . . . who told me something strange. When are you getting home from work, anyway? Call before you come over so I can draw the bath. And Richard, this message is not intended for you."

"Rei, this is your cousin Tom. An Englishman came to the hospital with a black eye and broken ankle. He may be a lunatic, I think. Anyway, he asked me to contact you—"

Tom's message was cut off. Richard must have intercepted at that point, and now I knew why he hadn't gone to work. I tore off my stockings and work clothes, slipping gym socks over my feet blistered from the pumps and sliding into jeans and the Love Cats Friendship T-shirt. I pulled my wig into a ponytail, grabbed my parka, and ran.

I found Richard at St. Luke's Emergency waiting room an hour later, Mariko at his side.

"If it wasn't for that hideous parka I wouldn't recognize you," he said, touching my artificial hair and wincing. "What do you think, Mariko?"

"I should have made you leave the bar last night because I knew the reporters were there. But I didn't. I screwed up," Mariko mumbled.

The scene came together. The salarymen flashing a camera around at the next table must have been a journalist team. They had probably followed Hugh and me from Club Marimba back to Roppongi Hills. Thank God the living room blinds had been drawn. Still, they nabbed me bright and early the next morning.

"Kiki was scared. She couldn't have you coming back upsetting things—" Mariko's voice broke.

"Keiko sent a couple of thugs to break Hugh's legs," Richard added. "Luckily, they just got the weak ankle."

A nurse at the main desk had put down her clipboard to stare at us. Perhaps I was so notorious from television that she could recognize me, wig and all. Then I heard someone next to her whisper "Shimura-sensei" and I realized my connection to the hospital heartthrob was the overriding interest.

"Is my cousin taking care of Mr. Glendinning?" I marched up to the desk and didn't bother with the usual conversational softeners.

"Not at the moment. Endo-sensei is looking after him now, but Shimura-sensei said to page him when you arrived."

"Will you?"

"We already have." She gave me a comforting look. I thanked her and shuffled back to Richard and Mariko.

"Have the attackers been caught?" I asked.

"Your cousin advised Hugh not to give a description or press charges, given that it was ya-san," Richard whispered.

"Brilliant. The one chance we had to get Keiko arrested and tied to Setsuko's murder is gone." I put my head in my hands.

"Why do you and Richard keep calling Kiki by the name Keiko?" Mariko interrupted, sounding cross. Richard and I exchanged glances.

"Because they're the same woman." I had no

time for soft words. I was furious with Mariko for leaving us and causing the resulting chaos.

"No. My mother was a gorgeous person, not a Mama-san!" Mariko shook her head so violently that one of her dreadlocks hit Richard in the mouth.

"You're right that she was gorgeous," Richard assured her. "You inherited that part."

Mariko looked skeptical. I took a deep breath and said, "Setsuko was your mother."

"That's not a funny joke, with my aunt dead and everything."

Feeling sorry about my earlier bluntness, I told her, "Setsuko was very young when you were born— just seventeen. Keiko offered to take care of you, and Setsuko never forgot you. Look at the way she stayed part of your life."

"But I don't look like her. I'm so dark . . ."

"You are beautiful," I said, and Richard put his arms around her.

"What about my father, then? That story about him going off to work in Australia . . ."

"We think he was an American war hero who died in Vietnam. We have a photograph, and perhaps a lawyer could help you trace his relatives . . ."

"I don't believe in tracing people who don't want you. And I don't believe this crap." A tear slid out of Mariko's eye, leaving a dark line. She broke out of Richard's hold and stumbled away, her small, black leather clad frame cutting a crooked path down the glossy gray hallway. A small black starling fallen from her nest, maybe forever.

"Go," I told Richard, and he did.

❊   ❊   ❊

Ten minutes later, Tom brought me back to see
Hugh, eliminating all rules about relatives-only with
a wave of his white-jacketed arm.

"Have the reporters arrived yet?" I whispered.

"No, and they won't be allowed inside. We'll protect him using every rule about patient confidentiality.
And I've alerted security about the possibility of, uh,
ya-san."

Hugh was resting on a gurney that looked a half-
foot too short. Tom brought me to the side and
drew a privacy curtain around, separating us from
the room at large. Together, we watched Hugh
breathing easily in sleep. He was nowhere near
death, it was clear, although his left leg was elevated
in a sling.

"He'll be here for at least a week," Tom said.

"For a broken ankle?" I was incredulous.

"It's the Japanese way," Tom shrugged. "Believe
me, one week is a modest estimate. I'll try to get him
out earlier, but he's probably safer relaxing here than
anywhere."

"He might still be indicted, so he needs time to pre-
pare with his lawyer. He doesn't have any time to relax!"
I was irritated by Tom's cheery bedside manner.

"Yes, he was complaining about that before
surgery. This is the guy who wanted you to translate
the autopsy, I suppose?"

When I nodded, my cousin's face turned into
something resembling Aunt Norie's when she was
unhappy with the quality of vegetables at the farmers

market. "So this is the man who was jailed in Shiroyama for a while, returned to Tokyo, and was seen with you in a filthy hostess bar?"

"You watch tabloid television?" I wouldn't have thought my brainy cousin had the time.

"My mother does." Tom scowled. "Don't worry, she won't call your father. Frankly, she's ashamed this kind of thing happened when she had responsibility for you."

"She doesn't have responsibility for me," I protested. "I've been living on my own in Tokyo ever since I arrived."

"That's the problem. As the man of our family, I want to ask you to move in with us for reasons of safety. They tried to break your friend's legs. He's a big man, very strong, and he fought back. Imagine what they could do to you. And your boy roommate, he is very small . . ."

Hugh stirred, and I came closer to the bed, put my hand over his. His grip was tight, although his green-gold gaze was unfocused.

"You're going to be fine, Hugh," I whispered. It was an effort to keep from swooping down on his lips.

"Do we know each other?" Hugh murmured.

"He's got three different drugs in him, Rei," Tom said. "It probably wasn't a good idea to have you see him."

"Rei," Hugh said, as if trying out the sound of the word. "*Reizōko*. It means fridge." I waited for more but my lover cut himself off with a giant yawn. Asleep again. I looked at Tom helplessly and let him lead me out.

27

Aunt Norie made no mention of how strange it was I'd come visiting at midnight. Showing me to the small bed crowded with stuffed animals in my absent cousin Chika's room, she was full of gentle suggestions: a simple dinner of miso soup, rice, and pickled vegetables, a soak in the bath afterward. She was impressed that I'd brought my own toiletries and nightgown. How perfect, what a nice visit it would be!

Not even my own mother treated me this lavishly, I thought while watching my aunt move rapidly around her small kitchen, serving the Zen diet to me and a larger meal to Tom. When I rolled into bed an hour later, Aunt Norie tucked plush bath towels around me for extra warmth, her own version of Smother love. She must be missing Chika, who was away at Kyoto University. I began wondering how long Aunt Norie expected to keep me.

❊   ❊   ❊

Tom didn't have to go to work until mid-afternoon, but rose early to jog and then eat breakfast with me. Aunt Norie grilled us each a small mackerel accompanied by more *miso* soup, rice, and *natto*, the pungent, fermented soybeans that Tom had adopted as the cornerstone of his new diet.

"I'm getting better, don't you think?" Tom pinched a corner of his waist, which I found ridiculous. Tom didn't need to be thin to get a wife or anything else he desired. When I told him what a big attraction he was at his workplace, he laughed.

"That's what I don't like—the word 'big'. Why not 'slim'? Dr. Tsutomu Shimura, slim attraction at Saint Luke's?"

Aunt Norie was smiling at our jokes as she brought in the morning paper. Then she looked at the front page and stopped.

"Don't worry. If it's Japanese, I can't read much," I reassured her.

"Give it to me, please. Rei should know what's being said about her," Tom said. He translated two stories. The first was an interview with Captain Okuhara about the lack of progress in the ongoing murder investigation. The shorter feature was all about me, illustrated with a sketch my ex-boyfriend Shin Hatsuda had drawn about a year ago. Wearing a half-open *yukata* and combing my short, wet hair, this image of me was blatantly inspired by a wood-block print by the early twentieth-century illustrator Hashiguchi Goyō. I wondered if the paper had paid Shin for the picture or the mean-spirited comments about how I had been a nice girl at first but turned out to be extremely bossy.

"Can we watch the news?" I picked up the TV remote control.

"Do as you like!" Aunt Norie was hanging out laundry on the sun porch and beat each piece extra-vigorously as if to show her disapproval. The frown on her face deepened as *News to You* opened with sinister, drum-heavy pop music.

Mr. Nanda, the man who had left a message on my answering machine, reported that Rei Shimura, a Nichiyu Kitchenware employee, would likely be a witness for the defense should Glendinning be arrested again. Over footage of me looking horribly panicked outside Roppongi Hills, the reporter went on to say that the Japanese-American party girl had enjoyed drinks with Hugh and another foreign man at Club Marimba two nights ago.

On the public television channel, a more serious story described the apparent disappearance of Hugh Glendinning about which Tokyo police refused to comment.

"The police know he's at Saint Luke's. I called them," Tom said.

"How kind of you." I rolled my eyes.

"I had to! It's dangerous to have such a patient. In fact"—he looked suddenly inspired—"Rei, if you're going to be some kind of witness, maybe you can receive twenty-four-hour police protection for yourself."

"I'm very safe now that I'm in the public eye. With cameras following me, who would possibly have a chance to harm me?"

"I think the best thing is to stay home with my

mother. No gangster would look for you in a suburban family home."

"I've got to get back to the hospital and
Nichiyu." My shock had passed, and I was finding the
suburbs less than charming. At five in the morning
I'd been awakened by screaming blackbirds, a sound
more frightening than anything I'd ever heard in
north Tokyo.

"Teaching should be the last thing on your mind,
and if your employer has any compassion, he will
understand your need for a leave of absence," Tom
insisted. My cousin, protected in his medical ivory
tower, knew very little about the contract worker's
life. A leave of absence for me would mean a loss of
salary. I wouldn't be able to keep up my share of the
apartment, and Richard would find a new roommate.

My worries multiplied as I picked up an assortment of English language dailies at the train station.
The *Japan Times* ran a photograph of me taken at a
Nichiyu holiday party with a beer in hand. Courtesy
of some student, no doubt. I prayed the panties picture wouldn't make it into print. The *Japan Times*
journalist described me as refusing to comment,
which made me look really guilty. I would have stayed
away from Roppongi Hills if I knew I would have to
do anything with Hugh's defense. Why hadn't Hugh
thought about that? Then the ugly thought came to
me that perhaps he had slept with me expressly for
that reason— because, once firmly in hand, the little
English teacher from Nichiyu would surely say and do
whatever he wanted.

When I walked into orthopedics, the chip on my

shoulder had grown as large as Ueno Park. I pushed aside the curtain that guarded the entry to Hugh's room, inspecting a large arrangement of white roses with a card that said "Love from Winnie and Piers" and yellow tulips from Hikari Yasui before reaching Hugh, who lay shielded by the *Japan Times.*

"I'm not ready yet, Nurse," he muttered. When I pulled the newspaper away, he brightened. "Rei! I thought you were one of them, forcing bed pans on me every quarter of an hour. This is the most humiliating experience of my life."

"Wasn't prison worse?" I didn't return the charming, lopsided smile he gave me.

"Close the curtain, will you?" He patted the edge of the bed for me to sit down. I did, leaning assiduously away from his outstretched arms. He sighed and said, "I see you're living up to the terms of our agreement."

"What's that?"

"My punishment. It happens to me every time we start to get close. I find it rather tiresome, especially at a time like this."

"I don't hate you," I whispered, conscious of the open door. "I just had a rather rude surprise on television and in the newspapers this morning. Something about me being called as a witness for your defense."

"Wouldn't you testify for me?"

"No! Not when all of Tokyo knows I left your apartment at eight-fifteen in the morning. I look like your mistress, not an objective observer."

"I see." Hugh paused. "I know it's rotten for your image to be wrapped up with mine. That's a good part of why I tried to hold myself off you for so long."

"It would have been nice if you had asked me whether I'd be willing to testify."

"Darling, that's not the way lawyers work. They don't ask, they subpoena. And if I had asked and you'd agreed, the prosecutor would have asked all about what we'd concocted together. It was the best thing, really."

He was bluffing. Searching the Nakamura house and spending the night together had compromised my credibility beyond repair. We both knew it.

"We're not going to talk about defense or trials at all. Starting now, for your good and mine." Hugh flashed me the look that had led to my last meltdown. "I have enough on my mind with the bastards who beat me up."

"That attack was my fault. I am so sorry I provoked Keiko—"

Hugh flicked my apology away. "Actually, it could serve me rather well. If I have to show up in court in a wheelchair, Mr. Ota has a powerful visual argument that evil forces are trying to hush up the truth about Setsuko's death."

"But we still aren't sure Keiko was behind Setsuko's death. Mariko said she was in Tokyo on New Year's Eve, too far from Shiroyama to do anything," I reminded him.

"The gangsters could have followed Setsuko's car north to Shiroyama, just as they followed me yesterday. I saw their Cadillac near my building and then outside the travel agency when I stopped to make that call to you. They jumped me after I left the phone booth."

"If you collapsed so publicly, why is it that nobody knows you went to the hospital? The press aren't here and there's nothing about it in the papers or on TV."

"Everyone scattered before the police pulled up. Nobody wanted to be a witness."

"I'd tell about what happened between Keiko and me." I put my hand over his. "You know I'll defend you."

"We won't talk about it." Hugh squeezed my hand. "Anyway, I was glad I had the sense to say I hadn't seen the guys' faces. Your cousin—rather a helpful guy, that Tom—confirmed that. He's also told me all kinds of startling things about you, things I'd never have guessed."

"Like what?" I felt my stomach lurch, and I started worrying whether Tom had described just how ungainly I was at fifteen.

"That your poverty is self-chosen. Your father's a psychiatry chief or some such thing in the States—"

"Does that make me more appealing to you?" I froze.

"It makes me think that there's absolutely no reason for you to be camping out in that wretched neighborhood."

"At the moment, I'm staying with Tom and my Aunt Norie."

"Why don't you sleep in my flat? The building has doormen and a concierge and loads of police, now that I'm so notorious. In a hurricane, the safest place is in the eye of the storm."

"You haven't met my aunt Norie, a most formidable guardian." I smiled, remembering how she hadn't allowed me to leave without a freshly ironed handkerchief and nutritious box lunch.

"I worry she might guard you from me." Hugh pulled me close and began toying with the buttons on my blouse. I pried his hands off as the curtain slid open and a young nurse holding a bedpan gasped.

"Let me give you some time to yourself." I jumped up to leave.

"I've nothing to give you." Hugh shook his head at the nurse.

"Shampoo and shave, sir?" She sounded anxious to serve him in any possible way.

"Mm, maybe." He rubbed a hand across his stubbly jaw.

It was a good time to go. I placed two video-cassettes I'd picked up on the way to the hospital between the flower arrangements.

"What are you leaving me, one of Richard's sexy videos?"

"Sorry. I brought Akira Kurosawa's *Seven Samurai* and *Yojimbo*." I explained about Japan's founding father of film, adding, "These are a couple of black-and-white classics about the samurai era, and they've even got subtitles! So you can work on your Japanese."

"I'd rather work on you." His voice sent a suggestion through my body that I didn't need to hear, not with nurses bouncing into the room like balls in a pachinko machine.

"I'll be back tomorrow. Can I bring you anything?"

"How about my mail, my laptop, and all the Nakamura discs? The concierge will let you in." His face brightened. "Wait. Get Yamamoto's copy of the key."

"My life's complicated enough," I protested.

"We haven't seen sight nor sound of him since he went home. Why don't you corner him and ask some of your infamous questions? If your work with Keiko was any indicator, you'll probably get something worthwhile out of him."

Perhaps I'd get someone else's legs broken. I took the telephone number and waved good-bye from the door, afraid to get near again.

28

Kenji Yamamoto lived with his parents in Sunshine Mansions, a white-tiled apartment tower surrounded by a sea of shining parked cars in the upper-middle-class suburb of Setagaya. I had telephoned ahead of time and convinced his mother to let me speak to him. When I arrived, he popped his head out the door before I even had time to ring the bell. He had Hugh's key in hand and was stretching it out to me. Things were going too fast.

"Here you go—see you later, Miss Shimura—"

"It's so good to come in from the cold!" I exclaimed, starting to take off my coat and smoothing down my silky wig. Yamamoto's mother, who had been standing behind her son, moved as if programmed to take my coat and hang it in a faux French armoire.

"Please come in, Shimura-san. My son tells me you met on holiday, before his terrible accident," Mrs. Yamamoto gushed.

"So desu neh," I agreed. "Isn't this a nice apartment!"

"Oh, it's terribly small." She waved a dismissive hand around the living room, its fussy set of matched green velvet furniture and walls were covered with framed vistas of European landscapes.

"Are these all originals? They're enchanting." I stepped close enough to discern two were paint-by-the-numbers.

"We bought them on last year's holiday to Europe," Mrs. Yamamoto said. "My husband's and my lifelong dream was to see Venice. So many talented artists on the street, selling their work for very little! I said to my husband, you never know who will be the next Da Vinci!"

"Very true. How I love the Italian painters!" I settled myself on the end of a small sofa and coughed into my hand. "Oh, excuse me. My throat is a little dry from the cold winds outside."

"I will make tea!" Mrs. Yamamoto announced.

"Please don't go to the trouble," I demurred, playing my part to perfection.

"Kenji-kun, it was terrible of you not to tell me your nice friend was coming. Now, I will just be a few moments—enjoy visiting together—" As Mrs. Yamamoto floated off to the kitchen, I realized she might be harboring hopes for her bachelor son.

I smiled cozily at Yamamoto and patted the seat next to me.

"May I call you Kenji-kun?" It literally meant "Kenji-boy."

"Okay." He didn't look happy as he sat down with me.

"What have you told your mother?" I asked in English.

"She thinks I had a ski accident and some kind of nervous problem where I cannot work. Hugh-san helped me figure it out," he whispered back.

"What's the latest from the police?"

"The National Police Agency is conducting a covert investigation. I'm sure nothing will come of it." He leaned forward to pick up the television's remote control from the rosewood coffee table.

I grabbed the remote away. "How do you know that?"

"Ichiro Fukujima has many friends in high places."

"Are you sure you aren't jumping to conclusions about this blackmail thing?" I asked. "Could Mr. Nakamura have needed the design for another purpose?"

"No! Nakamura is a horrible person, and only I see it!"

"That's not true." I would have gone on, but Mrs. Yamamoto came in bearing green tea. I accepted an earthenware cup, not taking a sip until her son had.

"You must speak as much as possible to my son, to help retrieve his memory. The doctors believe it will come back, given time," she said. From the way she was smiling at me, it was obvious she hadn't connected me to the girl in the newspapers.

"What doctors?" I asked Yamamoto when his mother had departed.

"The police arranged something." He shrugged.

"Everyone arranges things for you, don't they?" I

decided he was the most passive young man I'd met. "How did your problem with Nakamura start, anyway?"

"I don't know. Maybe when our section had after-work drinking."

"How often did you have to go?" At Nichiyu, it was the custom for workers to spend time drinking with colleagues at least twice weekly. Things that couldn't be said within the confines of the office were expressed here, often with a great deal of vulgarity. Drinking myself under the table with people who already bore some hostility toward me wasn't my idea of fun, so I declined all but the holiday affairs.

"In Mr. Nakamura's section, we went about three times a week." Yamamoto paused. "The problem is that alcohol makes me sick. I get dizzy and can't control my breathing. So I always pretended to be drunk, hoping people wouldn't give me more."

"And Mr. Nakamura noticed?" Now I remembered Yamamoto's untouched whiskey at Hugh's and how he'd hardly drunk any beer on New Year's Eve.

"Unfortunately. One time he saw me pouring Scotch into a potted plant behind the table and told me I was a baby." Yamamoto stared at me morosely.

"You should have ignored him."

"You don't understand." Yamamoto's voice rose. "He thought I wasn't part of the team and was starting to tell people. He would insult me in front of Mr. Sendai, saying I was more interested in myself than the company. So when I went to Nakamura's desk, I was searching for my employment file. I was very worried."

"And you found it?"

"Yes. It said that I was lazy, morally lax, at the bottom of my class . . ."

"He is horrible," I agreed. "But what happens to you now? Surely it's stupid to throw away a job thousands of young people would die for." I stopped, aware of my bad choice of words.

"I can't go back to Sendai unless Mr. Nakamura leaves. I don't like the atmosphere he creates. Drinking at lunchtime, or going out at five for a few hours' pleasure in Kabuki-cho . . ."

I recalled the black teddy in his bedroom closet and decided to ask Yamamoto if he thought Nakamura had been seeing a prostitute.

"Who knows? Guys like him go after office ladies, too."

"He's a pervert, all right," I agreed. "He really seemed to enjoy telling me about the man who touched me on the train."

"Maybe now I should apologize." Yamamoto sighed heavily.

"Huh?" He must have misunderstood my English.

"I had no idea how you'd react. I've been sick about doing it since New Year's Eve."

"Doing what?" I still couldn't follow.

"I went to the temple and prayed for forgiveness. Please do not tell Hugh. Just let me go on—"

As Yamamoto carried on, the truth finally hit me like a sack of nonburnable garbage. He had been on the same train as me New Year's Eve. I recalled the figures I'd seen in the window's reflection, including that of the young salaryman half-obscured by a newspaper. It had to have been him, moving his hand underneath the pages.

"You're sick," I whispered. He was young, educated, good-looking. He could date a nice-looking girl like Hikari Yasui if he wanted.

"I would never have done it if I knew you were a foreigner." Yamamoto's face flushed red, and he wouldn't meet my eyes.

"It was okay because you thought I was Japanese?" Each apology outraged me a little more.

"Look, a lot of guys do it," he said defiantly. "Some women don't mind. And I know you like to be touched. I've heard with my own ears."

Hugh would go crazy if he knew what his assistant had done, but Kenji Yamamoto needed to learn that women could fight their own battles. I gave the young salaryman a forgiving smile as I refilled my cup with lukewarm green tea, not bothering to strain it. His mother was walking in when I threw it in his face.

Before going to work, I removed the long-haired wig I'd been wearing so the security guard at Nichiyu would recognize me. I shouldn't have worried. Employees who'd never shown the slightest interest deluged me with greetings. I made my way into the language-teaching section and nervously waited Mr. Katoh.

"It's all very simple, really," I said, jumping to my feet when he came through the door. "Sometimes one gets caught up in circumstances beyond one's control—in this case, a death. I apologize for leaving early the other day, and you probably have heard I may need time to testify in court. For the trouble I've caused you and the company, I am so very sorry." I ended it all with a bow deep enough to contemplate that my navy flats really needed a polish.

"I appreciate your courtesy, Miss Shimura." Mr. Katoh looked unnaturally calm as he ushered me into the small conference room and closed the door. "I have good news for you."

"To be forgiven is enough," I stammered.

"You can get away from all your troubles in Osaka. Dormitory accommodation will be assured at no cost to you. You can go next week!"

"Osaka?" I repeated dumbly.

"Remember, we talked about it. They need you there, and will not know much about your reputation . . ."

"Mr. Katoh, I said I wanted to think about it." I stared at the buffed surface of the teak table where he, Richard, and I had spent many long hours going over student progress reports.

"I see." From his dour expression, I could tell he didn't. "Miss Shimura, if you wish to remain with Nichiyu . . ."

Spell it out, I wanted to say. Although part of me knew that if he were any more blunt, I'd be faced with no other option than giving my notice.

"I tried very hard to lobby for you," he continued. "At the emergency public relations meeting, I spoke against the wisdom of several other executives because of my gratitude for your steadfast service. Our sales force knows more English, can speak in the conversational style, even."

"Please don't say any more," I begged. "My class starts in five minutes and I must not be late."

"Don't you understand this is already decided?" His smile was completely gone.

Without answering, I bolted.

I taught in a sort of vacuum that afternoon, shocked enough over Osaka that the undercurrents of my students' curiosity didn't hurt me anymore. I corrected grammar and syntax to the most minute levels, wanting no time left over for free conversation or for their thoughts. My own were trouble enough.

I collared Richard in the employee lounge at eight. When I told him about my transfer, he didn't look surprised.

"They asked me if I wanted to transfer, but I said no thanks. I'd shrivel up and die if I had to sleep in a dorm with a curfew. I should have figured they'd force you."

"Well, I'm not going to do it," I said. "I'm saying no tomorrow, and if that means I'm fired, so be it. I'll find something else."

"You could live with Hugh."

"Without his job at Sendai, he'll be out of the glamour-pad soon enough." I made a face at Richard. "I'm coming home. I think it's safe. You've been there for days and the only thing that's died, probably, is my ficus plant."

"Actually, I'm sleeping in your room now." He folded his arms across his chest. "We'll have to share it."

"What?"

"It's a necessity. I talked Mariko into coming back but she demanded her own room. Besides, I always liked your room better."

"For its view of the sandal factory?" I asked, unbelieving.

"Look, you're hardly around anymore. You're driving me crazy with your indecision. And your phone calls! The people you blew off keep calling back."

Reluctantly, I took the scrawled list he handed me. I still wasn't ready to speak with reporters, nor my mother. I did call Joe Roncolotta. When he picked up, I was distracted by a hollow, banging sound on the line. I asked whether construction was going on, and Joe chuckled.

"I'm applauding you, doll, over the speaker-phone. You are becoming the most notorious young woman since Rie Miyazawa—come to think of it, your names are mighty similar—"

"If you're trying to flatter me, she's not the one." Rie Miyazawa was an actress/model who had once been the toast of Tokyo for her starring role in a book of artistic nude photos. Now she allegedly battled anorexia and declining public opinion.

"Oh, everybody knows you're really a nice little English teacher. In fact, one of my friends wants you to leave Nichiyu and open a new language school for him."

"I hope you told him I wasn't interested." I never wanted to teach again.

"Yeah, I did. I've already started managing you."

"Managing me?" I was incredulous. "I'm trying to keep a low profile, Joe. I'm wearing a wig and hiding out with my relatives because the *yakuza* put Hugh in the hospital—"

"Don't say that word on the telephone," he snapped.

"Where were you the Wednesday evening before New Year's Eve, by the way?" I asked.

"Don't tell me someone else got murdered?" he asked sarcastically.

"Assaulted. At Club Marimba."

"Check my alibi with my secretary, hon, and can you keep safe until Friday night? I've got someone meeting me at TAC with information that may relate to your situation. It's the black-and-white party. Meet me there at eight."

"Should I pick up Mrs. Chapman on the way?"

"This should be just us. Given that the information's confidential."

"Okay," I said, thinking it over.

"Plan on a long night and wear your slinkiest black or white dress. And leave the wig at home. I want Rei Shimura to appear as herself."

"I'm moving back to my apartment tomorrow," I told Aunt Norie as I fiddled with the oysters she had sautéed for dinner. She had been upset I'd traveled home without Tom, who was still at the hospital.

"Rei-chan, you aren't thinking clearly about this." She pushed a small saucer filled with my favorite pickled plums toward me.

"I can't stay here forever. It's not fair to you," I popped a shriveled plum in my mouth, thinking its sour-sweet taste was like saying good-bye.

"You are my husband's brother's child. If anything happens to you—it's bad enough, the news about you—"

"Was I on TV again?"

"Not you, but Glendinning-san was. The TBS network reported he is in the hospital with injuries from the *ya-san*. Now everyone knows!"

"That's good. The *yakuza* are smart enough to know not to attack in front of a dozen camera crews. Haven't you heard the safest place is in the eye of the hurricane?" I appropriated Hugh's words for my own purpose.

"You received a telephone call today from a police chief. Long distance." She pursed her lips, and I kept chewing. I'd never liked the flavor of oysters, nor the watery stuff in the middle. "Aren't you going to call Captain Okuhara?" She went into the living room and came back with the cordless telephone.

"I'd rather enjoy my dinner first."

"It's urgent, he advised." Aunt Norie slapped the phone in front of me.

I pushed my plate aside and began dialing the number she had written on a Hello Kitty notepad. It took three minutes to get transferred to Okuhara. By the time he came on, I was very tense.

"Miss Shimura! How surprising that you have a real Japanese family! Now it is so easy and pleasant to leave messages for you."

"I'm sorry I couldn't get back to you earlier," I said. "The circumstances I've been going through have been difficult."

"No trouble at all, although we have some questions for you, things that need to be followed up."

"Go ahead." I was starting to sweat.

"No, we'd rather see you in person. In Shiroyama."

My chopsticks clattered on the table.

"We can arrange police transportation, or you can travel here on your own. It's up to you, Miss Shimura." Captain Okuhara's disingenuous courtesy flowed over me like a chill rain.

"It's not a good time for me. The problem is I have a teaching career here, and Shiroyama is very far." If I showed up, they could incarcerate me immediately, just as they'd done with Hugh.

"But I'm very interested to learn what you were doing at the Nakamura house on Tuesday!"

Only Kenji Yamamoto could have told. I thought briefly about my open ticket back to San Francisco. No, I had to stay calm.

"Of course I'll come. Just let me ask my boss."

"We want to see you tomorrow."

"I'm teaching. I must fulfill my commitment before I can come. I'll be there this weekend, most definitely." I could bring him the disc with the marketing plan for Taipei and whatever Joe Roncolotta had to offer me Friday night.

He was silent for a while, then spoke. "No evasion, Miss Shimura. No tricks. They'll be watching for you at the airport."

"They'll be very bored." I hung up before he could make me commit to anything more. Then, ignoring Aunt Norie's exclamations, I went in the bathroom and threw up.

29

The next morning, I zipped over to Roppongi Hills before eight to get Hugh's laptop. I decided to brazen my way past the front desk without saying anything.

"Shimura-sama?" The concierge's language was as polite as possible, his bow very deep. "In order that you don't suffer any trouble, you should know that TBS television usually arrives in the next fifteen minutes for their stakeout. The side exit may be more convenient."

Hurrying down the hall toward Hugh's apartment, I wondered at the strangeness of the incident, how the man had known me and where I was headed. *Big Brother*, I thought as I picked up a small stack of newspapers and letters that had piled up outside Hugh's door. There was a smell to the place that I had forgotten, a mixture of leather furniture, pine-scented cleaner, and something indefinable. A gray wool sweater was tossed across the couch along with one of the American phone books. I could picture him lying there, plodding through it.

The small Nichiyu water heater on the kitchen counter was still plugged in, so I hit the re-boil button and brewed myself a cup of Darjeeling. Searching for milk in the fridge, I found a bottle of Cristal champagne and a basket of perfect hothouse strawberries. He had obviously been planning something delicious.

I drank the tea as I went into the study and collected the laptop. There were too many discs to fit in the laptop's padded case, so I put them in an empty Paul Smith shopping bag I found in the bedroom closet. In the kitchen, I put my cup in the dishwasher and although it was only half-full, started it.

The Japanese word for nostalgia, *natsukashii*, is touched with more sadness than joy. This kind of melancholy swept over me now. I knew suddenly that Hugh might never come home to pull on his sweater or drink a cup of tea or make love to me again, given what Okuhara had learned about our break-in at the Nakamura house.

I heard myself making a gasping noise I barely recognized as crying, I hadn't done it for so long. I sat at the kitchen table with Hugh's *Asian Wall Street Journal* still open and cried a river that could have floated me back to Shiroyama. I understood now why I should have run from Hugh: because the problem with caring about someone was the pain it brought, the possibility of loss.

Somewhere, the phone was ringing. I went to the living room and grabbed the cordless off the glass table before realizing how rashly I was behaving. If the reporter from *News to You* was on the other end, he'd have a nice tape to air of a blubbering mistress.

"Who's there?" Hugh asked. "Rei, is that you?"

"How did you know?" I let out a sob of relief.

"Well, I was actually calling in to check my messages. If you had let the telephone go on ringing, the machine would have picked up."

"I'll hang up if you want."

"No, no. So you moved in! But why are you crying?"

"I have a cold, damn it, and I didn't move in, I'm just here picking up your laptop. I'll have to bring it to you this afternoon—gosh, I've got to go now—"

"All right, then. Come as soon as you can and will you bring me some take-away? The hospital food is killing me. I complained to Mr. Ota about it, but he just brings me Japanese noodles."

Talking about telephones made me recall my own answering machine messages.

"What happened at Setsuko's travel agent?" I asked. "You were going to tell me something important before you were attacked."

"Oh, that. It turned out the agent spoke very little English, so she handed over the folder to me with all the receipts. Setsuko paid for our rooms in advance using the Sendai credit card."

"More fuel against Mr. Nakamura?"

"That's not the point. I found something very interesting: a receipt for an unrestricted, one-way ticket to Dallas for use in the new year. A thousand dollar ticket issued in her maiden name and paid for in cash I assume she received from me."

"Really!"

"I'm thinking that she obviously knew something disastrous was going down with her husband and the *yakuza* and the Eterna battery and wanted to get out."

"Or she wanted to see her father," I said.

"Possibly," Hugh said grudgingly. "But there could be other men, too."

Could there have been another man in Setsuko's life? She had been young and beautiful, with a handbag full of cash. She had more opportunities than most women, including myself.

After hanging up, I moped around Hugh's apartment for ten more minutes. I added the strawberries to the things I was bringing him and lumbered out the side entrance. On Roppongi Dori, the marquee of Mrs. Chapman's hotel loomed bright and welcoming. Perhaps I could find an hour's solace within. My work schedule wasn't really as pressing as I'd told Hugh.

"Rei, let me turn off the exercise video, and I'll be right down!" Over the house telephone, Mrs. Chapman greeted my surprise visit with delight. Minutes later, she stepped off the elevator in a turquoise velour jogging suit I'd seen at Mitsutan. Maybe she and Joe worked out together. How wonderful it would be to have a boyfriend with use of both legs.

"Honey, you're crying!" Her arms went around me like comforting steel girders.

"I'm not." I broke away.

"I haven't had breakfast yet, have you?" Mrs. Chapman took one of my heavy shopping bags and tucked my free arm under hers.

"Yes, but I was hoping to spend some time with you."

Mrs. Chapman led me out on the street and into a coffee shop, going straight to a quiet area in the back. She was a regular customer, I deduced from the way the waitresses chorused a welcome.

"Breakfast set?" A young girl wearing an apron and a cropped haircut very much like mine came up to serve us. She stared at me and giggled.

"Salad set, because of my diet. For two," Mrs. Chapman ordered, not giving me a chance to warn her what was coming: a single slice of pale gold toast and a saucer of lettuce, tomato, and cucumber topped with mayonnaise.

"Inside the hotel they do the same thing at double the price," she said, digging in with gusto when breakfast arrived.

"Are you still seeing Joe Roncolotta?"

"Yes indeed. But I'm worried about you! Where did you come from so early in the morning?"

"Hugh's place." Looking at her prim expression, I realized my mistake. "I mean, I went over to his apartment, but he wasn't home."

"The *Japan Times* says he's in the hospital."

"Yes. It's a long story, none of it good." The coffee here was bitter, tasted like it had been brewing for hours. I put the cup down and stared into its murky depths. "My roommate says that I always choose the hard road. I swear I didn't want anything like this."

Mrs. Chapman clucked and squeezed my hand in her coarse, larger one. "How bad is his injury?"

"It's a mild fracture, but it will keep him off his feet for a long time. I'm bringing him some things today. There's a feeling I have—" I stopped.

"What's that, honey?"

"I feel like we were getting close to figuring out the *why* of Setsuko's death, if not the *who*. But now Hugh's in the hospital, I have to do it all myself and have so little time."

"Joe and I can help you," Mrs. Chapman chided. "Why did you turn down his invitation for drinks the other day? He was so hurt."

I thought about how he'd invited me without her to the black-and-white party. I couldn't let that out. Instead I said, "It's a scandal to be seen with me, and I don't want to trouble him anymore. Besides, I think I'm going to have to leave Tokyo anyway."

"Oh, dear. What's that all about?"

"A job transfer I don't want to take. My becoming a murderer's mistress. A variety of things."

"Not your garden variety." Mrs. Chapman pressed her lips together. "Maybe it's a message from God."

"God?" I repeated dumbly. Then I remembered she was a church-goer, devout enough to seek out the English-speaking congregation in Omotesandō.

"God sometimes gives us a message that it's time for a change in our lives. Maybe it's time for you to go home to the States," she said.

"I hope not," I said, standing up and collecting my bags. "And God knows I'm going to be late! I'm sorry, but I have to go."

I dragged my feet as I approached St. Luke's that afternoon, was slow enough that a photographer was able to nicely frame her picture of me. I stopped dead to look at her—she was the first camerawoman I'd seen in Japan and looked considerably tidier in her vest and khakis than the men in blue jeans who had pursued me earlier in the week. Caught off guard, she bowed to me almost in apology for what she had to do. I bowed back. A camera shutter clicked as I came up. Good. Princess Masako couldn't have behaved more demurely.

At the nurses' station on the surgery ward, I was told Hugh had changed rooms. "The publicity problem," whispered the young nurse who had begged to shave him the day before. She insisted on accompanying me to the high security floor, keying in a code before we were admitted to the long hall. I spotted a tall figure in a blue robe loping along on crutches.

"Hugh?" I called out and he swung around, losing his balance and wiping out on the floor.

"I'm so sorry!" I apologized in English and Japanese as nurses shrieked and orderlies converged on the sprawled body.

"I was just clumsy. I'm not hurt," Hugh protested, although a scratch on his arm was bleeding.

It took half-a-dozen staffers to settle Hugh properly in bed and elevate his leg. When we were finally alone Hugh took my face in his hands and kissed me long enough that I almost forgot where we were.

"I have really bad news," I whispered.

"Let me eat first," he said. "You brought a peculiar aroma with you. Indian?"

"From Moti," I confirmed, setting it up on the swing-arm tray and sliding it into place before him. "I've brought you their best spinach curry with a side order of *naan*."

"Between you and the hospital dietitian, I'll be a vegetarian by the time I get out," he grumbled. Still, he ate ravenously, asking me belatedly if I wanted some.

"No, I ate a big breakfast. You'll never guess who bought it for me." I told him about Mrs. Chapman.

"She's a dodgy one, isn't she, still in Tokyo after all this time?" He raised his right eyebrow, and I stretched out a finger to nudge it down.

"Seeing her has been a great comfort to me."

"Why, Rei?" He drew me close again. "What upset you so much?"

"Captain Okuhara needs me to return to Shiroyama for questioning. He knows I got into the Nakamura house. He doesn't know you were there, too." I looked away from his worried face and down to my fingernails, which I'd begun to chew again.

"Mr. Ota will help you," Hugh said after a moment. "I'm sorry I made you go with me. Nakamura must have spotted you in the garden."

"Actually, Yamamoto told Captain Okuhara."

"How in hell?"

"It's my fault. When I met Yamamoto, I let something slip about going through Nakamura's closet. And Yamamoto was very angry with me. I think it was a matter of revenge."

There was a short knock and my cousin stuck his head inside the room.

"Doctor Tom!" Hugh greeted him. "You've come for my morning look-see."

Tom gave me an embarrassed look. Was it wrong for me to be there? I started to rise, but Hugh gripped my hand.

"So tell me, Tommy, what's going on?" His voice was jovial, but I sensed the anxiety underneath. "I walked a mile on crutches around the hospital today, but Dr. Endo won't say anything about letting me go."

"Walked a mile and fell, I heard," Tom said, studying Hugh's chart.

I got off the bed and stared out the window at the Sumida River. Being closeted in a small space with my cousin and my lover was making me irrationally nervous.

"You know what we call patients like you? Noncompliant." Tom's voice was light.

"Whereas you comply quite handily with the cops. *Yakuza* too, I imagine, seeming how everyone knows where I am—"

"Stop it!" I ordered Hugh, then turned on my relative. "Tom, I must to warn you that Hugh can't take jokes. He has a very undeveloped sense of humor."

"Hugh-san, please let me do my work." Tom picked up Hugh's foot and pressed gently on his big toe. "Do you feel any pain?"

"Nothing," Hugh said, although I saw him wince.

"You still have plenty of swelling, which is probably caused by your walking around on crutches. If

you rested, the swelling would subside and we could
finally apply your cast."

"Wait a minute. Dr. Endo gave me another
excuse. He told me I couldn't have a cast until next
Monday because that's when the orthopedic sur-
geon's available. Low priority, that's what I am!"

"We are very busy here, it's true. And it is no
problem for you to spend more time in the hospital.
We prefer to make sure the patient is fully recovered
before release."

"So what you're saying is it's the Japanese way to
over-hospitalize and run up big insurance bills?"
Hugh looked innocent, but his words hit their mark.

"You are good at arguing, *neh*? A real lawyer."
Tom shook his head and replaced Hugh's foot in the
sling. "Well, you'll get some action tonight, since
you'll be going down to X ray again to see if you've
done yourself any more damage. Rei-chan, your wig
is in a Mitsutan shopping bag at the nursing station.
I recommend that you wear it. And I'm off at eleven
again tonight—I don't want you traveling home
without me like you did yesterday."

"Actually, I'm going back to my own apartment
this evening. I already talked to Aunt Norie about it."

"You're staying in my flat," Hugh cut in.

"You think my cousin would sleep in your apartment?" Tom paused, seeming to struggle for words.
"Hugh-san, I must explain to you that in Japan, that
kind of behavior is not good for a young girl's image."

"Tom, I'm old enough to sleep where I want.
How can you, a cousin I've met less than five or six
times, tell me what to do?" I sniped.

"Tanin yori miuchi," Tom said under his breath.

"What's that?" Hugh asked.

"He says relatives are better than strangers." I scowled at my cousin, who delivered a similar expression back.

"I'll be a bona fide relative someday, I reckon," said Hugh, his smile almost an insult. They were both ridiculous, talking about me like I was a possession. I was gearing up to tell them both off when a nurse with a boyishly short hairstyle darted in, someone I could have sworn had long hair the day before.

"Shimura-*sensei*, do you think Mr. Glendinning is well enough for another visitor?" she chirped, all the while gazing at me.

"Who is it?" Hugh interrupted.

"Nakamura-san from Sendai Limited."

"That's fine. I need to get on with my rounds." Tom swept out without looking back. I knew he was furious.

"Ta!" Hugh waved after Tom and then whispered to me, "Please stay. I'm useless without you."

Seiji Nakamura had aged a decade in the three weeks since I'd first seen him at Minshuku Yogetsu. His skin had a sallow cast, and the bags under his eyes had deepened into pouches. I had written off the lines around his mouth to smoking but now realized it was due to his deep, permanent frown. He delivered it to me like a present before bending solicitously over Hugh.

"Glendinning-san has had so much trouble lately."

He made a sudden movement with his hands, which he had kept behind his back. I laughed inwardly as he set down a leather briefcase and proffered the real gift: a box of five jumbo-sized peaches, each cosseted in a protective foam girdle. What had I been expecting, a knife?

"These are grown in a special hothouse, but probably Glendinning-san does not care for peaches . . ." He was going through all the right motions, showing the obvious value of his gift while deprecating it, the hated ritual I knew by heart.

"Rei will like it. She just eats fruits, nuts, that kind of thing," Hugh said instead of thanking him in a straightforward manner. I took the peaches, since Hugh appeared unwilling to, and placed them on the tray alongside the Indian carryout meal.

"I read the newspaper this morning. I was sorry to hear about my friend's terrible injury," Nakamura said.

"Being here's really quite pleasant and relaxing," Hugh replied. "When I was searching for Yamamoto on the slopes and then thrown into prison in Shiroyama, that's when I needed a friend."

"Circumstances were difficult for me—"

"Your wife had passed away," I murmured, shooting Hugh a reproving glance. "You had enough trouble of your own."

"That is why I am here tonight." Mr. Nakamura gave me a *get-out-of-here* look that probably worked with his office ladies. "I made many prayers to resolve things, but my troubles keep increasing."

"How's that?" Hugh's voice was deceptively casual.

"We started out with a simple suicide verdict. Then this nosey girl became involved, and it turned to murder. Half the people invited to the farewell ceremony did not show up. Mostly the wrong ones came." He glared at me. "Like you, Shimura-san. Don't think I didn't recognize you with those impertinent eyes and that teen-ager's body."

"You must have been very angry," I said, feeling Hugh's body tense under the blanket. I knew that I had not deceived Mr. Nakamura that night, just as I hadn't gotten away with the housecleaning.

"Why do you think I made you clean the toilet? I could not cause a scene at my house, but what I wanted to do!"

I began moving uneasily on the edge of the cot.

"And then I saw her again three days ago, hiding in my garden." He widened his eyes at Hugh in an expression of mock incredulity. "What have I done? Why can't I get this young woman out of my life?" He looked at me. "What is it? Do you want to become my second wife?"

"I would never be a salaryman's wife! I have far too much ambition." I was still thinking about the cheap teddy in his bedroom closet. It was small for Keiko, but I did have evidence he knew her. Now seemed like a good time to bring that up. "You've spent time at a place called Club Marimba recently, where Setsuko's sister works."

"My wife's sister is dead." His delivery was bland.

I shook my head. "Keiko's alive and well and in bed with the mob. Which means you are, too."

"What are you, crazy?"

"What's crazy is the way you thought you could get away with killing her." I spoke without fear, given the phalanx of nurses and orderlies just outside.

Nakamura gave Hugh a pitiful look. "We are friends! What kinds of things are you telling people?"

"It would have been friendly to let me know what you had planned for the battery." Hugh pulled a disc randomly from the Paul Smith bag, waving it as if it were the important one. *Watch it*, I wanted to say. I needed something to give Captain Okuhara.

"It's quite natural for me to have information about product development—I'm a senior manager, after all."

"If it's so natural, why didn't Mr. Sendai know about it?" Hugh put the disc back into the bag and smiled. "What a tremendous way for me to return to the company, saving the Eterna and exorcising a corrupt executive who would have sold it down the river."

"Send her out so we can talk." The salaryman inclined his head in my direction.

"I'm afraid I can't. Rei's become something of a partner." Hugh squeezed my hand.

"If you want to make a deal, it's between the two of us. Men."

"Why?" I asked. "You had no trouble dealing with Keiko."

"You're a very rude young woman, aren't you?" Nakamura barked.

"Rei, I'm sorry." Hugh's eyes seemed to be trying to telescope all kinds of things to me, but the only one I cared about was that he wanted me gone.

"Okay, I'm going. Good luck to you both in your man's world." I spat out the words and pulled my parka off the bed, inadvertenly knocking Mr. Nakamura's costly peaches to the ground. Four of them rolled under the bed, and the one in my path got a savage, bruising kick as I sped to the door.

30

To my surprise, Richard and Mariko were back together in his room. This meant I slept comfortably and late. It was almost eleven when I ran into the Family Mart to get a rice ball for the road.

"Long time no see, Shimura-san! I thought you had moved away to the beautiful people downtown!" Mr. Waka greeted me with exuberance.

"It has been a long time," I agreed. "Too long."

"Look, look!" He held up the brand-new edition of the tabloid *Friday*, which had a cover photograph of me bowing to the camerawoman outside the hospital. The headline was "*Rei no Rei!*" or "*Rei's bow*," a pun on a second meaning of my name.

"It's quite a good article. They interview your students, your friends, your cousin at the hospital all to discuss your true nature—whether you will bow to the needs of justice—which I'm sure you will! It was a very positive story, considering the circumstances."

"Hmm." I popped open a hot can of green tea I'd bought at the machine just outside his door.

"Young ladies are adopting your haircut, do you realize? They call it *the Rei-Styru*. It costs six thousand yen at a salon in Harajuku."

"Oh, no." I ran my fingers through my hair still wet from the shower.

"You must read this. I'll give you the magazine for free because it's such a special event. Please." Mr. Waka looked so upset that I finally took the tabloid, rolling it up and sticking it in my backpack.

"You're too kind to me," I mumbled dutifully as I left.

"I'm not kind at all. Just a fan."

On the way to the train station I took out *Friday* and began trying to read it. I couldn't believe Richard had talked to them. And Tom. If only I could read more *kanji*; it was maddening not to understand what people were saying about me.

My face buried in the paper, I slowly climbed the metal stairs leading up the pedestrian overpass. The smell of diesel fuel was especially overwhelming because of the morning rush hour. The sputtering and roaring sounds of cars on the street below were a stark contrast from the peace of Aunt Norie's neighborhood. A smart person would not have given up free room and board there.

A sharp gust of wind tore *Friday* out of my hand and as the slim magazine skipped through the air, I noticed the roaring traffic sounds were louder, as if there were a car behind me. I glanced over my shoulder and saw something completely illegal: a huge black motorcycle soaring up the ramp for bicycles and onto the overpass itself.

The shiny black vehicle appeared to be heading straight for me. I moved out of its way and the driver, an anonymous, helmeted figure, adjusted his direction and increased speed. All these things I noticed in a matter of seconds; I heard people in the background crying out, but what pressed deep into my mind was the sound of the cycle, a horrible cross between a roar and a whine.

I was backed up flat against the security railing, like almost everyone on the pedestrian bridge. The *kamikaze* motorcyclist was now less than ten feet away. I was the undisputed target with nowhere to escape. Unless I jumped.

Desperation pumped through me and I scrambled over the railing, remembering belatedly that the huge safety net on the outside had been removed for repair. My idea was to hang on until danger had passed. I was halfway over as the motorcycle buzzed against the railing.

A black-gloved hand reached out and shoved me hard. I toppled over and reached wildly for the railings. My right hand fastened around a steel bar, but the rest of me dangled thirty feet above the railroad tracks.

It had happened fast, but I felt each detail in exquisite slow motion. My low-heeled pumps slipped off my feet and hit the ground; next went my backpack, which had been dangling off my left shoulder. I was beginning to feel extremely heavy. Every part of me seemed to sag downward. I swung my left arm uselessly; I wanted to grab the railing, but didn't have the strength. I was rotten at pull-ups, had failed that part of my junior high gym class.

I was too scared to cry, too scared to do anything but breathe fast and watch the motorcycle rider execute a wheelie and zip back down the pedestrian ramp into the street.

"Be careful," a woman in a business suit called to me from the safe side of the pedestrian bridge. A whole group of commuters was with her, making concerned sounds and arguing about what to do. Should they call the police or the fire department? It didn't matter, I wanted to say, my grip could never last that long.

A rag-tag band of homeless men had moved directly under me, holding out various bags and pieces of their cardboard shacks, as if that would provide a safe landing net. In the distance I heard traffic and maybe a siren.

"Take this." I heard a rough voice and looked up to see the grimy face of a street-sleeper I'd once stumbled over and given dinner. He was dangling the rope he used to secure blankets around his body.

The rope flew down and bounced off the rails. After a few misses, I caught it with my left hand. My rescuer and someone behind him began tugging ·upward. My left hand came back up to the railing, and strong hands reached under my arms and hauled me over.

I was safe. I lay hyperventilating on the steel walkway.

"*Sumimasen deshita. Sumimasen.*" Between short

breaths, I whimpered my apologies. I knew it was ludicrous, but I couldn't stop. Maybe I was hysterical.

"That guy was probably *Bōsōzoku*," my rescuer spat. "Damn motorcycle gangs!"

"Did you see his license plate?" I gasped.

"There was no license plate!" The man leaned in and whispered so close to my face I smelled sake on his breath. "And don't try to find out. *Bōsōzoku* are friends with the *ya-san*."

A pair of policemen were jogging toward us, their feet making the pedestrian bridge spring up and down under my back. I struggled into a sitting position and my shaggy friend got up and melted into the crowd of commuters. As the policemen took their notebooks out, I started in a slow, shaky voice to tell them about the phantom cyclist.

The senior officer interrupted me. "Your alien registration card, please?"

I should have expected they'd fixate on that. I pointed at my backpack lying with my shoes on the tracks below and told them to get it.

I arrived at Nichiyu dusty and late, but went straight to the English teaching office and slapped an envelope on Mr. Katoh's desk. His secretary Mrs. Bun kept her eyes on me, and I wondered if she'd investigate. Fifteen minutes later, I saw her whispering to the personnel director and knew she had.

I cleaned up in the lavatory but remained shell-shocked as I went in to teach my lunch-hour class. Everything was different. My teaching style had become formal and by-the-book. It was ironic that at a time when Tokyo's reading population was entering a first-name relationship with me, I was holding distant the people I'd worked with for years. At the end of class, a few students bowed and said *sayonara* to me instead of the more typical "see you next week." Perhaps they also sensed something was over.

Mr. Katoh called me into the conference room after I finished teaching. He spoke about the bad weather and made some disparaging comments about the way the media had behaved lately. Finally, he looked at me and said, "So you want to leave us."

"I feel compelled." I stared at the wall decorated with framed posters of Nichiyu's proudest products. The bean-grinder combination coffee maker. The water heater with fuzzy logic. I wouldn't be around to see the "caffe ratte" maker ascend to its rightful framed position.

"You wrote about wanting to spare the company shame and humiliation. I feel directly responsible for the trouble, you know." Mr. Katoh bowed his head. "It was I who suggested you take your holiday in Shiroyama."

"That wasn't your fault—"

"I don't understand why you had to involve yourself so. There were other guests, but I do not see their names in the newspapers anymore. Only you and this Englishman."

"He's Scottish, not English." I stopped, aware I was veering away from the business of my resignation. "Mr. Katoh, I've had a very good experience working here, but I am no longer effective with my students. Like I said in my letter, they are distracted by what I've become."

"When do you want to leave?" His voice was mournful.

"I have to see the police in Shiroyama next Monday."

"Oh, no, Miss Shimura. Do you have a lawyer?"

"Yes," I lied.

"It could all work out, I suppose." He sounded less than hopeful.

"I'm very sorry about how this is all turning out," I said.

"When you get out of this questioning, please call me. Maybe I can find something for you part-time. You recorded such a beautiful voice-over for the Caffe Ratte video. Surely none of our overseas vendors would know about your problems here."

My brusque, paternal boss was trying to help me in a most unorthodox manner. Feeling moved, I tried to thank him, but he brushed it off.

"We still need to make changes in the language program. Having been here so long, you can advise me about . . . how best to encourage Mr. Randall to like Osaka?"

All I wanted to do was go home and bury my injured body under blankets, but I couldn't forsake my appointment at Ishida Antiques. When I stepped inside, Mr. Ishida put the closed sign on the door and went back to his mini-kitchen to fill the kettle.

"So where were you yesterday? I telephoned a few times," I complained when he came back out to clear his abacus and business receipts off the low *kotatsu* table and set it for tea.

"I was having a second meeting with my friend at the Tokyo National Museum. Honda-san is a man with many responsibilities, so I must go when he has time for me." Mr. Ishida laid out a dark red Kutani teapot, cups, and a small strainer. Such special pieces; it was amazing he used them daily.

"And?"

"Patience, Miss Shimura." My mentor went into the kitchen to take the whistling kettle off the stove. I toyed with the china, looking on the underside for its stamps.

When he came out, he poured me the first cup.

"Please try it," he said.

"Itadakimasu." I said grace before sampling the steaming, pale green liquid. "A little grassy tasting. Fresh."

He looked pleased. "It is *gyokuro*, the highest grade of green tea. It comes from a farm that is eight generations old in Shizuoka Prefecture. I brewed it for exactly one minute."

I drank more, remaining quiet. His strange behavior might be influenced by my notoriety; perhaps he was checking to see if I were still the same person he knew.

"I've done something I'm not sure you will be pleased about," he said when we were drinking our second cups. I knew then he must have been contacted by the press, tried to stick up for me, and had it go wrong.

"I understand," I said. "Everyone's talking, my colleagues, my old friends . . ."

"Talking?" He looked confused.

"You know, to the tabloid reporters."

"Tabloids?" His face looked as dour as it had the time a shrine sale vendor had tried to sell us some reproduction wood-block prints. "I stopped reading all but my art magazines five years ago. Is there some new trouble?"

"Yes, there is. But nothing that relates to our friendship," I said carefully. "Please tell me what you thought might upset me."

"It is about the box from Shiroyama."

I sighed. So it was a fraud, after all.

"You see," Mr. Ishida continued, "Although the box is not my property, I have arranged for its sale. I was unable to reach you to ask permission, so again, my apology."

"Tell me—" I leaned toward him, putting both elbows on the tea table. Realizing my etiquette lapse, I jerked them off. Patience.

"The Shiroyama Folk Art Center is the buyer. My friend at the National Museum sent a close-up photograph and his appraisal of your box and they made a bid. It's as simple as that."

"Your friend authenticated it as Princess Miyo's?"

"As well as anyone could. Princess Miyo was an odd young lady, *neh*?" Mr. Ishida smiled. "One strangeness was that she used her left hand for eating and writing. My colleague believes the carving was done by a left-handed person living in the mid-nineteenth century."

"Is that enough to identify something? Surely—"

Mr. Ishida held up a hand, stilling me once again.

"Even today, most left-handed people must use the right. You know that."

That had been my father's ordeal. Half a world away from his proper Yokohama upbringing, he at last felt free enough to write left-handed. Still, he would never dream of using the left hand for chopsticks.

"The box itself, as you recognized, was not espe cially high quality, and was produced at the workshop of Koichi Hashimoto between 1850 and 1860 in Hakone. At that time, it would have sold for just a few *sen*. My friend believes Princess Miyo was proba bly given the box by a relative or friend of the family, someone who had stopped in Hakone while traveling along the Tokaido Road."

How ironic the antiques business was! For years I had strived to buy the finest quality I could afford; now I'd bought a piece of nineteenth-century junk and it meant something. Something major, in fact, to the small town where it came from.

"The reason I suggest you sell the box is that it has limited interest and won't appreciate in value," Mr. Ishida told me. "It is, however, of great signifi cance to the Shiroyama Folk Art Center."

"I'd be happy to donate it, since I hardly paid any thing and took it from the town where it belongs," I suggested.

Mr. Ishida was shaking his head. "And have your reputation as an antiques dealer vanish like a trace of smoke? I will not allow it."

"But I'm not a dealer," I said, although I had started thinking about the money.

"Miss Shimura, I insist on payment. I have arranged everything, and it would be a massive loss of face if you cancel this agreement."

"May I ask how much they'll pay?" My blunt question hung in the air, embarrassing me.

"One-point-two million yen. At first they were hesitant to exceed the million yen mark, but they changed their mind. That's why I'd be embarrassed if you decline."

I made him repeat the figure to ensure I'd gotten it right. He was talking about ten thousand dollars for a box that had cost me fifty dollars, the going price for a *Rei-Styru* haircut.

"They can afford that?" I was amazed, remembering the small gallery.

"The center is supported by descendants of the Shiroyama family, who have a significant lumber fortune. And the trustees know that what they pay you will be easily surpassed through increased admissions. They plan to use the box as a focus for a new public relations campaign, with articles and advertisements in the local and national press and a search made for the family that once owned the treasure you unearthed."

"People will finally know that Princess Miyo escaped. Maybe even who she became." It was oddly similar to my search for Setsuko.

"This is the contract I drafted. If you like, you can bring it to a lawyer first." Mr. Ishida held out a packet of papers.

I shook my head. Hugh wouldn't be able to make heads or tails of it, and Mr. Ota had more serious matters on his agenda. I also knew the price was astronomical for a cheap pine box not even 150 years old.

"If you give me a line-by-line reading of what it says, I'll sign now."

Mr. Ishida began, and the joy in his voice as he went through the dry words was apparent. Not even the knocking of a customer at the door would make him hurry.

As I pulled out a ballpoint pen to sign the document, he shook his head.

"Don't you have a *hanko*?" He was talking about my personal name stamp. A *hanko* was considered more secure than a handwritten signature; it also had its roots in hundreds of years of tradition.

"Of course." I dug around in my bag and found the slim, capped stick with my name carved out of rubber. My father had given it to me as a good-luck present for my new life in Japan.

"Ambition. An auspicious *kanji* to celebrate the start of a new career," Mr. Ishida said, surveying the first character in my surname.

I blushed and merely said, *"Okage samade"*; *because of you*, the ritual way to show gratitude toward others for your own success. I'd been running around like a lunatic while Mr. Ishida and Taro Ikeda had spent time analyzing my purchase. I'd have to find a way for them to be credited.

Outside St. Luke's, a thick crowd of reporters greeted me. After a bath at Karen's and a run through her closet, I was a new woman wearing a white leather trench coat over a cream-colored stretch satin evening dress she had borrowed from a magazine shoot. "Don't even think of staining this outfit!" my friend warned while I swore up and down nothing would happen. Now I tugged the skimpy coat over my thighs and refused the shouted questions about my accident at Minami-Senju Station and hurried into the warmth of the hospital.

"A vegetarian who wears leather. How refreshing," Hugh said when I arrived at his bedside.

As I slipped off the coat, he stared at the sleek evening dress. "Whose is it? This isn't your usual."

"Karen's. Well, it really is on loan from *Classy*." I was glad he was focusing on my clothes. I had decided not to tell him about the motorcycle attacker, because I had a feeling if he knew he wouldn't let me out of his sight.

"What I mean is—" he sighed at the language gap that remained between us—"who designed the dress? It's not your usual tomboy or missionary drag. Come closer so I can have a good look."

"It's an Hervé Léger." I suddenly felt very naked.

"You look like a kinky bridesmaid." His face didn't tell me whether it was a success or a disaster. "All those straps and cut-out patches."

"Karen said that because it's expensive and French that makes it all right, but I don't know—"

"It depends on what you're doing, and with whom." He slipped his hand into the bodice, and I shivered as his fingers glided over my bare skin.

"Someone's taking me to the black-and-white party at TAC."

"This is a game you're playing with me, right?" Hugh asked, pulling his hand away. "A jealousy thing."

"No, this is just a man I met who's got a lead for me about the American—"

"Who's the guy?"

"Joe Roncolotta."

Hugh was silent for a minute. When he spoke, he sounded cranky. "Since when have you been pals with the czar of the *gaijin* business establishment?"

"I called him up a few weeks ago. We've had dinner once. He's helping me."

"Given his age and girth, I suppose he's harmless enough. But he can't give you anything on the American that I don't have."

"What do you mean?" I lounged precariously on the bed, afraid to wrinkle the dress by sitting.

"The deal I made with Nakamura last night was rather simple. After I promised not to report him to Sendai, he agreed to abandon his plans for the sale of the Eterna battery. He will also tell Captain Okuhara we entered the house with his permission. Finally, he's delivered what we needed all along: Setsuko's father's letters."

"Are they real?" I asked, thinking of Mr. Ishida's handwriting expert.

"They're in their original envelopes, all postmarked from Texas over a period of twenty-five years. Kind of hard to fake that, I think. These were the valuables Setsuko was keeping in the safe."

"He knew about her father?"

"Sure. It turned out to be one of the things that

made her an attractive marriage candidate." He smiled wryly. "So much for my chauvinist's theory that beauty was her sole asset."

"How did Mr. Nakamura know we would want the letters?" I was uncomfortable with the idea of him as an ally.

"It turns out one of my friends at work has been something of a double agent—"

"Hikari. She was his mistress," I said.

"You knew?"

"Remember the black teddy? I recognized the smell of Hikari's deodorant. Obviously you didn't notice."

"I never got close enough to sniff." He looked at me with awe before continuing. "Nakamura said his gangster pal Mr. Fukujima knew about the thing with Hikari and casually gossiped about it. The news made its way to Keiko, who sensed Setsuko finally had the grounds for a decent divorce settlement. Keiko used the threat of telling Setsuko about Hikari to blackmail Nakamura."

"Did he pay?" Blackmail was a crime, but I couldn't help savoring the thought of the arrogant executive under a woman's command. Breaking Hugh's ankle and sending me over the pedestrian bridge was another issue, of course.

"A half-million yen was the first installment. It explains his abuse of the company credit card."

"But now that Setsuko's dead, there's no need for blackmail. He can do whatever he wants with Hikari, so why would he help you?"

"He suspects Keiko was behind the death but

doesn't know what to do about it without revealing his *yakuza* ties. So when I called Hikari, desperate for her help, the two of them hatched the idea of our breaking in and doing the work for him. He even moved the photo album to a prominent place, hoping we'd take it."

"It sounds like you think he's innocent," I said, disappointment mixing with relief that I wouldn't be prosecuted for burglary.

"Relatively innocent," Hugh said. "When he was away from us on New Year's Eve and told vague lies about his and Setsuko's whereabouts, it was because he was in a closet making an hour-long telephone call to Hikari. I went through my cellular phone bill today, and it all checked out."

"Ah. The missing telephone you were grumbling about on New Year's morning!"

"Bull's eye, Miss Shimura." With a flick of his hand he tipped me off balance so I rolled against his body. I was stunned to feel his arousal and the strength of my reaction.

"Are Setsuko's father's letters still here?" I said, rising to preserve Karen's dress and my willpower. Hugh gestured toward the briefcase I'd seen Mr. Nakamura carry in yesterday. I opened it and looked down on a sheaf of old letters, many of the envelopes patchworked yellow and green with mildew.

"It looks like the father wrote to her every six to eight weeks. Recently there was a gap of four months before he began writing again on a word processor. He said his arthritis had gotten to him."

"You've read them all?"

"There's not much to do during the daytime when no one comes except Winnie."

I picked up one of the older-looking handwritten letters by the edges, the way I'd learned in my museum internship. It was dated October 11, 1975.

> My dear Setsuko,
>
> I'm glad you and little Mariko were able to use the $800 toward her nursery school education. It is amazing to think my granddaughter is already four years old. I am looking forward to receiving her photo. You haven't sent me any since she turned one, so I am anxious to see how she is coming along. I remember when you were small you had the cutest dimples . . . it is difficult for me to realize you are now almost twenty and working hard at your nursing studies.

"He seemed to think she was raising Mariko herself," I said.

"Almost every letter is a variation on this, talk of money sent and pleas for photographs and school reports."

"And was Setsuko a nurse?" I asked.

"Not according to her husband. I think she believed calling herself that satisfied her dad, who comes off in the letters as a rather sentimental fellow. She mentions a husband abandoning her, seeming even more the innocent victim."

I read on, speeding through some bland references

to the beautiful fall weather in Texas and down to the
signature, which was simply "Father." I refolded it
and placed it back in its envelope.

"His name appears nowhere in the letters. I
expect he didn't really want her to know," Hugh said.

"Do you mind if I take a few of these with me?
Maybe some of the later typed ones?" I asked.

"No chance. Unless, perhaps, you'd be willing to
perform a very loving service." He shifted the blankets and winked at me.

"Well, then, I'm going." I pulled the coat over
me, hiding the letter I had in the pocket.

"You certainly have no guilt about taking time
away from our work to traipse off to a party!"

"Joe's got something on the American, I'm positive of it." I got up and headed for the door.
"Besides, I quit my job today. I need him."

"You're leaving Nichiyu? It's because of this mess,
isn't it?" Hugh sounded contrite. After a minute, he
said, "You should go back to America and do law or
medical school. I could write you a reference for law
and Tom could do the other—"

"Are you delirious? I'd never leave Tokyo to do
something so boring!"

"Darling, it hurts me to say this, but I can't very
well support you if I'm unemployed. I'll lose the flat,
the car, everything."

"This is my city, and I'll live here on my terms, okay?
I've got something new, I keep trying to tell you."

"What's your scheme?" Hugh closed his eyes as if
the sight of me was becoming tiresome.

"Antiques. I'm going to work as a freelance buyer

for private clients." I liked the way it sounded in contrast with "shopper," Joe's original term.

"Too risky. Why don't you gather a few clients first and build a nest egg? I'd hate to see you get discouraged." If Hugh were any more dubious, he could pass for my father.

"This afternoon, I sold a piece I bought in Shiroyama for one-point-two million yen. A decent nest egg, wouldn't you say?"

Hugh's eyes flew open. "Tell me I'm not dreaming!"

I put my hands on my hips and stared down at him with my most severe expression. "I'm having the cash wired to my bank account, if you want to see a receipt."

"You'll want to incorporate if you're going to run a business in Japan. You'll need a lawyer—"

"I'll need a lawyer who's not in the hospital or prison. Ta, darling." I waved my fingers in a splendid imitation of him as I left.

31

The Tokyo American Club lies within spitting or kissing distance of the Russian Embassy, depending on your mood. Mine was definitely guarded. I had a fantasy of walking into the sprawling, California-style complex and being politely shown out. Winnie had said something to Hugh about buying tickets, and I had less than 2,000 yen in my evening bag.

Fortunately, Joe was waiting on a sofa in the understated but plush lobby, a copy of the *Wall Street Journal* open in his lap. Catching sight of me, he smiled and patted the seat next to him.

"How's life?" he asked. "You look good for someone doing combat with the police, gangsters, and tabloid writers."

"I put in my resignation at Nichiyu. My lower stress level must be showing."

"Superb." Joe leaned forward and kissed me. "Now you're going to have to let me convince you about starting your business. We'll order some champagne to get started—"

"No champagne is needed, and don't bother trying to convince me about anything," I told him. "I'm already there."

Joe looked amazed when I told him about my sale to the Shiroyama Folk Art Center. He immediately started planning. "Much more important than advertising will be word-of-mouth. When the gals in the international women's clubs talk about shopping, your name should be on somebody's lips. Businessmen traveling solo will ask you to buy for their wives, in part because you're a pretty little thing and they'll enjoy the consultation. Do I offend you?" he beamed. "It's simply the way men work and to your economic advantage."

"I wonder about the way men work," I said. "This thing with Mrs. Chapman—do you just turn on and off?"

Joe shook his head. "She came on too strong for me. When I saw you that Sunday outside of the church, I was so relieved. I thought you would help me out, but you didn't!"

"What's wrong with her? Your ages match, and you have the same kind of enthusiasm for life—" I was perplexed.

"I'm not really interested in American women."

I stiffened. "Well, I didn't come here for a date with a man older than my father."

"*Touché*. The source is waiting for you, Miss Shimura, but we need to circulate first." He rose and gestured toward the sound of big band music, clinking glasses, and applause.

"I should warn you that I'm terrible at small-talk," I muttered, feeling a painful shyness come over me as we headed into a ballroom filled with elegantly dressed *gaijin*, the party page come to life.

"All you have to do is smile." Joe held out his hands for my coat. "Say, that's some number you're wearing." He blinked several times before he was elbowed out of the way.

"It's Ric Shimura!" A slim, red-haired woman held out her hand. "I'm Molly Mason! My husband Jim's over there. He wants your autograph but is too shy to ask."

"My name is Rei, not Rie," I corrected. "I believe you're confusing me with the actress Rie Miyazawa— I could understand your husband wanting her autograph—"

"I saw your picture in *Friday*," another woman interrupted. "I had to get my maid to translate the whole story. *Rei's bow*, it was called. Completely adorable!"

"Hugh's a squash buddy of mine, I suppose he hasn't mentioned it—I'm Jerry Swoboda." A well-fed, Rotary Club-type had a glass of champagne for me in one hand, his business card in the other.

"So, is Hugh good in bed or better off dead?" The last comment was whispered rather waspishly by a woman behind me. I began feeling dizzy and retreated into the arm Joe put around me.

"Hold on, what's this nonsense? Damn rude of you to talk like that." Joe attempted to cut a path for us across the room. We encountered a photographer en route, an Australian in a little black dress who

identified herself as a photojournalist on assignment
for the *Tokyo Weekender*.

"I know you aren't taking questions about the
murder, but I have to ask . . . your dress? Whose is
it?" She spoke while focusing her lens.

This time, I knew the verbal shorthand. "It's a
Léger."

"Of course! One of his bandage dresses—some
say he copied Azzedine Alaïa."

"Really? I thought that kind of thing only went
on in the art world!" I was fascinated.

"I can't believe you—here—with Hugh on his
sickbed!" Winnie Clancy stage-whispered from the
side. The society photographer turned to snap
Winnie's angry face, and I couldn't help imagining
how it would look on the party page.

My mischievous thoughts faded as Joe steered me
down a spiral staircase and into a small lounge. This
could be trouble, being alone with him. He pushed
open the door, and I made out the silhouette of a
man looking out the window at the sparkling Tokyo
night landscape. He wore an ill-fitting gray suit that
didn't follow the evening's black-tie dress code. As he
turned, the weathered face with dark blue eyes
snapped into my memory. He was the leader of the
veterans who had stonewalled me in Yokosuka.

"Master Chief Jimmy O'Donnell, meet Rei
Shimura." Joe's voice was hearty.

What did one say in a case like this? *Pleased to see
you again?* I took a sip of wine and shifted from foot
to foot until Joe told me to sit down.

"I can leave you two alone if you like," Joe offered.

"Please don't," I begged. As nervous as I was about Joe, Jimmy O'Donnell was a totally unknown entity.

"I had to sort some old business out before I could talk to you. Do you understand?" O'Donnell's voice rasped.

"Yes. I'm glad you decided to trust me." I settled down in a plush chair across from him and after a second, he also sat down.

"I thought you weren't being straight. I didn't understand why you cared more about the grandfather than the gal who claimed to be his offspring. The whole thing rubbed me the wrong way." He cast a glance at Joe. "We talked about it, and he told me you were the real thing."

"I'm not the granddaughter," I said quickly.

"No, but you're the genuine article. You support yourself in Tokyo without any handouts. You're asking questions because you're in love with that fellow who's in trouble, the Englishman."

Mrs. Chapman must have exaggerated wildly to Joe, who in turn was feeding the rumor. I shook my head. "There has to be a link between the American father and Setsuko's death. I think he'd stopped sending her money about six months ago."

"Five months ago, a guy called Willie Evans died. We got a copy of the obituary at Old Salts for our scrapbook," O'Donnell said. "Kind of a sad hobby we have, keeping track of the dead."

"Did you know Mr. Evans well?" I asked.

"Not at all. There were so many sailors around, three times as many as there are now. I knew most of the gals who worked the bars and was sorry when the big stores drove them out. I guess I felt as much loyalty to them as I do my own people."

I knew what Jimmy O'Donnell was talking about. He was as in love with Japan as Joe and I were. The three of us sat quietly for a minute, as if appreciating that.

"In the early fifties, he had a girlfriend here who worked in the bars. She already had one kid, but he didn't care. They got a house together and lived like they were married. They had a baby. Evans's name didn't go on any birth certificate because he didn't want his commanding officer to know."

"Typical." Joe nodded. "So how did he leave her?"

"His tour of duty ended and he just went back to the States, met some gal at a church picnic. They were together thirty-three years before she passed away, breast cancer, I think."

"Did the American wife know about his first love in Japan?" I asked.

"I have no idea. The two sons might be able to help you. They're still living in the Boston area, as the obituary says." He handed me a blurry photocopy of a notice in the *Boston Globe*. Skimming it quickly, I saw no mention of Texas—it appeared Willie Evans's entire life before and after Japan took place in Framingham, Massachusetts.

"You should call them, Rei," Joe said, as if hearing my silent question. "You've got dates and other locations to check by them. There's no need to jump to conclusions, but it's worth acting sooner than later."

"You're right." I folded the paper into my evening bag, where I caught sight of the envelope I had not returned to Hugh. "Actually, I have a letter from the father—"

Joe was practically on top of me to get it, ruining my hopes of keeping off fingerprints. "Let me see." He looked up at O'Donnell. "There's a Texas postmark here. Not Boston."

"You know, he could have retired to the West . . . a lot of guys do, for the weather," James O'Donnell said lamely. "I can start looking into folks from Texas. I suppose I should get going."

"No, you're staying for a drink and spending the night with me in Aoyama," Joe coaxed. "After we drop the young lady off, you and I'll paint the town red, just like we used to."

Back in the ballroom, Jimmy O'Donnell stayed busy holding up the *hors d'oeuvre* table while Joe took me out on the dance floor. I had some trouble with the Blahnik heels and the fact I'd never swing-danced before. I was whirled from Joe into the arms of a small, dark man who kept telling me he'd gone to Princeton. After that came a lean young Japanese whose name I recognized as connected to a powdered soup fortune. My final partner was Molly Mason's husband Jim, who swore he hadn't confused me with Rie Miyazawa and wondered how the Imperial Hotel sounded for lunch next Tuesday. . . .

I excused myself to tell Joe I was going home.

"The glorious reality of the party page has hit

you, huh?" he teased. "Now you see why I lead a quiet life devoted to my business."

"But you don't! You're in the *Weekender* at least every other issue. Tonight we had our picture taken two dozen times."

"Not my picture. Yours," he corrected.

"I don't normally look like this—"

"You should from now on," Joe said. "While you were dancing, I was spreading the word on your upcoming antiques venture. I tickled them a little about the box you sold to the museum, and the upshot is I have five gals who want appointments as soon as possible."

"That's wonderful." I was unable to concentrate. "Joe, if I go home now, I can figure out my strategy for the Evans brothers. I have to call them early tomorrow morning."

"You're hopeless." Joe brought my coat and escorted me outside and into a taxi, kissing me good-bye in front of a battalion of Japanese media. The taxi driver seemed ecstatic until we started moving and I directed him to drop me at the nearby Kamiyacho station. It looked cheap, I guess, for a woman wearing Hervé Léger. Still, the sale of the box had been a fluke. It could be a long wait for my next influx of cash. In the meantime, budget was going to be my mantra.

As had become my custom, I scanned the crowd exiting Minami-Senju station with me. A few motley bands of drunken men got off. Trailing a safe distance behind them, but not totally alone, I wrapped the

thin leather coat around me and started over the steel
pedestrian bridge for home. I waved at Mr. Waka
through the window at Family Mart but didn't go in.
My feet were killing me. I wanted to get home and
stick them in the bathroom sink.

My street was silent except for a drip coming from
somewhere high above. Paired with my footfalls in the
unusually high shoes, the sounds formed a rhythmic
percussion. After a few minutes, I realized a quieter,
clipped noise was marring the rhythm. I stopped,
feigning a look in the window of the closed fishmon-
ger, and it ceased.

I started walking again, sorry that I hadn't taken
the taxi all the way home. To return to Mr. Waka's
shop, I'd have to run toward my stalker. Where was
Kenji Yamamoto tonight? I wondered. Or Keiko's
yakuza friends?

I slipped off Karen's shoes and took them in my
hands so I could walk faster. The street was freezing
cold and rough against my feet, with disgusting wet
spots that soaked through my pantyhose. As the footsteps fell faster behind me, I spun around and a slight
figure leaped into the gas company's doorway. He
was shorter than Joe Roncolotta and Yamamoto, but
maybe it was the man who had tried to run me over
with the motorcycle.

"*Yamete,*" I said loudly. *Quit it*. There was no
response. I broke into a run, my apartment looming
like a beacon just fifty feet away. I made it in and took
the stairs two at a time, cursing the fact there was no
lock on the vestibule door. My stalker could run up
the stairs behind me if he wanted.

When I turned the key into the lock of my door and fell inside, I was trembling so violently that Richard got up from eating an octopus–corn pizza with Mariko and put his hand on my forehead.

"What is it? The flu or something? Poor baby—"

"No, it's the guy who rode the motorcycle at the train station. He came back to get me," I said as I ran to the telephone and dialed 110. An English-speaking officer came on halfway through my conversation with the sergeant who had answered the call.

"Excuse me, miss, but how long will you remain in Japan?"

"I'm not a tourist, I live here!" I gave my name and street address again. When they realized I was the *Friday* girl who had been involved in an accident at Minami-Senju station earlier, the English-speaking officer asked if Hugh Glendinning was with me. I said no.

The policeman decided to dispatch a car to my street, all the while warning me an arrest would be unlikely, given that it wasn't a crime for a person to walk around at night. "Unless, of course, the person is carrying a weapon—in our country, unlike yours, guns are not allowed!" the officer huffed.

I hung up and asked Richard to make me tea. He gave me a can of Pocari Sweat, insisting the soft drink's ionization action would settle me better than caffeine. But I didn't want to sleep.

We sat by the window with the lights off watching for the stalker. All that appeared was the police cruiser, which double-parked in a manner so obvious and unusual that lights started snapping on in neighboring windows. Two cops got out. They peered in doorways and roused a few street people, but left after twenty minutes with nothing to show for it.

"When you came in, he must have given up. He probably was just a lecher who followed you from the station," Richard told me.

"But I only noticed him on our street. It was almost like he was here first, waiting for me to arrive."

"The guy was probably sent by Keiko," Mariko said grimly. "Earlier this evening I called Esmerelda at the bar. She said a punk wearing a motorcycle helmet showed up asking for payment."

So the attack was Keiko's doing and had nothing to do with Joe Roncolotta or Kenji Yamamoto. I should have told the police . . . or would that have made things worse? I felt clammy and realized that I was sweating into the Léger. Karen would kill me if I stained it. I shooed Richard and Mariko back to their room, then undressed and gently sponged the armholes with a mixture of water and baby shampoo.

The silk felt good under my fingers; it really was a nice dress. And what my mother always told me about quality fabrics had proven true. The material was implausibly unwrinkled, even after my battles with the piranhas of the Tokyo American Club and the phantoms of the East Tokyo streets.

32

I hit the alarm clock's SNOOZE button twice before struggling into a sitting position at six-thirty on Saturday. I couldn't figure out why I was awake. Through blurred eyes, I saw the evening dress on its hanger and the memory of my wild night came back.

I turned on all possible sources of heat—my kerosene heater, the water tank, broiler, and range—before showering fast and sliding into jeans and Hugh's white shirt, which had been washed and ironed by someone. Richard didn't usually do my laundry. I chuckled a little as I made coffee and dialed California.

My father picked up the phone on the second ring.

"It's Rei on the telephone, Catherine! She's all right." Then he started in on me. "Rei-chan, there's a crazy rumor about your name being on Japanese television! Eric Hanada saw something on cable, and

his granddaughter says she's going to mail a magazine called *Friday* with you on the cover."

"Baby, it's time for you to come home." My
mother had gotten on another extension. "Cash in
that ticket we sent you last year or just buy a new
one—"

"Stop, will you?" I snapped before realizing how I
was falling into my old, ungracious patterns. I took a
deep breath and started again. "Sorry, I can't fly out.
The police are watching for me at Narita Airport."

The story took half an hour to tell. My mother
gasped at the story of Setsuko's murder, but seemed
equally curious about matters relating to Hugh.

"Married or divorced?" she asked casually.

"Neither. Mom, that's not important"

"Sendai? Hmm," my father said.

I felt it my duty to confess he was on indefinite
leave. There was an uncomfortable lull.

"You see, everything hinges on finding Setsuko's
killer," I said, trying to get back on track. "If we can
prove there were other people in Setsuko's background, these awful questions and the possibility of
the indictment will be over."

"Something like ninety-nine percent of the people who stand trial in Japan are convicted. Did you
know that?" My father demanded.

"Yes, Dad." As if I hadn't heard it a dozen times
already.

"Hugh's an attorney, not a killer," my mother cut in.
Ordinarily, that kind of generalization would have
drawn an argument from me, but I kept my mouth shut.

There was a silence on my father's side. I pictured

him sitting on the edge of his walnut desk with the phone cradled between his shoulder and ear, staring through the study's glass doors at the rock garden my mother and I built together. He could ponder the swirls of gravel and small, moss-covered boulders for hours. I preferred the garden from outside, with the fresh air around me and the birds in the trees. I remembered how I'd spent a long-ago afternoon there, deciding whether I would risk coming to Japan without a job. The garden had told me yes.

"Dad, are you looking at the garden?" I asked him.

"Yes." He sounded faintly surprised.

"It's special because the stones and plants all followed a plan. There's a pattern here, too, in what happened to Setsuko. And I've got it drawn in my mind, all but the last few pieces."

"What do you need from us, Rei? Should we come?" my mother pressed.

"You can help me best from where you are." But as I started to talk about calling directory assistance in Boston and Texas, it was my father who asked for the Evans brothers' first names. My father, my champion.

After I hung up, Richard and Mariko drifted in, talking about making pancakes. From the way Richard looked at Hugh's shirt on me, I could tell he had planned on wearing it. Mariko was wearing a pair of his long johns with her own Ranma sweatshirt. Standing at the stove with a spatula, she looked very much like she belonged.

The pancakes she produced were perfectly golden, fluffy, and all about the size of a 500 yen coin.

"Mariko's such a perfectionist," Richard said, watching her arrange a square butter pat on each cake. I thought of getting some maple syrup but she had something else in mind: strawberry jam.

"You probably wonder why I'm staying with Richard again," Mariko said, watching me cut into a diminutive pancake.

"It's better for you here than at the Marimba, isn't it?"

"Yes. Even though this neighborhood is horrible." She shot Richard a sidelong glance. "We're friends again. I like him, you know? At first it was just his looks. Now I know his heart, and he is the only man who wants more than my body."

"Are you planning to continue living together?" I asked cautiously.

"Well, I'm actually moving out of here." Richard ran his fingers through his hair so it stood straight up. "Simone has a lead on a place in Shibuya and figures we could afford it together."

"Shibuya's pretty ritzy," I said, envy running through me along with the awful feeling I wouldn't be his best friend anymore.

"It's one bedroom, but I said I'd take the living room." Richard shrugged. "It's similar to the way we live here, but it will be a thousand times neater with me out front."

"How stupid to leave such a cheap apartment in Tokyo!" Mariko, who had previously mocked our neighborhood, exclaimed.

"I'll be earning more money now that I'm leaving Nichiyu!"

"You have a new job?" I was incredulous. He really had locked me out of his life.

"Hugh and I were shooting the breeze at Marimba, and he told me about some French businessman who wants to back a new language school. It's going to be an expensive place oriented to people going on European tours, and I'll do English and Simone will teach French. She was getting sick of selling bracelets in Ueno Park anyway."

"So where am I going to live?" Mariko demanded.

"Doesn't your bank have a dormitory?" Richard sounded nervous.

"That's for full-time workers. I'm trying to get them to give me more hours, but . . ." Mariko trailed off, looking like she was going to cry.

"As boring as you find this neighborhood, there's no reason you can't stay with us a while longer. Richard, you aren't quitting Nichiyu right away?" I asked.

"Nope. We've got to save up for the key money and realtor fees, and I don't want to send old Katoh off the deep end just yet."

"As I told you before, Mariko, you're welcome to sleep in my room," I offered.

"But Mariko and I are living in harmony." Richard squeezed her hand. "We lie head-to-toe on our futons so no one gets tempted, and she tells me Japanese ghost stories!"

Mariko showed her dimples, and I had an uneasy feeling her ardor had not completely cooled.

"I'll be moving out," I said, my mind made up. "I have to go to Shiroyama but when I get back, Hugh will probably have returned to his apartment to convalesce. I want to be there."

"Well, it is centrally heated. I can't blame you," Richard said. "Will you have us over for dinner in the fabulous white kitchen?"

"As long as you don't mind facing the *paparazzi* outside the building."

"No! Really?" Richard had loved giving quotes to the tabloid reporters, and was miffed when all they had wanted were snapshots of me.

The phone rang as we were finishing breakfast.

"I can hardly understand the way these people speak in Boston, but I think I've located one of the men you're looking for," my father.

"Which son?"

"Roderick Evans. He seemed excited, actually, to hear that my daughter in Tokyo needed to contact him on a matter regarding his father."

"He doesn't know what's coming." I worried aloud. "To find out one's father had a second family in Japan . . . how can I tell him?"

"You'll be fine, Rei," my father said. "Trust yourself."

Trust yourself. I brushed my teeth and walked around straightening things as I willed myself to call Roderick Evans. I wrote out a list of questions. I did fifty sit-ups and drank three glasses of water. Finally, I dialed Boston.

"Mr. Roderick Evans? This is Rei Shimura calling from Japan . . ."

"My late father's favorite place in the world! I tell you, I'm sorry he isn't here to talk to somebody living there. Call me Rod, will you?" Evans's voice was warm and free of suspicion. My father must have done some job on him.

"I'm calling because I saw a copy of his obituary. It made its way over to the Navy community, some old chiefs saw it . . ."

"The Veterans' Association, right? I mailed them the notice just as my father would have wanted. So, do you want information on his retirement years for the military newspaper or something?"

"Well, I'd love to hear about what happened." I tried to stay evasive.

"He came back home and got married to Mom—the former Peg Miller, as the obit said—and he bought his own garage, had a real good business with that."

A garage didn't sound like big money to me. "Did he spend any time in Texas?"

"Nope. Well, he had a buddy who moved there. I think he visited once, but maybe that was for a mechanics' convention. Why?"

"Well, there are some papers here . . . I work in the historic preservation field and have come across some letters without a proper signature. I have reason to believe they might be from your father."

"We have a fax at the garage. Just send it and I'll give you an answer Monday morning."

"The fact is it's rather sensitive. I was actually hoping you could send me his handwriting sample."

"I don't know about that." His voice became more guarded. "What are you really looking for?"

"I'm trying to determine whether your father was connected to a Japanese woman." I paused. "She was half-American, actually. Her name was Setsuko Ozawa Nakamura."

"So what?"

"Well, she had no father listed on her birth certificate." I held my breath, hoping he'd stay on the line.

There was a brief silence, and then Rod cleared his throat. "Are you trying to say my dad was her father? Of all the . . . I should just hang up." He didn't.

"I don't know for sure, but someone at the Veterans' Association thought maybe it could be him. I'm really sorry." I gulped.

"I always wondered," Rod said. "I always wondered why he looked at Oriental women on the street, right in front of my mom like she wasn't even there."

"I'm sorry," I repeated.

There was another pause, and then Rod gave me a fax number. "You send me that letter. I'll go in tonight to wait for it."

"You will?"

"But if there are people out there making claims to his estate, tell them to forget about it. He's got nothing, he recognizes nobody else in his will other than me and Marshall—"

"Nobody's trying to sue anyone," I said. "It might be the case that Setsuko was blackmailing him. Knowing what I do about her, that wouldn't be surprising at all. Your father could be a victim of sorts—"

"Don't patronize me, okay? Send the goddamn letter, and I'll tell you what I think."

⊠   ⊠   ⊠

I buried my face in my hands after it was over. What a screw-up I'd made of things. Roderick Evans had been so injured, so naked in his outrage. He couldn't have had enough cunning to fly to Japan and kill Setsuko. I'd hit another roadblock.

I picked up the phone again and dialed the St. Luke's number I now knew by heart.

"Room four-twenty-three, please," I said.

"That room is unoccupied," the operator told me.

"Did Mr. Glendinning change rooms again? This is Rei Shimura calling."

"Oh, the cousin of Shimura-*sensei*! Don't you know Mr. Glendinning is not here anymore? He left against doctor's advice with a friend."

"A friend?" I panicked, thinking how dangerous Yamamoto had become.

"Yes. He left with a woman in the early morning hours," the receptionist confided. "The charge nurse was furious about it! This lady must have helped him down the stairway and out the front. By then it was too late to do anything."

"Was the woman foreign or Japanese?"

"*Gaijin*. Shimura-*sensei* noticed her often during visiting hours. A blond woman in a long black-and-white gown and a fur coat."

"Thank you very much," I said, starting to hang up.

"Anytime, Shimura-san, and your cousin wants to know if you'll be stopping in today? He's working the afternoon shift and wants to see you."

"Tell him I'll try to come in." I would have to

make a major apology for my last outburst if I wanted to remain part of the Shimura family.

"Since the photographers aren't outside anymore, visiting will be a lot more convenient for you!" the receptionist chirped, and even I had to laugh.

I kept my eyes out for stalkers on the way to Family Mart. When I made it inside, I made a silent, thankful prayer.

"A great picture today." Mr. Waka held up the *Yomiuri Shimbun* with the page folded back to show a photograph of me being handed into the taxi by Joe the previous evening.

"Rei no ka rei sa," Mr. Waka said. It was another play on the many meanings of my name—this time, it meant something like *Rei's beauty*.

"No doubt an attempt at satire. What does the story say?" I scrabbled for change in my pocket to photocopy the envelope and letter.

"Well, it says you are very much a girl of adventure. You had an accident at the train station yesterday? Please be more careful. And there's plenty of talk about your escort, Mr. Joe Roncolotta, the elderly Tokyo businessman. The journalist believes he bought the dress you were wearing because a teacher surely couldn't afford it. There is mention of Mr. Roncolotta's deceased Japanese wife and the various ladies he has known since that time—he is sixty-two years old! Frankly, I don't think it's a good idea!"

"Nothing's going on," I soothed, but he didn't look happier.

"What about poor Mr. Glendinning waiting in the hospital room alone? Popular opinion has turned in his favor. People are feeling sorry for him now that you are going out with many men."

"He's not in the hospital anymore. He left with another woman. You'll read about it if tomorrow is another slow news day." I looked at the page in my hands, trying to determine if it was clear enough to fax through to America. Then my eyes lit on the moldy envelope.

"Do you want me to read the article to you?" Mr. Waka prodded. "Or the latest survey on Mr. Glendinning's image?"

"Wait a minute." I needed to hold on to the idea that was beginning to emerge. Why hadn't I seen it before?

"What are you looking at?" Waka-san came out from behind his cauldron of *oden* and looked over my shoulder. "A letter from America?"

"This letter is addressed in care of the post office in Kawasaki."

"Sure. There's a private post office box number right there."

I had gone to Kawasaki looking for a house when the post office was what I'd needed to find all along. The post office, which was probably harboring more mail for Setsuko, the last vital clue to her past.

"I didn't know people in Japan even used post office boxes."

"It's unusual," Mr. Waka nodded. "However, many people use the post office for their savings accounts— same rates as the bank and right in the neighborhood!"

"I bank at Sanwa," I said absently. "I've got to go there now—it closes at noon—"

"You're going to Sanwa Bank?"

"No, the post office!"

"What about your fax?" Mr. Waka asked.

"Could you put it through for me? I'll pay you when I get back."

"But this is an international telephone number! I can only fax domestically." He sucked the air between his teeth, the quintessential can't-do-it gesture.

"What?" I grabbed him by the shoulders. "Please. Can't you re-set the fax? I'll pay anything."

"If I reprogram this, it will be so much trouble—"

"Waka-san, when everything works out the *Yomiuri* will be interviewing *you*."

I put the pages in the proper order with a short note that included my telephone number. *I hope I'm not ruining your life*, I wrote and signed my name.

As I hurried through the tidy gray streets of Kawasaki, I thought about how the post office was a perfectly logical place for Setsuko to conduct her private mail liaison. It was a convenient stop on the way from Hayama to Tokyo, yet devoid of any chance of running into the neighbors. And she'd kept it for years, shielding her father from the knowledge she'd moved to a very pricey neighborhood.

I'd affixed my wig ahead of time, and riding the bus to the post office, my shiny tresses received a few approving glances. I hoped people would believe a woman my age was likely to have her own mailbox. Post Office Barbie, I thought.

I roamed the post office briefly before I saw the steel block of mailboxes with combination locks. When I located box 63992, I began twisting the dial. It didn't work. I tried the combination six times before breaking down and taking the code out of my handbag to look at it again. Was there some trick in Japan? Weren't all combinations right-left-right, the way every gym locker in my lifetime had worked?

Other customers were beginning to watch my struggle, so I gave up and went as innocently as I could to the main desk. I took a number and waited my turn with the others. It was a quarter to twelve when I was called up front.

"Excuse me, but I'm having some trouble getting into my post office box." I threw up my hands as if that were the silliest thing in the world.

"Box number?" The clerk wearing a trainee button pulled a metal box with index cards from under the counter. Uncomputerized, as much of Japan still was.

"Six-three-nine-nine-two," I said.

The woman rummaged for a minute, came up with a card, and read it with a sober expression. "Mrs. Ozawa, your box is closed because the last two months' rent was not paid."

"I'm sorry, I was away," I said, which was true enough. "What do I owe you?"

"Eight-thousand yen."

I winced at the figure and dug fruitlessly into my bag for cash. Why hadn't I stopped at my bank first?

"I'm sorry, I don't have that much money with me."
And even if the Japanese post office accepted charge
cards, mine said Rei Shimura.

The clerk looked surprisingly sympathetic. "If you
like, we could start automatic deductions from your
savings account. That way you won't have this problem again."

"My savings account?" I asked, feeling slightly
giddy. "What a great idea!"

"I can fill out the application for you now—"

She scribbled on a form laden with *kanji* and
pushed it toward me. As I took out a pen she made a
command that stopped me cold.

"You must use your *hanko*."

I would have looked for Setsuko Nakamura's
name seal in her house if I had known what was coming. As it was, I'd have to bluff and use my own. If I
could somehow manage to blur the seal, it might go
unnoticed.

I took out my seal and plunged it into the plush ink
pad set on the counter. Then I stamped where she indi-
cated, applying more pressure than needed. What I'd
made looked like a Rorschach blot; it was pretty hard to
make out that it said anything. To my relief the clerk
just filed it and gave me a receipt. I stared down at the
paper, reading Setsuko's remaining account balance:
3.2 million yen. Here was the result of all those traded-
back dresses, safe from her husband's hands.

"We'll take the interior lock off the mailbox, and
on Monday you can use it again. In the meantime,
here's a claim slip for your mail. Go to counter number five."

I obeyed her, noting that it was now five minutes to noon and almost everyone was gone. There were two customers waiting ahead of me in line when the public address system began playing "Auld Lang Syne." The clerk slapped a closed sign on the counter, and the smattering of customers dispersed. I went straight up to the counter.

"I'm sorry, maybe *okyaku-sama* didn't hear we are closed." Even though the male clerk was referring to me as an honorable customer, his tone was decidedly starchy.

"I cannot leave until I pick up my mail." I placed the claim slip in front of him.

"This section is closed," he repeated.

I didn't move until he finally shrugged and walked off with my slip. He came back with a slim packet of letters. "Next time, come before the last minute, please."

I thanked him profusely with a toss of my plastic mane and hurried out the post office, scanning the envelopes. Two were addressed in Japanese and one was in English, from a Miami law firm called Mulroney, Simms, and Schweiger.

I wanted to read the English letter fast. I ran across the intersection just as the pedestrian crossing music had stopped and charged into a Mosburger shop where I sat down at the counter. In the midst of teen-agers munching odorous hamburgers, I slit open the envelope and pulled out a crisp sheet of paper dated December 20.

Dear Ms. Ozawa:

This letter is to update you on developments regarding the institution of a patrimony suit against the estate of Mr. R.P.S.

Our office has conducted some preliminary investigations, as per your request on November 3 about the basis for bringing about a suit and the likelihood of its success. Although the possibility that you might prevail cannot be ruled out entirely, we do not think that the evidence is strong enough to support your contentions.

The documents you sent to our office, personal letters spanning 25 years, were all signed as "Father." Without a formal signature or other evidence of identity, the case would be dismissed for failing to meet the burden of proof necessary to institute an action against the estate. It may be possible to conduct handwriting analysis; however, even this approach would have to overcome strong objections and contrary evidence that would be produced by the defense. Additionally, since there is no mention of you in the will, the estate will make the obvious argument that the deceased had no intention of including you in his will.

On a side issue, regarding your communications with the wife of the deceased, I urge you to not make further

efforts to contact her. My private investigator has determined that, contrary to
your beliefs, she is not a frail widow with
a passive attitude toward your views. It
was our impression that she is a rather
vigorous person who has expressed considerable anger upon learning of you and
the letters you have written to her son and
daughter.

I trust you will let matters rest as I
have recommended. Please feel free to
contact us if you are in need of further
assistance.

Very truly yours,

James R. Mulroney
Attorney at Law

I jammed the letter back into its envelope, cursing
myself for all the work that could have been spared
had I gotten to the post office faster. I found a pay
phone and inserted a telephone card which just had
four units left. I wouldn't have time for a long conversation with Hugh.

An answering machine came on in an English-
woman's cool tones. I would have thought it a wrong
number, but for the fact I recognized the voice as
Winnie Clancy's. Had she moved in to take care of
Hugh? I left a brief message and told him I'd call
from home.

"It's me," I said when Mr. Waka appeared to look

straight through me after I walked into Family Mart thirty-five minutes later.

"Your hair—" his eyes bugged out.

"It's a wig." I flipped the long hair back over my shoulders.

"You look more Japanese now." From the way he pressed his lips together, I could tell it wasn't something he approved of. "I'm tired of your running in and out. Won't you stay for a cup of *oden*?"

The pot looked even murkier than usual. "I'm on a New Year's diet, so I better take a couple of rice-balls. Did the fax go through?"

"Yes, but if you waste away, you won't be able to hold up those fancy dresses. Do you miss your American food? How about a *hotto doggu*?"

"No thanks, I don't eat meat," I said, unwrapping the sweet tofu and rice snack.

"It's no good, not healthy. In Japan, we believe in eating thirty different foods every single day! Meat, fish, rice, pickles, soy beans—"

"I've got to hurry. But I've a feeling that the next time you see me I'll be in a better mood," I promised, discarding the plastic wrappers in his waste basket.

"Come back then, *neh*? And stay out of the tabloids," Waka-san called after me.

33

It was two in the afternoon when I arrived home, midnight in Miami. I would call and leave a message on the law firm's answering machine.

Opening the unlocked door to my apartment, I looked toward my answering machine and saw the message light was on. Hurriedly kicking off my shoes, I started to trip and reached out a hand to steady myself on a tall lantern. My hand went through *shōji* paper, taking the lantern down with me. I moaned, feeling as bad about the ruined antique as the pain shooting through my knee.

"Careful."

I looked up and saw Marcelle Chapman in her familiar zebra coat.

"Oh! Richard must have let you in," I said, thinking how strange it was for her to be looking down on me like this.

"No, he went out an hour ago. But Mariko's here."

I followed Mrs. Chapman's gaze to my futon. Mariko was lying in a fetal position, her wrists and ankles bound with electrical tape. She did not move.

"It didn't have to happen. If it wasn't for your meddling, I would have been out of here weeks ago." Mrs. Chapman's voice broke.

"Is she dead?" I whispered, panic rising.

Mariko twisted around so I could see her face. Her mouth was taped, but her eyes blazed.

"I'm not dating Joe Roncolotta, I promise," I said wildly. "Neither is Mariko. None of us mean you any harm—I think we should all sit down and talk calmly."

"It's bath-time, but you have no bath in this apartment. I forgot that detail." She pursed her lips.

The bath. I suddenly realized this visit had nothing to do with Joe Roncolotta.

"Because there's no bath, I think the two of you will have to jump."

"Jump?" I repeated dumbly.

"Things have been going pretty bad for you lately, haven't they?" Mrs. Chapman stepped over my prone body, keeping one foot on each side. "You're having trouble at work. The gangsters have a contract out on you. Your boyfriend's going to prison for life."

"He's not!"

"Not going to jail? Well, I suppose you could save him if it turns out you did all the killing."

"Nobody knows about you," I said, thinking fast. "Why don't you just leave while you have a chance to get out of the country? No one suspects you."

"You're a liar, Rei Shimura." She drew out my name

in an exaggerated accent that must have sounded Japanese to her. "It's the Japanese half of you."

"What's making you act this way? You're a caring person. You helped me from the beginning." It was a risk to continue talking. If I irritated her, she might gag me like Mariko. Without a mouth, I would be a little less human, more like a corpse. Easier to kill.

Instead of answering me, Mrs. Chapman went to the answering machine and pressed play. As I struggled to rise, her Reebok connected with my jaw. I curtailed my groan so I could hear the recording.

"Rei, this is Rod Evans. I'm relieved to tell you that handwriting is nowhere near my dad's. You gave me a hell of a scare." He paused. "I may have a lead for you, though. The postmark on the envelope made me think of Bob Smith, a guy who served with my dad in Japan. Mr. Smith left a girlfriend and daughter there and always felt bad about it. He tried to provide for them by sending money and all. I know because my dad told me, kind of a warning when I was headed to Nam, but that's another story. Smith was a Texas rancher, real high profile. He couldn't acknowledge the Japanese girl and keep the business. The wife he married turned out to be mean as pig shit. He always said—" The machine beeped, cutting the rest of the message off.

Mrs. Chapman pressed erase with a black-gloved finger.

"Your passport said Smith, not Chapman." I remembered how, at her urging, I'd explained away the glaring discrepancy to Captain Okuhara. I'd saved her, when she could have been caught.

I looked up at her, waiting. A time would come

for me to move. My right leg hurt but I was pretty sure it would work for me, given the opportunity.

"For heaven's sake, I came to talk to that Nakamura woman, to put some sense in her head!" Mrs. Chapman exploded. "I even brought my checkbook."

"What did you want her to do?" I asked.

"To stop. To get the hell out of our lives, now that Bobby's dead." Pain flashed across her face. "The two of them carrying on with post office boxes in different cities, different states—you'd think they were having an affair or something. It wasn't until after the cancer took him that I figured out what had been happening to Binnie's money."

"Whose money?"

"My granddaughter's. Every dollar Bob spent on Setsuko was one he stole from her inheritance."

"That must have made you pretty upset," I said, attempting to soothe her.

"Setsuko found out he died through a detective or lawyer or somebody. She was going to make a claim on the estate. I sent her a note saying we needed to talk things over, just the two of us. She called me on the telephone and told me not until after the holidays. Like she was in control. I asked about her plans and she let it slip where she was headed. With just five hotels to call, she was pretty easy to find." Mrs. Chapman smiled tightly.

"Why didn't you just meet her in Tokyo?" I asked.

"I needed to see what kind of a personality I was up against and I got a load of her, all right. At dinner that night, she was whispering about me in that fool language with the innkeeper."

"They just didn't like foreigners! I could have told you that it wasn't personal." In hindsight, my own worries about how I'd been treated seemed very petty.

"Aren't you Miss Know-It-All?" Mrs. Chapman kicked me again, this time close to my eye. I held my hand on my throbbing cheekbone and listened to Mariko struggling on the bed, her body rolling against the quilt.

"I decided to talk to her when I had the advantage," Mrs. Chapman continued. "I went into the bathroom, fixing the door so no one would disturb us. She was shocked to see me. Then she laughed and told me she had a fancy lawyer set up to beat the hell out of me. You can imagine who I thought it was."

"Hugh," I said.

"I hung around afterwards to see what he would do. I concluded nothing. It was you who turned out to be the snoop."

"How did you kill her?"

"I didn't mean to. She was standing up in the bath, skinny and shameless, like she was going to walk out on our conversation. I hit her with a bath cover. She fell down and I grabbed her feet. Her head stayed under. It just took a minute."

"The pearls. Did you plant them in Hugh's room?" I had to know.

"I confused his room with the young Japanese assistant's, but the necklace wound up in the right place anyway. God moves in mysterious ways."

"You're a woman of faith." I faked a smile at her.

"I think it's time for a prayer. Maybe if we pray together we can see a way through this thing—get some help for you—"

Mariko gave me a scathing look, so I stopped.

"Get up." Mrs. Chapman kicked at me again, and I pulled myself awkwardly to my knees and stood up. The telephone was near, but I didn't dare move toward it because she had my chef's knife in her right hand.

"About Mariko," I continued, talking loudly in the hopes someone would hear. "You knew she worked at the bank and also at Marimba. It must have been tough because you couldn't identify her."

"That's right. When you dropped the hint she was staying at your apartment, I had to bide my time till you and the little blond boy left her alone." Mrs. Chapman was behind me now, binding my wrists with the thick tape. Just as she started to tighten the tape, I kicked backwards. Her knee rammed me in the buttocks and I found myself sailing through the air, falling against Mariko and the edge of the futon with a painful thud.

"I can't stand your Japanese face, you know that? It reminds me of her. Even after she's dead, you haunt me—"

I rolled over on my back and kicked at Mrs. Chapman, who towered over me once more.

"Who would believe this is a suicide with my hands tied?" I asked, imagining *yakuza* would be the first thing Hugh and Tom would think about, that all attention would focus in that direction while Marcia Smith slipped out of the country.

"Good point. I'll untie them."

"Why did you kill Mrs. Yogetsu?" Soon I would run out of ways to delay her.

"I used an interpreter to call there earlier in December to make sure the Nakamuras were staying at the inn. Even though my name wasn't mentioned, I think the innkeeper guessed I was behind the telephone call. When Joe Roncolotta dropped you off after dinner, I saw her. I followed her back to the train station. I saw a train coming, the perfect solution."

As she talked, I could hear something strange going on in the stairwell, a heavy, irregular rhythm. Someone or something was out there. *Yakuza* henchmen? I positively longed for them. I shot a glance at Mariko. Her eyes flickered.

"I want you to get up now. Nice and easy," Mrs. Chapman ordered.

"I'm not doing anything to Mariko." My confidence in being saved was waning because the person in the stairwell seemed to have stopped on the second landing.

"I don't care. Just get up."

I did and was marched over to my kitchen table, where she brought the knife to my wrists and began sawing at the tape with which she had bound me.

"Time to write a note about how sorry you are to have to do this, but it's time for you to leave the life."

"It's time for me to leave the life? No one would believe I'd write that. It's so overblown and maudlin!" I didn't know where the words were coming from, but I had to keep talking.

She stopped unhitching my hands. "I was giving you a few extra minutes. A favor in exchange for what you've done for me. If you'd rather just jump, we'll go straight to the window."

She pushed me to the side window and slammed it open with one easy move of her left hand. Cold air tinged with gasoline and rotting vegetables blasted my face. The trash heap was ten feet to the right of my window. If I were a magician, I could waft myself toward it and land safely atop the garbage bags. Otherwise it was four stories to concrete.

"I won't jump. You'll have to throw me out." I turned to face her, making calculations. Even though she was taller and heavier than me, it was unlikely she was spry enough to lift me. All she'd carried off so far was hitting Setsuko over the head and shoving Mrs. Yogetsu before a train. She'd certainly not be able to pick up a body and throw it. But it turned out she had something else in mind.

"Good-bye, Rei." Her face was tranquil as she began moving the knife in a straight path toward my throat. I rushed at her, causing her to overshoot her mark, the knife slicing through fine cotton and glancing off my collarbone. I felt the cut but was seized by adrenaline as I slid under her arm and toward the door.

"You fool." She slammed her body into mine, and we both landed on the floor.

The telephone began ringing. I lunged for the receiver as Mrs. Chapman's knife nicked my biceps, drawing a beaded line of blood. Then there was a loud cracking sound, and I knew she had gotten me on the head, the place she should have gone for in the beginning.

Things went black for a second. Then, Mrs.

Chapman emitted a yowl that told me I was still alive. The telephone continued to beep. I crawled toward it and knocked the receiver down to the floor with my shoulder.

"Who is it?" I said, disoriented because of the bizarre scene unfolding before me. Mrs. Chapman lay on her back like a beached whale, a long sword touching her throat. I squinted and realized the sword was really a metal crutch. The crutch was connected to Hugh Glendinning, looking very much like a Celtic hero on his last breath. He had only one crutch left for support and was leaning dangerously to one side.

"Easy, now," Hugh said to Mrs. Chapman, and then to me, "That's blood on my shirt, darling. Something tells me this is the last time I'll lend you anything good."

I didn't reply, concentrating on the faraway voice on the telephone.

"Hallo, this is Winnie Clancy. May I speak to Hugh, please?"

"I think he's—indisposed." This was no fantasy world if Winnie was calling, I thought with a catch of joy.

"Fast worker, aren't you?" Winnie said in her clipped accent.

"Mrs. Clancy, would you do me a favor?"

"What?" She sounded exasperated.

"Call 110," I said with a bit of swagger and my best American accent. "Tell them to come to three-fourteen-nine Nihonzutsumi, apartment 4B. Come over yourself if you want to see Hugh. But call the cops first, if you want his Scottish ass alive."

34

Hugh was using soap in the tub, something I had never seen done in Japan. Thin swirls of old soap floated in the water, ghosts of unlawful baths past. I shuddered, thinking of the damage he had done to his bath's heating mechanism.

"You'll look like a boxer tomorrow." Hugh turned on the cold water tap briefly to refresh the wash cloth before returning it to the bruise under my eye. He hadn't exaggerated about being the king of sports injuries. He'd made sure the nurses gave me an ice pack for my face during the time I'd waited for Tom to come out of surgery, shoot Hugh an accusing look, then take it all back when he heard the story.

"I still haven't figured out how you knew Mrs. Chapman was the one." I settled back against Hugh's chest, resigning myself to the fact I would allow him the soap and anything he wanted that night.

"I broke out of that damn hospital at four A.M.

and went home to have my first decent sleep in a half-
week," he said, beginning to massage my shoulders.
"When I woke up, Winnie and Piers were there. They
made me watch a videotape of news footage showing
you leaving my building the morning after you stayed
over. Piers was nattering on about the unsuitability of
our relationship as I lay there, eating up the vision of
you looking so lovely in my shirt. Then I had a nasty
shock."

"That I stole the old man's taxi?" I leaned forward, enjoying the feel of his fingers on my back.

"No, darling. In the background I spotted somebody tall and foreign. I backed up the tape and recognized our dear old friend. I started quizzing myself
about why Mrs. Chapman, who likes you so much,
would have watched you without making herself
known." His voice was rueful. "I fell asleep again. I
was taking Demerol for my ankle, which thanks to
your four flights of stairs, is now even worse."

"Poor Hugh," I said, stroking his left thigh. From
knee to foot he was encased in a fiberglass cast, carefully elevated along the side of the tub. Getting him
in had been a rather complicated maneuver I worried
about repeating; we'd have to drain the bath before
he could stand up.

"It must have been hours later that the telephone
woke me, and I had a chat with Mr. Naruse."

"Who?" I touched my aching head. Hugh's
crutch had knocked against me in his wild drive to
pinion Mrs. Chapman, and although there was no
concussion, I had a monster bump.

"Mr. Naruse is the private investigator I put on

your street. Richard and Mariko told me about your mishap at the train station, so I decided you needed someone to follow you, given that I couldn't."

"There was a man stalking me through the neighborhood last night. If you mean to tell me that was him— "

"You called the cops, he reported. I thought you realized I'd hired him and were enraged. That's why I asked Winnie to help me leave the hospital."

"Did you know she re-recorded your answering machine message? She's moved in and taken over your life!"

"Don't distract me from the story." He kissed my wandering hand and folded it into his. "Mr. Naruse called to report the morning's activity. Various people came and went, but at one o'clock an older *gaijin* woman entered the building. With his binoculars, he was able to track her entering your apartment. For a variety of boring legal reasons he was unwilling to go inside, so I drove over myself."

"Mrs. Chapman, I mean Smith, must have waited until Richard and I were gone to ring the doorbell," I said. Mariko probably figured because she was an older foreign woman, she was safe to let in."

"I wonder." Hugh sighed. "I wish I could have been in the room where Marcia Chapman-Smith gave her confession. You could have interpreted for us again."

"Nope. This is Tokyo, where the police do things professionally." I stretched against him, thinking about how good it had been to sit together in the police waiting room and give our statements. Captain Okuhara had arrived and bowed deeply to Hugh and me, asking what he could do to atone for his oversight.

"Press conference," Hugh had ordered with a grin.

Mariko hadn't been so cheerful about things. Once the tape has been removed from her lips, she had choice words for us, the police, and the pack of press who'd tagged along.

"This woman killed my mother and tried to kill me. I don't want anything to do with her people and I don't give a damn about what's in her husband's will. I wouldn't take a dollar if they handed it to me on a silver tray," she shouted, tossing her dreadlocks for the camera.

But there was Setsuko's secret savings account at the post office—money I was sure she would have wanted her daughter to have. I'd make sure Mariko got it, and if Mr. Nakamura didn't see my point, Hugh, back in power at Sendai, would help.

Mr. Nakamura had decided to testify against Keiko regarding her blackmail plot, so Sendai would get back the half-million yen that he'd given her. Club Marimba would close, and Mariko would be in the market for a new job.

"You're too quiet, Rei. I'm not used to it." Hugh interrupted my thoughts.

"I'm plotting." I smiled at him.

"So am I. We'd best go to bed early, I think."

"Very early," I agreed, heart beating a bit faster.

"Yes, we've got one long Sunday to get through," he said, surprising me with his train of thought. "Up at seven so I can make you a proper Scottish breakfast.

Winnie laid in some eggs and sausages—oops, scratch the meat. Eggs and toast okay?"

I nodded, and he continued. "If I'm still ambulatory, I'll hobble after you to one of those Sunday morning shrine sales you're always going on about."

"You'd go shopping with me?" I was touched.

"All the better if you find another bauble worth over a million yen and bring it to the twelve o'clock press conference. Or so Joe Roncolotta suggested. He's invited us to brunch at TAC after we're done with the police."

"So my *gaijin* escorts are getting along?" I shifted around to face him.

"Let's say we care deeply about the same investment, albeit for different reasons."

"I'm going to let that ridiculous comment pass on account of my headache, but watch it," I warned.

"Relax, it's just a figure of speech. Continuing with our schedule, we'll lunch and drive to your flat to pick up the clothes Richard promised to have ready: the few decent things you own, in his words."

"What are you talking about?" I was suddenly worried. "Captain Okuhara said I didn't have to go to Shiroyama after all."

"You're moving in with me, aren't you? Richard said you wanted to." Hugh's voice had a tenderness I never would have expected.

"That was because of your injury and problems with police. I wanted to be with you for the little time we had left. But now that there are no extenuating circumstances, I hardly think it's necessary—"

He held up a hand to stop me. "Let's be practical,

then. I could provide you with a great business address. All I ask is that you collect me every night along with your faxes."

A great wave of laughter swept over me then, and I looked into his green-gold eyes, warm with something I had seen before but finally realized was all for me.

"You're incorrigible," I said. "A capitalist Scot who's far too proprietary—"

"But you want me anyway?"

Water sloshed over the side of the tub as I landed on him, giving my answer.